P9-DID-300

SOUTHERN LITERARY CLASSICS SERIES

C. Hugh Holman and Louis D. Rubin, Jr.
General Editors

Previously published:

CHITA, *by Lafcadio Hearn, introduction by Arlin Turner, Duke University*

IN OLE VIRGINIA, *by Thomas Nelson Page, introduction by Kimball King, The University of North Carolina at Chapel Hill*

ADVENTURES OF CAPTAIN SIMON SUGGS, *by Johnson Jones Hooper, introduction by Manly Wade Wellman*

TIGER-LILIES, *by Sidney Lanier, introduction by Richard Harwell, Smith College*

THE LETTERS OF THE BRITISH SPY, *by William Wirt, introduction by Richard Beale Davis, University of Tennessee*

In preparation:

THE VALLEY OF SHENANDOAH, *by George Tucker, introduction by Donald R. Noble, University of Alabama*

THE KNIGHTS OF THE GOLDEN HORSE-SHOE, *by William Alexander Caruthers, introduction by Curtis Carroll Davis*

THE PARTISAN LEADER, *by Nathaniel Beverley Tucker, introduction by C. Hugh Holman, The University of North Carolina at Chapel Hill*

THE
PLANTER'S NORTHERN BRIDE

THE

PLANTER'S NORTHERN BRIDE

by

MRS. CAROLINE LEE HENTZ

"I saw her, and I lov'd her—I sought her and I won;
A dozen pleasant summers, and more, since then have run;
And half as many voices now prattling by her side,
Remind me of the autumn when she became my bride."

Thomas Mackellar

"Nothing shall assuage
Your love but marriage: for such is
The tying of two in wedlock, as is
The tuning of two lutes in one key: for
Striking the strings of the one, straws will stir
Upon the strings of the other; and in
Two minds linked in love, one cannot be
Delighted, but the other rejoiceth."

Lilly's Sappho

With an Introduction by

RHODA COLEMAN ELLISON

THE UNIVERSITY OF NORTH CAROLINA PRESS
Chapel Hill

Southern Literary Classics Series

Manufactured in the United States of America
Cloth edition, Standard Book Number 8078-1131-9
Paper edition, Standard Book Number 8078-4051-3
Library of Congress Catalog Card Number 72-108136

The copy of the first edition of 1854 used in duplicating this work is in the Kentucky Library, Western Kentucky University, Bowling Green, Kentucky.

INTRODUCTION

When *The Planter's Northern Bride* was published in 1854 it became popular overnight, and it continued to be read during the remainder of the century. The work of a New Englander transplanted to the South, it seemed to many of her contemporaries to be both a charming love story and a convincing answer to *Uncle Tom's Cabin.* After the Civil War it provided escapist readers with one of the more credible pictures of the Old South. In an age not given to its brand of sentimentality, it merits interest because it records the cultural patterns of the antebellum period. As a popular plantation romance, it reflects the literary taste of the 1850's as well as the characteristic reasoning about slavery, yet it achieves a greater degree of immediacy and reality than many other specimens of its genre.

Two years before the publication of *The Planter's Northern Bride*, Mrs. Harriet Beecher Stowe had fired the first shot in an extraordinary literary war that engaged many novelists besides Mrs. Caroline Lee Hentz. One apologist after another rose to defend the South's "peculiar institution" against the attack in *Uncle Tom's Cabin.* The year 1852 alone saw the appearance of such titles as *Aunt Phillis's Cabin, or Slaves and Masters*, by Charles Jacob

Peterson; *Uncle Tom's Cabin Contrasted with Buckingham Hall, the Planter's Home, or A Fair View of Both Sides of the Slavery Question*, by Robert Criswell; *Northwood: Life North and South, Showing the True Character of Both*, by Sarah J. Hale; *Life in the South*, by W. L. G. Smith; *The North and the South, or Slavery and Its Contrasts*, by Caroline E. Rush. In this same year Mrs. Hentz contributed the first of her two proslavery novels, *Marcus Warland, or The Long Moss Spring*, a less vigorous counterattack than *The Planter's Northern Bride.*

Of all those who joined battle with Mrs. Stowe, Mrs. Hentz was one of the best qualified from many points of view. Her own background and experience reveal many surprising parallels to Mrs. Stowe's. Not only was she a native of Massachusetts but she too married a scholarly, unprosperous husband, emigrated temporarily to the Midwest, and became a teacher with her husband. Both women moved to Cincinnati in the same year, 1832, and, according to Mrs. Hentz's son, Dr. Charles A. Hentz, were members of the same literary society there.[1] Later both joined what Hawthorne called "the damned mob of scribbling women" and produced fiction prolifically to help support their families. In all these circumstances the experience of the two novelists was remarkably similar.

In their observation of the Southern plantation, however, Mrs. Hentz had an advantage over her old acquaintance. Instead of merely visiting across the Ohio River, like Mrs. Stowe, she made her home in Kentucky for two years. While Mrs. Stowe, after eighteen years' residence in Cincinnati, returned to New England and allegedly learned most of what she knew about slavery from her reading,[2] Mrs. Hentz followed the rolling-stone career of

1. Charles A. Hentz, "Autobiography," North Carolina Collection, Library of The University of North Carolina at Chapel Hill.

2. Her chief sourcebook is said to have been Theodore Weld's

her brilliant but eccentric French husband about the Deep South for the rest of her life. When, as Caroline Lee Whiting, she married Nicholas Marcellus Hentz in 1824, he had already begun the restless roaming that was to familiarize her with so many strange scenes, particularly in the South. He had emigrated with his father from France on the fall of Napoleon, studied medicine briefly at Harvard, and become an instructor at George Bancroft's Round Hill School in Northampton, Massachusetts.[3] Two years after his marriage he secured the professorship of modern languages at The University of North Carolina at Chapel Hill.

By the time he resigned in 1830 to organize a school for girls in Covington, Kentucky, the pattern of their future life seems to have been established. Mr. Hentz never remained in any location for more than three or four years except in Florence, Alabama, where he and Mrs. Hentz conducted a school for nine years, from 1834 to 1843. Their son, Dr. Charles A. Hentz, speculated in his autobiography that his father's unreasonable jealousy of his attractive wife was more than once the cause of those sudden removals. He related the melodramatic incident of a challenge to a duel, which precipitated their departure from Cincinnati after they had resided there for only two years. It is not surprising that the plots of several of Mrs. Hentz's

American Slavery as It Is: Testimony of a Thousand Witnesses (1839). See Kenneth S. Lynn's introduction to *Uncle Tom's Cabin* (Cambridge, Massachusetts, 1962).

3. Mr. Hentz did important research in entomology, his work on spiders being published by the *Boston Journal of Natural History*, January, 1842—December, 1847. The biographical facts for both Mr. and Mrs. Hentz are derived from the *Dictionary of American Biography*, s.v. "Hentz, Caroline Lee Whiting," and from Mrs. Caroline Mays Brevard in *The Library of Southern Literature*, eds. Edwin Anderson Alderman and Joel Chandler Harris (New Orleans, Atlanta: The Martin & Hoyt Company, 1908-13), VI, 2375-79.

novels revolve around a jealous hero.[4] From Florence the Hentzes moved for the usual brief period to Tuscaloosa, to Tuskegee, and then to Columbus, Georgia, where in 1851 Mr. Hentz's health, always uncertain, finally failed. After five strenuous years of nursing and writing, Mrs. Hentz died in their last home, Marianna, Florida, on February 11, 1856. Over a period of twenty years she had lived in five Southern states.

In addition to her broad acquaintance with the South, Mrs. Hentz had professional experience that fitted her for the writing of *The Planter's Northern Bride* and a professional reputation that assured her of an audience through the rest of the century. From time to time she had composed poems and stories for magazines and newspapers, an unsuccessful novel, and three plays, one of which was produced in Philadelphia and Boston, a second in New York, and a third in Cincinnati and New Orleans.[5] In 1850, recognizing the imminent failure of her husband's health, she resorted to her pen as a source of livelihood and published her first successful novel, *Linda, or The Young Pilot of the Belle Creole.* By the time *The Planter's Northern Bride* appeared four years later, she was the author of four other novels and two volumes of short stories. She turned out her fiction with amazing speed and consistency, averaging almost two volumes a year up to the publication of *Ernest Linwood* in the week of her death. All of her books enjoyed a wide popularity, 100,000 copies being sold in three years, and the fact that the publishers kept some of the titles in print until the last decade of the century indicates that they continued to be

4. See Rhoda Coleman Ellison, "Mrs. Hentz and the Green-eyed Monster," *American Literature,* XXII (November, 1950), 345-50.

5. Arthur Hobson Quinn, *History of the American Drama,* 2nd ed. (New York, 1946), pp. 264-65, and *Dictionary of American Biography,* s.v. "Hentz, Caroline Lee Whiting."

in demand. A Philadelphia house, under the successive names of Carey and Hart, A. Hart, and Perry and McMillan, was Mrs. Hentz's original publisher. After her death the stereotype plates of all her volumes were purchased by T. B. Peterson and Brothers, also of Philadelphia, who then issued "Peterson's Uniform Edition of the Complete Works of Mrs. Caroline Lee Hentz," guaranteed to be printed on better paper than heretofore. The last discoverable imprint of this edition is in 1889. None of her books received a new edition in Mrs. Hentz's lifetime, and it is possible that even if she had had the opportunity of revision she would not have used it. Not only the personal and economic pressures under which she wrote but her own temperament might have discouraged the laborious art of polishing. It is recorded of her: "Composition cost her no effort; she could write in spare half-hours, in a room filled with children, or with friends looking on and reading over her shoulder."[6] At any rate, her stories remained popular in the form in which she first wrote them.

In spite of the preference of Mrs. Hentz's biographer, Mrs. Caroline Mays Brevard, for her last novel, *Ernest Linwood*,[7] *The Planter's Northern Bride* seems more significant today. It continues, with variations, the sentimental characters and certain elements of the plot and style of the typical plantation romance of the 1850's, yet manages to come closer to reality. It is distinguished from most of its kind by the author's position as a native of the North who argues for slavery and who creates the impression of an authentic regional setting for her proslavery story. Like *Uncle Tom's Cabin*, it was written with a sincerity that sometimes transcends the artifices of its genre and

6. *Dictionary of American Biography*, s.v. "Hentz, Caroline Lee Whiting."

7. Brevard, *The Library of Southern Literature*, VI, 2379.

brings it to life a century later to readers of very different convictions.

The pattern of the planation romance was already firmly set by the decade in which *Uncle Tom's Cabin* and *The Planter's Northern Bride* were published. Mrs. Hentz, like Mrs. Stowe, inherited a cast of stock characters that had begun to charm readers as early as 1832 in John Pendleton Kennedy's *Swallow Barn* and have retained their fascination for over a century, as witnessed by Margaret Mitchell's *Gone with the Wind.* The most familiar of the white stereotypes in this popular tradition are the hospitable, humane old slave-holder, the gay Southern belle, the gallant young gentleman who wins her love, and the favorably impressed visitor or governess from the North. The stock Negro characters include the faithful man-servant, the devoted and domineering black mammy, the beautiful mulatto, and the story-teller. In her romances Mrs. Hentz utilizes many of these stereotypes. In *Marcus Warland* and *Eoline, or Magnolia Vale* (both published in 1852), she presents the traditional old planter, the Southern girl, and the young gentleman lover, with the devoted slaves in the background. In *The Planter's Northern Bride*, however, the white cast is altered to fit the demands of a drama in which the chief conflict is ideological rather than personal. Among the conventional characters, only the faithful male house-servant and the credulous Northern visitor are portrayed according to specifications. The kindly master who dominates the action is represented as neither venerable nor youthful; actually he appropriates the functions of both of the white male types, being lover and host. There is no Southern belle on the scene, and no plantation story-teller. The attractive mulatto stays far in the background, and the Negro mammy is properly retiring.

In its cast of characters *The Planter's Northern Bride*

actually has more in common with *Uncle Tom's Cabin* than with many other plantation romances, even those of its own author. Perhaps the parallels result from Mrs. Hentz's deliberate attempt to counter Mrs. Stowe's argument with similar characters and situations presented from a different point of view. As the kindly master, her Moreland (the pun is appropriate) parallels the more complex St. Clare and Shelby, though demonstrating more of the condescension that W. J. Cash found almost inevitable in the Southern planter.[8] His Northern bride is the visitor from New England, less austere but no less religious than Mrs. Stowe's Miss Ophelia. Paul, the black preacher, is a lesser Uncle Tom who, unlike his prototype, is tempted but redeems himself dramatically. Among the house servants, more delicately bred and colored, Albert matches the facile Adolph, and his "yellow girl" occupies the nobler Eliza's position. In addition, each novel introduces the recalcitrant little girl, but in Mrs. Hentz's narrative both her race and her character deficiency are different from Topsy's. Although Mrs. Hentz's canvas is not as broad as Mrs. Stowe's, she too creates many variations of these types, for example, the weak Crissy and the ugly free Negro, Judy. Naturally her proslavery novel demanded a special kind of villain; her crafty abolitionist-missionary has little in common with Mrs. Stowe's slave-driver except his villainy. Again, perhaps in an effort not to over-simplify, Mrs. Hentz introduces variations. Besides the abolitionist who is a hypocritical rascal, she presents two other types: the good man who rides a hobby and the busybody who is determined to free the slaves against their will. The fact that most of her characters are intended to represent types is evidenced by the Dickensian names she gives them. Not only is her landowner called Moreland, but the three men whose think-

8. W. J. Cash, *The Mind of the South* (New York, 1941), p. 69.

ing on slavery he tries to correct are Hastings, Grimby and Horsely, the plotting abolitionist is Brainard, and the couple who hypnotize Crissy into stealing away from her owners are Mr. and Mrs. Softly—names that for eccentricity eclipse those of Mrs. Stowe, who was also an admirer of the Great Boz.

In addition to certain stereotype characters, readers of the plantation romances expected sensational action and extravagant sentiments. Violence and horror were the stock-in-trade of such popular novelists as Mrs. E. D. E. N. Southworth,[9] and they were useful even to Mrs. Stowe. *The Planter's Northern Bride*, however, is less typical in this respect. In Mrs. Hentz's other fiction the plot often hinges on a spectacular accident, such as the explosion of a steamboat in *Linda, or The Young Pilot of the Belle Creole*, the burning of a plantation home in *Marcus Warland*, or the encounter with a savage Indian in *Robert Graham* (1855). In all of these events the hero courageously saves a life at the risk of his own. The principal crises in *The Planter's Northern Bride*, however, are the planter's verbal challenges of those who attempt to violate the institution of slavery, and in only one case does his confrontation become physical. Even in Crissy's escape across the Ohio at Cincinnati—apparently intended as an ironic reversal of Eliza's leap to freedom—the reader is likely to be more concerned about Crissy's inner conflict than about her physical danger.

In the exploitation of sentimental conventions, the story of Moreland and his Northern bride and Southern slaves is more characteristic of the romantic formula of its day. Undoubtedly it introduces no situation as ludicrous as the melodramatic Ernest Linwood's punishing himself by fasting for forty days in his library in imitation of

9. See, for example, her *Redemption*, in which a quadroon is sold into the horrors of slavery in the Deep South.

Christ's fasting for forty days in the wilderness. Moreover, its one death scene is more realistic than either little Eva's or St. Clare's; no visions of heaven or departed ones are accorded its expiring consumptive.[10] Nor does Mrs. Hentz labor the importance of religious conversion as constantly as Mrs. Stowe, although she does maintain a firm Christian stance, in keeping with her own principles and the fictional standards of her day. Yet *The Planter's Northern Bride* satisfied the popular taste by means of its Cinderella beginning, its dramatic contrast between the lives of the very rich and the very poor, and its glorification, with Biblical overtones, of family ties. Since the author had a keen sense of the individual scene, her narrative moves forward frequently by dialogue, but often dialogue that is heavily ceremonial, lacking in Mrs. Stowe's irony and humor. In sentimentality even more than in stereotype characters and plot, Mrs. Hentz's novel is typical of its genre in the antebellum period.

The reasoning in defense of slavery is also fairly typical, yet the author's New England origin made an interesting difference. In reviewing *The Planter's Northern Bride*, Mrs. Sarah J. Hale, editor of *Godey's Lady's Book*, observed that, having lived in the North, West, and South, "Mrs. Hentz has learned the wisdom of loving her whole country above any particular state or section." The New York *Mirror*, after recommending this novel because "the incidents are well varied, the scenes beautifully described, and the interest admirably kept up," added: "But the moral of the book is its highest merit. The 'Planter's Northern Bride' should be as welcome as the dove of peace to every fireside in the Union. It cannot be read without a

10. In answer to Mrs. Stowe's implication that tuberculosis is a Southern disease, Mrs. Hentz counters with two examples of fatal cases contracted in the North and with another prevented from a fatal conclusion only by a sudden removal to Georgia.

moistening of the eye, a softening of the heart, and a mitigation of sectional and most unchristian prejudice."[11] This lack of narrow sectional bias and this ultimate purpose of bringing the North and the South into harmony through a calm reasonableness about slavery distinguish the novel from much of the plantation fiction of the 1850's. "Being a native of the North and a dweller of the South, with affections strongly clinging to both," as she herself said,[12] she attempted to mediate between the sections. Her intention was to defend slavery, not merely as a humane institution and a beneficial arrangement for both white and black in her adopted section, but also as a system essential to the economy of the North. The *American Courier* declared that she had "developed new views of golden argument,"[13] although it appears that she was taking a leaf from the politicians' book. The difficulty of dramatizing the economic argument led her to present it chiefly in long speeches by the planter and in occasional auctorial outbursts.[14]

For the action of her story Mrs. Hentz had to depend on the more dramatic values of the theme of humaneness. Again she made some efforts toward a moderate point of view and tone. In *Marcus Warland* she had not entirely ignored Mrs. Stowe's basic contention that Negro family life was unprotected by law, for she portrayed one master as being compelled by the collapse of his fortunes to sell his slaves, and another planter as coldly refusing to purchase his slave's wife before moving his chattels to Texas. More on the defensive in *The Planter's Northern Bride*,

11. Both of these editorial accolades appear on a flyleaf advertisement of the novel in *Robert Graham*, published in the following year.

12. Hentz, "Address to the Reader," *Marcus Warland*, p. 7.

13. Flyleaf advertisement in *Robert Graham*.

14. Her planter's speeches are not so long, however, as those of Walwroth, who argues for twenty or thirty pages at a time in W. L. G. Smith's *Life in the South* (Philadelphia, 1852).

she yet showed sympathy for a runaway slave. She also refused to approve of the original enslavement of the race, even though she could allow her planter to view it as the will of God. Her method of defending slavery was the stock one of dramatizing the difference in the condition of laborers in the North and the South and demonstrating the manner in which skeptical or hostile Northerners were converted when they became eye-witnesses of plantation paternalism. Just as Mrs. Stowe had made certain Southerners the severest critics of slavery, so Mrs. Hentz introduced thoughtful Northerners to support it as the most beneficial system for any laboring class. She herself maintained the moderate tone that she gave these Northern spokesmen.[15] Feeling herself called to the role of peacemaker, she persuasively marshaled all the arguments at her command—paternalistic, fatalistic, and pragmatic—in defense of a system she had never known except as an outsider.

Her readers will doubtless always be curious about this outsider's commitment to the cause for which she debated with Mrs. Stowe. The manner in which she first came to accept slavery is not known. Mrs. Brevard reported hearing that when Mrs. Hentz moved to Chapel Hill, her first home in the South, she "came without prejudice against Southern institutions."[16] Mrs. Hentz's letters are not available, and the diary she kept during 1836 in Florence, Alabama, makes only two allusions to slavery. On May 20 she observed wryly of a certain Mrs. Dickey, "She is not handsome, not even pretty,—nor witty, but her father has 4 or 500 negroes and that makes her lovely in this southern land." On May 24, during reverberations from the Creek

15. She would never have permitted herself the anger of such a novelist as Mrs. V. G. Cowdin, who also wrote of the experiences of an abolitionist's daughter in *Ellen, or The Fanatic's Daughter* (Mobile, Alabama, 1860).

16. Brevard, *The Library of Southern Literature*, VI, 2378.

Indian uprisings in southern Alabama she exclaimed, ''Oh! that we were far removed from the red men of the wilderness as well as from the children of Africa.''[17]

The pattern of her changing interest in slavery is clearer in her fiction than in her life. Like most other plantation romances, her novels which antedate Mrs. Stowe's masterpiece seem unselfconscious about Negro bondage and introduce the black man only as an occasional bit of local color. *Eoline*, published in 1852, ignores the slavery issue entirely and introduces only one slave by name. In *Marcus Warland*, which appeared in the same year, though probably later, she declared: ''It is not our intention to write a work in defense of the peculiar institution of Southern life; but in delineating pictures of Southern life, where the negro character occupies so conspicuous a place and exercises so commanding an influence, we would draw from nature alone.''[18] In this novel she introduced her first full quota of black characters and her first digressions in defense of slavery, but her plot was unaffected. Plans for its composition may have been well under way before she read *Uncle Tom's Cabin*, which was not available in book form until March of that year. Her argument against abolition doctrine was given to Mr. Bellamy, the stereotyped old planter, who refused for altruistic reasons to free his slaves. ''He felt that by turning hundreds of helpless beings adrift upon the world, he would be rather exposing them to want and temptation than administering to their well-being.''[19] Certain short stories published in 1853 repeat the paternalistic theme, as in the tale of Dilsey, a ''sable attendant'' whose stolen child is returned through the as-

17. Mrs. Hentz's unpublished diary is preserved in the North Carolina Collection of the Library of The University of North Carolina at Chapel Hill.

18. Hentz, *Marcus Warland*, p. 17.

19. *Ibid.*, p. 60.

sistance of compassionate whites, even though, it is insisted, she is a free Negro. Mrs. Hentz records this allegedly true story as "one of many instances of Southern kindness and humanity to a lowly race—whose feelings the Southron is too often accused of disregarding and trampling under foot."[20] The following year *The Planter's Northern Bride* brought Mrs. Hentz's proslavery efforts to their climax. In her subsequent novels she returned to the romantic formula, unaffected by the great debate of the decade. None of her novels is more remote from concern over slavery or from reality than her last, *Ernest Linwood.*

Perhaps one reason for *Ernest Linwood*'s receding into unreality is its lack of a recognizable setting. On the other hand, one element that distinguishes *The Planter's Northern Bride* from the commonplace plantation romance and gives a greater impression of reality is its careful eye for local color. Besides enabling her to argue temperately as one who knew and loved both sections, Mrs. Hentz's New England origin gave her an advantage in describing the Southern scene and its picturesque inhabitants. As an outsider, she retained an awareness of the peculiarities of landscape, architecture, and customs, and portrayed them in nearly all her novels. Especially in *The Planter's Northern Bride*, her trees are authentically Southern, not merely the "shining-leaved magnolia" but also "the sturdy blackjack, the graceful willow oak," often decorated by "hoary moss that hung in gray loops" or by coral honeysuckle. Although her mocking bird with its "rills of melody, clear, silvery, liquid," might have sung anywhere in the South and her cotton blossoms might have changed their delicate tints throughout the region, most of her pictures are drawn from accurate observation in the Lower South, especially southern Alabama and Georgia and northern Florida.

20. Hentz, *Wild Jack, or The Stolen Child and Other Stories,* p. 34.

Moreland is described as traveling through piney woods and on a road that "was one bed of sand, in which the horses' feet plunged to the fetlocks, throwing off a cloud of dust at every step." The account of the planter's residence is authentic for this section, too, with emphasis on the breezeway and on the long porch that completely surrounds the house. In contrast, the white backwoodsman lived in a one-room, windowless log cabin, whose separate corners were used as sleeping quarters for overnight guests passing through the comparatively unsettled country.

Mrs. Hentz capitalized on the quaint manners and customs of two classes of uneducated people in the South of her time—the backwoodsman and the Negro.[21] In such earlier novels as *Linda*, the resident of the more untraveled areas plays the stock role of sinister villain in the journey of the planter's family. In *The Planter's Northern Bride*, however, Mrs. Hentz again moved toward reality, probably motivated partly by the desire to provide a "democratic" argument for slavery—the availability of slaves to even the hard-working poor white as he gradually accumulated and cleared his acres of land. The "true beauty of the backwood gripe" with which the backwoods family greet Eulalia and also the bacon and greens, hoecakes, and sweet potato pie that they serve her were as characteristic of the region as were the chills and fever from which these Georgia crackers suffered periodically. ("Shake a little one day, up and smart as a pipe-stem the next.") The mood may be more pastoral than the realities justified, but the pioneer farmer breaking in new land, himself chief workman as well as overseer, is authentic.

The backwoodsman, however, is incidental, and subordinate in histrionic value to the Negro. Beginning with

21. In *Linda* and its sequel, *Robert Graham*, she also pictured highly conventionalized Indians who evidently had only a literary origin.

Linda, Mrs. Hentz observed and carefully painted into the background of her stories the picturesque customs of the black race. As the Negro characters emerged from the background to take more significant roles in *The Planter's Northern Bride*, Mrs. Hentz gave greater attention to their quaint ways. The seriousness of her intention in this novel probably prevented her from lightening its mood with the carefully recorded cornshucking songs of *Linda* or the gay Christmas celebrations, including the now-forgotten custom of "catching the white folks' Christmas gift," seen pictured in *Marcus Warland*. But she observed such allegedly racial traits as the Negro's respect for a smooth, snowy-white bed, his capacity for sleeping soundly under almost any conditions, his enjoyment of hymn-singing, and his habit of spending money with no thought of the morrow. The backwoodsman provides a brief, grotesque contrast in the story of the cultured planter, but the happy, childlike slave exists throughout the novel as the most picturesque element in his life. Mrs. Hentz did fuller justice to the externals of the existence of both characters than did most writers before the postwar local-color movement.

In *The Planter's Northern Bride*, more than in any of her other novels, Mrs. Hentz sketched the landscape and the folk customs of the Lower South as though she hoped an unusually definite and colorful setting might lend credibility to her story and its thesis. In this respect both she and Mrs. Stowe took more pains than most of their contemporaries, but of the two authors Mrs. Hentz, perhaps because she had more opportunity for observation, was more generous with details. She was too ambitious when she hoped that, by defending slavery as a New Englander, she might help prevent the war which, according to a half-joking acknowledgment of Abraham Lincoln, Mrs. Stowe caused. Her novel pales beside the vitality of *Uncle Tom's*

Cabin. Yet it remains an interesting variation of a durable genre, one of the more conscientious and successful attempts to picture plantation life in the last decade of slavery.

THE
PLANTER'S NORTHERN BRIDE

PREFACE.

It was the intention of the author to have given this book to the world during the course of the past season, but unforeseen occurrences have prevented the accomplishment of her purpose. She no longer regrets the delay, as she believes it will meet a more cordial reception at the present time.

When individual or public feeling is too highly wrought on any subject, there must inevitably follow a reaction, and reason, recovering from the effects of transient inebriation, is ready to assert its original sovereignty.

Not in the spirit of egotism, do we repeat what was said in the preface of a former work, that we were born at the North, and though destiny has removed us far from our native scenes, we cherish for them a sacred regard, an undying attachment.

It cannot therefore be supposed that we are actuated by hostility or prejudice, in endeavouring to represent the unhappy consequences of that intolerant and fanatical spirit, whose fatal influence we so deeply deplore.

We believe that there are a host of noble, liberal minds, of warm, generous, candid hearts, at the North, that will bear us out in our views of Southern character, and that feel with us that our *national* honour is tarnished, when a portion of our country is held up to public disgrace and foreign insult, by those, too, whom every feeling of patriotism should lead to defend it from ignominy and shield it from dishonour. The hope that they will appreciate and do justice to our motives, has imparted enthusiasm to our feelings, and energy to our will, in the prosecution of our literary labour.

When we have seen the dark and horrible pictures drawn of slavery and exhibited to a gazing world, we have wondered if we were one of those favoured individuals to whom the fair side of life is ever turned, or whether we were created with a moral blindness, incapable of distinguishing its lights and shadows. One thing is certain, and if we were on judicial oath we would repeat it, that during our residence in the South, we have never *witnessed* one scene of cruelty or oppression, never beheld a chain or a manacle, or the infliction of a punishment more severe than parental authority would be justified in applying to filial disobedience or transgression. This is not owing to our being placed in a limited sphere of observation, for we have seen and studied domestic, social, and plantation life, in Carolina, Alabama, Georgia, and Florida. We have been admitted into close and familiar communion with numerous families in each of these States, not merely as a passing visiter, but as an indwelling guest, and we have never been pained by an inhuman exercise of authority, or a wanton abuse of power.

On the contrary, we have been touched and gratified by the exhibition of affectionate kindness and care on one side, and loyal and devoted attachment on the other. We have been especially struck with the cheerfulness and contentment of the slaves, and their usually elastic and buoyant spirits. From the abundant opportunities we have had of judging, we give it as our honest belief, that the negroes of the South are the happiest *labouring class* on the face of the globe; even subtracting from their portion of enjoyment all that can truly be said of their trials and sufferings. The fugitives who fly to the Northern States are no proof against the truth of this statement. They have most of them been made disaffected by the influence of others—tempted by promises which are seldom fulfilled Even in the garden of Eden, the seeds of discontent and rebellion were sown; surely we need not wonder that they sometimes take root in the beautiful groves of the South.

In the large cities we have *heard* of families who were cruel to their slaves, as well as unnaturally severe in the discipline of their children. (Are there no similar instances at the North?) But the indignant feeling which any known instance of inhumanity calls forth at the South, proves that they are not of common occurrence.

We have conversed a great deal with the coloured people, feeling the deepest interest in learning their own views of their peculiar situation, and we have almost invariably been delighted and affected by their humble devotion to their master's family, their child-like, affectionate reliance on their care and protection, and above all, with their genuine cheerfulness and contentment.

This very morning, since commencing these remarks, our sympathies have been strongly moved by the simple eloquence of a negro woman in speaking of her former master and mistress, who have been dead for many years.

"Oh!" said she, her eyes swimming with tears, and her voice choking with emotion, "I loved my master and mistress like my own soul. If I could have died in their stead, I would gladly done it. I would have gone into the grave and brought them up, if the Lord had let me do it. Oh! they were so good—so kind. All on us black folks would 'ave laid down our lives for 'em at any minute."

"Then you were happy?" we said; "you did not sigh to be free?"

"No, mistress, that I didn't. I was too well off for that. I wouldn't have left my master and mistress for all the freedom in the world. I'd left my own father and mother first. I loved 'em better than I done them. I loved their children too. Every one of 'em has been babies in my arms—and I loved 'em a heap better than I done my own, I want to stay with 'em as long as I live, and I know they will take care of me when I get too old to work."

These are her own words. We have not sought this simple instance of faithful and enduring love. It came to us as if in corroboration of our previous remarks, and we could not help recording it.

The history of Crissy and the circumstances of her abduction are true.

The character of Dr. Darley is drawn from life. Though death has now set the seal of eternity on his virtues, we would not violate the sanctity of private life by bringing his real name before the public. Should those he loved best on earth recognise the lineaments we have attempted to draw, may they accept this imperfect tribute to his exalted worth, his brilliant and commanding talents, as well as his pure and genuine philanthropy.

Many of the circumstance we have recorded in these pages are founded on truth. The plot of the insurrection, the manner in which it was instigated and detected, and the brief history of

Nat, the giant, with his domestication in a Northern family, are literally true.

If any one should think the affection manifested by the slaves of Moreland for their master is too highly coloured, we would refer them to the sketch of Thomas Jefferson's arrival at Monticello on his return from Paris, after an absence of five years. It is from the pen of his daughter, and no one will doubt its authenticity.

"The negroes discovered the approach of the carriage as soon as it reached Shadwell, and such a scene I never witnessed in my life. They collected in crowds around it, and almost drew it up the mountain by hand. The shouting, &c., had been sufficiently obstreperous before, but the moment the carriage arrived on the top it reached the climax. When the door of the carriage was opened, they received him in their arms and bore him into the house, crowding around, kissing his hands and feet, some blubbering and crying, others laughing. It appeared impossible to satisfy their eyes, or their anxiety to touch, and even to kiss the very earth that bore him. These were the first ebullitions of joy for his return, after a long absence, which they would of course feel; but it is perhaps not out of place to add here, that they were at all times very devoted in their attachment to their master. They believed him to be one of the greatest, and they knew him to be one of the best of men, and kindest of masters. They spoke to him freely, and applied confidingly to him in all their difficulties and distresses; and he watched over them in sickness and health; interested himself in all their concerns; advising them, and showing esteem and confidence in the good, and indulgence to all."

We can add nothing to this simple, pathetic description. Monticello is hallowed ground, and the testimony that proceeds from its venerated retreat should be listened to with respect and confidence. The same accents might be heard from Mount Vernon's august shades, where the grave of Washington has been bedewed by the tears of the grateful African.

But we have done.

If we fail to accomplish the purpose for which we have written, we shall at least have the consolation of knowing that our motives are disinterested, and our aim patriotic and true.

Should no Northern heart respond to our earnest appeal, we trust the voice of the South will answer to our own, not in a faint, cold, dying echo, but in a full, spontaneous strain, whose reverberations shall reach to the green hills and granite cliffs of New England's "rock-bound coast."

CAROLINE LEE HENTZ.

MR. AND MRS. MORELAND AND ALBERT.

THE

PLANTER'S NORTHERN BRIDE.

CHAPTER I.

Mr. Moreland, a Southern planter, was travelling through the New England States in the bright season of a Northern spring. Business with some of the merchant princes of Boston had brought him to the North; but a desire to become familiar with the beautiful surroundings of the metropolis induced him to linger long after it was transacted, to gratify the taste and curiosity of an intelligent and liberal mind. He was rich and independent, had leisure as well as wealth at his command, and there was something in the deep green fields and clear blue waters of New England that gave a freshness, and brightness, and elasticity to his spirits, wanting in his milder, sunnier latitude.

He found himself one Saturday night in a sweet country village, whose boundaries were marked by the most luxuriant shubbery and trees, in the midst of which a thousand silver rills were gushing. He was pleased with the prospect of passing the ensuing Sunday in a valley so serene and quiet, that it seemed as if Nature enjoyed in its shades the repose of an eternal Sabbath. The inn where he stopped was a neat, orderly place, and though the landlord impressed him, at first, as a hard, repulsive looking man, with a dark, Indian face, and large, iron-bound frame, he found him ready to perform all the duties of a host. Requesting to be shown to a private apartment, he ordered Albert, a young mulatto, who accompanied him on his journey, to follow him with his valise. Albert was a handsome, golden-skinned youth, with shining black hair and eyes, dressed very nearly as genteelly as his master, and who generally attracted more attention on their Northern tour. Accustomed to wait on his master and listen to the conversation of refined and educated gentlemen, he had very little of the dialect of the negro, and those familiar with the almost unintelligible jargon which delineators of the sable character put into their lips, could not but be astonished at the propriety of his language and pronunciation.

When Mr. Moreland started on his journey to the North, his friends endeavoured to dissuade him from taking a servant with him, as he would incur the danger of losing him among the granite hills to which he was bound:—they especially warned him of the risk of taking

Albert, whose superior intelligence and cultivation would render him more accessible to the arguments which would probably be brought forward to lure him from his allegiance.

"I defy all the eloquence of the North to induce Albert to leave me," exclaimed Mr. Moreland. "Let them do it if they can. Albert," he said, calling the boy to him, who was busily employed in brushing and polishing his master's boots, with a friction quick enough to create sparkles of light. "Albert,—I am going to the North,—would you like to go with me?"

"To be sure I would, master, I would like to go anywhere in the world with you."

"You know the people are all free at the North, Albert."

"Yes, master.

"And when you are there, they will very likely try to persuade you that you are free too, and tell you it is your duty to run away from me, and set up for a gentleman yourself. What do you think of all this?"

Albert suspended his brush in the air, drew up his left shoulder with a significant shrug, darted an oblique glance at his master from his bright black eyes, and then renewed his friction with accelerated velocity.

"Well, my boy, you have not answered me," cried Mr. Moreland, in a careless, yet interested manner, peculiar to himself.

"Why, you see, Mars. Russell (when he addressed his

master by his Christian name, he always abbreviated his title in this manner, though when the name was omitted he uttered the title in all its dignity),—"you see, Mars. Russell,"—here the mulatto slipped the boot from his arm, placed it on the floor, and still retaining the brush in his right hand, folded his arms across his breast, and spoke deliberately and earnestly,—"they couldn't come round this boy with that story; I've hearn it often enough already; I ain't afraid of anything they can say and do, to get me away from you as long as you want me to stay with you. But if you are afraid to trust me, master, that's another thing. You'd better leave me, if you think I'd be mean enough to run away."

"Well said, Albert!" exclaimed Mr. Moreland, laughing at the air of injured honour and conscious self-appreciation he assumed; "I do trust you, and shall surely take you with me; you can make yourself very amusing to the people, by telling them of your home frolics, such as being chained, handcuffed, scourged, flayed, and burned alive, and all those little trifles they are so much interested in."

"Oh! master, I wish I may find everybody as well off as I am. If there's no lies told on you but what I tell, you'll be mighty safe, I know. Ever since Miss Claudia"—

"Enough," cried Mr. Moreland, hastily interrupting him. He had breathed a name which evidently awakened painful recollections, for his sunshiny countenance became suddenly dark and cold. Albert, who seemed familiar with his master's varying moods, respectfully resumed his occupation, while Mr. Moreland took up his hat and plunged into the soft, balmy atmosphere of a Southern spring morning.

It is not our intention to go back and relate the past history of Mr. Moreland. It will be gathered in the midst of unfolding events, at least all that is necessary for the interest of our story. We will therefore return to the white-walled inn of the fair New England village, where our traveller was seated, enjoying the long, dewy twilight of the new region in which he was making a temporary rest. The sun had gone down, but the glow of his parting smile lingered on the landscape and reddened the stream that gleamed and flashed through the distant shrubbery. Not far from the inn, on a gradual eminence, rose the village church, whose tall spire, surmounted by a horizontal vane, reposed on the golden clouds of sunset, resembling the crucifix of some gorgeous cathedral. This edifice was situated far back from the road, surrounded by a common of the richest green, in the centre of which rose the swelling mound, consecrated by the house of God. Some very handsome buildings were seen at regular intervals, on either side of the road, among which the court-house stood conspicuous, with its freestone-coloured wall and lofty cupola. There was something in the aspect of that church, with its heaven-ascending spire, whose glory-crown of lingering day-beams glittered with a kind of celestial splendour, reminding him of the halo which encircles the brows of saints; something in the deep tranquillity of the hour, the soft, hazy, undulating outline of the distant horizon, the swaying motion of the tall poplars that margined the street far as his eye could reach, and through whose darkening vista a solitary figure gradually lessened on the eye, that solemnized and even saddened the spirits of our traveller. The remembrances of early youth and opening manhood pressed upon him with suddenly awakened force. Hopes, on which so sad and awful a blight had fallen, raised themselves like faded flowers sprinkled with dew, and mocked him with their visionary bloom. In the excitement of travelling, the realities of business, the frequent collision of interests, the championship of oft invaded rights, he had lost much of that morbidness of feeling and restlessness of character, which, being more accidental than inherent, would naturally yield to the force of circumstances counter to those in which they were born. But at the close of any arbitrary division of time, such as the last day of the week or the year, the mind is disposed to deeper meditation, and the mental burden, whose weight has been equipoised by worldly six-day cares, rolls back upon the mind with leaden oppression.

Moreland had too great a respect for the institutions of religion, too deep an inner sense of its power, to think of continuing his journey on the Sabbath, and he was glad that the chamber which he occupied looked out upon that serene landscape, and that the morning shadow of the lofty church-spire would be thrown across his window. It seemed to him he had seen this valley before, with its beautiful green, grassy slopes, its sunset-gilded church, and dark poplar avenue. And it seemed to him also, that he had seen a fair maiden form gliding through the central aisle of that temple, in robes of virgin white, and soft, down-bending eyes of dark brown lustre, and brow of moonlight calmness. It was one of those dim reminiscences, those vague, dream-like consciousnesses of a previous existence, which every being of poetic temperament is sometimes aware of, and though they come, faint shadows of a far-off world, quick and vanishing as lightning, they nevertheless leave certain traces of their presence, "trails of glory," as a great poet has called them, proceeding from the spirit's home.

While he sat leaning in silence against the window frame, the bell of the church began to toll slowly and solemnly, and as the sounds rolled heavily and gloomily along, then reverberated and vibrated with melancholy prolongation, sending out a sad, dying echo, followed by another majestic, startling peal, he wondered to hear such a funeral knell at that twilight hour, and looked up the shadowy line of poplars for the dark procession leading to the grave. Nothing was seen, however, and nothing heard but those monotonous, heavy, mournful peals, which seemed to sweep by him with the flaps of the raven's wings. Twenty times the bell tolled, and then all was still.

"What means the tolling of the bell?" asked he of the landlord, who was walking beneath the window. "Is there a funeral at this late hour?"

"A young woman has just died," replied the landlord. "They are tolling her age. It is a custom of our village."

Moreland drew back with a shudder. Just twenty. That was *her* age. *She* had not died, and yet the death-bell might well ring a deeper knell over her than the being who had just departed. In the grave the remembrance of the bitterest wrongs are buried, and the most vindictive cease to thirst for vengeance. Moreland was glad when a summons to supper turned his thoughts into a different channel.

There might have been a dozen men seated around the table, some whose dress and manners proclaimed that they were gentlemen, others evidently of a coarser grain. They all looked up at the entrance of Moreland, who, with a bow, such as the courteous stranger is always ready to make, took his seat, while Albert placed himself behind his master's chair.

"Take a seat," said Mr. Grimby, the landlord, looking at Albert. "There's one by the gentleman. Plenty of room for us all."*

"My boy will wait," cried Mr. Moreland, with un-

* A fact.

conscious haughtiness, while his pale cheek visibly reddened. "I would thank you to leave the arrangement of such things to myself."

"No offence, I hope, sir," rejoined Mr. Grimby. 'We look upon everybody here as free and equal. This is a free country, and when folks come among us we don't see why they can't conform to our ways of thinking. There's a proverb that says—'when you're with the Romans, it's best to do as the Romans do.'"

"Am I to understand," said Mr. Moreland, fixing his eye deliberately on his Indian-visaged host, "that you wish my servant to sit down with yourself and these gentlemen?"

"To be sure I do," replied the landlord, winking his small black eye knowingly at his left-hand neighbour. "I don't see why he isn't as good as the rest of us. I'm an enemy to all distinctions myself, and I'd like to bring everybody round to my opinion."

"Albert!" cried his master, "obey the landlord's wishes. *I* want no supper; take my seat and see that you are well attended to."

"Mars. Russell," said the mulatto, in a confused and deprecating tone.

"Do as I tell you," exclaimed Mr. Moreland, in a tone of authority, which, though tempered by kindness, Albert understood too well to resist. As Moreland passed from the room, a gentleman, with a very prepossessing countenance and address, who was seated on the opposite side of the table, rose and followed him.

"I am sorry you have had so poor a specimen of Northern politeness," said the gentleman, accosting Moreland, with a slight embarrassment of manner. "I trust you do not think we all endorse such sentiments."

"I certainly must make you an exception, sir," replied Moreland, holding out his hand with involuntary frankness; "but I fear there are but very few. This is, however, the first direct attack I have received, and I hardly knew in what way to meet it. I have too much self-respect to place myself on a level with a man so infinitely my inferior. That he intended to insult me, I know by his manner. He knows our customs at home, and that nothing could be done in more positive violation of them than his unwarrantable proposition."

They had walked out in the open air while they were speaking, and continued their walk through the poplar avenue, through whose stiff and stately branches the first stars of evening were beginning to glisten.

"I should think you would fear the effect of these things on your servant," said the gentleman,—"that it would make him insolent and rebellious. Pardon me, sir, but I think you were rather imprudent in bringing him with you, and exposing him to the influences which must meet him on every side. You will not be surprised, after the instance which has just occurred, when I tell you, that, in this village, you are in the very hot-bed of fanaticism ; and that a Southern planter, accompanied by his slave, can meet but little sympathy, consideration, or toleration ; I fear there will be strong efforts made to induce your boy to leave you."

"I fear nothing of that kind," answered Moreland. "If they can bribe him from me, let him go. I brought him far less to minister to my wants than to test his fidelity and affection. I believe them proof against any temptation or assault; if I am deceived I wish to know it, though the pang would be as severe as if my own brother should lift his hand against me."

"Indeed!—I did not imagine that the feelings were ever so deeply interested. While I respect your rights, and resent any ungentlemanlike infringement of them, as in the case of our landlord, I cannot conceive how beings, who are ranked as goods and chattels, things of bargain and traffic, can ever fill the place of a friend or brother in the heart."

"Nevertheless, I assure you, that next to our own kindred, we look upon our slaves as our best friends."

As they came out of the avenue into the open street, they perceived the figure of a woman, walking with slow steps before them, bearing a large bundle under her arm ; she paused several times, as if to recover breath, and once she stopped and leaned against the fence, while a dry, hollow cough rent her frame.

"Nancy," said the gentleman, "is that you?—you should not be out in the night air."

The woman turned round, and the starlight fell on a pale and wasted face.

"I can't help it," she answered,—"I can't hold out any longer,—I can't work any more;—I ain't strong enough to do a single chore now; and Mr. Grimby says he hain't got any room for me to lay by in. My wages stopped three weeks ago. He says there's no use in my hanging on any longer, for I'll never be good for anything any more."

"Where are you going now?" said the gentleman.

"Home!" was the reply, in a tone of deep and hopeless despondency,—"Home, to my poor old mother. I've supported her by my wages ever since I've been hired out; that's the reason I haven't laid up any. God knows——"

Here she stopped, for her words were evidently choked by an awful realization of the irremediable misery of her condition. Moreland listened with eager interest. His compassion was awakened, and so were other feelings. Here was a problem he earnestly desired to solve, and he determined to avail himself of the opportunity thrown in his path.

"How far is your home from here?" he asked.

"About three-quarters of a mile."

"Give me your bundle—I'll carry it for you, you are too feeble; nay, I insist upon it."

Taking the bundle from the reluctant hand of the poor woman, he swung it lightly upward and poised it on his left shoulder. His companion turned with a look of unfeigned surprise towards the elegant and evidently high-bred stranger, thus courteously relieving poverty and weakness of an oppressive burden.

"Suffer me to assist you," said he. "You must be very unaccustomed to services of this kind; I ought to have anticipated you."

"I am not accustomed to do such things for myself," answered Moreland, "because there is no occasion; but it only makes me more willing to do them for others. You look upon us as very self-indulging beings, do you not?"

"We think your institutions calculated to promote the growth of self-indulgence and selfishness. The virtues that resist their opposing influences must have more than common vitality."

"We, who know the full length and breadth of our responsibilities, have less time than any other men for self-indulgence. We feel that life is too short for the performance of our duties, made doubly arduous and irksome by the misapprehension and prejudice of those who ought to know us better and judge us more justly and kindly. My good woman, do we walk too fast?"

"Oh, no, sir. I so long to get home, but I am so ashamed to have you carry that bundle."

He had forgotten the encumbrance in studying the domestic problem, presented to him for solution. Here was a poor young woman, entirely dependent on her daily labour for the support of herself and aged mother, incapacitated by sickness from ministering to their necessities, thrown back upon her home, without the means of subsistence: in prospective, a death of lingering torure for herself, for her mother a life of destitution or a helter in the almshouse. For every comfort, for the bare necessaries of life, they must depend upon the compassion of the public; the attendance of a physician must be the work of charity, their existence a burden on others.

She had probably been a faithful labourer in her employer's family, while health and strength lasted. He was an honest man in the common acceptation of the word, and had doled out her weekly wages as long as they were earned; but he was not rich, he had no superfluous gold, and could not afford to pay to her what was due to her stronger and more healthy successor; he could not afford to give her even the room which was required by another. What could she do but go to her desolate home and die? She could not murmur. She had no claim on the affection of the man in whose service she had been employed. She had lived with him in the capacity of a hireling, and he, satisfied that he paid her the utmost farthing which justice required, dismissed her, without incurring the census of unkindness or injustice. We ought to add, without deserving it. There were others far more able than himself to take care of her, and a home provided by the parish for every unsheltered head.

Moreland, whose moral perceptions were rendered very acute by observation, drew a contrast in his own mind, between the Northern and Southern labourer, when reduced to a state of sickness and dependence. He brought his own experience in comparison with the lesson of the present hour, and thought that the sick and dying negro, retained under his master's roof, kindly nursed and ministered unto, with no sad, anxious lookings forward into the morrow for the supply of nature's wants, no fears of being cast into the pauper's home, or of being made a member of that unhappy family, consecrated by no head, hallowed by no domestic relationship, had in contrast a far happier lot. In the latter case there was sickness, without its most horrible concomitant, poverty, without the harrowing circumstances connected with public charity, or the capricious influence of private compassion. It is true, the nominal bondage of the slave was wanting, but there was the bondage of poverty, whose iron chains are heard clanking in every region of God's earth, whose dark links are wrought in the forge of human suffering, eating slowly into the quivering flesh, till they reach and dry up the life-blood of the heart. It has often been said that there need be no such thing as poverty in this free and happy land; that here it is only the offspring of vice and intemperance; that the avenues of wealth and distinction are open to all, and that all who choose may arrive at the golden portals of success and honour, and enter boldly in. Whether this be true or not, let the thousand toiling operatives of the Northern manufactories tell; let the poor, starving seamstresses, whose pallid faces mingle their chill, wintry gleams with the summer glow and splendour of the Northern cities, tell; let the free negroes, congregated in the suburbs of some of our modern Babylons, lured from their homes by hopes based on sand, without forethought, experience, or employment, without sympathy, influence, or caste, let them also tell.

When Moreland reached the low, dark-walled cottage which Nancy pointed out as her home, he gave her back her bundle, and at the same time slipped a bill into her hand, of whose amount she could not be aware. But she knew by the soft, yielding paper the nature of the gift, and something whispered her that it was no niggard boon.

"Oh, sir," she cried, "you are too good. God bless you, sir, over and over again!"

She stood in the doorway of the little cabin, and the dull light within played luridly on her sharpened and emaciated features. Her large black eyes were burning with consumption's wasting fires, and a deep red, central spot in each concave cheek, like the flame of the magic cauldron, was fed with blood alone. Large tears were now sparkling in those glowing flame-spots, but they did not extinguish their wasting brightness.

"Poor creature!" thought Moreland. "Her day of toil is indeed over. There is nothing left for her but to endure and to die. She has learned to *labour*, she must now learn to *wait*."

As he turned from the door, resolving to call again before he left the village, he saw his companion step back and speak to her, extending his hand at the same time. Perceiving that he was actuated by the Christian spirit, which does not wish the left hand to know what the right hand doeth, he walked slowly on, through an atmosphere perfumed by the delicious but oppressive fragrance of the blossoming lilacs, that lent to this obscure habitation a certain poetic charm.

During their walk back to the inn, he became more and more pleased with his new acquaintance, whose name he ascertained was Brooks, by profession an architect of bridges. He was not a resident of the village, but was now engaged in erecting a central bridge over the river that divided the village from the main body of the town. As his interests were not identified with the place or the people, his opinions were received by Moreland with more faith and confidence than if they issued from the lips of a native inhabitant.

When they returned to the inn, they found Albert waiting at the door, with a countenance of mingled vexation and triumph. The landlord and several other men were standing near him, and had evidently been engaged in earnest conversation. The sudden cessation of this, on the approach of Mr. Moreland, proved that he had been the subject of it, and from the manner in which they drew back as he entered the passage, he imagined their remarks were not of the most flattering nature.

"Well, Albert, my boy," said he, when they were alone in his chamber, "I hope you relished your supper."

"Please, Mars. Russell, don't do that again. I made 'em wait on me this time, but it don't seem right. Besides, I don't feel on an equality with 'em, no way. They are no gentlemen."

Moreland laughed.

"What were they talking to you about so earnestly as I entered?" asked he.

"About how you treated me and the rest of us. Why, Mars. Russell, they don't know nothing about us. They want to know if we don't wear chains at home and manacles about our wrists. One asked if you didn't give us fodder to eat. Another wanted to strip off my coat, to see if my back wa'n't all covered with scars. I wish you'd heard what I told 'em. Master, I wish you'd heard the way I give it to 'em."

"I have no doubt you did me justice, Albert. My feelings are not in the least wounded, though my sense of justice is pained. Why, I should think the sight of your round, sleek cheeks, and sound, active limbs would be the best argument in my favour. They must believe you thrive wonderfully on fodder."

"What you think one of 'em said, Mars. Russell? They say you fatten me up, you dress me up, and carry me 'bout as a show-boy, to make folks think you treat us all well, but that the niggers at home are treated worse than dogs or cattle, a heap worse. I tell 'em it's all one big lie. I tell 'em you're the best—"

"Never mind, Albert. That will do. I want to think—"

Albert never ventured to intrude on his master's thinking moments, and, turning away in respectful silence, he soon stretched himself on the carpet and sunk in a profound sleep. In the mean time Moreland waded through a deep current of thought, that swelled as it rolled, and ofttimes it was turbid and foaming, and sometimes it seemed of icy chillness. He was a man of strong intellect and strong passions; but the latter, being under the control of principle, gave force and energy and warmth to a character which, if unrestrained, they would have defaced and laid waste. He was a searcher after truth, and felt ready and brave enough to plunge into the cold abyss, where it is said to be hidden, or to encounter the fires of persecution, the thorns of prejudice, to hazard everything, to suffer everything, rather than relinquish the hope of attaining it. He pondered much on the condition of mankind, its inequalities and wrongs. He thought of the poor and subservient in other lands, and compared them with our own. He thought of the groaning serfs of Russia; the starving sons of Ireland; the squalid operatives of England, its dark, subterranean workshops, sunless abodes of want, misery, and sin, its toiling millions, doomed to drain their hearts' best blood to add to the splendours and luxuries of royalty and rank; of the free hirelings of the North, who, as a *class*, travail in discontent and repining, anxious to throw off the yoke of servitude, sighing for an equality which exists only in name; and then he turned his thoughts homeward, to the enslaved children of Africa, and, taking them as a *class*, as a *distinct race* of beings, he came to the irresistible conclusion, that they were the happiest *subservient* race that were found on the face of the globe. He did not seek to disguise to himself the evils which were inseparably connected with their condition, or that man too oft abused the power he owned; but in view of all this, in view of the great, commanding truth, that wherever civilized man exists, there is the dividing line of the high and the low, the rich and the poor, the thinking and the labouring, in view of the God-proclaimed fact that "all Creation toileth and groaneth together," and that labour and suffering are the solemn sacraments of life, he believed that the slaves of the South were blest beyond the pallid slaves of Europe, or the anxious, care-worn labourers of the North.

With this conviction he fell asleep, and in his dreams he still tried to unravel the mystery of life, and to reconcile its inequalities with the justice and mercy of an omnipotent God.

CHAPTER II.

MORELAND breakfasted in his own room, and the peace of the Sabbath morning brooded on his heart. He took his seat at the window, and watched the shadows of the trees playing on the white walls of the church, and the golden gleam of its vane flashing on the blue of the sky. He was glad when the deep-toned bell called the worshippers together, and the people began to ascend the grassy slope that led up to the house of God. Mr. Brooks, his new friend, offered to accompany him and usher him to a seat; an offer he gratefully accepted. The pew to which he conducted him was situated at the right hand of the pulpit, in one of the wings of the church, so that he was facing the congregation, and could see them without appearing to gaze, as they glided, one by one, up the central aisle, to their accustomed places.

The interior of the church was very simple and pure. The green curtains and hangings of the pulpit, and the green screen that ran around the gallery, made a charming contrast with the unsullied whiteness of the walls, and harmonized with the green boughs that shaded the windows, and the green grass that carpeted the common.

There was no organ, with gilded pipes and sounding bellows, to give dignity to the orchestra, but Moreland caught a glimpse of white robes behind the curtain of the gallery, and he was sure some beautiful daughters of Zion were assembled there to sing praises to their God. He wanted the service to commence, so that he could see the figures of that vestal choir, as well as hear their mingling voices. His ear was gratified before his eye, for while waiting the coming of the minister, an anthem began to roll forth from the invisible band, whose notes filled the intervals of sound between the echoing peals of the bell. The commencing words of the anthem were grand. Moreland had heard them before, but they came to him with a new sense, because he was prepared to receive new impressions.

> "Before Jehovah's awful throne,
> Ye nations bow with sacred joy;
> Know that the Lord is God alone,
> He can create, and He destroy."

Among the voices that gave utterance to these adoring words, was one which, though sweet and soft and feminine beyond expression, seemed to drown every other. It rose, like the imagined hymn of an angel, clear and swelling, and then died gently away, to rise again with richer, fuller harmony. Moreland, whose devotional feelings were always exalted by sacred music, listened with breathless rapture, wondering what sweet bird of song had folded its wings behind that green enclosure.

At the conclusion of the anthem, where it is affirmed that the truth of God shall stand firm as a rock,

"While rolling years shall cease to move,"

when again and again the sublime refrain was repeated, that single voice alone fell upon his ear. On that alone the "rolling years" seemed borne onward to eternity. Other voices sang, and their notes died away; but hers kept rolling and warbling round the arching walls of the church, till the house was filled with their melody, and Moreland kept looking up, almost expecting to see them forming into something visible, as well as audible, into silvery or crystal rings, sparkling and glittering on the eye. He held his breath so long, that the act of respiration became painful, when renewed, and so intensely had he listened that the moisture gathered on his brow.

The anthem ceased as the venerable minister walked up the aisle and ascended the pulpit. He looked congenial with the music that heralded his approach, with his silver hair, mild, benignant countenance, and deep set thoughtful eyes. He was just such a minister as on would associate in idea with that pure, simple church, and white-robed singing band. His prayer breathed the very spirit of devotion. It reminded Moreland of the "Lord, save or we perish" of drowning Peter—"God be merciful to me a sinner" of the weeping publican. After the reading of a beautiful opening hymn, the choir rose, and the eyes of Moreland rested on one fair face, which he knew, by intuition, belonged to the minstrel maiden whose voice had so charmed his ear. It rose above the green curtain like a lily from its bed of sheathing leaves, so fair, so spiritual, so serene, it was impossible not to imagine an atmosphere of fragrance surrounding its purity and bloom. He was right. The hymn commenced, and the same sweet strains gushed from the lips, on which he was now gazing. He could not see the colour of her eyes, for they were downcast, but he could see the soft shadow of long, dark, drooping lashes on her cheeks, and he could see the bright, deep hue of chestnut brown that dyed her hair. He remembered the vision that had flitted before him the preceding evening, and it seemed to him that he had met this maiden stranger in some of the dim-remembered scenes of a past eternity. He could not shake off this wild idea, born of a poetic temperament and excited imagination. What was there about this young female that so singularly attracted him;—him, who had lately abjured the very thought of woman, in a widowhood of heart, far deeper and sadder than that which death creates; who had torn from his bosom the wilted garlands of love, and cast them, in indignation and despair, at the feet of a fallen and degraded idol? She was not more beautiful than some of her companions, perhaps not as beautiful as some, and yet he gazed only on her, watching the lifting of her drooping lids, as the Persian watches the rising of the star of day. It was not till the close of the hymn, the beginning of the sermon, after the curtain was drawn on one side and the singers seated, that she raised her eyes and fixed them steadily on the evangelical countenance of the pastor. Though bent on another, Moreland felt their dark magnetism to his heart's core. This sudden, powerful attraction, exercised by the simple village maiden, would not have been so strange had he been a young, romantic boy; but he was a man of some sad experience, who, before he entered that church, believed himself cold and insensible to the most seductive charms of womankind. At length, roused to the reflection that he might attract observation by the intensity of his gaze, he turned also towards the minister and endeavoured to rivet his attention on the truths he uttered. It is not to be supposed that a distinguished-looking stranger would pass entirely unnoticed in a village church, and there was many an eye perusing his face, while his was bent on the gallery; and there were some who thought his fixed and earnest gaze the bold, free stare of conscious wealth and arrogance. They had heard that a Southern gentleman, accompanied by a mulatto slave, had stopped at the inn the preceding night, and they were not slow in identifying the individual with the handsome stranger before them. There were a few, however, who did not judge him in this harsh manner, who had heard—(strange how quickly such things are winged in a country village)—how he had carried Nancy Brown's bundle all the way home for her, and put in her hand a ten dollar bill, without saying a word about it, and they lifted up their hearts and blessed him, though he knew it not.

When the benediction was pronounced, and the congregation passed out, Moreland lingered in the vestibule waiting for the choristers to descend. SHE came at last, leading by the hand a little girl of about five years of age, whose countenance bore a strong resemblance to her own. So many people were crowded in the doorways, she was obliged to pass so close to Moreland that her white dress floated against him; and if it had been the wing of a seraph he could not have felt a thrill of deeper reverence. She did not look at him, but he felt, by the colour that glowed on the lilies of her cheek, that she was aware of his presence and his gaze.

"Eula!" said the little girl, "don't walk so fast; Papa is coming."

Eula!—blessings on that cherub mouth for pronouncing the name he so longed to know. But that large, bustling gentleman, with reddish-auburn hair and florid complexion, and small, keen, restless black eyes, was that Eula's father? To be sure, it must be, for does she not take his arm with an affectionate, confiding air; and does not the little smiling five-year old thing frisk round to the other side of him, catching hold of his hand as if it were an ingot of gold she was grasping, instead of four freckled fingers and one stout thumb!

"Who is that reddish-haired gentleman?" asked Moreland of Mr. Brooks, as they walked slowly in the wake of light the sweet-voiced maiden seemed to leave behind her.

"His name is Hastings," replied his companion, "one of the most conspicuous characters in the village. He is considered a very shrewd, intelligent man, and, although not at all popular, has nevertheless a great deal of influence in the community."

"What is his profession?"

"He cannot be said to have any exclusive profession. He prepares young men for college, edits a paper called the "Emancipator," writes essays, delivers public lectures on all the leading topics of the day, and, among these, as you are doubtless prepared to hear, slavery, or rather anti-slavery, occupies a very conspicuous place."

"Indeed!" cried Moreland, with an unaccountable feeling of pain at the intelligence; "and is that young lady on his right arm his own daughter?"

"Yes! that is Miss Eulalia Hastings, or, as she is often called, the Flower of the village. She sings like an angel. You heard her voice in church. She is highly educated and accomplished, though she is so modest and retiring she makes no display. She is universally beloved and admired, and makes friends even of her father's enemies."

"Of course, she inherits all her father's prejudices against the South?" remarked Moreland, in a tone that seemed to ask a negation.

"Very probably; though they must be softened by passing through such a medium. I heard him say once, that if wife or child of his were languishing in a consumption, and he knew he could add ten years to their lives by sending them to the milder climate of the South, his conscience would not justify the act, so utterly does he abhor its institutions."

"You think, then, he would not allow his daughter to marry a Southerner?" This was said in a light, sarcastic tone, which was followed by one more serious. "Is he a man of wealth as well as influence?"

"No, not at all. His father left him considerable property, but he has wasted it in fruitless speculations and visionary schemes for the improvement of the age. He always has a hobby which he rides without mercy or judgment. The one on which he is mounted at present is the immediate emancipation of the negro race. You must not feel slighted if he invites your servant (I do not like the word *slave*) to come and break bread with him, without extending towards you the rites of hospitality."

"Is there a possibility of his doing this?" asked Moreland.

"We can only judge of the future by the past," replied the architect. "Not very long ago, while travelling in a neighbouring state, he came across a runaway negro, one of the most repulsive objects I ever saw,—gigantic in stature, black as ebony, with coarse and brutal features, and manners corresponding to his appearance. He took him at once under his protection, gave him a seat in his carriage, brought him home, introduced him to his family, gave him a seat at table between his wife and eldest daughter, put him in their best bedroom, and appeared to feel himself honoured by having such a guest."

"I like this," interrupted Moreland; "it shows that he is sincere, and is willing to put his principles to the proof. But Miss Hastings, surely this must have been very repugnant to her feelings; she could not willingly submit to such an infliction."

He said this with a shudder of inexpressible loathing, as he looked on the delicate, graceful figure walking before him, and imagined it placed in such close juxtaposition with the rough, gigantic negro.

"I suspect Miss Eulalia did not relish it very much," said Mr. Brooks; "but filial respect closed her lips. She happened to fall sick immediately after his arrival, whether as a consequence I know not, and thus escaped further personal contact. But the best part of the story is to come. Mr. Hastings, after he had gained sufficient éclat for his philanthropy and great-heartedness, was very willing to transfer his protegé to some of his neighbours, but no one was willing to accept the responsibility, and the fellow liked his quarters too well to think of leaving them. He grew very insolent and overbearing, and his host was at last compelled to turn him out of the house. Since then, he has had a double bolt fastened to his doors; and his dreams, I suspect, are haunted by black spectres, armed and equipped for murder and robbery."

The attention of Moreland was diverted by the diverging steps of the party before him. They turned aside into a path leading to a neat, modest-looking dwelling, shaded by sycamore trees, beside whose deep green, the scarlet berries of the mountain ash gleamed with coral splendour. Like most of the other houses, it wanted the graceful verandah,—the pillared piazza of Southern climes,—and gave one an impression of glare and exposure; but the smooth, beautiful green that surrounded it, and the richness of branching shade that embosomed it, compensated for the want of these artificial embellishments. As Mr. Hastings opened the gate that shut in the front yard, and held it open for his daughters to pass through, the handkerchief of Eulalia dropped from her hand, and a light breeze blew it back directly at the feet of Moreland; he caught it with eagerness, and as she turned immediately, with a consciousness of the loss, he stepped forward and presented it, with a respectful and graceful bow. He was thus brought face to face with her, and the soft, electric-beaming eyes seemed to shed into his bosom a flood of living light. With an impulse bold as irresistible, he pressed the hand which received the handkerchief from his; and though he saw the startled crimson rush to her cheek, he could not repent of his presumption. He could not help doing it,—it was an expression of sympathy as involuntary as it was sincere. He felt as if a mighty barrier of prejudice separated him from one to whom he was irresistibly attracted, and he was forced in this, perhaps their only meeting, to give expression in some way to his suddenly awakened, but passionate emotions. It was like taking the hand of a friend through the grate of a convent, the bars of a dungeon, in token of a long farewell. He walked in silence the rest of the way; and his companion smiled to himself at the impression the Flower of the Village had evidently made on the Southern planter.

Moreland had the good sense to tell Albert to remain in the kitchen during meal-times, so that the equilibrium of the landlord might not be disturbed by an appearance of servility on one part, and aristocracy on the other. And, whether Mr. Grimby thought he had taken an ultra step the preceding evening, or whether he was influenced by Albert's warm praises of his master, and his evident attachment and devotion to him, he was much more polite in his deportment and respectful in his manners. Still, he was anxious to draw him into a political or sectional discussion, for he believed himself, in strength of argument, superior to even his oracle, Mr. Hastings.

So, in imitation of the play of the fox and glove, he went round and round, ready to drop the gauntlet at the most favourable moment. But Moreland's mind was preoccupied, and he did not think the Sabbath calm should be ruffled by the contentions of party, or the warrings of self-love.

He did not attend church the after part of the day. He was resolved to struggle with the weakness which he blushed to feel. He would not place himself again within the influence of that seraph voice, or that fair, music-breathing face. He could not bridge the gulf of prejudice that yawned between them; and he would not linger on the opposite side sighing for the flowers that bloomed in vain for him. So he seated himself at the window, with book in hand, respecting himself for the dignified stand he had mentally taken; but the position he occupied was very unfavourable for the strength of his resolution. The church was so near that through its open windows he could hear distinctly the venerable accents of the minister, and the sweet and solemn notes of the choristers. He could distinguish the nightingale-voice, which, once heard, never could be forgotten,—it came flowing out into the sunshine, mingling with and melting into the blue waves of ether, rolling in the "upper deep;" it came floating across the gulf, over whose bridgeless depths he had been lamenting, on soft and downy wings, like a messenger dove, bearing promises of peace and love; it hovered over the dim retreats of memory, and its thrilling strains blended with the echoes of a voice which had in other hours enthralled his soul;—but that had breathed of the passions of earth, this of the hopes of immortality. Of course he could not read, and, suffering the book to fall from his fingers, he sunk into a long, deep revery.

Intending to recommence his journey early the following morning, he thought he would walk out before sunset, and take his last look of the charming valley in which the village was set, like a polished gem. Not seeing his agreeable and intelligent new friend, the architect, he sauntered along without any companion but his own thoughts, turning into by-paths, without knowing whither they went, assured they would lead him only to green fields and tranquil waters, or, perchance, to some garden of the dead. He was surprised to find himself close to Nancy Brown's little cottage. He recognised the pale purple of the lilac bushes through the old dark fence, and the air was heavy with their fragrance. A natural movement of humanity urged him to enter, and see if he could do anything more for the poor invalid, who had interested his feelings so much. The door was open, and he stood on its threshold withou having his approach perceived. *She* was there, th white-robed, singing maiden worshipper of the temple, and she had already heard the story of his kindness and liberality from the lips of the grateful Nar y. She had just been listening to it, and the glow was on ler heart when he entered. A smile of welcome, involuntary as the heart-beat, which at that moment was quickened, dawned on her lips, but was instantaneously overcast by a cloud of reserve. It was probably the recollection of his presumptuous act in the morning, which drew the sudden cloud over her dawning smile. It is impossible to describe the effect of her appearance in that little, low, dark cottage, in contrast with extreme age and decrepitude on one side, and deadliness and emaciation on the other. She sat between Nancy and her mother, and each poor, pale, drooping figure caught something of life and brightness from her youthful and benignant aspect. She was pale too, but hers was the pallor of moonlight, so fair, so lustrous, it diffused around a kindred softness and repose. When Moreland first stepped upon the threshold, a very quick, slight, vanishing blush flitted over her cheek, then left it as colourless and calm as before.

Nancy, whose eyes were fixed on her face, did not perceive as quickly the entrance of her benevolent visiter.

"There is a gentleman at the door," said Eulalia, rising from her seat.

Nancy turned round, and, recognising the kind and liberal stranger, asked him to walk in, and offering him her own chair, took a seat on the side of the bed. Her surprise and embarrassment brought on a violent fit of coughing, whose hollow, wasting sound reverberated painfully in the narrow apartment.

"This is the good gentleman I was just telling you about," said she, as soon as she could recover breath. "Mother, this is the gentleman that carried my bundle for me, and gave me that money last night. Oh, sir, I don't know what to say to you. I never did know how to talk, but there are a heap of words here, if I could only get 'em out." Here Nancy pressed her wasted hand on her heart, with a great deal of expression, though with little grace.

"The Lord bless you, sir!" cried the old mother, her voice trembling and quavering with age and imbecility. "The Lord reward you for your good deeds! Well, well, I never would have believed such a fine gentleman as you would have carried Nancy's bundle for her. I never would. Well, it's a blessed thing not to be proud. Just like Miss Euly here. She ha'in't got one bit of pride. She's just as willing to wait on such a poor old creatur as me, as if I was of some account in the world."

It was pleasant to the ear of Moreland to find himself associated with Eulalia Hastings, even in the mind ot this humble, indigent creature. There was another thing that pleased him. The woman was not mercenary. She appreciated more highly the simple act of condescension, the carrying of the bundle, than the money which was given to relieve their wants. He had too much ease of manner, had seen too much of the world, to suffer himself to be embarrassed by this unexpected meeting. He thought there was something peculiar in it; the accidental arrangement of circumstances which brought him in contact with the lovely chorister. The distance between them seemed wonderfully diminished. When he first saw her, in her elevated position in the gallery, singing the praise of God in words of surpassing grandeur, his imagination exalted her into one of that celestial band who stand in white robes about the throne, day and night, chanting the eternal chorus, "Hallelujah! the Lord God omnipotent reigneth." Now, she was on a level with himself, seated near him in the abode of indigence and suffering; he heard her gentle, speaking accents, fraught with human sympathy and sensibility. He began to think it possible that he might defer his journey a few days longer. There was nothing particularly to hasten his return. It was far better for him to be away, far from the remembrances that darkened his home. He could not possibly find a more quiet resting spot than in this beautiful valley, where

"The green of the earth and the blue of the sky"

seemed to meet in gorgeous rivalship.

Would it not be well to seek an acquaintance with Mr. Hastings, and endeavour, with earnestness and deliberation, to remove his prejudices and give him juster views of his fellow beings? While he thus communed with himself, Mrs. Brown was not idle. In the innocence and curiosity of second childhood, she sat gazing on their elegant visiter, through the spectacles, which she wiped at least a dozen times with the corner of her checked apron, so as to assist her faded vision.

"May I make bold to ask your name, sir?" said she. "I know most everybody that lives hereabouts, but I don't think you live in these parts, do you?"

"I should ask your pardon for not introducing myself sooner, madam," was the courteous reply. "My name is Moreland. I reside in the distant South."

"The South!" repeated the octogenarian. "Well, that is far off. What part of the South?"

"I reside in Georgia."

"The South!" again repeated she, bewildered by the idea of such immense distance. "Ain't it there where they have so many black folks to wait on 'em, with great iron chains on their hands and feet? Well, well, who would have thought it? You don't look as if you come from among such a dreadful set of people—not one bit. Law me! you don't say so!"

Here she again took off her spectacles, wiped them laboriously, readjusted them, and fixed her dim, glimmering glance once more on the face of the Southern stranger. She was probably searching for those lineaments of harshness and cruelty, those lines of tiger grimness and ferocity, she had so often heard described.

"Mother!" exclaimed Nancy, whose natural delicacy of feeling and deep gratitude were greatly shocked by these remarks, "you'll offend the gentleman. She don't mean any harm, sir—no more than a child."

"Do not fear that I shall be offended," said Moreland, with an irrepressible smile at the old lady's persevering scrutiny. "I like to hear what people think of us. It may do us good. You are mistaken, madam," added he, addressing the mother; "our black people do not wear chains, unless outrageous and criminal behaviour force us to such severity."

Perhaps Moreland would not have thought it worth the effort, to refute the charges of a poor, imbecile, ignorant woman, who only repeated what she had heard from higher powers, had not the daughter of Hastings been present to listen to his words. But he could not bear that she should look upon him as one of that "dreadful set," represented as dwelling amid clanking chains and galling manacles, and banqueting on human blood. He saw, that though her eye was cast modestly downward, she was no inattentive or uninterested listener.

"Well," ejaculated the old lady, half in soliloquy and half in harangue—"I don't mean to give offence, to be sure. You've been mighty good to Nancy, and I can't take away the blessing that's gone up to heaven for you now, if I wanted to. But I'm sorry such a likely, kindhearted gentleman as you seem to be, should live where such a sinful traffic is carried on. I've hearn Squire Hastings tell such awful things about it, it e'enamost made my hair stand on end. He used to lecture and speechify in the school-house close by, and as long as I could hobble out doors I went to hear him, for it always helped me powerfully in spirit. He's a mighty knowing man, and has a way of telling things that makes one's flesh creep. He's *her* father, Squire Hastings is. She ain't ashamed to hear me tell on't."

Eulalia made a scarcely perceptible shrinking, backward motion, at this eulogium on her father. She had heard it many a time before, but it never had seemed so exaggerated or ill-timed as at the present moment.

"I am sorry you have been led to believe us so awfully wicked and cruel, my good woman," said Moreland, looking at Eulalia's evidently troubled countenance, though his words were addressed to Dame Brown. "I cannot wonder so much at yourself, who have probably lived secluded from the world, and received your opinions from those around; but that those, who have had abundant opportunities of knowing what we really are, beings of like passions with themselves, as upright in principle, as honest in opinion, as kind in action, should represent us as such monsters of iniquity, does indeed seem wonderful. We claim no exemption from the faults and failings of poor fallen humanity, but we do claim a share of its virtues. The clanking chains of which you speak are mere figures of speech. You hear instead merry voices singing in the fields of labour or filling up the pauses of toil. Sadly have I missed in my northern travels, the joyous songs and exhilarating laughter of our slaves."

"You don't say so! Well, well! One does hear such strange things. You don't say they ever sing and laugh! Why, I thought they did nothing but cry and groan and gnash their teeth, all the day long. Well, it is hard to know what to believe."

"I wish you were able to travel so far," said Moreland, looking compassionately at Nancy's hectic cheeks, "and occupy a cabin in one of my plantations, where the balmy air would restore you to health. One day passed in the midst of the negroes would be worth a thousand arguments in our favour. You would see there, age free from care or labour, sickness tenderly nursed, and helplessness amply provided for. The poor invalid is not compelled to leave the master whom she has served, when health and strength are exhausted, but, without any care or forethought of her own, is watched over as kindly as if born of a fairer race."

Nancy sighed. She thought of her days of servitude, her waning health, her anxious fears and torturing apprehensions of future want, and it seemed to her the mere exemption from such far-reaching solicitudes must be a blessing. She thought, too, of the soft, mild atmosphere that flowed around those children of toil, and wished she could breathe its balm.

"I wish it was not so far off," she exclaimed; "but," she added, with a deeper sigh, "I never could live to reach there. And if I could, mother is too old to bear the journey. And then we couldn't afford it."

Moreland was sorry he had suggested an impracticable idea. He did not intend to raise hopes which could not e realized, though so uncalculating was his benevolence e would willingly have paid the expenses of the journey, if by so doing he could have restored health to her frail and broken constitution.

"We've mighty good friends here," said the old lady, wiping away the falling tears with the corner of her apron. "Miss Euly is just like an angel to us; and there are others too, who, if they don't look as pretty, are 'most as kind as she is."

Eulalia rose to depart. She had lingered in the hope that Moreland would go, but the sun was darting his horizontal rays through the window, throwing rosy lines across her fair face, and she felt he was waiting her motion. She felt embarrassed when he also rose, doubting the propriety of being escorted by a stranger.

"I will see you again," were his parting words to Nancy and her mother. So it was evident he had made up his mind not to leave on the morrow.

"May I escort you home?" he asked, when he opened the gate for her to pass out. "Though we have had no formal introduction, I have announced my own name, and I know it is Miss Hastings whom I have the honour of addressing."

"We village maidens are quite independent," she

replied, with a smile; "we are not accustomed to escorts in our rural walks, especially when leading from such lowly dwellings. Strangers seldom find out as readily as you have done, sir, the abodes of poverty."

"It was accident," he answered, gratified by her manner, which implied approbation, if not interest, "I can claim no credit for seeking. Though you must have discovered that I am disposed to arrogate to myself all the merit I can possibly lay hold of, I hope you will not think me a vain boaster."

"I think you have the power of making the worse appear the better reason," she said, with a smile that softened the sarcasm of her words.

"You have no pleasing impressions, I fear, of our beautiful South, Miss Hastings. You have had dark and forbidding pictures drawn of it. You look upon it as a moral Aceldama, and shudder at the view. Is it not so?"

"I love to think of your sunny clime," she answered, while a dawning colour mingled with the glow of sunset on her cheek, "of your magnolia bowers and flowery plains. I have heard a great deal of your chivalry and liberality, and love to listen to their praises; but I do not love to think of the dark spot in your social system, that is gradually spreading and deepening, and destroying all its beauty and happiness. I do shudder when I think of this. I did not mean to say so much, but you have forced it from me."

"I admire your candour. I did not expect to hear you speak so mildly, considering the prejudices of birth and education. Your father is, I understand, an avowed champion of what he believes to be truth, and it is perfectly natural that you should respect his opinions and adopt them as your own. Yet, if you grant me the privilege of your acquaintance, I hope to be able to convince you that those opinions are erroneous, and that though we have a dark spot in our social system, like every other cloud, 'it turns its silver lining to the light.'"

"My father does not adopt his opinions lightly," said she, with modest emphasis; "he has been a great student from his youth up, and something of a traveller, too. He does not wish to believe evil of mankind, neither does he, until the conviction is forced upon him."

"But you would not regret, if I could prove to you that he was mistaken in his estimate of Southern character,—that there is far less of cruelty, oppression, and sorrow in our midst than you now believe,—would you?"

This was said with such irresistible frankness, that had Eulalia been a more obstinate adherent than she was to her father's sentiments, she could not have uttered a cold negation. Naturally as reserved as she was modest, she was surprised at the freedom of her conversation with an utter stranger. His morning boldness, which she had at first deeply resented (though she made no commentary on it to her father), now occurred to her as accidental; he had probably merely intended to take a firm hold of the handkerchief, and grasped her hand instead. She could not help being pleased with the ease and grace of his manners; and the kindness and condescension she had witnessed in Mrs. Brown's cottage were genuine passports to her favour. It was not often, in the retirement of her village home, that her exquisite sense of refinement was so fully gratified; she had lived in a world of her own, whose visionary inhabitants were very much such beings as Moreland. He did not seem like a stranger, but rather as the incarnation of her own bright and beautiful idealities. She wanted her father to know him, to hear him talk, and listen to his eloquent self-defence. She was astonished when she reached their own gate, the walk had seemed so very short, and wondered what had become of the setting sun,—she had not marked its going down.

"Sister Eula! have you come back?" exclaimed a sweet voice, through the bars of the gate, and a little sunshiny head was seen beaming behind it. She, Eula's morning companion, stood with her feet on the lower round of the gate, and, when it was opened, swung back with it, laughing merrily at having secured so brave a ride.

Moreland, who was very fond of children, caught her in his arms, promising her a better and longer ride than the limits of the gate could furnish.

"I've seen you before," said she, peeping at him through her bright hair, which fell shadingly over her brow; "I saw you this morning; you picked up sister Eula's handkerchief. Papa said—"

"Dora!" interrupted Eulalia, "here are some flowers for you. Nancy gave them to me. Don't you want them?"

"Oh, yes!" exclaimed the child, eagerly extending her hand, and forgetting what papa had said, which Moreland would have very much liked to hear.

Papa was standing in the door, looking very portly and dignified, not a little surprised at seeing the stranger whom he had so keenly observed in the morning, walking quietly up his own yard, in company with one daughter, and bearing the other, perched like a bird on his shoulder.

"Papa, don't you see me riding?" cried Dora, from her elevated seat, long before they reached the door.

Mr. Hastings descended the steps, and the child leaped into his arms.

"Little romp!" cried he, setting her down very kindly, "go to your mother." And away she flew to tell her mother of the stranger's coming, and her own marvellous adventure.

"Mr. Moreland, father," said Eulalia. "He met me at Mrs. Brown's cottage, and it being late, he accompanied me home."

Moreland felt something as if a gimlet were boring

in his flesh, while enduring the piercing glance of the philanthropist; but he did not wince under the infliction, though it somewhat galled him.

"Won't you walk in, sir?" said Mr. Hastings, holding out his hand. "Glad to see you, if you have time to sit down."

This was an unexpected condescension, of which Moreland unhesitatingly availed himself. He wanted to enter the home of Eulalia, and see her in the midst of domestic associations.

"He has not seen the tiger's claws," thought Moreland; "or, perhaps, like the keeper of a menagerie, he confronts the wild beast that he may have the glory of taming him."

They entered a very neat and modestly furnished parlour, curtained with white muslin and carpeted with domestic manufacture. The furniture was of the simplest kind, though there was an air of taste and even elegance diffused over the room. There was a pretty work-box inlaid with pearl and surrounded by handsomely bound books, on the centre table. These he set down at once as the property of Eulalia. There were beautiful flowers, not in gilded vases, but set in crystals on the mantelpiece. These, he was convinced, had been arranged by the hands of Eulalia. He looked in vain for a piano or guitar, as accompaniments to her enchanting voice.

"Take a seat, sir," said Mr. Hastings, trying to

draw forward a prim-looking arm-chair, which was known in the household by the patronymic of *old maid*, from its peculiarly precise appearance—"and make yourself at home. We don't use any ceremony here."

"Ceremony is the greatest enemy of enjoyment," said Moreland, waiving the chair of state, and seating himself in one of less ambitious appearance. "I trust I am not encroaching on your hospitality, by accepting your invitation too readily. This is a Sabbath evening, and you may be accustomed to pass it with your family alone. A stranger may intermeddle with your joys. If so, I would not, for any consideration, intrude."

"Not at all, not at all, sir," replied his host. "We commence our Sundays on Saturday night, and when the Sabbath sun goes down, we feel privileged to enjoy social intercourse with our neighbours and friends; quiet, sober intercourse of course, but we do not object to a friendly call. Stay and take tea with us. We will be happy to have you. Eula, tell your mother a gentleman will partake of our family supper."

How could Moreland refuse such a cordial invitation? Of course he did not, but accepted it with all imaginable readiness. He could not account for this unexpected hospitality, where he had looked scarcely for ordinary courtesy. He was unconsciously doing Mr. Hastings great injustice. It does not follow, because a man is narrow and one-sided in his views, and bitter and obstinate in his prejudices, that he is destitute of social graces and domestic virtues. Moreland had his prejudices too, though he did not know it. He had imagined there was very little hospitality at the North, and that strangers were looked upon with a cold and suspicious eye. He thought the hearts of people were cold in proportion as they receded from the burning sun of the tropics, and that passion, the great central fire of the human bosom, giving life and splendour to every other element, was wanting in the less genial latitude he was now crossing.

Mr. Hastings, like most men, was actuated by mixed motives. He believed in the good old scripture injunction of hospitality to strangers, and he was exceedingly fond of making *impressions*, and enlarging the bounds of his influence. He took great pride in his argumentative powers, and thought he should have a dazzling opportunity to display them. He saw in prospective a glorious field of disputation, where he would gather more laurels than he could possibly dispose of. His prophetic glance pierced still further, and he beheld one black wave rolling after another from the Southern shores, before the resistless gales of his eloquence.

He was very fond of distinction. He loved to have strangers call at his house, assured that when they left the place, they would carry the impression that Mr. Hastings was the greatest man in the village, nay more, the greatest man in the country. Then he was very fond of his children. Eulalia was the pride of his heart and the delight of his eyes. The simple attention of escorting her home pleased him. The caressing kindness to little Dora charmed him; and, though the stranger belonged to a class of men whom he denounced as devoid of humanity, principle, or religion, against whom he had commenced a deadly crusade, with all the fanaticism of Peter the Hermit, and the rashness of Richard Cœur de Lion; moved by all these blended motives, he smiled blandly upon him, giving a gentle friction to his hands, as if to warm and ignite his hospitable feelings.

It was not long before little Dora came into the room with a hop-skip-and-jump step, announcing that supper was ready; and Mr. Hastings, with a courteous bow, ushered his guest into an adjoining room, where the family board was spread; here he was introduced to "my wife,"—a very intelligent and dignified-looking lady,—and "my son Reuben," a handsome, bright-eyed, auburn-locked youth of about seventeen, who perused the stranger's lineaments with vivid curiosity,—"Eulalia, my daughter, you have already seen." Yes! he had seen Eulalia,—it was a circumstance he was not likely to forget. He had seen her in the house of God, surrounded by a halo of music and prayer;—he had seen her in the cottage of the poor, making the dark and lowly places of life beautiful by her presence;—he now saw her presiding with quiet grace and self-possession at her father's board, for she occupied her mother's seat at the head of the table, behind an old-fashioned, massy silver urn. This shining relic of antiquity reflected brilliantly the lamp-light that flowed from the centre of the table, and it also seemed to reflect the soft, virgin lustre of Eulalia's illuminated face. It was a real patriarch, this old tiger-footed silver urn, having descended through three generations, and it set off the table wonderfully.

Dora slided into a seat on the left hand of Moreland, who, in gratitude for the compliment, helped her most munificently to butter and honey, which a glance from her mother's eye admonished her not to eat too lavishly.

"We are accustomed to wait upon ourselves at table," said Mr. Hastings, as Moreland received his cup of coffee from Eulalia's hand; "I fear our independent mode of living cannot be very agreeable to you, sir, whose customs are so different."

"On the contrary, nothing can be more agreeable than a family circle like this, uninterrupted by the presence of attendants, oftentimes as useless as they are annoying."

'Indeed! I thought a table at the South was never considered properly set without a negro placed at the back of every chair."

"I do not think the number of chairs governs the number of attendants," answered Moreland, with a smile; "though there is usually a superfluity. Yielding to the force of habit, I allow myself to be waited on, without thinking of it, though I consider it by no means indispensable."

"I am glad you can conform so readily to our plain,

republican habits. How do you like our Northern portion of the country, sir?"

"I see much to admire in the luxuriance of your vegetation, your rich, blooming clover fields and cultivated plains. I admire it most as a proof of the energy and industry of the sons of New England, which can convert your hard and granite soil into regions of beauty and fertility, rivalling the spontaneous richness of the South. I am charmed with your delightful summer climate, so soft, yet invigorating; and I honour your noble institutions. But," he added, "I admire, most of all, the intelligence, refinement, and loveliness of the daughters of New England, to which description has never done justice."

Surely, Moreland was trying to ingratiate himself in the favour of the family, by this fine and flattering speech; but though it sounded very much like one prepared and polished for the occasion, it was nevertheless spontaneous and sincere. By *pluralizing* the daughter of Mr. Hastings, he had ventured to express an admiration becoming too strong for repression. He forgot the barriers which a few hours before had seemed so insurmountable; he forgot that Mr. Hastings was the avowed enemy of his dearest social and domestic rights and privileges; that probably the very seat which he now occupied was lately filled by a gigantic negro; that the fair hands of Eulalia had poured coffee for him from that silver urn; and that the smile of welcome beamed as kindly on one as the other. He remembered only the loveliness of her person, the sweetness of her manners, the inexpressible charm that drew him towards her.

"Sister Eula stamped that butter," whispered Dora, as his knife severed a yellow rose from its stem. "She made that plum cake, too."

Moreland smiled at the communication, imparted with the innocent desire of elevating Sister Eula in his estimation, and thought the butter and the cake had a double relish. No one had heard Dora's whispered secret but himself, she had brought her rosy little mouth in such close proximity with his ear.

"It is not polite to whisper at table, Dora," said her mother, gently, but reprovingly, and Dora hung her head and put her finger in her mouth, with suddenly-acquired awkwardness. Moreland, excessively amused by the remark and its consequences, glanced at Eulalia's hand, which happened to be raised at that moment to shade back a loosened ringlet from her cheek. The glance was suggested by the thought that the hand which had been employed in moulding and spatting that golden ball, and manufacturing that excellent cake, could not possess much feminine delicacy of colour or lineament, but he was pleased to see that it was fair and symmetrical. Not so dazzlingly white as Claudia's snowy, but perjured hand, but pure from the stains of labour, and harmonizing with the delicacy of her face.

The truth was, Eulalia knew nothing of the drudgery of housekeeping, and but little of its cares. She was wonderfully expert with her needle, as her father's and brother's shirts, her mother's and sister's dresses could testify, had they tongues to speak. But her mother who was very proud of Eulalia's beauty, and very careful to keep it in high preservation, had habituated her to sew in gloves, with truncated fingers, ingeniously adapted for such a purpose. She swept and garnished her own room every day till it was a miracle of neatness; but she had been taught, as a regular duty, to draw on a pair of thick woollen mittens before she wielded the broom and exercised the duster. Had it not been for her mother's watchfulness, Eulalia's hands might not have justified the admiration of the fastidiously observing Moreland.

Though no servant attended the supper table, and Mr. Hastings boasted of their independence, they had a woman of *all work* in the kitchen, whose labour would have shamed the toil of three of Moreland's stoutest slaves. She rose with the dawn of day, and continued her tread-mill course till its close. She baked and brewed and washed and ironed and scrubbed and scoured, hardly giving herself time to talk, or sitting down but to eat. It is true, Mrs. Hastings assisted her in many of these operations, but the heavy burden of toil rested on her, and they dreamed not, because she was willing to assume it for the weekly stipend she received, that they exacted too much of her health and strength. It is true, that every night, to use her own words, "she was fagged out and tired e'en a'most to death, but she had it to do, and there was no use in grumbling about it. If she didn't take care of herself, who would? If she didn't try and lay up something for a rainy day, she wondered how she was to be taken care of, if she was sick and had to be laid by." So Betsy Jones toiled on, and her one dollar and a half per week, supplied clothes for herself and orphan brother, who was incapacitated, by lameness, from earning his daily bread. The physician's fees, who attended him, were also drained from the same source. How much she had to lay up for a rainy day may be easily imagined. Betsy had none of the false pride which is often found in her class. She had no *ambition* to put herself upon a perfect equality with her employers. She did not care about sitting down with them at meal time, nor did she disdain the summons of a tinkling bell.

"I should look putty," she said, "sitting down in my dirty duds by the side of Miss Euly, fixed off in all her niceties. I don't care about sitting down till I've done all my drudgery and all my little chores, and then I'm too jaded out to think of primping and furbishing up for company. If I've got to work I'll work, and done with it, let alone trying to be a lady."

But with all Betsy's humility, she had a just appreciation of herself, and could assert her dignity, when occasion required, with due emphasis. When Mr. Hastings installed his sable protegé into the honours of the household, when she saw him introduced into the guest chamber, where he swathed his huge limbs in the nice linen sheets she had so carefully bleached and ironed, and she was called upon to make up the bed and arrange the room, she stoutly rebelled, and declared "she wouldn't do no such thing. She wa'n't hired to wait upon a nasty runaway, who she knew never had to work half as hard as she had. Great, lazy, good-for-nothing fellow, that he was. *He* talk about being abused like a dog! Why he was as fat as stall-fed beef, and as strong as a lion."

"Well, Betsy, I must do it myself then," said Mrs. Hastings, "rather than waste any more words about it. I am sorry, however, to see that you have no more compassion for a poor, hunted, persecuted being, whom my husband has seen fit to receive under his sheltering roof."

"If the kitchen is good enough for me, it is good enough for such as him," exclaimed Betsy, opening all the windows energetically, and whisking the counterpane and sheets over the sill.

"I shall make it myself, Betsy," said Mrs. Hastings, with heroic determination, "I don't want to hear any more grumbling."

"Just as you please, Miss Hastings," cried Betsy,

leaving the room with a resounding step. "He's no more parsecuted than I am, the Lord knows."

Whatever were Mrs. Hastings's feelings, she expressed no opposition to the will of her lord and master, whom she looked up to as the great philanthropist of the age, as one of those martyr spirits who, though they may weave for themselves a crown of thorns in this world, will exchange it for a diadem of glory in the next.

After this unexpected digression, caused by little Dora's whisper, we will return to the supper table, or rather to the parlour, for there is no one at the table now but Mrs. Hastings and Betsy, who are both busy in putting away the best china, the cut glass preserve dishes, and silver urn, brought out for the occasion.

"Now, that's a real gentleman," said Betsy, peeping into the parlour through the crack of the door. "I'd as lieves wait upon him as not. He's as handsome as a pictur, and he don't look a bit proud neither, only sort of grand, as t'were. If I was Miss Euly—la sus!"

"Betsy!" said Mrs. Hastings, in a tone of grave rebuke, "you had better attend to your dishes."

Betsy flourished her napkin, but she would peep a little more.

"La me!" she exclaimed, "if they ha'n't got the singing books out, and, there, they are all sot round the middle table. Did you ever? Well! Miss Euly does sing like a martingale."

As there is no use in peeping through an aperture

when we have the freedom of the house, we will enter the parlour and seat ourselves in the *old maid*, which, being too heavy to be moved with convenience to the centre table, chances to be standing vacant in the corner.

Mr. Hastings was proud of his daughter's singing, as well he might be. It was really music to his soul, as well as his ear. He had a fine voice himself, and so had Reuben. And even little Dora had been taught to sing the praises of her God and King, with childhood's cherub tones.

"It is our custom," said Mr. Hastings, rubbing his hands slowly and gently, "it is our custom, Mr. Moreland, to have some sacred music every Sunday evening. We have no instruments but those which God has given us, and which we try to tune to His glory. My daughter, here, has a tolerable voice, my son sings a pretty good bass, and I myself can get through a tune without much difficulty. Will you join us, sir? You look as if you could help us, if you pleased."

"With all my heart," replied Moreland, taking a seat at Eulalia's side, and appropriating a singing book for their mutual benefit. "If I can do nothing better, I can at least turn the leaves, as I listen."

But he could do a great deal better, and it was not long before his voice was heard mingling with the sweet hosannas of Eulalia, while bending over the same book, so near, that her warm, pure breath floated against his glowing cheek. He was carried back to the days of his childhood, when his mother taught him the songs of Zion, while cradled in her arms or pillowed on her knee. The recollection softened and moved him to such a degree that his voice choked and then ceased. Eulalia involuntarily turned and looked in his face, and, surprised at the emotion she saw depicted there, her own voice faltered. There was something so exquisitely soft and sympathetic in the expression of her dark hazel eyes, so innocent, yet so full of intelligence, that Moreland felt bewildered by the glance.

"Oh!" thought he, and it was with difficulty he refrained from expressing his thoughts aloud, "I am oppressed with a sense of beauty and sweetness unknown before. All that is pathetic and holy in the past rises up to hallow and subdue the intoxication of the present moment. Strange, that I, born amid the sunny groves of the South, should come to the cold clime of New England to find an influence as warm, as powerful and instantaneous as is ever felt under the glowing skies of the tropics."

"We do not seem to make out quite as well with that tune as the others," said Mr. Hastings, thinking Moreland was probably out of practice and could not help stumbling over some difficult notes; "perhaps we had better try another; or perhaps we had better stop altogether. This must be dull amusement to you, sir."

"On the contrary, my feelings have only been too deeply interested," replied Moreland, ashamed of the interruption he had caused. "This sweet family music, these words of adoration and praise, heard under the stranger's roof, reminded me so vividly of my own early home, that my heart is softened to almost boyish weakness. I pray you to continue."

After singing some charming anthems, in which Mrs. Hastings, whose voice was only less sweet than Eulalia's, also joined, the books were closed, the chairs moved back, and Moreland reluctantly rose to depart.

"No hurry, sir," said Mr. Hastings; "happy to have you sit longer. Happy to have you call again. How long do you think of remaining in our village?"

"I did think of leaving to-morrow," replied his guest; "but," involuntarily looking at Eulalia, "I may probably remain a few days longer."

"You stop at Mr. Grimby's?"

"Yes."

"Well, I shall call and have a few hours' chat with you. I like you, sir—excuse my frankness—and I want to do you good. I think I can. I am a man who have read and studied and reflected a great deal, and have arrived, I flatter myself, at very just views of men and things. In the mean time,"—here he opened a secretary, whose glass doors were lined with green silk, and took out a bundle of papers,—"allow me to present you with these papers. Give them, if you please, a careful perusal, and if you are a candid man, as I trust you are, you cannot fail of being a convert to my opinions.

Yes, sir," continued he, warming with his subject, "you will find my arguments unanswerable. They are founded on truth. 'The eternal days of God are hers,' and it is in vain to contend against her omnipotent power."

Moreland reddened; he saw the package consisted of numbers of the "Emancipator," edited by Mr. Hastings himself. The gauntlet was now thrown down; he must take it up and enter the lists of controversy, *coute qui coute.*

"I am an earnest seeker of truth, myself," replied he, "and, as you say, I trust a candid one. Should you prove to me that my preconceived opinions are erroneous, I will most ingenuously acknowledge it. But I, too, have read and studied and reflected, and if I have arrived at different conclusions, I shall call upon you to examine mine, with equal frankness and impartiality."

"Certainly, certainly," cried the philanthropist;—"there's not a more impartial man in the world than myself, or one more open to conviction. But once convinced I am *right*, you might as well attempt to move the everlasting hills from their base, as shake the groundwork of my firm and rooted opinions. I will call and see you to-morrow."

And thus, after exchanging the usual courtesies of the parting moment, terminated Moreland's first visit to the home of Eulalia Hastings.

CHAPTER III.

When Moreland returned to the inn, not seeing Albert, and feeling very thirsty, he walked through the passage leading to the back part of the house to a bench where a bucket of water was usually standing. In so doing, he had to pass the kitchen, which, unlike those of the South, belonged to the main suite of apartments, and was only separated from the dining-room by an apartment which served as a store-room or pantry. Though it was a warm summer evening, the blaze roaring in the large chimney illuminated the whole passage through the open door. A woman was seated on the hearth stirring something in a large oven with a long stick, and, as she stirred, the aromatic smoke, which rose from the iron censer, was impregnated with the rich odour of burning coffee. Albert was standing on the opposite side of the fire-place, with a very *nonchalant* air, watching the operation and inhaling the aroma in his expanded nostrils. The perspiration was dripping from the poor woman's brow, which she kept wiping with one hand, while she plied with the other her oaken wand. Moreland recognised the landlady, Mrs. Grimby, whom he had seen bustling about the house, though she had never made her appearance at table. His chivalrous regard for woman was quite pained at seeing her thus unpleasantly and laboriously occupied, while his boy stood idly gazing by; and, stepping across the threshold, he accosted the landlady, much to her surprise and embarrassment. She had no cause for shame, for nothing could be more neat or well arranged than the kitchen furniture; and the white floor, unstained by grease, bore evidence of a thorough Saturday's scouring. Rows of shining tin utensils, bright and glittering as burnished silver, adorned the walls on one side, shelves of white crockery the other. It was altogether an attractive, rejoicing-looking room; and had it been a December instead of a June evening, and the atmosphere sparkling with frost instead of silvering in a summer mist, Moreland could have made himself very comfortable in the midst of that culinary finery.

"Why don't you make my boy assist you, madam?" said he; "he has nothing else to do, and can stand the heat much better than yourself."

"Thank you, sir," she replied, dusting a chair, and placing it near the door while she was speaking; "I couldn't think of setting him to work, I'm sure. This is nothing but play, to what I've been doing these several days,—my best help is gone home, Nancy Brown, she did the work of two common girls; but she got sick, and I do think she's done her last job in this world. I hain't been able to get any one in her place yet, and somebody's got to do the work; it's, as Mr. Grimby says, them that keeps tavern are as bad off as the slaves are, and I know it's true; but folks are obliged to live."

"Albert, stir that coffee," said his master; "I am astonished you have not offered to do it yourself."

The mulatto sprang forward, seized the stick, and, giving it first a graceful flourish round his head, began to stir, with vigorous hand, the brown and smoking kernels.

"Why, Mars. Russell," said he, with an apologetic smile, "you must 'xcuse me this time; I have been conversing with the lady, and forgot all about offering to help her; I'm willing, though."

"Yes," said Mrs. Grimby, "he seems mighty kind. It is warm work," she added, drawing back from the glowing hearth, and exposing her fervid face to the evening breeze that came in through an open casement.

"I beg you will take the liberty to call upon my boy whenever you wish his assistance," said Moreland, pitying the poor overtasked woman; "he can do almost anything; you will find he has a light foot and an active hand."

"Who's going to wait on you, Mars. Russell?" asked the mulatto, with a slight shrug of the shoulders. "Who's going to brush your clothes, black your boots, and do a heap of things beside?"

"You can do all that I require, and have a great deal of time left, Albert," replied his master. "I expect you will conform to my wishes, and do credit to your Southern training. Do you find it difficult to supply yourselves with servants, madam?" said he, addressing the landlady, not from mere curiosity, but a desire to inform himself of the true condition of the labouring class.

"We never think of calling them servants," replied Mrs. Grimby; "they won't allow us to do that. They wouldn't stay with us if we did. We speak of them as *help*, *hired help*, but never as servants. Yes, it is sometimes next to impossible to get anybody for love or money. All the girls are for going to the factories, where they have higher wages and lighter work. I don't think we can blame them much, though for my part, I'd rather, a great deal, do housework, than stand all day long behind the wheels and looms, with the cotton fuz choking the lungs and stopping up the nostrils. They think it more genteel; but I don't see any difference, for my part. I never did think there was any disgrace in work; if I did, I should lead a mighty mean life of it.

"You took tea at Squire Hastings', didn't you?" said she, first making the assertion, and then asking the question.

"Yes," replied Moreland, with a sudden bounding of

the heart, which it was well the landlady could not see. "Are you acquainted with the family?"

"To be sure I am. There's not many families in the village that I don't know. I used to visit Mrs. Hastings, but since Mr. Grimby took the tavern I've no time to go nowhere. Squire Hastings is the knowingest gentleman anywhere about, and Miss Eulaly is the nicest girl I ever saw in my life. I don't suppose there's a girl in the county that's had as many good offers as she has; but she don't seem to take to anybody. I don't blame her for setting store by herself, for beauty is her least merit."

Moreland thought the landlady a very discerning as well as industrious woman, and felt more than ever disposed to give her the assistance of his leisurely servant. He also thought her a woman of delicacy; for in the course of their conversation she had neither directly nor indirectly attacked those habits and customs, so at variance with her own. He would willingly have remained longer, listening to the praises of Eulalia, but he did not care about Mr. Grimby's coming into the kitchen and finding him so familiarly established there; so leaving Albert at his post of honour, he retired to his own chamber, and began to peruse the documents which Mr Hastings had placed in his hand.

At first he glanced over them carelessly, as if fulfilling an irksome task imposed upon him; then his attention became fixed; sometimes a disdainful smile curled his lip, then a hot flush rose to his temples, or an indignant frown contracted his brow. The articles were well written, and calculated to give an impression of extreme candour and philanthropy. There was much truth in them, but the true was so ingeniously woven with what was false, none but the most experienced eye could detect the tinselry from the gold. There were facts, too, but so distorted, so wrenched from their connexion with other extenuating facts, that they presented a mangled and bleeding mass of fragments, instead of a solid body of truth.

"Is it possible," he exclaimed, "that such things can be published and circulated and read by a rational and intelligent community as truth, as Christian truth, published, too, under the broad banner of philanthropy, nay, more, under the banner of the cross of Christ? Were they speaking of the dark ages of the world, over whose sanguinary archives the dim and mouldering veil of antiquity is floating, we might not wonder; but that such misrepresentations should be made of our own times, of our own country, by those who might inform themselves of the reality, is indeed incredible. Why, if I believed one-fourth part of what I see stated here, I would forsake my native regions, the grave of my mother, the home of my youth, the friends of my manhood, property, reputation, everything, making my whole life an expiatory sacrifice for the involuntary sins of my bygone years. I should think every gale wafted from our sweet jessamine bowers was laden with pestilential exhalations, and every sunbeam darting from our lovely skies would turn into a burning arrow, fastening into the soul."

He rose, greatly excited, and walked to the window that looked out upon the village church. He drew back the curtain and gazed on the tranquil beauty of the night scene. He could see the outline of the lofty dome, crowned with the jewelry of heaven, and a little farther, he distinguished a lighted window, glimmering through the foliage, which he believed belonged to the chamber of Eulalia. How peaceful it looked, that solitary light, streaming through the dewy shades and mingling with the stellar splendours of the heavens! Gradually he raised his thoughts above that solitary light, above those stellar glories, above the deep, ethereal blue of the zenith, till, ascending higher and higher, they reached the great Source of all. For a few moments his soul seemed to bask in the blaze of eternal truth. The passions of men, their vain strife, their petty controversies and warring interests, dwindled down into little specks, scarcely distinguishable in the full blaze of the Godhead. "He who sitteth in the heavens shall laugh," thought Moreland, during his brief apocalypse. "He shall laugh at the pitiful devices of man, and sweep away every refuge of lies. In the great golden scales of immutable justice our *motives* will be weighed, and when they are found wanting, as they too oft will be, frail and fallible beings as we are, the angel of mercy will plead in our behalf.

Oh, glorious thought! that we are to be judged hereafter by God, not man."

With this sublime reliance he fell asleep, and dreamed that he was wandering in his own native bowers, by the side of Eulalia Hastings.

At a rather late hour of the next afternoon, Mr. Hastings called and was received by Moreland, with due courtesy and cordiality. He invited him into the parlour, but Mr. Hastings suggested a seat in the passage, where a fine current of air was flowing. Moreland would have preferred a less public place, for the passage of a country inn is a thoroughfare for loungers and smokers and drinkers, who feel that they have as good a right to be there as the greatest nabob in the land. But Mr. Hastings was so accustomed to speak in public and to feed on public applause, that he did not like to confine to the individual ear, sentiments which would undoubtedly enlighten and regenerate mankind. He required the excitement of numbers to elicit the latent enthusiasm of his intellect. His arguments, like the claws of the lion, were embedded in a soft covering, and it was only when he came in collision with others that their strong gripe was felt and their clenching power acknowledged.

"Well, sir!" said he, applying the usual friction to his ready matches, "I hope you are pleased with the papers I gave you for perusal?"

"Pleased!" repeated Moreland, and, in spite of his desire to keep it back, a haughty flush swept over his brow; "you did not expect that I should be pleased with what, if true, would make me one of the veriest scoundrels on the face of the earth."

"Softly, softly, sir. We make no individual remarks, —conscience may apply them, but they are of general signification. The man who is not willing to merge all personal feelings in the good of the human race, is unworthy the name of a philanthropist or a Christian. We are the champions of truth, justice, and humanity, and wage eternal war with falsehood, oppression, and cruelty. Like the ancient warriors, who went forth in their war-chariots, from which a thousand scythes were gleaming, ready to mow down all opposing ranks,—we suffer the wheels of justice to roll down, though the votaries of error be crushed in their majestic evolutions."

"You have made a very happy comparison, sir," answered Moreland, from whose brow the angry flush had entirely faded; "your blows are as indiscriminate and aimless as the bristling weapons to which you allude. As you seem to have so much respect for ancient authorities, suppose we imitate the famous example of the Roman and Alban brothers, who decided, by their threefold combat, the destinies of their countries. I am willing to stand forth as the champion of mine, for you compel me to draw a dividing line between the North and the South, thus anticipating that division of interests which your uncalculating zeal will surely bring about."

By this time, the bar-room, which was nearly opposite them, was filling up with eager listeners, whose ears were open and distended, but from whose mouths the fumes of tobacco were steaming, till the hall was clouded with this incense of the tavern. Moreland was glad to see his friend, the bridge architect, making his way through the crowd and taking a quiet seat by the door.

"Well, let us begin the combat by one plain, positive question?" said Mr. Hastings, his keen black eyes sparkling like ignited coals. "Do you justify slavery?"

"Were you to ask me if I justified the *slave trade*, —that traffic forced upon us, by that very British government which now taunts and upbraids us with such bitterness and rancour for the institution whose corner-stone itself has laid,—I would answer *No!* but if you mean the involuntary slavery which surrounds me and my brethren of the South, I reply, I can justify it; we had no more to do with its existence than our own. We are not responsible for it, though we are for the duties it involves, the heaviest perhaps ever imposed upon man."

"Do you assert that you are not responsible for its *continuance;* that you have not the power to break the chains another's hand has forged; to restore the freedom which was as much the birthright of their ancestors as your own?"

"We have the *power* to do many things which reason and right forbid. We have the power to cast thousands of helpless, ignorant, reckless beings on their own resources, or to commit them to the tender mercies of those who, while they rave of their injuries, hold out no hand to redress them; but we believe it our duty to take care of them, to make the life of servitude, which seem their present destiny, as much as possible a life of comfort and enjoyment; and, while we reap the benefit of their labour and the fruit of their toil in their day of vigour, to nurse them in sickness, provide for them in old age, and save them from the horrors and miseries of want."

"I should like to know how many masters believe this their duty," interrupted Mr. Hastings; "or, believing it, fulfil the obligations you have described. I should like to have you explain the tales of cruelty and suffering, the cries of anguish that have rent the very heavens, and moved the spirit of men to a resistance that can never again be subdued to passiveness."

"That there are hard and cruel masters," replied Moreland; "that there is in consequence much suffering and wrong, I grieve to acknowledge; for wherever human nature exists, man has abused his privileges, and the cry of human suffering pierces the ear of the Almighty. But no sufferings which they can possibly endure, n degradation to which they are ever forced in their present condition, can compare to the misery, the degradation and hopelessness of their lot, in their native Africa, where they are doomed to a slavery more galling than imagination can conceive, and steeped in a superstition so dark and loathsome that the soul shudders at the contemplation. Have you never read of the hecatombs of human victims slaughtered at the grave of a barbarian chief, or the shrieks and groans of wives, sacrificed with the most terrific rites, to the manes of their husbands? I will not speak of the horrors of cannibalism. There is no need of calling up such revolting images. I only wished to present before you a faint picture of the native African, and contrast it with even the most degraded of our Southern slaves."

"Sir," exclaimed Mr. Hastings, "pardon me for saying it—you are begging the question. You could give no better proof of the weakness of your cause, than the manner in which you elude our arguments. I do not pretend to speculate upon their condition in their native country. We know but very little about it, and I doubt not the accounts we hear are highly coloured and monstrously exaggerated. I never presume to arraign the Almighty for any of his arrangements and dispensations. He placed the negro in Africa, and there he ought to remain, in spite of the avarice and cupidity of his white brethren."

"Indeed!" replied Moreland, "I am astonished that you do not question the justice and mercy of God, in creating this subservient and benighted race, with lineaments so devoid of beauty and grace, and swathing them in a skin, whose hue is the blackness of darkness, making a boundary line between us, as distinct, yea, more distinct than that which severs the noonday from midnight. The mulatto, in whose veins the blood of the white man is flowing and brightening their dusky tide, partakes of the beauty and intelligence of our race,—but take the native African, examine his lineaments, features, and peculiar characteristics, and say if he came from the hands of God in a state of equality with ourselves, endowed with equal physical and intellectual powers, intended for our bosom companions and familiar friends."

"If you are about to hide yourself in the counsels of the Almighty," cried Mr. Hastings, with increasing excitement of manner, "I give up the discussion. I see you close up every avenue to conviction, and indulge in a sophistry I consider unworthy of an honest, upright mind. Sir, we might talk in this way for six thousand years without changing my immutable conviction, that, as long as you allow the existence of slavery, you are living in sin and iniquity, that you are violating the laws of God and man, incurring the vengeance of heaven, and the retributions of eternity. I use strong language, sir, for the occasion justifies it. I am a philanthropist, sir, a champion of truth, and I have sworn to defend it at any sacrifice, yea, that of life itself, if the offering be required."

"But if you could be convinced," said Moreland, becoming more calm and energetic as his opponent grew fiery and vehement, "that, by your premature efforts, and overheated zeal, you increase the evils, which time alone can remedy; that you only rivet more closely the bonds you rashly attempt to wrench asunder by the hand of violence; that, instead of being the friends, you are in reality the worst enemies of the bondman whose cause you espouse; that, by adopting a kinder, more rational course, you would find in us co-labourers and brethren, instead of antagonists; if you could be convinced of all this, sir, would you not lay down your weapons, and reflect on the consequences that may flow from your present course of action?"

"I never can be convinced, sir; it is utterly impossible. I know that I am right, and that you are wrong. This conviction is one of those first, great truths, which are learned by intuition, not by the slow process of reasoning. God is both the teacher and the judge. You are wasting breath, sir. I am sorry to inform you of it, but you are wasting much precious breath on me."

"I have not sought this discussion," replied the Southerner, "and I have no wish to prolong it, at the risk of kindling feelings of personal animosity. I came among you, a peaceful stranger, pressing upon you no claims, assuming no privileges, but what you all freely share. It is true I have met with much liberality and expansion of feeling, much hospitality and generous appreciation, especially among the princely-spirited Bostonians, where I found many a brother in heart and soul. I have become acquainted, too, with noble, liberal, and candid men wherever I have travelled in your Northern regions; but I have also met with those whose vocation it seemed to trample on our rights, to tread upon them as they would grapes in the winepress, though blood instead of purple juice gushed up beneath their feet. It has been mine to oppose the shield of defence to the sword of aggression, though I would gladly lay aside all belligerent weapons, and cultivate that friendly communion, which no sectional interest should disturb or destroy."

Moreland had an exceedingly clear, sweet, and finely modulated voice. He never lost the command of it by passion or excitement, it never became indistinct through diffidence or confusion of ideas; but, swelling like a well-tuned melodious instrument, charmed the ear, while it riveted the attention. In this respect he had a great advantage over Mr. Hastings, whose voice often shivered and broke, when pitched on too high a key, or became thick and incoherent in the vehemence of argument. The loungers in the bar-room, who had long been accustomed to the eloquence of the latter, listened with a keener, deeper interest, to the thrilling accents of the former. The tones, the manner, the sentiments were new. They began to think there could be two sides to a question; that there was a possibility, though Squire Hastings was certainly a remarkably great man, one of the greatest men that ever lived, that other men had some sense too. The stranger had a good deal of *spunk*

—they liked to see it. They liked a man who knew how to stand up for himself, even if he wasn't on the right side of the argument. They were for giving him fair play, sea-room and land-room, and waited, with segars suspended in the air, and necks stretched eagerly forward, for the continuation of the scene; but Mr. Hastings, fearful of the fascinating influence of his opponent on the minds he considered subservient to his own, closed the discussion by a sudden and unexpected stroke of policy. Advancing with great frankness of manner towards Moreland, he held out his hand, saying,

"We had better renew our conversation some future hour. We are both getting a little too warm for the season. I hope, however, you will not believe me actuated by personal hostility. On the contrary, as I said before, I like you very much as a man. Come and see me again while you stay, and I have no doubt we shall understand each other better. I do not want you to go away with the impression that Northern hospitality and liberality are confined to the walls of our metropolis."

Moreland did not forget that it was the father of Eulalia that thus addressed him, and he suffered his hand to close over the hand of the philanthropist, and promised to renew the social pleasures of the preceding evening.

"Well," said Mr. Grimby, after Mr. Hastings had retired "I never saw the squire in such a tight fix before. He's got somebody now that knows how to talk about as well as he does, and I'm glad to see him pushed a little. I shouldn't wonder if you deserved the most credit, for it is harder to be smart on the wrong side than the right. Ha! ha! ha!"

The laugh was echoed in the bar-room, for the landlord had the reputation of being a *wit*, and all his sayings received their full amount of credit. Moreland was not sorry to escape from so uncongenial an atmosphere; and joining his friend, the architect, he recovered, in a long walk through the skirts of the village, the serenity of his temper and the equilibrium of his mind. There was something in the clear good sense and calm rationality of Mr. Brooks, inexpressibly soothing to his chafed and wounded spirit. It was pleasant to meet with one who had broad and comprehensive views of men and things, views which were not confined to the narrow horizon of the present, but extended into the boundlessness of the future.

That night, as he stood near the window in deep meditation, deliberately drawing on his gloves, Albert came and stood before him, with a very dissatisfied countenance.

"Mars. Russell," said he, putting his left hand in his bosom and giving a kind of flourish with his right, "please, how long you going to stay here, in this little, mean, no-account place?"

Moreland started. It was the very question he was

asking himself, though put in a very different manner, and he had no answer ready for either interrogator.

"Why, are you tired, Albert?"

"Yes, master, that I am. And if I've got to work for Mistress Grimby all this time, I don't care how soon we start. She's kept me on the go ever since the day broke, a scrubbing and scouring on all fours, till I can hardly stand up straight. She took you at your word, Mars. Russell, I can tell you. She's had a real day's work out of my bones."

Albert sucked in his breath, and, stooping down, rubbed his knees, with a significant gesture. "Then, I'm so dirty, master. I'm really ashamed to look you in the eye. I'm willing to do anything for you, Mars. Russell, but I have no opinion of making myself a dog, for folks that ain't no quality after all."

Moreland could not help thinking that his politeness had been understood in its broadest sense, and he regretted the benevolent impulse which had urged him to make the offer. He knew he should give more offence by withdrawing his services, than he had won gratitude by their spontaneous offer. He sympathized, too, with Albert's wounded aristocracy, which had never bled so copiously before.

"My poor boy," said he, smiling at Albert's half-comic, half-rueful look, "you have not been used to such hard usage, I must acknowledge. It is well to have a taste of what the Northern bondwomen have to endure, so that you may be more contented with your own lot. I suppose the good lady herself worked as hard as yourself."

"Yes, master, there's no denying that, and she didn't grumble neither, not much. I do have a feeling for women, and am willing to do as much for them as anybody else—but there's bounds, Mars. Russell."

"I will see about it, Albert. You need not do anything more to-night; I shall not be abroad late."

He was about to close the door, when Albert's "Mars. Russell," in an unusually deprecating tone, arrested his steps.

"Please, master, how long you going to stay?"

"I cannot tell, Albert,—are you getting home-sick?"

"Yes, that I am, master; I'm most pined away to a skeleton aready. They give me a plenty to eat, but not of the right sort. I hain't set eyes on a mouthful of bacon and greens since I ben here. I've got nobody to sing and dance with; and I've most forgot how to laugh. Hi, Mars. Russell, if I ever get back home again, the way I'll jump Georgia motions will be a caution."

"We will be at home soon," cried Moreland, laughing, while a vision of bright ebony faces, dancing and singing by the light of the moon, under the boughs of the old pine-trees, rose to his remembrance. A few minutes later, he stood under the dewy branches of the sycamores, which seemed, as they rustled in the night gale, to whisper the sweet name of Eulalia.

He was invited into the family sitting-room, and welcomed with great cordiality. There was a delightful home-atmosphere diffused around every object. Mr. Hastings was sitting, with a book, in which he seemed earnestly engaged, in his right hand, while his left arm was thrown round Dora, who was enthroned on his knees. Reuben, the student youth, was bending over a heavy and venerable-looking tome that was spread open before him; his head was leaning on his hand, which was half buried in a mass of dark red, glowing curls. Mrs. Hastings was busily engaged in knitting, that most cosy and domestic of all occupations; and Eulalia's hand held a roll of snowy linen, in which her threaded needle was brightly glittering. The graceful paraphernalia of woman's industry was round her. Her dress was the perfection of neatness and taste; she rose at his entrance, while her soft yet thrilling eye beamed with the welcome her modest lips dared not think of uttering.

Dora bounded from her father's knee with the lightness of a fawn, and openly expressed her rapture at seeing him again. Moreland's warm heart responded to her joyous greeting. No barrier of ceremony interposed its cold restraint between him and his sweet child friend. He could take her in his arms, kiss her blooming cheek, and feel drawn closer to Eulalia by these tender, innocent caresses. He could take many a liberty, under pretext of amusing his little companion, which he would not have done without her participation. He would not have dared to penetrate into the mysteries of Eulalia's rosewood work-box, but Dora drew it towards her, and displayed her politeness by exhibiting, one by one, its hoarded treasures. Almost everything it contained had a history, which the young chatterbox was eager to tell.

"My dear, I fear you are troublesome," said her mother. "You had better get down and sit in a chair. You must not appropriate Mr. Moreland's visit to yourself."

"Who did you come to see?" asked the child, looking smilingly into his eyes—"Sister Eula?"

Every one laughed at this abrupt question, even Eulalia, though the pale blush of her cheek indicated a transient confusion.

"What makes you think I came to see Sister Eula, more than yourself?" asked Moreland, thinking the child had most marvellous penetration.

"Cause you look at her so hard," cried Dora, in a confidential half-whisper, "and cause she's so pretty."

The pale blush-rose on Eulalia's cheek turned to crimson, and Moreland himself was conscious of an uncomfortable glow, while the student youth actually shouted with laughter.

"My dear," said Mrs. Hastings gravely, "you are entirely too forward. You talk too much for a little girl. You must go to bed immediately."

"Please, ma, I won't talk any more," exclaimed the little culprit. "I ain't a bit sleepy."

Moreland pleaded eloquently in her behalf. He said she deserved a reward for calling such a bright and beautiful colour to her sister's cheek; that he admired her discrimination, and thanked her for giving him credit for so much good taste and judgment. So sportively and gracefully did he bear himself through the awkwardness of the moment, that it was soon forgotten, and conversation flowed on without pause or interruption. There was a cluster of flowers standing in the centre of the table.

"You like flowers, do you not?" said he to Eulalia.

"*Like* is too cold a word," she replied. "I love them next to human beings. They have a language to me, deeper than words, sweeter even than music."

"If you want beautiful flowers, you must come to the South," he said. "All that you cultivate here with so much care, grows wild in our forests and enamels our green savannas. The yellow jessamine gilds our woods with its blossoming gold, the virgin's bower twines its soft purplish wreath with the rosy clusters of the multiflora, and the coral honeysuckle rivals the scarlet bloom of your mountain ash-trees. You have no conception of the beauty of some of our Southern landscapes, the luxuriance of our gardens, the fragrance of our flowers."

"As I never expect to witness these beautiful scenes," replied Eulalia, "I must be content with the productions of our colder soil. As I cannot compare them with yours, I enjoy ours as far as my taste has been developed, though I am conscious of capacities of beauty which have never yet been exercised—and probably never will be."

As she said this, her voice saddened, and her eye looked pensive under the shade of its drooping lashes.

"I wish *I* could see those pretty flowers!" said Dora. "Do you live a great way off?"

"A great way," replied Moreland; smiling, "but I'll take you home with me, if you'll go. I'll make you a bower of roses, and you shall be Queen of the blooming year!"

"Will you?—may I?" she exclaimed, then jumping down, she ran to her father, who seemed in profound meditation. "Pa, may I go home with Mr. Moreland, and live with him in a beautiful bower?"

"Foolish, foolish child!" he cried, "you know not what you ask."

The words were nothing in themselves,—they might refer to the distance to be overcome, to the impracti-bility of the thing; but Moreland felt there was a deeper meaning, and if literally translated would read thus:—

"Foolish child! you know not that beneath those beautiful flowers is concealed the bite of the serpent, the sting of the adder. Though fair and smiling to the eye,—thou bright and sunny land!—yet it shall be better for Sodom and Gomorrah in the day of judgment than for thee."

"*I* should like to travel in the South," cried Reuben, lifting his eyes from his book, and speaking with great animation. "I should like, of all things, to visit the Southern States?"

"Why, my son?" asked Mr. Hastings, in a tone of grave surprise.

"I have heard so much about them, I want to judge for myself," replied the youth, with decision.

"Come and visit me," said Moreland, observing a fire and intelligence in the countenance of the youth which he had not noticed before, "the woods of Carolina and Georgia furnish rare sport for the hunter, and our streams abound in fish."

"Reuben has tasks before him somewhat less fascinating than hunting and fishing," said his father; "but rather more indispensable. We have not quite as much leisure here as you gentlemen of the South. Time, with us, is wealth; and we realize, in its fullest sense, the meaning of golden moments and the diamond sands of the hour-glass. Sir," added he, fixing his keen eyes steadfastly on Moreland's face, "I presume, from the hospitalities you are offering my children, that you are a married gentlemen."

"I have been married," replied Moreland, turning very pale, then reddening even to the hue of crimson.

"Your wife is dead?" continued Mr. Hastings.

"No, sir; she who was my wife still lives; but she no longer bears my name. I am free from the marriage bond, but not by death."

There was a pause after these unfortunate questions. Mr. Hastings hemmed and cleared his throat, and Moreland, perhaps fearful of being probed still deeper, turned towards him and said—

"It is very painful to me to allude to these circumstances. Being a stranger, I cannot explain them. I therefore prefer to remain silent. It was more to escape from sad and bitter recollections, than to attend to the demands of business, that I left my Southern home and became a wanderer here."

He paused in great agitation. The soft, dark eye of Eulalia met his own, beaming with sympathy and glistening with sensibility. There was no reproach, no suspicion in its clear depths of light. Her delicacy was wounded by her father's abrupt inquisitiveness. She wanted to apologize for him, to soothe the pain he had inflicted,—but what could she say, or do? She felt, too, an inexplicable shock. She had never dreamed that Moreland was a married man; true, he was divorced, but that was so shocking. He had loved and wedded. The ties were broken; but could hearts be wrenched asunder by the hand of violence, without for ever bleeding? She wished she had not known it, or knowing so much, that more could be revealed.

"I am sorry that I touched upon an unpleasant

theme," said Mr. Hastings. "I had no intention of intruding on domestic misfortunes. We Yankees are accused of being inquisitive, and perhaps we are a little so. It is natural, however, for us to feel some interest in those who are brought in contact with us. You see us here in the bosom of our families—just as we are—without disguise or mystery. In this respect you have a decided advantage, who give us nothing but your name in return."

"You are right, Mr. Hastings. A stranger should always bear credentials with him, proving his claims to a hospitable reception. I have these in my trunk, which I would be happy to show you, if it would not trespass on your attention. I brought letters of introduction from some of the first men of the South, which have given me a passport to the best society of New York and Boston. I would be glad if my private history were fully known, knowing that your sympathies would be all enlisted in my favour; but I cannot win them by a process so exquisitely painful."

"Let us say no more about it," said his host. "I intended this evening to avoid every unpleasant subject, every national difference, and have a real social, free and easy time. Supposing we have a little music. We can have some *songs* to-night. Eula, give us one of your little simple Scotch airs—one of the melodies of Burns. Burns is my favourite poet, sir. He wrote as if there were burning coals upon his heart. He was a *man* as well as a *poet*. Come, Eula, you are always ready. You have no instrument to tune. I believe you are fond of music, Mr. Moreland?"

"Passionately so—especially the music of the human voice."

And Eulalia sang till the very air seemed to ripple as her melodious breath mingled with its waves. She needed no accompaniment. Why should she? The nightingale has none.

CHAPTER IV.

Day after day passed away, and still Moreland lingered in the village, unable to break the spell that bound him to the spot. Week after week passed away, and still he lingered, feeling the spell that bound him stronger and still more strong. He no longer sought to liberate himself from the enchantment. He resolved that Eulalia Hastings should be his wife, if he had the power to win her affections, in spite of the terrible warfare her father was making against his principles and practice. In spite of the awful declaration, he so well remembered, recorded in one of her father's written documents, "that he would rather a daughter of his should be laid in the deepest grave of New England than be wedded to a Southern slaveholder," he resolved to triumph over all opposition, and transplant this Northern flower to his own sunnier clime.

"For many virtues had he admired several women," and *one* he had loved, with all the vehemence of passion—loved "not wisely, but too well." He had loved, in spite of the resistance of reason, the warnings of prudence, and trusted against the admonitions of friendship and the pleadings of affection. Now reason and prudence justified, instead of opposing his choice. Eulalia possessed every qualification wanting in the brilliant, but misguided Claudia. There was about her a pure, sweet, fresh womanliness, a virgin delicacy, a strong but guarded sensibility, a deep, genuine, but unobtrusive piety. She was fair without vanity, intelligent and highly cultivated without pedantry or display, admired, caressed, and beloved, without pride or vain-glory. Yet with all these charming and engaging quailties, he could see that her character was only half developed; that there was a latent strength and enthusiasm, a sleeping power, which, like lightning, is born only of the night-cloud and the storm. The good landlady, while boasting of her many lovers, had remarked "that she took to none of them," and it was probable, that the portals of her heart, that temple adorned with such pearls and precious gems, had never yet opened and closed on the divinity destined to be enshrined and worshipped there.

And what were Eulalia's feelings? Her youth had been gliding over a smooth, unrippling stream, calmly and quietly, yet monotonously. Now the current quickened and swelled, and sunbeams and shadows chased each other over the surface. New life was born within her. She lived in a new and more glorious world. All that her pure heart had ever imagined of manly excellence, or imagination dreamed of manly grace, she found realized in Moreland. His homage humbled, while it exalted her; for she deemed herself unworthy to receive it.

She began to believe in the existence of a second love, stronger than the first. He offered to tell her the history of his former ill-fated attachment, and the causes which had destroyed it; but though her curiosity had been strongly excited, she refused to hear what she knew would give him pain to reveal. With implicit confidence in his honour and truth, she believed him blameless in the transaction, and she shrunk with unconquerable repugnance from hearing from his lips the name of Claudia. It was mentioned no more.

It is not to be supposed that village gossip was mute, when there was such abundant fuel to feed its loquacity, or that parental solicitude was slumbering, when there was so much to excite and alarm it. Mr. Hastings found himself in a most awkward and distressing situation. He was an exceedingly ambitious man—ambitious for himself and his children. Had wealth been at his command, he would have loved to make a display of magnificence and pomp, that would have dazzled the eyes of the more lowly and obscure. He wanted his daughter to marry a distinguished man, who would give consequence to the family, and increase his own influence. Here was a gentleman of wealth beyond his most sanguine expectations, of most refined and captivating manners, intelligent, accomplished, and bearing the highest credentials of his birth and standing—a man of whose alliance he would be proud; but he belonged to a class which, for years, he had been denouncing as unworthy of the fellowship of Christians; he dwelt in a portion of the land doomed by him as the Sodom and Gomorrah of modern times, over which the God of retribution was brooding in the awful might of coming vengeance. His principles, his consistency, his reputation were at stake. He had always believed the Southerners a selfish, aristocratic, lazy, self-indulging, cruel set of people; he had whetted and sharpened his prejudices on the rough grindstone of popular ignorance, till they had acquired the edge and keenness of the razor. The unexpected appearance of a Southern gentleman in his own immediate circle, the first with whom he had ever become familiarly acquainted, was an exciting incident in the village monotony of his life. He could not help admiring him as an individual, he could not help acknowledging the truth and candour of many of his arguments; but the champion of truth must never admit the possibility of his having been in error, and the character for consistency must be preserved at any sacrifice.

"What, marry my daughter!" he exclaimed, when the crisis arrived for which he had been preparing all the ammunition of his intellect. "Sir, I am sorry, very sorry, but it can never be. There is a great gulf between us,—one that I fear will never be filled. Were I to consent to this union, I should destroy, by a single act, the labour and devotion of years. Were you a poor New England farmer, I would willingly receive you as my son; but holding the position and advocating the principles you now do, you can never be to me more than you have hitherto been,—the guest of my household, the companion of the passing hour."

"Is the future happiness of your daughter a question of no interest in your mind?" asked Moreland, who had nerved himself to encounter the most vigorous opposition; but who believed that patience and perseverance and will could finally overcome it.

"Does she know of your application?" asked the father, anxiously.

"She does. It is with her sanction that I come; and I am authorized to say, that her happiness as well as my own is involved in your decision."

"You should not have done this. You knew what my sentiments were. You had read from my own pen a sentence I know you must have remembered, 'that I would rather see a daughter of mine laid in the deepest grave of New England than wedded to a Southern planter.' You had received my answer before making the proposition. You have trifled with my daughter's affections, and endangered her peace. You should not have done this—you should have made your first appeal to me, sir.

"I have done nothing clandestine, sir," replied Moreland, proudly; "from my very first visit, you must have perceived my admiration of your daughter. I have never attempted to conceal my feelings,—they have been as open as the day. I had read the awful declaration to which you refer; but I did not, could not believe it the real language of your heart. I looked upon it as a figure of rhetoric, and nothing more. Sir, your daughter's heart is mine,—I have won it by no subtle arts, no secret means. It is the reward of my pure affection,—my strong and ardent love. Give her to me, and I will receive her as the dearest, holiest trust ever given to man. Give her to me, and I will bear her to a clime more congenial to the delicacy of her constitution than this, where eastern blasts wither so early the fairest flowers of life; I will guard her with a tenderness and devotion equalled only by her loveliness and worth."

"Mr. Moreland," cried Mr. Hastings, putting his hands behind him and walking up and down the room with short, quick steps, "you agitate me very much. Eulalia is a dear child to me—a blessed child. From her cradle to the present hour she has never, to my knowledge, deserved reproof or blame. I love all my children, but Eulalia is the darling of my heart. God forgive me if I have sacrificed her happiness to my imprudence!"

"You have not sacrificed her happiness, you have secured it, sir. She will be the centre of a happy home

She will be surrounded by affluence and comfort, the mistress of faithful, affectionate beings, by whom she will be beloved and adored. She will bring light and joy to scenes darkened by domestic disappointment, and exercise a mother's holy influence over the child, doomed to the saddest of all orphanages."

"Ah! I am glad you mentioned this. Were there no other objection, I could not consent to her marriage with one who has been divorced. She might be exposed to much sorrow and misconstruction. Besides, it proves that your affections are easily excited, and probably easily subdued. You will soon forget my daughter."

"I cannot wonder at your want of faith in my stability and constancy, but I have been more unfortunate than blameworthy. I was very young when I married, and if I erred in my choice I may be forgiven on the plea of youth and inexperience. Passion may die away, but love, such love as I bear Eulalia, can never change. She was created for me in the great counsels of eternity. The moment I saw her my soul claimed her as its own. I was led here for no other purpose but to find her, my heart's immortal counterpart. I have remained for no other purpose but to win her, and I will stay till love, stronger than the trumpet blast of Israel's priests, shall break down the Jericho of prejudice and fanaticism."

Moreland was losing his usual self-possession. A hot flush crimsoned his cheek; his voice became husky and tremulous. He was beginning to feel as proud as Lucifer. Mr. Hastings seemed a very insignificant object to be placed in opposition to the mightiness of his will. Mr. Hastings felt the influence of this regal passion of the moment, and a dark reddish spark kindled in his ye.

"Do you threaten me?" he exclaimed, looking steadily in the face of Moreland. "I tell you, young man, that lofty tone will have far less effect than the one you used awhile ago. I am a sturdy, independent Yankee, and high words have no more power on me than the summer wind on the century-rooted oak. When I believe I am in the right I am as firm as my own granite hills, and you might as well attempt to move them as me."

Moreland, who had never withdrawn his eye one moment from the dark red spark burning so intensely on him, felt the power of an inexorable will grasping and clenching him, till a cold numb feeling came over him. The hot colour died away on his cheek, leaving him as pale as marble. He could not, would not, even for Eulalia's sake, humble himself before this obstinate, immovable man, only to be trampled on and crushed. He moved towards the table and took up his hat. There was a wild rose in it, which he had plucked by the wayside, intending to give it to Eulalia. It was wilted, but surpassingly sweet in odour. The sight of that withered flower softened his feelings, and turned them in a new channel. It seemed an emblem of Eulalia, doomed to a heart-blight, beneath which her youth and beauty would languish and fade. He thought less of his own sorrow than hers, of whose love he had every assurance ingenuous modesty could impart.

"Am I to understand that your decision is unalterable?" he asked, in a tone far less regal than that which had so exasperated Mr. Hastings. "Is it your inexorable resolution that I shall not wed your daughter?"

"It is."

Moreland laid his hand on the latch and was passing out, when Mr. Hastings added, with an entire change of manner—"I am sorry to part with one unpleasant feeling on either side. I do not wish to give you pain. You have paid my daughter a great compliment, which we shall all appreciate. You must perceive that I am actuated by principle alone. I am a poor man, and you are rich. Were my judgment to be influenced by personal accomplishments, yours would be irresistible. I have but one objection, but that is insurmountable. Were you an humble missionary to some heathen land, I would give her to you in the name of the living God; I would give her as the firstling of my flock; I would devote her as a lamb without spot or blemish, to a good and glorious cause."

"I look upon myself as a missionary," replied Moreland, with a kindling countenance. "I look upon every master and mistress in our Southern land, as missionaries appointed to civilize and christianize the sons and daughters of Africa. To them Ethiopia is stretching out its sable hands, and through them they are lifted to God. If all the efforts of all the missionaries in our country were concentrated in the dark regions of Africa, they could not, judging of the success of their labours elsewhere, make one-tenth part of the number of converts that are found in our households and plantations. In our towns and villages, the churches of the negroes rise side by side with our own. Their prayers of faith, their hymns of praise, ascend on the same breeze, and are borne upward to the same heaven. Once more, then, I entreat you, give me your daughter, and look upon her evermore as the wife of a Christian missionary."

"I cannot consent to evil that good may come," was the emphatic reply. "But one condition I will make. Liberate your slaves; remove the curse from your household and your land; come to me with a pure, unburdened conscience, and I will oppose no barrier to your love."

"I have offered many of them their freedom, on condition that they go to Liberia, but they will not listen to the proposition. And I cannot, even to secure Paradise itself, cast upon the Northern world the large family dependent upon me for comfort and support. Under such circumstances, the freedom for which you plead would be their direst curse, instead of their greatest blessing. I believe, in God's good time, the day of liberation will come, if man will wait his leading. No, sir, I cannot accede to your proposition; nor is it from mercenary motives that I refuse. Heaven knows I am above such considerations. If I can purchase happiness only at the sacrifice of duty, then I must be for ever wretched."

"May you live to have very different ideas of duty from what now govern you! You have decided the question yourself, and I am glad of it. You can no longer reproach me for destroying the happiness of Eulalia."

"You might have spared me that," exclaimed Moreland, with irrepressible bitterness. Then, fearing to trust himself to say more in his present maddened state of feeling, he made a silent bow and left the house.

As he passed through the yard he met Dora, with her hands laden with flowers. She sprang to meet him, with a bright and joyous smile; but on seeing his pale, stern, and agitated countenance, she seemed bewildered and frightened, and the flowers dropped from her hands.

"What's the matter?" she cried. "What makes you look so sorry and angry? Don't you love me any more?"

Without saying a word, he took the child in his arms and pressed her to his bosom, with a wild passion, of which he was not aware. He identified her for the moment with Eulalia, and felt as if he could no longer restrain the overflowings of his love and despair.

"Please don't!" said the little girl, entreatingly—skrinking from the arms which had always before so gently encircled her—gazing earnestly and fearfully in his face.

"Dora, I am going home," he exclaimed. "I am going, never to return."

"Going? when?" cried the child.

"To-morrow."

"Let me go and tell Eula," said Dora, running two or three steps from him in her eagerness to tell the tidings,—then returning and taking hold of his hand, she burst into tears.

"What makes you go when we all love you so? Why can't you live here all the time?"

"It is because I love you that I must leave you. Tell Eula—but it is no matter—I must see her once more before I go."

Bending down and kissing the fair forehead now clouded with grief, he passed from under the shade of the sycamore boughs, through the white gate and into the open street. He thought he caught a glimpse of a pale face, at an upper window,—a white, faint gleam, like a vanishing star,—but he dared not look back again. He dared not think of the anguish he was leaving behind,—he could hardly bear the weight and intensity of that which he was bearing away.

"Albert," said he, as soon as he found himself in

his own room, "get everything ready; we shall go to-morrow."

"Bless you for the news, Mars. Russell!" exclaimed the overjoyed mulatto; "I'm mighty glad to hear it. Won't I see old Georgie again? Wont I say howdy to all the blessed old darkies? But,"—pausing abruptly, while a sudden seriousness settled on his bright face,—"what the matter, master? Anything happened to worry you? Any bad news from home?"

"No! I only wish to be perfectly quiet. Don't talk to me."

Throwing himself into a chair by the window, he leaned his throbbing temples on his hand, and fixed his gloomy gaze on the God-devoted temple,—the birth-place of his love and his sorrow. There he sat, without change of position, till supper was announced.

"I want no supper," said he, without moving.

"Indeed, Mars. Russell, you'll be sick, at this rate," said Albert, watching with increasing anxiety his pale and altered countenance; "indeed, you are sick now," he added, laying his hand humbly but affectionately on his master's burning forehead; "you've got fever, sure enough, this minute. 'Spose I go and get a doctor, master?"

This act might seem too familiar, to those unaccustomed to the caressing freedom of manner often permitted to a favourite slave. One of Albert's chief delights was to brush his master's hair, and bathe his temples, when suffering from a sick and aching head.

"Don't be foolish, boy," he cried; "I tell you again, there's nothing the matter with me."

"But, Mars. Russell, you don't know how hot your head is." The smooth, bronze-coloured fingers gently threaded the dark hair that fell heavily on his master's brow.

"You shall see how easily I can cool it," said Moreland; and, wishing to relieve the anxiety of his humble friend, he rose and approached the wash-stand, intending to plunge his aching temples in the brimming basin; but he reeled, and would have fallen, had not Albert's arms supported him.

"I do feel strangely here," said he, putting his hand to his head. "I had better lie down awhile."

Albert smoothed the pillow under his head, as gently as a woman could have done; then bringing the basin to the bed-side, he bathed his forehead and moistened his hair, till the throbbing veins seemed less wiry to the touch. He stood, dark and gentle as the twilight, now stealing soft and stilly round the room, and hanging a dusky curtain over the bed.

That night, when the family of Mr. Hastings gathered round the supper table, the place of Eulalia was vacant—she had a sick headache—she was lying down—she did not want any supper. Mrs. Hastings looked very sad; Mr. Hastings had a grave, contracted brow, and even Dora's sunny brow of childhood wore the gloom of solemn thought. The first word uttered was by her, after looking at her father.

"Papa, is it right to say grace if one isn't thankful?"

"What makes you ask such a strange question, child?"

"I thought you didn't look thankful to-night, papa, that's all."

Reuben laughed, but Mrs. Hastings drew a deep sigh. She felt that the blessing was wanting at the board, from which the sweet face of Eulalia was banished by reason of sorrow. She knew the sorrow must be deep and full, which she had not the power to confine within her own unselfish bosom. The submissive and unquestioning wife was merged in the anxious, sympathizing mother, and her heart instinctively rebelled against her husband's cold and harsh decree. She admired and esteemed the gentle and gallant stranger, whom she would probably never more behold, and loved him, because he loved her Eulalia. He had come among them like a beam of light, and what darkness and chillness he would leave behind!

"How sorry I am Mr. Moreland is going away!" exclaimed Dora, again breaking the heavy silence. "Papa, what makes him go? And what made him look so strange and sorry when he went away?"

"He wanted to take your sister Eula away with him,

and I would not let him," replied the father, laying down his knife and fork.

"But he would bring her back again, papa!"

"He wanted her to live there all the time. You would not be likely ever to see her again. We should no more hear her sweet voice in the temple of God or at the altar of home. She would be to us just as if she were dead; for the places that now know her would no more be gladdened by her presence."

He looked at his wife while he was speaking, and the words sunk deep in her soul. He had touched the right chord. She shuddered at the desolation of the prospect he presented, and wondered she had not realized its dreariness and darkness.

"I am sure he is rich enough to bring her home to visit us, every year or two," cried Reuben, whose heart Moreland had completely captivated, "and I think him good enough to do it, if you ask him."

"Evil was the day the Southern stranger came among us," exclaimed Mr. Hastings sternly, "if he has made all my children aliens from their father's principles."

"You have always encouraged us, sir, to express independent opinions," said Reuben manfully. "I must acknowledge that I have a very different opinion of the South and Southern people, since Mr. Moreland came here. When I am a man I intend to travel among them, and judge for myself."

"Really, young man, you are mapping out a glorious

future," exclaimed his father, sarcastically. "Perhaps you are looking forward to the time when you can purchase a plantation, fill it with live human stock, and flourish your whip with as much grace as any other lordly slave-master. Perhaps you have been thinking the sacrifice of your sister a trifling thing in comparison with your own advancement."

"Father, you know I am above such meanness," cried the youth, his keen black eye actually corruscating as he spoke; "besides, I do not think my sister would be sacrificed by marrying such a man as Mr. Moreland. If she ever sees another like him in this part of the world, it is more than I imagine."

Reuben, too much excited to command his temper, got up suddenly and left the table, followed by the gentle reproach of his mother's eyes. Mr. Hastings seemed thunderstruck at this first outbreak of independence in his son, whom he still looked upon as a mere child, bound to think exactly as he thought, and to do exactly as he did. It was altogether an uncomfortable meal, and when Betsy came to clear away the dishes she found them nearly as full as when she put them on the table. Shrewd and intelligent as she was, she had not been unobservant of the signs of the times, and was not without her suspicions of the cause of Eulalia's sudden indisposition. She had reasons of her own for wishing to see her; so, upon the pretext of bearing her a hot cup of tea, she entered her chamber.

The lamp was placed upon the hearth, burning against a back-ground of odorous, fresh pine boughs, that filled with dark green shade the place occupied in winter with glowing flame. The bed on which Eulalia lay was in a kind of twilight, and her pallid face was hardly distinguishable from the pillow, save by the dark framework of her dishevelled hair.

"Here, Miss Eula, is a cup of tea," said Betsy, softening her voice to its lowest key, and approaching the bed; "it will do your head good. I couldn't get along no how in the world, if it wer'n't for my tea o'nights. It helps one mightily."

"No, I thank you, Betsy," answered Eulalia, covering her eyes with her hand, to hide the moist and swollen lids. "I shall be well in the morning. Don't trouble yourself about me."

"It's mighty strange," said Betsy, seating herself and absently sipping the fragrant beverage rejected by Eulalia, "it's strange how it happened, but Mr. Moreland's sick, too. While the folks were at supper, I run over to Miss Grimby's to borrow a handful of hops, and they all seemed in a powerful fright. Albert was running after a doctor, saying his master was in an awful way, taken all of a sudden, or so."

Eulalia started from her pillow and leaned eagerly forward, as if to catch the lowest sound of Betsy's nasal tones.

"Oh! Betsy, are you sure this is all true?" she

exclaimed, pushing back her hair with both hands, and gazing wistfully in her face.

"To be sure it is true, or I wouldn't be the one to say it," replied Betsy, emphatically.

Now Betsy had a habit of exaggeration, in which she unconsciously indulged, and she used the epithets *powerful* and *awful* without meaning all that the lexicographer attributes to them. "I declare," continued she, "*that* Albert is the lovingest creatur I ever beheld. The way he loves his master, I couldn't begin to tell,—and I don't wonder at it, for a nicer gentleman never came into these parts. He's given away ever so much money to the poor, besides what he's done to Nancy. It's well Albert's there to take care of him. Mrs. Grimby's got a new gal to help her, the awkwardest thing I ever set eyes on; and she's been working so hard lately, she looks herself as if she'd been dragged through a knot-hole."

While Betsy's tongue ran on, with a kind of railroad speed, Eulalia had risen and thrown one arm around the bed-post, against which she stood leaning. Her heart had been faint and sick before, under the cold burden of disappointed hope; now it ached and throbbed with sudden anxiety and dread. Moreland sick, and perhaps dying, at an inn! Had he come, had he lingered only for this!

"Does father know of it?" she asked. "No! I

know he does not. Tell him, Betsy, and he will go and see him."

"I expect there's not much use in the Squire's going," muttered Betsy, "unless he'll give him the right medicine. I've seen all that's been going on; and, tho' I've no right to say it, I'm desperate sorry, at the way things have turned. He'd make you a grand, good husband, and you'd live like the lady you was born to be. As for the stories they tell about whipping and slashing the niggers, I don't believe a word on't. Albert says they are all lies,—that he'd a heap rather live there than here, and be as free as the rest of us. Free!—I wonder what they call free?" continued Betsy, feeling of the knots and callouses of her toil-worn hands. "I know I ain't free, or I wouldn't work, like a pack-horse, from one year's eend to another. I'm obliged to work to live, and to make others live, and God knows I'm willing; but I should like to know what rest and pleasure I have? I haven't sot down before since I got up this blessed morning. Albert says the niggers sing and dance as much as they please, when their work is done up. I wonder how I would look singing and dancing! Now, don't be angry, Miss Euly, but the Squire's standing in his own light this time. There ain't a lady in the land but what would envy you, not one. You'll never get such another chance, as sure as you're born."

"Betsy" said Eulalia, sinking down on the bedside,

still embracing the post with the clinging hands, "I know you mean to be kind, but you must not talk in that way. Please go and tell father how very sick he is."

"I'll tell him," she answered reluctantly, and slowly rising, with the now empty cup in her hand, and taking a step or two towards the door. "I'll tell him, though it's no use. You are as sick as he is, I dare say. You look as white as a ghost, and as limber as a wet rag. I'll tell you what I will do, Miss Euly, if it will be any comfort to you. I'll run over to the tavern again, after I've done up all my chores, and see how the gentleman really is, and if he needs watchers I'll set up with him myself, for I know nobody can beat me nussing, when I try—my poor lame brother knows that's true."

"You are too tired, Betsy. You have been working too hard; but you are a kind nurse—I know it well myself."

"Albert can spell me," cried Betsy, nodding her head, "and if I do set up at night, it don't make me lazy next day. Folks can do with a heap less sleep than they think they can, if they only try it."

Mrs. Hastings entered, and Betsy withdrew, having rested herself from the toils of the day by pouring into Eulalia's ear her affectionate sympathy.

Mr. Hastings was really troubled when he heard of the illness of Moreland, and immediately walked over to the inn to ascertain the truth of the statement. He found the physician there, who talked professionally of inflammatory symptoms, of a tendency of blood to the brain, and the necessity of perfect quietude. He pronounced it a most sudden and violent attack, one that would require great skill to conquer, and experience to understand. Mr. Hastings was not so much alarmed as he would have been, had he not known that almost all the Doctor's patients had very violent and dangerous attacks, and that he pronounced their cure as little short of a miracle. Still he felt very uncomfortable, and walked homewards with slow and heavy steps. The image of Eulalia, when he had told her of the decree which had gone forth; the deadly pallor of her complexion; the unutterable anguish of her glance, turned from him to heaven, as if appealing to its mercy; the sudden pressure of her hand upon her heart, as if an arrow were quivering there—came to him in the darkness like accusing phantoms, and would not vanish away. The countenance of Moreland, too, when he asked him "if that was his unalterable decision," so pale, agitated, and stern, would rise before him, drawn only too vividly on the shadows of night. He could not help asking himself, if he were doing right to separate those whom God seemed to have united by a love so passing strong, so transcending all he had ever witnessed in the romance of life. He questioned his own principles, his own motives, and wondered if it were really his duty to sacrifice his daughter's happiness to his own reputation. He seemed much less in his own estimation, walking alone, under the great dark dome of night, whose starry hieroglyphics proclaimed an antiquity deep as eternity; he felt much less, we repeat, with these solemn influences around him, than when acting as the demagogue of a party, and feeding on the husks of popular applause.

CHAPTER V.

The Parsonage! what a sweet, lovely spot it was! Parsonages almost always are lovely. They are selected with a view to the sacred character of the inmate, far from the noise and bustle of the working-day world, with a smooth, green lawn stretching out in front, a profusion of shade trees sheltering that green lawn from the bronzing sunbeams, and a pure white paling running all round it. Such was the dwelling-place of Parson Ellery, as he was called by the country people, and if goodness and piety could consecrate a spot, it was indeed holy ground. But though the good country people called him parson, he owned a loftier title, which the villagers preferred—Doctor Ellery, he having been honoured with a D. D., by the faculty of a neighbouring university. Though now a somewhat aged man, he had never married, a circumstance which continued to excite wonder in those who knew him best. He had come among them, a stranger, in the meridian of his days, and no one knew the history of his youthful life. He was what may emphatically be styled a man of God, devoting himself to His service with apostolic simplicity and evangelical devotion, dividing his time between the seclusion of the study, the homes of the poor, and the chambers of the sick and the dying. He was also a man of peace, and grieved when any jarring elements were set in motion in the heart of the community. He did all he could to counteract the blind fanaticism which Mr. Hastings had kindled and continued to fan with his fiery breathings; and in so doing, he had excited in the latter feelings of personal animosity, the more bitter, because policy induced him to conceal them. He did not wish to appear at variance with a man so popular and universally beloved; therefore he smiled blandly upon him, was a constant attendant on public worship, and a respectful observer of all the ordinances of religion. Still, the minister knew that Mr. Hastings disliked and distrusted him, feared his influence, and did all he could, in secret, to weaken and undermine it.

Though unmarried, as a most excellent and respectable housekeeper presided over his establishment, he was visited by all the matrons and maidens of the parish. Among these none was so welcome or beloved as Eulalia Hastings. She had grown up under his eye, from a lovely young child into a still lovelier young woman, and, forgetting the lapse of time, she was still to him the innocent and confiding child, who always seemed to him, sweet as the rose of Sharon and fair as the lily of the valley. She it was, who brought him the first flowers of spring, the first strawberries of summer, and the first fruits of autumn. He had accustomed all the children to call him father, and Eulalia still addressed him by that endearing name.

He was now seated in his study, in a large arm-chair, with a slab, covered with green baize in front, which served as a table, and on which paper, pen, and ink were laid. But though the paraphernalia of writing was before him, the pen lay idly by the pure blank paper, and his hand supported on its palm, his drooping head. He seemed lost in sad and profound meditation, when a low, sweet voice, breathing his name at the open door, roused him from his deep revery.

"Eulalia, my child, come in."

"Do I intrude, father?" It was thus that, from childhood, she had addressed him, and never did her spirit cling with more yearning fondness and sacred trust to all that name implies, than at the present moment.

He answered by rising, taking her kindly by both hands, leading her to a seat near the window, and taking another near her. She looked so pale and sad, so fair, so delicate, he felt as if he must place her as he would a wilting flower, where the summer breeze could fan her. She sat awhile in silence, but the quivering of her lip and the tears glittering on her long, dark, drooping lashes showed, more eloquently than words, the sorrow that sighed for consolation. The good man knew all her history. It was that on which he was pondering when she entered. He had been bearing her in the arms of faith and prayer, to the mercy seat of heaven; and when he told her of this, in gentle, soothing words, she bowed her head, and the tears rained down her cheeks.

"Oh! dear father," she cried, "my soul is oppressed with the burden of its sorrow. I came to you for comfort and support. The clouds are very dark around me. You have told me that religion would sustain me in life's saddest trials; but, oh, in vain I pray. I sink lower and lower. Hope, joy, and faith, all—all are leaving me."

"Ah! my child, you have basked in sunshine till this hour, while thousands have sat cold and weeping behind the hidings of God's countenance. I fear your religion is indeed built upon the sand, if the first wave of suffering that beats against it shakes it from its foundation. The children of God must all pass through some ordeal to prove their divine affiliation. Some pass through the fire, some the flood, and some are cast into the lion's den of oppression; yet, strengthened by angels, they faint not, but triumph, and look back upon every trial as a stepping-stone to glory and happiness."

"I think I could bear any suffering that affected me alone," said Eulalia, raising her tear-dimmed eyes; "but to be the cause of misery, sickness, and perhaps death to others,—there is something so crushing, so terrible in the thought."

"Sickness and death are the ministers of God," replied the pastor, "and they always stand ready to do his bidding. The illness of this unfortunate stranger may have been excited by contending passions, but not produced. Change of climate, and a thousand causes unknown to us, may have brought about this result. I learn from his servant, that he has had a similar attack, and that then, as now, his case was considered hopeless. *You* have no cause of self-reproach, my child; and, whatever be the issue, you have nothing left but submission."

"You have seen him to-day, father. Do you indeed give up all hope?"

"No! while an omnipotent God watches over him. To-night, I am told, will be the crisis of his malady. We must pray,—we must wrestle in prayer for his recovery, but always with one reservation, my dear Eulalia, "Not my will, but thine, O, God! be done."

"One thing, let me ask, father,—did he speak?—did he know you?"

"No! my child,—he lies still, pale and unconscious as the unbreathing marble. His faithful slave stands weeping and sobbing by his bedside, an image of the truest and fondest affection I ever witnessed. Friends are waiting round him, ready to administer to his sufferings, when awakened to their consciousness. Be comforted, my daughter,—all that man can do has been done; but it is in moments like these, man feels his impotence, and can only prostrate himself in sackcloth and ashes, at the feet of infinite wisdom and mercy."

"In your presence, I do feel the possibility of submission; but I dare not tell you all my rebellion and despair, when there is no one near to soothe and sustain. How kind, how sympathizing you are!—you, who never knew the tumult of earthly passions. What gentleness and tenderness you manifest for weaknesses you never felt!"

The minister raised his mild gray eyes to heaven, then turned them on Eulalia with an unutterable expression. There was a sudden glow, a lighting up in them, that sent a flash over his brow and warmed with transient colour his pallid cheeks.

"Perhaps the history of passions subdued, of weaknesses overcome, and sorrows endured and sanctified through grace, may teach you how to subdue and endure your own," said he in a low, agitated voice. Eulalia looked at him with a countenance of the most earnest interest. It glowed with the reflection of his own emotions.

"Calm and passionless as you see me now," he added, "nature moulded me out of very strong and warring elements. My father was in affluent circumstances, and I, being an only son, was indulged to an extent that I have never seen equalled. Had it not been for the counterpoising influence of a pious, restraining mother, my extravagance would have been as boundless as my means were unrestricted. When I became of age my mother died, and it seemed to me that the star of home set for ever behind her death-cloud. I became restless and ambitious. I longed for new scenes of action. I wanted to travel, to see more of the world and mankind. While in college I had become acquainted with several young men from the South, one of whom was the intimate friend of my youth."

Here Eulalia bent forward in an attitude of deeper attention.

"This young man," continued the minister, "whose name was Livingston, was a Virginian, and he had so often described his home to me, in bright and glowing colours, that I resolved to visit it, and become familiar by personal observation with those manners and habits, which, I am sorry to say, are so often misrepresented and painted in the darkest and most forbidding colours. My father gave his consent, and I accompanied my friend over the mountains of Virginia to his home, in one of the loveliest valleys of the world. I shall never forget the greeting we received. Had I been a son or brother I could not have been more warmly, cordially welcomed—not only by the white family, from whom I expected hospitality and kindness, but by the household negroes and the plantation slaves, who constituted one large community in themselves. I had heard many a tale of the woes and sufferings of this enslaved race; but I looked in vain for scars and stripes and chains. I saw comfortable cabins erected for their accommodation, comfortable raiment and food provided for them. They went forth to their labour with cheerful faces, and returned at night to pastime or rest, often with the song upon their lips. I was not prepared for such a state of things, nor for the kindness and familiarity with which young Livingston treated these dependants, who on their part seemed to adore their young master. With the recollection of these scenes still vivid in my memory, it is not strange that I have mourned deeply over your father's prejudices, and the zeal he manifests in a cause he is only injuring by his vehemence. It is not strange that I should have regretted the recent decision he has made, and sought with all my influence to induce him to change it."

"And have you done so?" exclaimed Eulalia. "Oh! I did not know. I feared you might blame my want of filial submission. Oh! bless you, sir, for this last, this greatest kindness."

"Far be it from me to lessen your filial reverence," continued Doctor Ellery. "Your father has many virtues, and, I doubt not, thinks he is doing God service by the course he is pursuing. I wish I could turn his zeal and talents into a different channel; but I am placed as a watch-light on the hill of Zion, and must keep myself, as much as possible, aloof from the storms and strifes of contending parties. Eulalia, that was a happy home to which young Livingston bore me. The father was a warm-hearted, hospitable, genial gentleman, fond of hunting and fishing, a noble equestrian, a Nimrod in the chase; a kind, just master, an indulgent father, a tender, affectionate husband. The mother, a dignified, intelligent lady, who looked well to the ways of her household, directing and superintending everything with the eye of a mistress, yet never sacrificing one lady-like grace or accomplishment. And the daughter, Emma Livingston,—" here his voice faltered, and he paused. A faint red began to tinge the cheek of Eulalia. A strong sympathy drew her still nearer her evangelical friend.

"Emma Livingston," he resumed, "I will not attempt to describe. She had the bloom, the beauty, the gayety, and innocence of youth; but a bloom so soft, a beauty so winning, a gayety so tempered by modesty, and an innocence so exalted by wisdom, that her character presented a rare and lovely combination. Eulalia, you have heard a great deal of the selfishness and hard-heartedness of Southern females; and so had I. Here was a young girl, an only daughter, brought up in the midst of attendants, to whom her slightest word was law. You, my dear child are not more gentle and self-sacrificing than she was. You do not speak more gently to your little sister than did she to her household slaves. I have seen her lavish the tenderest caresses on their little infants. I have seen her hang in anxious watchfulness over their sick-beds. I have seen her weep over their humble graves. She taught them to read. She read the Bible to them herself, and never seemed happier than when administering to their necessities. Surely it was not wrong to assimilate her to an angel of light, as she glided among these sable beings, twining with the roses of affection, their links of bondage. I could dwell for hours on those days of love and happiness, for I feel as if I had lifted a heavy stone from the fountain of memory, and that I cannot stay the gushing waters. For years I have not uttered her name; and now,—when moved, by a strong and holy impulse for your soul's good, to break the silence that has so long closed over my sorrows,—it seems as if I must breathe it alone, and breathe it for ever. I was then young and impassioned, and all that youth and passion ever breathed of love, I felt for Emma. I was the beloved friend of her brother, the favoured guest of her father,—every circumstance was propitious to my wishes. Her own heart was mine. The esteem and affection of her kindred were mine. I wrote to my father, who gave his cordial consent to a union which the gifts of fortune as well as nature so liberally blessed. We were to divide our time between the North and the South. In the summer I was to bear my bride to my native North. In the winter we were to return to her beloved Virginia. What was wanting, my child, to complete my felicity? Nothing but the consent of Almighty God? I did not ask for that. I dreamed not of its being withheld. Why should I dream? The rose of health blushed on the young cheek of Emma, and its sunbeam sparkled in her clear azure eye. Exercise in the open air gave vigour to her frame and elasticity to her step. She delighted most in riding on horseback, as the daughters of Virginia are wont to do. She had her own favourite horse, black and shining as ebony, which, though fleet and spirited as the deer, seemed gentle as a lamb. She would ride with her brother and myself over mountain and plain, swift and fearless as the eagle. And now, my daughter, I come to that dark era of my life, which I must hurry over, lest reason plunge headlong in the grave of memory. I cannot relate the particulars; but, once, during those mountain rides, just two weeks before our appointed nuptials, her horse took fright and leaped over a precipice, whose brink—God of heaven!—was covered with wild roses and flowering vines."

The minister rose and walked the length of his study, back and forth, and back and forth, with clasped hands, and eyes darkened by the memory of despair. Eulalia could not speak. She was gazing, in imagination, on the mangled body of Emma, at the foot of that awful precipice,—on the horse and the rider, both quivering and bleeding in the agonies of death,—on the anguish of surviving friends; she was dwelling on the appalling uncertainty of every earthly blessing,—the terrible penalty love is doomed to pay for its short dream of joy,—on the sad, sad doom of mortality; she wept as if her heart would break,—wept for herself, wept for her minister, and for all the sons and daughters of humanity.

The sound of her suppressed sobs roused the minister from his own paroxysm of grief. He resumed his seat, and wiped the cold moisture that had gathered on his brow.

"I can never tell you," he added, "the anguish that succeeded the first tempest of sorrow,—the despair that brooded over my mind. For a long time, I thought I should die. I prayed but to die, to throw off the cold, heavy burthen of life. I prayed to die, not because I sighed for the joys of heaven, but that I was weary of the gloom of earth. I thought not so much of meeting the spirit of my Emma above, as losing the remembrance of her awful fate below. Had I then died, dark indeed would have been my doom; but I lived for repentance, for faith, and hope. One of those blessed servants of God, who are anointed for a peculiar mission, found me, and dragged me up out of the depths of the abyss of blackness in which my soul was plunged; he poured oil and balm into my wounds, bound them in the swaddling bands which wrapped the babe of the manger, and left me not till he had laid me a weeping penitent at the foot of the cross. Then a divine warmth penetrated my heart. I looked upon this world only as the dim vestibule of a great and glorious temple, and I said, 'I had rather be a doorkeeper in the house of my God, than to dwell in the tents of wickedness.' I looked upon it as a frail bridge over the river of time: and I said, 'Let me guide my fellow-pilgrims over the tottering planks to the beautiful shores of the promised land,—that land whose celestial beauties my eyes have been opened to behold.' I said, 'O, my God! I dedicate myself to thee, body and soul, in life and death, for time and eternity.' Eulalia, I have been true, as far as poor frail humanity can be, to the solemn vows of my great consecration. I see now why I was led through such a thorny path. My soul was so wedded to earth, nothing but a mighty wrench could have torn it from my grasp. It was all right. 'Be still, and know that I am God.' We must sooner or later obey this mandate; if not in the sorrows and tribulation of time, mid the thunders and lightnings of eternal judgment."

Eulalia sat pale with awe, listening to the solemn accents of the minister, and gazing on his countenance, now flashing with a sublime fire. She felt humbled by the selfishness of her grief, the rebelliousness of her will, the conviction she had brought with her, that "there was no sorrow like unto her sorrow."

"My father," at length she said, "I will try to profit by this sad lesson; but pray for me, for I am very weak."

A short time after, she rose to depart; but, after she

had bidden adieu, she lingered on the threshold, as if something still remained unuttered.

"Whatever be the event of this night," she said, in a faltering voice, "remember, father, that *he* is a Christian."

"To the Christian's God let us commend him, in faith and hope, and, above all, in entire submission; and should our prayers be heard, my daughter, as something whispers that they will, I believe Providence has a mission for you to perform, the way of which will be made smooth beneath your feet. You will be a golden link of union between the divided interests of humanity, and inherit the peculiar blessing reserved for those who shall be called the children of God."

Those prophetic words remained with Eulalia and strengthened her through that long, long, sleepless night.

CHAPTER VI.

Poor Albert! with what faithful affection, what unwearied devotion and unutterable sorrow did he watch night and day by his sick and apparently dying master! He would not leave him, though every kindness and attention was lavished upon the stranger, so far from home and friends, that compassion could dictate or sympathy impart. Though others watched, he could not, would not sleep. The only times he would leave the room, was when his grief was wrought up to a paroxysm that was perfectly uncontrollable, and he feared to disturb the patient by his bitter cries. Then, he would rush out doors, throw himself upon the ground, and give vent to the most heart-rending lamentations. The idea of his master's dying, and leaving him alone in that strange land, filled him with the wildest terror as well as the deepest anguish. He shrunk with horror from the sight of Mr. Hastings, whom he believed his master's enemy; though whenever he entered the chamber he watched him with the keenness of the basilisk.

He could not bear to see him look at his master, and could he have done so, he would have interposed a screen before his pallid face, to save it from the influence of what he fully believed to be an *evil eye*. In the architect, Mr. Brooks, who devoted every moment he could spare from professional labours to the sick-bed of his friend, he had the most affectionate confidence, and he loved the good minister, who was now his daily visiter. He would watch their countenances with the most intense eagerness, as if he could read in those solemn tablets the secret of his master's fate.

Nothing could exceed the interest manifested by the whole neighbourhood in the sick stranger, whose humanity and courtesy had softened many a bitter prejudice, and inspired feelings of warm personal regard. The charm of romance, which even the most matter-of-fact beings appreciate, gave an attraction to the sufferer, that deepened the sympathy he awakened. The story of his love for Eulalia Hastings, of his rejection by her father, of Eulalia's own love and sorrow, were known far and near. Perhaps Betsy's garrulous tongue had told the secret; but through whatever channel it came, it had been circulated from house to house, till it was the theme of every tongue. Various were the commentaries it called forth. Some condemned the stern fanaticism of the father; others praised him as a glorious martyr to truth and humanity. Eulalia was too much beloved to be envied, save by a jealous few, and even envy was transformed to pity in the contemplation of her blighted hopes.

Quite an affecting incident occurred the very evening that Eulalia visited the minister. Nancy, who had heard with great sorrow of the illness of her benefactor, and who had for days been confined to her bed, felt one of those sudden revivals of strength peculiar to the victims of consumption. She heard that morning that the Southern stranger must surely die, and she resolved to see his face again, before it was hidden by the clods of the valley. In vain her poor old mother told her she was too weak, too ill to go. She dragged her feeble footsteps to her former home, stopping every now and then to rest by the wayside, and stooping to pick up the wild flowers that grew in her path, thinking they might gladden the sick man's fading sight. When she presented herself before the landlady, she started as if a spectral illusion were bewildering her senses.

"Why, Nancy—where in the world did you come from?" exclaimed Mrs. Grimby, giving her a chair as she spoke, into which the wearied creature sank breathless and exhausted.

"How is the sick gentleman? Is he really going to die?" was Nancy's first interrogation.

"So the Doctor says," replied Mrs. Grimby, "and he knows best. Poor man! I feel so sorry for him. It is so hard to be taken away, when none of his kin can be near him. He's such a kind, pleasant gentleman, one couldn't help liking him. Albert, too, that poor yellow boy, takes on so desperately, it is enough to make one's heart ache to hear him. I never would have believed it if I hadn't seen it—never in this world. It sometimes seems as if he would go raving distracted."

"May I see him?" asked Nancy, while a tear dropped upon the wild flowers she held in her poor emaciated hand.

"Lord bless you!—they won't let anybody but the Doctor and the minister and Mr. Brooks go into the room now. They say it's the criticallest time of his whole sickness. He don't take no notice of anybody or anything; but looks just like a piece of white marble. No, Nancy, I wouldn't dare to let you in, to save my life."

"I'll just look at him and come out, without saying one word," pleaded the invalid. "If he's going now I shall follow soon—and I want to see him only once. I got out of my bed to come, though mother tried hard to keep me from it. You don't know how good he has been to us. He gave us money, and what is more, the kindest words and the most pitying looks. He doesn't despise the poor."

"Yes—he's been kind to me," said Mrs. Grimby, and her voice choked.

Nancy hailed this symptom of sensibility as propitious to her prayer—and she pleaded so earnestly, with her large hollow eyes fixed so mournfully on her, with that burning hectic spot on either cheek, that Mrs. Grimby consented, on condition that she should walk on tiptoe, stay but one moment, and not open her lips while she remained. The affectionate, grateful heart of the sick girl swelled almost to bursting as she gazed on the inanimate and altered countenance of her friend. Where was the kind and sunny smile, the darkly-beaming glance, the glow of life and health, which had so lately lighted up their humble cottage and left their bright reflection on its gloom? And Albert, too, who stood at the bed-head mute as a statue—how dim and ashy looked his golden skin—how dull and melancholy his bright black eye!

"Come," whispered Mrs. Grimby, seeing Nancy's bosom heave, and fearing the commencement of one of her racking coughs. "Come, you must not stay any longer."

Nancy slid softly down on one knee and laid her flowers on the pillow, as reverently as one scatters them over the shrouded dead; then, rising and putting her handkerchief to her face, left the apartment.

"Stop, and let me give you a glass of wine before you go, Nancy," said the landlady, "and bite a piece of cracker with it. You mustn't take on so. It's the Lord's doing, and we must all die at last."

Mrs. Grimby felt very sorry for the poor girl, who had entered her service a strong, blooming maiden. She remembered how faithfully she had laboured, even after the clutch of the destroyer was on her. She feared she had let her work too hard, that she had not been as kind and considerate as she ought to have been. She feared she had sometimes spoken quickly and harshly to her, and though she had never spared herself, she thought she ought to have spared her more.

"I wish I could send you home, Nancy," said she, following her to the door. "I do hate to see you walk."

"Thank you. I don't mind walking. I won't forget how kind you've been, Mrs. Grimby. I hope the Lord will bless you for it."

She did not mean the wine and the bread, which had really strengthened her exhausted frame, but the transient glimpse she had given her of the pale face and scarcely breathing form she never more expected to behold.

And what did the morning bring to the anxious watchers round that still couch, over which the shadows of death seemed slowly, darkly gathering? What did it bring to the throbbing heart, which had counted the weary moments by its own wild beatings? It brought hope—hope born from the bosom of despair; and the tidings was like a resurrection from the dead. As the minister had said, there *is hope*, as long as there is an omnipotent God to watch over us.

The convalescence of the invalid was slow, but cheered by so many acts of kindness, he could not murmur at his imprisonment. As soon as he was able to be moved,

Doctor Ellery insisted upon taking him to the Parsonage, where, in perfect quietude, he could wait his com plete restoration. Albert, whose joy was as demonstrative as his grief had been, was enraptured at the change, for he could not hear a slamming door or a resounding step in the house, without trembling for his master's weakened nerves. The change was indeed a grateful one from the bustle of an inn, to the deep tranquillity of that pastoral home. The minister treated him with even parental tenderness; and the good housekeeper made for him the nicest panada, the most delicious wine whey, and every delicacy medical wisdom permitted the invalid to taste. And Dora, sweet little Dora, came every day to see him, laden with flowers, with which she decorated his room, and sometimes playfully adorned the folds of his dressing-gown. She told him how sad and sorry they all were, when he was so sick, and that even now, sister Eula never smiled.

"Do you know," said she, in a low, confiding tone, "that I heard mamma talking to papa about sister Eula, and she said she was afraid she would fall into a consumption. Oh! wouldn't that be dreadful? Poor Nancy Brown has got it, and don't she look bad?"

Moreland felt icy-cold shivers run through his frame.

"And what did your papa say?" he asked.

"He didn't say nothing; but put his hands behind him, so, and walked up and down, and up and down, just as he always does when anything pesters him.

Then mamma said, if Eula was only in the South, there wouldn't be any danger."

"Did your mother say that? God bless her!" exclaimed Moreland, drawing the little chatterer closer in his arms; "and what did your papa say then?"

"He kept saying, 'God knows, God knows,' and went right out of the room. Then I saw mamma was crying, and I went and kissed away her tears."

While Moreland listened to the artless prattle of the child, a new and powerful motive of action was born within him. The proud spirit which had told him never to hazard a second rejection should be subdued. What were the hazard of a thousand rejections to Eulalia's danger? He *would* snatch her from a clime where the damps of death are so often mingled with the soft dews of night,—he *would* save her from a doom, the very thought of which froze his veins with horror,—if there was power in man or help in Heaven, he would do it. The energy of his purpose gave him strength. He rose and sought the minister; he told him all his past history, his present intentions, his future hopes. He besought his influence and co-operation, his counsels and his prayers. All these were promised, and they were all given.

No one knew what passed between the minister and Mr. Hastings; but every day the former was seen to visit the latter, and after long private interviews they would separate, with the impress of deep thought on

MR. HASTINGS AND THE MINISTER.

their brows. They also took long walks together in sequestered by-paths, and sometimes they wandered to the graveyard, and, leaning on some old gray tomb-stone, would converse earnestly and gravely with each other. The villagers, who were well aware of the want of harmony in the sentiments of the two parties, wondered at this unwonted communion, though many were shrewd enough to divine the cause; and they shook their heads, and said that the good minister might talk till every hair of his head turned to silver, and he never would make such an obstinate man as Squire Hastings change his purpose.

As soon as he was able to walk abroad, Moreland called at Mr. Hastings's. Dora flew to the gate to meet him, almost wild with joy, and ushered him into the sitting-room, with delighted eagerness.

"Mamma, sister Eula—here's Mr. Moreland come again. Ain't you glad?"

Mrs. Hastings came forward and extended her hand, with a most heartfelt expression of pleasure. Eulalia, too, while a bright rosy cloud swept over her lovely face, suffered her hand to linger in the greeting pressure of his, and her eye, so soft, yet thrilling, mingled for a moment its glad rays with the languid but now kindling fires of his own. In vain he assured them that he disclaimed all the privileges of an invalid. The easy chair was brought forward; a glass of sangaree, rich with the aroma of the nutmeg, prepared for his refreshment. He was even threatened with a pillow, for the repose of his head, but this he strenuously refused. He was forced, however, to acknowledge that he was weary from his walk, and that there was much comfort in the soft depths of that "old arm-chair." He looked very pale and interesting; and there was a grace in his languor, more attractive than the vigour of health.

He had no reason to be displeased with his reception. Mr. Hastings came in rubbing his hands, with his "very happy to see you" air. Reuben shook his hand most vehemently, and Betsy's honest face shone upon him through the half-opened door.

"You look a little the worse for the wear," said Mr. Hastings. "I am sorry to see it. I fear you will carry away with you unfavourable impressions of our climate."

"I had a similar attack at home," replied Moreland; "so I must think my malady independent of the latitude where I dwell. I sometimes think," he added with a smile, "that I might have escaped this last infliction had not the alarmed affection of my boy placed me in the hands of the doctor."

"I believe you are free from the scourge of our climate—consumption," observed Mr. Hastings. "Your mild, uniform temperature is favourable to the lungs."

"Yes," replied Moreland, looking at Eulalia, from whose transparent complexion the rosy hue had faded, leaving it of waxen delicacy. "The frail and delicate from other regions are safe when they breathe our genial atmosphere. The consumptive sometimes finds a grave beneath our flowers; but it is when they come too late for restoration."

Here a slight cough from Eulalia made Moreland start. He gazed long and anxiously upon her. She was thinner than when he first saw her—and so exquisitely, so delicately fair! The faint blue meandering of her temple veins was visible through her alabaster skin. Then her eyes of such velvet softness, such languishing brightness—had they not the fatal beauty which marks the victims of consumption? Those long, pensive, dark lashes—did they not seem to weep over the radiance doomed to an early fading? Eulalia looked up, and meeting his earnest gaze, understood its meaning.

"If you were as familiar with colds," she said, with a sweet, assuring smile, "as we are here, you would think a cough of very little consequence."

"Did you ever read the story in the 'Diary of a Physician,' called A Slight Cold?" asked Moreland. "It is made of some consequence there."

"If you are not too much fatigued," said Mr. Hastings, rising with considerable embarrassment of manner, "I would like you to walk into my study with me a few moments, Mr. Moreland. You will find an arm-chair there also, for my wife has an eye to my comfort as well as that of her guests."

Moreland rose with alacrity, and obeyed the movement of the Philanthropist. As he passed out of the doorway, he saw Eulalia cast a look at her father so tender and beseeching, he thought he must be made of stone to resist the mute appeal. When they reached the study, Mr. Hastings went through every possible preliminary, to retard the conversation he had sought. He moved the chairs, the books and papers on the table, opened the windows, wiped his face with his handkerchief, and dusted the knees of his pantaloons.

"Mr. Moreland," said he, at length seating himself, drawing a heavy volume towards him, and poising it over the table, "circumstances have arisen since our last conversation, which have somewhat modified the views I then expressed. My principles are unchanged, my views of your Southern institutions are unchanged, but I am led to believe that the will of God demands of me a sacrifice, and to that will I am constrained to bow. Do not interrupt me. I wish to explain myself, so that you may understand I am not acting in an inconsistent manner. I did not know, when I conversed with you last, the strength of your attachment to my daughter. I did not know that her happiness was involved in this union. I find that your hearts are drawn towards each other in a very strong and peculiar manner; and I begin to see the dealings of Providence in this dispensation. Eulalia is a delicate child. I have brought her up in fear and trembling. In short, she is a tropic flower, born to be nurtured beneath milder skies than ours. To preserve her health, to prolong her life, I am willing to hazard the high social position I at present occupy. Sir, I shall falsify myself to save my daughter. I have said in public and in private, that I would never suffer wife or child of mine to live at the South, even if I could add ten years to their existence; and I meant what I said—but we are all weak and fallible. I thought I had more firmness; but so many counter influences have been acting upon me! Your dangerous illness immediately following my rejection; my daughter's fading health; the prayers of my wife; the counsels of our minister; the opinions of my best friends, all have actuated me to revoke the decision I had made. There is another motive. You said you looked upon yourself as a missionary, appointed by heaven for the good of a benighted race. That remark has had great weight with me. More than all else, it has induced me to sacrifice my daughter."

"Call it not a sacrifice!" exclaimed Moreland, who had waited with glowing impatience for the conclusion of this long harangue, "call it a gift, the most precious gift of Heaven, and I bless you for the bestowal. Believe me, sir, you never will repent this yielding of your will to the pleadings of affection, the urgings of reason. Eulalia, I will watch over and cherish her, as never yet was woman loved and cherished. She will be adored by the affectionate community over which she will preside. Yes! I feel that her lot will be a happy one. As for your son, consider me from this moment as his elder brother, the joint guardian of his best interests. And should your darling Dora ever need a father's care, that sacred care be mine. Oh! sir, you have made me a very happy man; I thank you, I bless you for it. I feel new life, new health, flowing into my veins. Let me go. I am but half blest till Eulalia shares my joy."

"No, no!—I will send her to you," replied the father, clearing his throat of a strange huskiness. He was softened by the outgushings of that warm, generous heart; he was pleased with himself, for the great sacrifice he thought he had made—he was exalted in his own estimation. And now he had actually passed the Rubicon of his prejudices, he could not help contemplating the worldly advantages of the union. It would be a fine thing for Reuben to have a rich, influential brother-in-law; it would be well, if himself and Mrs. Hastings should be called away, to have a fair and opulent home for the orphan Dora. Eulalia, cradled in the lap of wealth and fanned by the fragrant breezes of the South, would bloom like its wild-wood blossoms. Then, she would go forth as a missionary, to bind up the bleeding wounds and smarting stripes of the poor slaves (for he had dwelt so long on the picture his imagination had drawn, it was an indelible reality to him),—she would teach their darkened minds the way of salvation, and draw them out of their bondage and chains, into the glorious liberty of the children of God.

These thoughts comforted him, and gave a benignant

expression to his countenance, as he sought Eulalia, which was beautiful to her as the sunshine of heaven. She knew that all her earthly happiness hung on the issue of that hour. She had waited in trembling apprehension its close, hoping, fearing, doubting; and now when her father opened the door and beckoned her to him, with a smile, she felt sick and giddy with the excess of her emotion. She rose to meet him, but seated herself again, for the room darkened around her.

"Come, my daughter," said he, approaching her, and putting one arm around her,—"come into the fresh air; it will revive you."

He led her through the garden path to the door of the study. He was silent, preparing a speech for the occasion, which would be a striking display of philanthropy and parental tenderness combined; but when he placed her hand in that of Moreland, his voice choked, his pompous declamation utterly failed, and he turned abruptly and left the room. Though privileged to remain, we will follow his example.

Joy is the best physician, after all. From this hour Moreland gained strength and elasticity. Eulalia's cheek recovered its soft oval outline, and the pale virgin rose once more blushed under its transparent surface.

The rumour of the approaching wedding circulated through the village, and there was more than the usual amount of admiration and interest. Mr. Hastings found himself a perfect *lion*, and was of course pleased, in spite of his great sacrifice.

"Well, Squire, I hear you're going to give your daughter to a Southerner, after all. How are you going to reconcile it to your principles?"

"I am only yielding to a higher power. Man proposes, but God disposes. The life of both was at stake, and had I persisted in my first decision I might be arraigned hereafter for the crime of murder. Besides, I send my daughter forth as a missionary, just as much as if she were bound for Burmah or Hindostan. I trust my friends will not accuse me of inconsistency."

Thus his neighbours addressed him, and thus he answered. He was establishing the reputation of a martyr. The fiery locks that wreathed his brow were assuming the character of a flaming crown of glory.

CHAPTER VII.

MORELAND sat in the same seat he had occupied many Sabbaths before. The same majestic anthem rolled round the walls of the church, consecrating it for the approach of the minister. It was the last Sunday he expected to worship there; the last Sunday the angel voice of Eulalia would mingle with her sister choristers in hymns of praise and hosannas of adoration. In the midst of the closing strains, when in clear, sweet, ascending, and sublime accents, she repeated the burden of the anthem,

> "When rolling years shall cease to move,"

there was a sudden trembling and faltering, then a pause, and a silence, as if the song of the morning stars were instantaneously hushed. Moreland listened breathlessly. He thought he heard a faint sob behind that green curtain—and his own bosom heaved. He began to realize all that Eulalia was resigning for him; the strength of the ties she was severing; the dear and holy associations she was rending asunder. Could he make up to her all that she relinquished? Father, mother, brother, sister, pastor, idolizing friends, the scenes of her happy childhood, her sheltered, peaceful youth? Yes! his love, passing as it did the love of man, should indemnify her for all. And in that heaven-dedicated place, he made a vow before God, that her happiness should be the first aim of his existence.

Eulalia sat behind the curtain, her face bowed on her hands, which covered her falling tears. Her companions respected her emotions, and, even after the minister commenced the solemn rites of the day, they suffered the green screen to remain, that concealed her from the gaze of the congregation. Their own eyes glistened, when they thought that, on another Sabbath, that fair form and sweet face and celestial voice would be wanting in the village choir.

Eulalia sat behind the curtain, oppressed with the solemnities of the place, and borne down by the weight of her own feelings. Her thoughts wandered from the past to the future, forgetful of the purposes of the present hour. The minister seemed to be repeating in her ear the tragic story of his early love, instead of the mysteries and glories of revelation. The sighing boughs of the elms, as they whispered through the windows of the gallery, told her sweet histories of her youth, and breathed a sad and lingering farewell. She was going to a land of strangers, to be surrounded by a girdle of darkness, from which there was no escape,—where, she had learned to believe, the fires of insurrection were for ever smouldering. But she was going with Moreland, and the companionship of such a being would make a Paradise of even the frozen regions of Nova Zembla, —how much more of the beautiful and flower-enamelled South! How unworthy was she, the humble village maiden, of the love of one so gifted and so noble! Was she indeed to become his wife, the mother of his child? She, the young and inexperienced? Like the handmaid of the Lord, she pondered on all these things, while the deep-toned voice of the minister fell in grave and solemn music on her ear. Forgive her wandering thoughts, for she is passing the great crisis of her being. She tries to bring them home to God, but in vain. She feels, in imagination, the child's soft arms clinging round her neck, its fair head cradled on her breast. She is breathing up to Heaven prayers for its helpless innocency,—prayers for wisdom to guide, for strength to guard, for power to go before it, in the purity and light of a Christian example. She sees its tender, appealing eyes lifted lovingly to her own. Are they the eyes of Moreland, or of the unhappy Claudia? She cannot bear the suggestion. That name always comes chillingly over her glowing heart. It is not jealousy, but dread. She dreads to think of one, who, once blessed with the heart of Moreland, could cast away such a gem.

As they walked home from church, Mr. and Mrs. Hastings arm and arm, Moreland by the side of Eulalia, with Dora's hand clinging to his; not a word was spoken by either, till Dora, as usual, broke the silence.

"What's the reason you didn't sing, sister Eula—? and what's the reason you don't talk any now? 'Tisn't a sin to talk going home from church, is it?"

"No, my child," said her father, turning round; "many things are lawful, which are not expedient under particular circumstances."

"I don't know what you mean!" cried Dora.

"I mean that your sister feels more like thinking than talking just now, and so we all do. Supposing you try to think of what good Doctor Ellery said, till we reach home."

"I love to think loud," replied the child. "What good does it do to think, if we don't tell anybody of it?"

"She is right," said Moreland, in a low voice to Eulalia; "it is not good to brood too long over our own solitary thoughts. I think I understand your feelings; but if you have one unexpressed regret, if you have one wish concealed, breathe it now, assured it shall be gratified, if it be in the power of man to do it."

"I have wept over the blessings I am about to resign," replied Eulalia; "for they magnify like the sun, when his parting rays shine upon us. But at this moment I regret, most of all, my unworthiness of the blessings for which I exchange them."

Had Eulalia been a fashionable belle, she never would

have made this meek, depreciating speech; but she was truth, simplicity, guilelessness, and purity—and Moreland loved her all the more for these unworldly attributes. If he did not reconcile her to herself, it was because the heart has no rhetoric, language no inspiration.

The wedding was to be very simple. It was to take place on the morning of their departure, without any display, waiters or attendants. But though no bridal pomp accompanied her nuptials, Eulalia was not suffered to depart without the most abundant tokens of affection and appreciation. Gifts were showered upon her—not costly ones, such as diamonds and precious stones, but heart-tokens far more precious in her estimation. The Sabbath-school children whom she had taught so faithfully and lovingly, brought her bouquets of flowers and trifles of their own manufacture. Even the poor, whom her bounty, restricted as it was obliged to be, had so often relieved; and whom her sympathy and cares, which were ever unlimited, had so often blessed, crowded round her with their blessings and their homely offerings. One poor woman, whose hands were half paralyzed, gave her an ironing-holder, which she had made of patchwork and quilted; another, near eighty years of age, presented her with a comb-case, framed of pasteboard and covered with calico, manufactured by her own aged and tremulous fingers. Very homely as were these gifts,

Eulalia received them with a tear and a smile, and promised to keep them as long as she lived.

"What shall I do," said a feeble octogenarian, wiping the tears from her silver lashes—"what shall I do, when you are gone? Who will read me God's blessed word, and talk to me so sweetly of a Saviour's love and the joys laid up for the righteous in Heaven?"

"Dora shall take my place. She can read now as well as I can, and in a few years she can talk to you of all these things, and you will teach her lessons of meekness and piety, even as you have done to me."

"What shall I do," exclaimed a poor sick mother, reclining on a couch of pain, by which Eulalia had ofttimes knelt and prayed—"when you are gone so far away? Who will love and care for my orphan children as you have done? Who will teach them to be good and keep them out of bad company as you have done?"

"My mother will still be your friend, and as Dora grows older she will do all that I have done, and I trust far more. I am going to leave her a precious legacy, which, young as she is, she will consider sacred."

"It is so hard to give you up," said another. "It seems as if I could be willing, Miss Euly, if you weren't going among such awful people. But I am so afraid you'll repent on't. You are going to have a fine husband, to be sure, and you'll ride in a fine carriage and live in a grand house, and you'll never be obliged to wet your fingers' ends; but the riches that don't come righteously won't bless a body. I wouldn't use money that was got by selling a human being, any more than I would take up live coals out of the chimney and eat 'em."

"You need not fear for me," said Eulalia, gently. "I do not expect such trials as that."

The evening before her marriage she accompanied Moreland to Dame Brown's cottage, for Nancy could not come to her. The walk she took to visit the apparently dying Moreland had accelerated the progress of her fatal malady, and she was now confined to the house, and most of the time to her bed. Albert had told him of that visit, and he never recalled it without the deepest emotion. Albert, with a delicacy of feeling seldom found in the uneducated, had picked up the wilted flowers she left upon his pillow, after they had fallen under the feet, and preserved them in water till his master's brightening vision could rest upon the gift.

"This is very good of you to come and see me, when you have so many friends to take leave of," said Nancy, leaning forward with eagerness to greet her. "And you too, sir," she added, holding out to Moreland her wasted and burning hand. "I never expected to see you in this poor cabin again—never; but it's wonderful what the Lord can do!"

"She looks dreadful bad, don't she?" asked Dame Brown, who sat in an old arm-chair by the side of Nancy's bed. "She can't hold out much longer. She coughs all night long, and you can hear her breathe e'enamost out of doors."

"I feel easier now, mother," said she. "Don't worry them by talking about what can't be helped. Every pain helps me on my journey home! I shall soon be there! Oh, yes! I shall soon be there!"

She lifted up her large, intensely bright eyes, with a smile that gleamed wildly on her sunken features.

"You are willing to die, Nancy?" cried Moreland, seeing that Eulalia was too much affected to speak, and on whose face she now turned an eager, wistful gaze. "You are not afraid of the sting of death? You look upon Heaven as your everlasting home?"

"Oh! sir," she replied, solemnly, "my Saviour has taken away the sting of death, and given me victory over the grave. Why should I fear to die? why should I wish to live? I've struggled with poverty all my life, and it has been a bitter warfare. When I was strong and could labour for my poor mother, I was willing to work the livelong day, though it seemed ever so long. But I havn't had much pleasure in life, even at the best, for the life of the poor and toiling has many a thorn and but few roses. Oh! sir," she cried, suddenly raising herself in the bed and clasping her thin hands over her knees, "I am so glad you are going to take her away from here! She might get the consumption, for she's one of the fair and beautiful ones that are sure to be singled out. I used to have round, blooming cheeks, and the people of the tavern praised me for my looks."

One sigh to the memory of her departed beauty convulsed the breast of the dying girl.

"Yes!" said her mother, "they used to call her pretty Nancy. Her cheeks were as rosy as you ever saw, and she had pretty holes in them, when she laughed; and now, they are so hollow, and such an awful round red spot right in the middle. Oh! Lord a marcy, what will become of me when she's gone, and you not by to comfort me, Miss Euly?"

"God will take care of you. God will comfort you," said Eulalia; "you will never want for friends."

"Only to think," said the old woman, following the lead of her rambling thoughts, as she looked from Eulalia to Moreland, and forgetting, for the moment, her own sorrow,—"only to think of the Squire's letting you go off with a furrener, after making such an ado about the way they carry on. I don't see how he can get over his speeches and writings, and the awful things he's told the people about the South folks. Well, well, I am glad for one account,—Miss Euly's going to have a kind, handsome husband, if there ever was one, and a rich one; and she'll do a power of good with her money. I know you can't be cruel to anybody, sir; and if she sees folks happy about you and her, she'd better not fret and worry about other folks. Do all the good you can, and leave the rest to Providence. I'm nothing but a poor old creature now, and havn't any business to talk and advise my betters; but I was reckoned smart in my day, and sometimes it seems as if I could see through a kind of loophole, brighter than I ever did before. I've been thinking a mighty deal about these affairs since you've come among us, and have been so good to us, and your yellow boy has brought us so many nice things, and Miss Euly is going off with you; and I know there's been wrong said and done. Your boy told us how kindly you treated 'em all, and how they all loved you, and how everybody round you was good, and didn't practise the iniquities they tell us of. Lord a marcy,—how monstrous difficult it is to get at the truth!"

The good woman fairly paused for breath, and Nancy repeated, as she had often done before,

"She don't mean any harm, any more than a child."

When Eulalia rose to depart, Nancy drew her down and whispered to her to open the upper bureau drawer and bring her a breast-pin, fastened to a little round pincushion.—It was a low, old-fashioned bureau, and the breast-pin was also old-fashioned, being in the form of a heart, set round with pearl. It had a glass in the centre, beneath which hair was intended to be set. Eulalia brought it to the bedside, well divining her purpose.

"And now," said Nancy, "please take the scissors hanging by the window, and cut off a lock of my hair and have it put under that glass when I am dead and gone, to remember me by. The one that gave me that breast-pin is dead, so there's no harm in my giving it away."

Moreland and Eulalia exchanged a quick flashing glance of intelligence. A history of love and fidelity was contained in those few words. The form of the heart was emblematical; even the pearls were significant of the tears of sorrow, which had probably bedewed this simple pledge. It was henceforth sacred in Eulalia's eyes. She took the scissors, and Nancy, bending forward, shook down the matted tresses of her long black hair, once so smooth and shining. Eulalia separated one from the rest, and attempted to sever it from the head it once adorned, but her eyes were blinded by tears, and her fingers had no strength. Moreland took the scissors gently from her hand, and cut two locks from the heavy mass that shaded the pillow.

"One for her, Nancy, and one for myself."—"Oh! sir!" exclaimed Nancy, bursting into tears. Not another word was spoken before they left the cottage, for the hearts of all were full. They knew that, in all human probability, they would not meet again, till they met in the light of eternity.

Moreland left with Mrs. Hastings a sum for the support of Nancy. If it lasted longer than her life, it was to be given to the poor and aged mother. Every token of love to Eulalia was also paid with usury. The patchwork holder was transmuted into gold, and the calico comb-case went through the same chemical process.

That night, when Moreland bade adieu to the family and turned his steps to the parsonage, Mr. Hastings accompanied him.

"I know how it will be in the morning," said he. "There will be no time for talking in the midst of sad leave-takings; and I feel as if I had much to say. As far as you are concerned, I have confidence to believe that you will make my daughter happy; but, when I think of the entire change in her mode of living, and the peculiar sensitiveness of her character, I have many misgivings. I think she has a remarkable antipathy to negroes. I have tried to conquer it in every possible way, but it, nevertheless, still exists."

"Indeed!" cried Moreland, in a tone of surprise and regret. "How has she manifested this unusual repugnance? She sees so few of the race here, I can hardly conceive how this antipathy could develop itself."

"About a year ago," continued Mr. Hastings, "I met in my travels a poor runaway negro—half-clothed, half-starved, the victim of an inhuman master, who, like the persecuted Son of Man, had not literally where to lay his head. Sir, I had compassion on him. I looked upon him as a man and as a brother. I took him into my carriage, brought him to my home, welcomed him to my board and my best household cheer. He told me the story of his sufferings and wrongs, and they were enough to move the very stones to cry out for vengeance. He remained with me for weeks, and during all that time Eulalia manifested a loathing so unnatural that it distressed me beyond expression. She could not eat seated at his side; she actually languished and sickened, and did not revive till he left me."

"I have heard the history of your hospitality to that vagabond," cried Moreland—and he could not help speaking in an excited and indignant voice—"and I have traced him from the beginning of his infamous career. He is a vile scoundrel, who, having first robbed and then attempted to murder his master, fled and hid himself from pursuit in the Dismal Swamp of his native state. His whole story was a lie. I am sorry your compassion was called forth by so unworthy an object. I am sorry your hospitality was degraded so low. I do not wonder that Eulalia shrunk with horror from the approach of such a wretch; that her intuitive delicacy and purity felt the contamination and withered under its influence. Why, I am told you were obliged to turn him out of doors for his insolence."

"Granting that I was deceived in him, it does not follow that the principle upon which I acted was wrong. I should do the same thing, under the same circumstances. My fellow men shall never call upon me in vain for redress or protection."

"I am glad to hear you utter that sentiment," exclaimed Moreland; "and on its faith and strength I call upon you, in the name of my Southern brethren, for redress and protection. Believe not all the tales of the vagrants, who are mostly fugitives from justice, not oppression. In your zeal for one portion of humanity forget not the interests of another, to which you are more closely allied. And one thing let me tell you, sir; if Eulalia's happiness and life are dear to your soul, if you would not arm the hand of the assassin, and kindle the brand of the incendiary, suspend your fiery efforts in the cause of emancipation. You are blowing the flames of insurrection, and no language can convey the faintest conception of the horrors that may ensue. You know not what you are doing. The time will come when waves of blood may roll over the land—and where will Eulalia be? Can my single arm hold her up above the crimson billows, my single breast shield her from the unimaginable horrors of servile warfare?"

They had reached the grove of the Parsonage—and they both stopped involuntarily and gazed upon each other. The moon at that moment came out from behind a cloud, and the dark eyes of Moreland flashed back its resplendent lustre. Mr. Hastings looked very pale in the silver light—

"I cannot expose my daughter to the possibility of such a fate," he cried. "Thank God, it is not too late!"

"Your word is pledged, and, as a man of honour you cannot retract," exclaimed Moreland, startled into a consciousness of his imprudence. "I was only lifting a warning voice. I was endeavouring to arrest a course of action which must inevitably result in ruin. I did not intend to express myself so strongly. Indeed, so firm is my reliance on the fidelity and affection of my own negroes, I believe, if an insurrection really took place, they would die in my defence."

"So every one thinks of their own," was the caustic reply. "Self-love,—nothing but self-love, Mr. Moreland. This is a serious view of the subject,—a very serious view. I must take time for reflection. The wedding cannot be consummated on the morrow."

"Good Heavens!" cried Moreland, "I never will submit to this wanton trifling with my hopes and affections. Why, it is worse than the tortures of the Inquisition!"

At this critical moment, when angry passions were swelling in the bosoms of each, the slender but majestic form of the minister came gliding, in his student's robe of flowing black silk, under the boughs of the trees, now involved in thick shadows, now illuminated by the white moonbeams, and stood before them, with his serene, thoughtful brow, and religious-beaming eyes. He had heard their excited tones, and he came to soothe and to reconcile. And there he stood, talking with them long and earnestly, regardless of the night-chill to which he so seldom exposed himself. He spoke with the benignity of the Christian, blended with the authority that invests his divine office. He would not suffer them to separate till harmony was restored, promises renewed, and the hopes of the morrow born anew.

Eulalia, in the mean time, unconscious of the agitating interview between her father and her lover, was sitting a her chamber window, with no light but that of the moonbeams which streamed in through the casement. She had extinguished the candle, lest it should bear witness to her tears; but she could not extinguish the greater glory of the heavens. It gushed in through the muslin curtains, and flowed round her as she sat in her loose white robes, making her look like an angel of light. It flooded one side of the bed, where little Dora lay sleeping, as tranquilly as if there were no such thing as parting in the world. Mrs. Hastings had just left the apartment, and Eulalia had been breathing out all her filial love, gratitude, and sorrow on her breast. Who can wonder that she wept the last night she was to sleep under that dear, paternal roof she might never again behold! Who can wonder that she trembled in the prospect of that long, long journey, when she had never travelled more than twenty miles from home before!

How she wished she could live over again her youthful years; that she might show more love and devotion and tenderness to her parents, more affection to her brother and sister, more consideration for all around her! How much more she might have done for others, how much less for herself!

"How selfish I have been!" thought she; "how absorbed in my own thoughts and feelings! I might have saved my dear mother so many weary steps, if I had only thought of it. Poor Betsy, too! How hard she has been working for me! I ought not to have permitted it. I wish father could afford to hire another woman, to lighten her labours. And I—I shall have more servants than I know what to do with. Surely toil divided among so many cannot be so wearing as it is here."

The door slowly opened, and Betsy stole in, shutting it very softly behind her. She came near the window where Eulalia was sitting, and sunk wearily on a trunk, all packed and strapped for travelling.

"Poor Betsy! how tired you must be!" said Eulalia, and her voice, always sweet and gentle, never sounded so sweet and gentle before to Betsy's weary ears.

"Yes, that I am, Miss Euly; but I thought I must creep in and see you a few moments to-night. There'll be such a bustle in the morning, I couldn't get in a word edgeways, I know. I'm dreadful sorry to lose you, but I hope our loss will be your gain. I guess you'll be well off—a powerful sight better off than the rest of us. Your pa has to scuffle mightily to get along, and if your ma was not the best manager in the world, he couldn't make the eends of the year meet. I save all I can, gracious knows, tho' I tries to have everything in a genteel style. I thinks more of the appearance of the house than Miss Hastings does herself."

"Yes, Betsy, I know how faithful and economical you are, how industrious and good. I shall feel happy in thinking my mother has such a helpmate and friend. Promise me, Betsy, for my sake, that you will not leave her. I know she never could supply your place. I only wish she could afford to keep more help, so that you would not have to work so hard. But you will have less to do when I am gone, Betsy."

"No, that I sha'n't, for you're always helping me about my little chores. Besides, it dont seem work, what I do for you. Your washing is as easy as nothing. When folks is sweet-tempered, like you, their clothes just go in and out of the water, and they're as nice as a snow-ball. As for leaving your mother, I ain't thinking on it. She's a good woman, and I guess I'm as well off here as anywhere else, as long as I have to work—and that I shall have to do as long as I live. Some helps is always dissatisfied, grumbling, and changing about; but I'm not of that sort. Some wants to sit down at the first table, and primp up and make believe they are ladies; but I'm not of that sort, either. You don't know, Miss Euly, what a discontented set most helps is. They never know when they're well off, and think everybody that employs 'em is beholden to 'em."

"They are not all so, Betsy, I am sure. You and Nancy are exceptions—and many others besides. And now, Betsy, let me thank you for all your kindness to me, and forgive me, if I have ever exacted too much of you. I have been thoughtless, I know, but never intentionally unkind."

Betsy, whose heart was brimful, just ready to run over, could not stand this appeal. She bowed her head down into her checked apron and wept aloud.

"Don't, Betsy!" cried Eulalia, putting her arm over her neck, thus prostrated in grief. "You'll break my heart if you go on in this way. Don't!"

"You've allers been just as good as you could be, and as innocent of harm as a baby in the cradle. You mustn't talk in that way to me, Miss Euly. It makes me feel too cheap. I come to tell you what Mr. Moreland done, and I got to talking so it clean went out of my head for the time. I declare, if he ain't the most significant man that ever was seen in this part of the world. To-night, when I was milking, under the great big appletree the cows love to stand under, he come along and stopped, and spoke to me as chirp as a bird, 'Betsy,' says he, 'here's a trifle, if you will accept of it. You sat up with me when I was sick. Not that money could pay such a service; but it may do you some good, and help you to take care of your lame brother.' How in the world did he hear about that? He slipped this piece of silver in my hand and went off, 'fore I had time to thank him. How much is it, Miss Euly? A quarter, ain't it? It was kinder dark when I took it, and I've been too busy to look at it since."

Eulalia took it, well knowing that Moreland would not

give so small a boon, and as the moonlight gleamed upon it, it gave back a bright, golden gleam.

"This is an eagle, Betsy. It is worth ten dollars. You might know Mr. Moreland would give you more than a quarter, if he gave you anything."

"Well! did you ever? you don't say so? I declare it seems like robbery to take so much—most equal to ten weeks' wages. Really, it don't seem right to keep it. Ain't he a gentleman? I was thankful for a little, but so much as this makes me feel really queer."

"Keep it; he is rich, and can well afford it. It makes him happier to give than you to receive. And now, Betsy, you are tired and ought to go to bed. You will have to rise early, and so will I. We must all be cheerful in the morning—remember that, Betsy. I would not sow in tears, though I trust to reap in joy."

Betsy retired, gazing fondly through her tears at the golden eagle, almost believing it an optical illusion—and Eulalia laid herself down by the sleeping Dora, and pressed her cheek against the warm and glowing cheek pillowed so sweetly there.

Albert was quite mortified that his master's wedding should be such a plain and matter-of-fact business. He remembered the splendour of his former marriage,—the festal pomp, the crowding guests, the wreathing garlands, the illuminated halls, and the exhilarating dance. He remembered the jubilee among the negroes; the cake and lemonade distributed among them, the music of the banjo, the muffled thunders of the tambourine. He was not at all pleased with the idea of his master's marrying a poor Yankee girl, especially a daughter of Mr. Hastings, for whom he had conceived a supreme dislike. Then, to be married in the morning, and start right off on a journey. Albert could not "see one bit of fun in that." He did not express his dissatisfaction; but he comforted himself by expatiating to Betsy on the splendid style in which they had such things got up at home,—how many barbacued pigs they had, stuffed hams and roasted turkeys, to say nothing of cakes, confectionaries, and wines.

"I'm sure," said Betsy, jealous of the family dignity, "there can't be any nicer cake than that, if I did make it, with Miss Hastings's help, myself; that in the middle of the waiter is made of loaf sugar, and it's as light as a feather, and as white as the driven snow. There never was nicer cake in this world, I guess."

Betsy pointed to a waiter, which rejoiced in the burden of various kinds of cake, in the centre of which rose one, in the form of a pyramid, covered with a dazzlingly white coat of icing, and crowned with a cluster of white rosebuds. This was Betsy's pride and glory,—the bride-cake, the dream-cake, the cake of all other cakes. She looked at Albert, expecting a burst of admiration.

"Is that all the cake you're going to have?" he asked, with a supercilious smile. "Why, we give more than that to the niggers. We've had more than a dozen cakes baked at once, a heap bigger than that."

"Well, you must be the extravagantest, wastefullest folks that ever lived," cried Betsy, her brown face reddening with mortification, "that's all I can say. What's the use, I want to know, of having such a sight of things, when there's no company and people; going right off, too,—after breakfast, besides, when folks have eat all they want to. Let alone," jerking the napkin from his hand. "You needn't help me. You're too smart."

Albert laughed, excessively amused at Betsy's anger. Having succeeded in impressing her with an exalted idea of his aristocratic mode of living, he condescended to say, that the cake looked very nice, what there was of it.

"Talk about the black folks at the South having such a dreadful time!" muttered Betsy, half to herself and half to him. "I want to know who has an easier time than this fellow? If I hadn't more to do, I should get so lazy I'd want somebody to laugh for me. I'm ten times more of a slave, this minute, than you are, and have been all my life."

"That's the truth, Miss Betsy. You'd better come and live with Mars. Russell. 'Spose you do."

"I wish I could go with Miss Euly," she answered, with a sigh; "but there's no use in pining. The Lord knows best."

Brief, yet solemn, was the marriage rite. The carriage stood at the door, which was to bear them on their first day's journey to meet the railroad, the trunks were strapped on, everything was ready for their departure, before Doctor Ellery pronounced the thrilling words, "that what God had joined together let no man put asunder." Eulalia, in a simple travelling dress, and pale from suppressed emotion, bore little resemblance to the brilliant and magnificently decorated being who had once before clasped Moreland's plighted hand in hers; but the vows she pledged were pure and holy, to be broken only by death—second only to the covenant that bound her to her God. She had taken her real farewell of her own family the night before, and resolved, if possible, to spare her parents the anguish of seeing her weep at parting; but when her minister came, and, taking her trembling hand, blessed her and committed her to the keeping of her Heavenly Father, with so much tenderness and affection and solemnity; borne down by an irresistible, reverential emotion, she knelt before him and bowed her head on his hand. Inexpressibly affected, he bent down, imprinted a kiss on her fair, drooping brow, and left the room.

Albert, notwithstanding his objections to the marriage, had too chivalrous a sense of politeness, not to seize the fitting moment to come forward and congratulate his master.

"Albert," said Moreland, "I introduce you to your

new mistress. You will henceforth devote yourself to her service, with all zeal and fidelity, even as you have done to mine."

Eulalia held out her hand, with a countenance of such angelic sweetness, lifting, at the same time, such a grateful, confiding look to Moreland's face, that Albert's prejudices were quite melted away. He was insensibly won by the divine charm of goodness, exalted by loveliness, and forgot that she was nothing but a poor Yankee girl.

Dora was so excited and mystified by all around her, so pleased and astonished at being dressed in her best white frock, and having cake to eat so early in the morning, that she looked on in wondering silence. Then, she was to ride with Reuben, in a one-horse carriage, behind the big carriage, as far as the next town, a great event in her young life. She got into the vehicle before the horse was fastened to it, she was so afraid it would start without her. She did not know yet, poor child, what it was to miss such a sister as Eula.

When Eulalia took leave of her parents, her face was as white as marble, one moment, the next, it was flushed and burning. She found herself in the carriage without knowing how she was placed there—her husband at her side; she felt the motion of the revolving wheels, she saw the sycamore boughs wave towards her, then vanish, the scarlet berries of the mountain ash flash a moment, and then vanish. She realized that the home of her youth was forsaken for the stranger's hearth.

"Do not hold back your tears, my Eulalia," said a gentle voice, while the arm which was henceforth to be her shield and support, fondly encircled her. "You have wrestled nobly with your sorrow. But think me not so selfish as to be jealous of a daughter's tenderness, gratitude, and devotion. I feel the sacrifice you are making. Accept in return the consecration of my life."

The tears thus sanctioned, hallowed by an embrace so tender, by soothings so kind and words so endearing, flowed in a gentle, relieving shower. The tension of her nerves relaxed, the girdle that pressed upon her heart loosened, and the morning twilight of joy stole on the shadows of grief.

CHAPTER VIII.

It is not our intention to describe with minuteness the journey of our Northern heroine to her Southern home; but some of the impressions of so artless and inexperienced a traveller have a novelty and freshness that cannot fail to inspire interest. She had never seen a car, and when she first saw a train rushing towards the depot, with the iron monster at its head, belching fire and smoke and screeching like a tortured demon, she started as if a fiend from the infernal regions was approaching her. But when she found herself borne along with such supernatural velocity; when she felt herself winged over hill and dale with equal speed; when trees, rocks, and buildings went racing by, at a rate that mocked her credulity, she was exhilarated, excited—she felt the joy of motion. And, though the thundering sound of the machinery drowned the accents she most loved to hear, she was seated at her husband's side—his hand was clasped in hers—his eye ever answered, with assuring love, the timid glance of hers. She now dwelt far less on the memories of the past than the hopes of the future.

She had never been on board a steamboat. She had never even seen those eagles of the river, with beaks of fire and breath of smoke, skimming the foaming waters. Born in a little inland town, whose winding stream bore no heavier vessel than the school-boy's light canoe, and confined by circumstances to one peculiar spot, it is not strange she knew so little of the world beyond. The first time she entered a boat it was in the night—and it was in the dark night. The river looked of inky blackness, in contrast with the blazing light proceeding from the fiery bowels of the machinery. The black smoke rolled above in long, serpentine convolutions, spangled with glittering red, while the imprisoned steam howled in its iron tubes. As Eulalia walked the narrow plank that bridged the water between the boat and the shore, and which vibrated at every step of her light foot, she clung impulsively to the hand of her husband, and dared not cast her eye down to the cold abyss below.

"You are but a young traveller," said Moreland, smiling at her childlike apprehensions, "but by and by you will mind it no more than rambling by moonligh on your own green lawn."

As they stepped upon the deck, there seemed a commotion and a crowd that impeded their progress. A man, bearing a torch, walked by the side of half a dozen others, who seemed bending under the weight of a heavy burthen.

"Move one side," said one of them, "don't you see there's a lady coming?"

"Who is this?" asked Moreland, seeing that it was the body of a man they were bearing, and moving so as to intercept Eulalia's view of it.

"It is a negro," answered one, "who fell into the river just now. The mate jumped in and got him out, but I expect the poor fellow is drowned. He is a runaway, and somebody told him his master was behind. In running over the plank his foot slipped, and in he went."

"He may be resuscitated," exclaimed Moreland. "I once restored a man to life, myself. Carry him on, and I will follow immediately."

Eulalia, as her husband almost carried her by, caught one glimpse of the face, on which the torchlight threw a strong, red gleam, and recognised the features of the gigantic negro whom her father had once made his guest.

"Good heavens!" she cried, "it is Nat, The Giant!" (By this name he had announced himself, and the villagers always added the apposition of Nat.)

Sick and faint, she turned from the dripping form, and leaned on her husband's shoulder for support.

"I must leave you now," said he, when they reached the ladies' cabin. "If we succeed in resuscitating the poor fellow, I will return and tell you. I grieve for the shock you have received; but let it not, I entreat you, depress your spirits. Retire to your berth, and you will sleep as gently as if rocked in a cradle bed."

"Oh, no, I shall not sleep to-night—but do not think of me. Do what you can for the drowned man. Poor fellow! I am not afraid of him now."

Eulalia lingered at the door, listening to the music of Moreland's retreating footsteps, for it was music to the dreary blank of her feelings—then entered the cabin with a sinking heart. Could she only have sat up on deck with him, with nothing but the starless night around them, she would have been happy; but she felt so strange, so very strange, so unaccustomed to the scene in which she found herself, she hardly knew what to do. The berths were all occupied but one—an upper one, which the chambermaid directed her to occupy. She did not like to commit herself to this very smart and independent-looking girl; but the idea of mounting so lofty a couch was quite terrific to her. She expected to see some steps or ladder for her accommodation; but she discovered she must do without, unless the angels came down and made her one, as they did in Jacob's dream.

Most of the passengers were unawakened by the bustle on deck; but one old lady had risen and was seated in a rocking-chair, which seesawed one way, while the boat rocked another, in the strong gust of the swelling wind. She presented a very extraordinary figure, and had not Eulalia's mind been saddened by the dreadful accident which had just occurred, she would have found it difficult to suppress her smiles. A loose wrapper enveloped her person, and over this a large blanket shawl was pinned, so that the folds rose above the ears, making her appear as if her head were sinking out of sight. A broad strip of flannel passed over the top of her head and was pinned under her chin. As her face was very pale and long and meagre, this band gave her a most shocking and corpselike appearance. Eulalia, disposed as she was to view everything in its fairest light, thought she saw the Nightmare embodied before her; and not knowing the lady's name, she identified her by that in her mind. She did not like to look at her, though she perceived that she was an object of intense scrutiny herself. Unwilling to retire till she had heard the tidings her husband had promised to bring her, she took a seat at a respectful distance from the formidable lady, and taking off her bonnet, began to arrange her beautiful but somewhat disordered hair.

"This is going to be a stormy night," said the Nightmare. "There isn't a star to be seen, and the clouds are as black as charcoal. Don't you see how the boat rocks?"

"Does it rock more than usual?" asked the ignorant Eulalia.

"Why, can't you tell, yourself?"

"It is the first time I was ever in a steamboat. I thought they always rocked in this manner."

"No, indeed. You ain't much of a traveller, then."

"This is my first journey, madam."

"Indeed! Where did you start from?"

"I came from Massachusetts, and"—anticipating the next question—"from the town of ——."

"How far are you going to travel?"

"As far as Georgia."

"Ah! you are going South, are you? Well, I am sorry for you; for a meaner country there never was on the face of the whole earth. Are you going to teach school there?"

"No, madam."

"A governess in a private family, perhaps?"

"No, madam," answered Eulalia, a mischievous smile playing on her lip.

"You are not travelling alone, are you?"

"No, madam."

"You look too young to be married!"

Eulalia was silent.

"May I ask what you are going to the South for?"

"For a home."

"Ah, poor thing! you are an orphan, I suppose. Take my advice, and try to get a living where you are. They are the proudest folks there that ever lived, and they look upon poor people as no better than white negroes. I lived a year there myself, and know what I am saying. I have a daughter married in North Caro lina, and I went on to make her a visit. Her husband is not a Southern man himself. He was born in Vermont; but, when he was quite young, he went to the South and taught school. He made a good deal of money that way (it is a good place to make money, there's no denying that),—bought a farm and some negroes, and then came home and married my daughter. They had been engaged three years. Nothing would do, but I must come on and see them, and I was fool enough to go."

"What did you dislike so much?" asked Eulalia, early impressions crowding on her mind.

"Oh! everything,—the country, the people, their way of living, their style of building, and, worse than all, the lazy, dirty, good-for-nothing negroes! They did not do as much work in one week as a white servant will accomplish in one day; you have to look after them all the time, and keep everything under lock and key."

"They were not unkindly treated, then," said Eulalia, "or they would have worked harder, I suppose?"

"They were treated a great deal too well, I think. I went there, expecting to see a great deal of cruelty; but it was not so, excepting now and then I would hear of such a thing, but I never saw it. My son-in-law used to bluster and threaten a great deal, but his threats were never put in execution; and my daughter was a timid, inexperienced thing, ten times more afraid of them than they of her. I tried to set matters right, while I stayed, but they only grew worse. I could not put up with the saucyness of the negroes. They would not call me anything but *old mistress*, and my daughter Miss Lucy, as if she was not a married woman."

"Did your daughter seem very unhappy?"

"No! It provoked me to see her so contented, buried in the pine-woods, living in a log cabin, no neighbour within a mile's distance, no visiters, except those who came to stay all day or all night. To be sure, she had everything that was comfortable and plentiful; her husband is very kind, and she thinks there is nobody like him. She even seems attached to the negroes, and says she takes pleasure in providing for their wants."

"I thought you said she was afraid of them. I should think that would make her very uncomfortable."

"She will not acknowledge it, though I know she is, by the soft tone in which she always speaks to them. Who is that?"

A tap at the door made Eulalia spring from her seat, for she was sure it was her husband. And so it was. His thoughtful, serious countenance suggested what his lips confirmed, their efforts were unavailing. Nat the Giant had indeed finished his wanderings, and was destined for a gloomier home than the Dismal Swamp of Virginia.

"I fear you may be sea-sick," he added; "for the night is very tempestuous. I have told Albert to bring you a glass of brandy, which is said to be a sovereign remedy."

Eulalia shook her head and smiled; but she, nevertheless, took the glass from Albert's hand, because Moreland had prescribed it, and she would not seem ungrateful for his soothing attentions. She was certain she would not need it herself, but perhaps her friend the Nightmare might, who was listening eagerly behind the half-open door.

"Who is that gentleman?" asked she, when Eulalia returned into the cabin.

"My husband, madam."

"Why, I thought you said you were not married."

"I did not deny the fact."

"You did not say anything, which was the same thing. Who was that with him?"

"Albert, his servant."

"His slave, you had better say."

"His slave, then," replied the weary young bride, placing the glass on the table, for the boat rocked so, the dark, amber fluid threatened to overflow.

"What's that in that tumbler?" continued the persevering inquisitor, though fully aware of its generous contents.

"A remedy for sea-sickness, my husband says. Are you troubled with it?"

'Yes, dreadfully! I have been sick ever since the wind began to blow, but I never make any complaint.

That is the reason I left my berth, I thought I should feel better sitting up. Oh! mercy, how the boat pitches, I am as sick as death."

Her lower jaw fell down so frightfully, her eyes rolling upwards at the same time, that Eulalia was alarmed, and hastened to offer her the brandy. She swallowed a copious draught, which seemed to revive her.

"I ought to have diluted this with water," said Eulalia. "You must pardon me, I did not think of it. It must have burned your throat very badly."

"It has more effect that way," answered the old lady; "and I can bear anything better than this awful sickness. Your husband is a thoughtful man."

Eulalia devoutly hoped the anodyne would compose her new friend to sleep, for her own eyelids began to be heavy from fatigue. While preparing for rest, she cast many a glance at her airy bed, wondering how she was to attain so undesirable an elevation; but the difficulty, like most others, vanished in the act of overcoming it. A light spring was all that was needed, and she looked down in triumph on the flannel-girdled head, sinking in its dark recess. As she lay perfectly still, she supposed the old lady imagined her asleep, for, before she deposited herself in her own berth, she stole to the table and took another portion of the *sovereign remedy*. It was probably caused by a sudden tilt of the boat, but the last drop went down her throat, and an empty glass was left upon the table.

"Do you feel worse?" asked Eulalia, thinking her throat must be a chimney, to bear such a fiery draught, and willing to let her know that she observed the appropriation of the fluid.

"Oh, yes, a great deal worse. I don't think I could have lived till morning, if it had not been for this medicine. Your husband is a good man—a thoughtful, kind-hearted man. I am grateful for his goodness. Oh! mercy! how my head aches! I have the rheumatism in my head terribly. I must have caught it in North Carolina, for I never had it before I went there."

The old lady continued to talk, till her voice seemed to mingle with the wail of the night-gust, the murmur of the waters, and the heavy plunging sound of the engine, so monotonous and dreary. Eulalia could not sleep. That large, black, dripping form, with glazed, half-opened eyes, and mouth through which the ghastly ivory gleamed, seemed lying before her, huge, cold, and still. Was it not an evil omen, that it should thus meet her on the very first step of her watery way? Moreland had told her the history of his crimes, but the last victim is the one most deeply pitied. She tried to rid herself of the hideous image that haunted her couch. There it lay—a black, gigantic barrier between her and the fair, flowery land to which her bridegroom's hand was leading her. The excitement of her imagination was owing, in a great measure, to the close, oppressive air of the cabin, which was made still more oppressive by the odour of the burning oil. Could she have seen the waters dashing round the paddle wheels, and roaring behind the boat; could she have seen the trees rustling and bowing in the wind, as they went hurrying and thundering by, the sense of sublimity would have absorbed that of terror; but her inexperience magnified the rushing sound of the river, into the wrath of whitening billows, and the moan of the stormy night-gust into the wail of the wrecking tempest. At length, a mistiness stole over her mind, and it seemed as if she heard low, soft, sweet strains rising on the rising blast,

> "Softening the raven down of darkness
> Till it smiled."

The melody, at first indistinct as a mist, condensed into a rich cloud of music, and then came down in a shower of divine words—words such as often ascended from her own household shrine, breathed by her mother's gentle voice and Dora's cherub lips. She fancied she could hear them gliding in that close, stifling cabin, bringing messages of earthly and heavenly love—

> "Through all the changing scenes of life,
> In trouble and in joy,
> The praises of my God shall still
> My heart and tongue employ."

"Oh! how sweet! Oh! how comforting!" thought Eulalia. "Bless thee, gentle mother—thou art following in spirit thy wandering daughter. Bless thee, too, sweet sister-child! I feel thy little arms entwining my neck—thy loving head nestling in my bosom. And, oh! I feel too that a love stronger even than thine, my mother, or thine, my darling sister, is near to protect and bless me. And God over all—the God of my fathers—the God of my home. Let me sleep when such blessings make a golden guard around me."

And sweetly, soundly did the young traveller sleep, till the awakening day.

What a change did the morning sunshine bring! Eulalia, with the elastic feelings of a child, rebounded from despondency to rapture. Leaving all her companions still asleep in their berths, her voluble friend, the old lady, fortunately passive under the influence of the "sovereign remedy"—she stole on deck and joined her husband in a morning promenade, delightful and exhilarating beyond expression. The stormy wind was lulled into a gentle breeze that curled the face of the river into ten thousand dimples, and in every dimple a silver sunbeam sparkled. Not a solitary cloud, not even a white one as large as the wing of a dove, flecked the blue of the heavens. Bright, clear, resplendent they bent their eternal arch above;—bright, trembling, sparkling, they looked up from the sunlit depths below. All the time the boat went gliding onward with a motion graceful and uniform as the bird's, whose pinions were cleaving the azure sky, and the green shores smiled and the tall trees bowed as they passed. Eulalia, leaning on the arm of

Moreland, and borne on without any will of her own, through the most enchanting scenery she had ever witnessed, felt the happiest of human beings. The love-light kindled in her eye, and coloured with a brighter tint the pale rose of her cheek. That grand, that beautiful river, how it swelled in comparison with her own native stream, she had once thought so broad and affluent! How the world enlarged upon her vision! How her spirit amplified within her!

The bell which summoned them to the breakfast table opened upon her a new and less attractive scene. Glancing along the line of strange faces that margined the board, she recognised her old friend, who nodded very familiarly, and pushed forward to a seat nearly opposite. Instead of the swathing band of flannel, she wore a black silk kerchief over her head, the ends of which were fastened under her chin by a large glass breast-pin. The white border of a cap peered from under this gloomy head-gear, and contrasted as strongly with the sallow hue of her complexion as it did with the sable folds that so nearly shrouded it. Near her, but evidently having no connexion with her, was a young and blooming girl, whose bright, ingenuous eyes rested on the bridal pair with such undisguised admiration, they could not but forgive the scrutiny, for the sake of the sentiment which inspired it. Eulalia's heart felt drawn towards her by a congenial charm, and, by the magnetic telegraph which passes from soul to soul, they understood each other's thoughts and emotions. There was a gentleman on her right, whose thoughts she could also read, and they were not an agreeable study. He had a coarse, vulgar look, self-satisfied and pompous withal; satisfied with himself but at variance with the rest of the world. There were two perpendicular wrinkles between his brows, and the strong lines round his mouth and at the corners of his eyes denoted habitual discontent. He was well dressed, but that air of unmistakeable refinement which marks the gentleman was wanting. In the course of the breakfast, Albert came in, and, standing behind his master, said something to him in a very low, respectful tone. The eyes of the *bourgeois* gleamed with a peculiar expression. They fastened upon Moreland, and perused his lineaments with an insatiable stare. They devoured the features and figure of the mulatto, with a kind of malicious curiosity mingled with triumph. Moreland did not notice this rude and prolonged gaze, being engaged in earnest conversation with a gentleman whom he had met in Boston, and whose intelligence, liberality, and courtesy had then made a deep impression on him; but Eulalia did, and she was sure Moreland had an enemy in this scowling stranger, though he knew it not. She wanted to put him on his guard, but sought in vain for the opportunity. The old lady, whose name was Haskell, fastened herself upon her like the old man of the sea, in the cabin, on the deck, wherever she went. She talked to her till her ears grew dizzy with the continuous buzzing. Fortunately the effect of her proximity was somewhat neutralized by the companionship of the bright-eyed, blooming girl, who beautified, with the garlands of her youth, the hoar ruins of age.

In the mean time, Moreland found himself drawn into a vortex which he vainly endeavoured to shun. He disliked coming in collision with the rough and ignorant, and for this reason avoided, as far as was compatible with politeness, his frowning neighbour of the breakfast table. But he would not be avoided; he forced himself into his path, followed him into the social hall, and dragged him into the depths of disputation. Nor was this all. It was only preliminary to a direct personal attack, which the high-spirited Southerner, driven to the defensive, indignantly repelled.

"Sir," said the man, who bore the name of Horsely, "I believe you are from the South?"

"I am."

"There are a great many Southerners travelling North now-a-days."

Moreland was silent.

"I should not think they would like coming into this part of the country so well. They must meet with a great many things that are not agreeable to them."

"They do," was the emphatic reply.

"I wonder they ever think of bringing their slaves with them. It seems to me downright madness. Sir, there are men who think it their duty to enlighten these poor, degraded beings, and let them know what their real condition is. Sir, I am one of that class; I am no hypocrite; I do nothing in the dark. I give you fair warning. I would tell your mulatto to his face, if he were present, that he was a free man,—as free as I am, as free as you are yourself, sir, and that you have no right to hold him in bondage."

"Tell him so," replied Moreland haughtily. "I am not intimidated by such a threat. He has been told so a hundred times already. He has been told so in the city and the country, in the bar-room and the street,—it has been rung in his ears with trumpet-tongues. He has heard all that you can tell him, yet you may repeat it a thousand times more, if you will. He will not leave me."

"It seems that all your slaves are not as faithful," replied Horsely, with a sneer. "The poor fellow who was drowned last night, preferred, it would appear, the river's bed to the tender mercies of the master from whose pursuit he was fleeing, and whose approach drove him to desperation."

"Do you imply that I had any interest in that wretch, beyond what humanity inspires?"

"A master's interest, as far as that goes. At least, I have been told so."

Moreland's face reddened, but he preserved his calmness of tone.

"You are mistaken, sir. I know the master of that man,—a kind, just, humane man. This negro, whose herculean strength was only equalled by his dark, strong passions, was a very dangerous individual. For the robbery and attempted murder of his master, he fled, and has long imposed upon the credulity of the public, by his false, demoniac tales. He, who deserved the hangman's rope, has been exalted to the honours of martyrdom, and all the opprobrium of his crimes transferred to their innocent victim."

"This may be so," cried Horsely, with an incredulous shrug of the shoulders; "but you cannot deny that many and many a poor fugitive slave has escaped from cruelty and oppression, to our free and sheltering institutions. These are facts that stare you in the face. You cannot shut them out. The eyes of the North are opened to the wrongs of the slave, and as sure as there is a God of justice and mercy, those wrongs will yet be redressed. Why, I have heard stories told by some of these poor starving fugitives myself, that almost turned me to stone. You do not pretend to say they are all lies?"

"I grant that some of these tales of cruelty are true; for, that man is sometimes a deadly tyrant, the annals of history too darkly prove. But, generally speaking, they are nothing but gross fabrications, invented to enlist the sympathies of credulous fanatics. Why, if we opened our homes and our hearts to all the criminals and vagrants of the North; if we enticed them by hopes of gain, and bribed them by promises of reward, our beautiful South would soon become a Botany Bay, and its orange bowers peopled with the vilest convicts. I'll tell you what I saw, not many weeks since, in passing Charles's river bridge—not in the darkness of night, but the blaze of day. There was a rushing sound of trampling feet; a dark cloud of men gathering and hurrying on in the eagerness of pursuit. A fugitive was borne on before that cloud, as if on the wings of a mighty wind. He was a white man. The cry of "murder" rose from the mob and rung over the river. One moment and the fugitive would have been arrested; but he vaulted over the railing, plunged into the water, and was drowned, even like the gigantic felon, the responsibility of whose fate you have been endeavouring to roll on me. Did I condemn the Bostonians as a cruel, bloodthirsty people, because the cry of blood for blood, which rung in the ears of the first murderer, went up in their midst? Did I attribute this crime to their institutions, or to the strength of man's unlicensed passions, which, whether at the North or the South, scatter ruin and death in their path? I heard of worse things than this—of men in the high walks of life, butchered like the beasts of the stall, mangled and cut up and burned, till every trace of the human form was extinct; and I did not impute it to the social system to which they belonged, but to that spirit of man, which, when divorced from

God, is given up to the dominion of demons and the powers of darkness. One would suppose, to hear you talk, that the North was one wide garden of the Lord, where nothing but the peaceable fruits of righteousness grow—and the South a howling wilderness of sin and crime and pollution."

"You draw your own conclusions," said Horsely, knitting his brows with vexation. "I said no such thing. I do say, however, that the North is a peaceable country—the best country in the world. Here, every man attends to his own business—"

"Pardon me," interrupted Moreland; "there certainly are some exceptions."

Some of the auditors who had gathered near to listen to the conversation laughed aloud at Horsely's disconcerted and angry countenance. Looking fiercely at the offenders, he withdrew, resolved to whet his weapons for a new conflict. Meeting with Albert, he gave vent to his exasperated feelings, lashing the master over the slave's back. He told him that he was a fool to stay in a state of bondage, when freedom was in his reach; that he had only to claim his birthright, and he would find himself surrounded by a body-guard of friends and supporters. Albert laughed, and said that he was as free as any one whom he saw—that he would not change places with anybody. He had money enough and leisure enough, and the best master that ever lived.

"Can't catch this boy with chaff, master," said the

mulatto, turning on his heel and showing his white and glittering teeth.

Shall we follow our travellers wave by wave, till the boat is exchanged for the thundering car, the car again for one of the floating palaces of the river? Shall we describe Eulalia's parting with the garrulous old lady and the rose-cheeked maiden, whose faces she never expected to behold again, but which would long remain in the picture-gallery of memory? Or shall we pass over these varying yet monotonous scenes, and arrive at the moment when the planter welcomed his Northern bride to his home in the dew-dropping South? One more scene on a boat, by way of contrast. A night of moonlight gentleness and peace, when drawing nearer and nearer the wished-for haven; the soft, bland atmosphere of a Southern clime smoothed and uncurled the wrinkled surface of the water, as soon as the vessel had ploughed its liquid face. They were on the sea—the deep, deep sea, and though gliding comparatively near the coast, it was invisible to the eye, and the view had all the boundlessness and grandeur of the ocean's midst. Eulalia sat on deck, by her husband's side, with glory above her and glory below, and both the downward and the upward glory were reflected on her soul, making an intense inward glory, which was again reflected resplendently from her face. Gently rocked on the undulating waters, cradled on the arm of Moreland—that arm which seemed to her as the wing of an angel, protecting and sheltering her—bathed in that calm, celestial light, that deep, tranquil, silver ocean, whose horizon was another silver ocean, distinguishable only by a kind of quivering splendour, fanned by a pure and inspiriting breeze, Eulalia approached nearer a state of beatitude than she had ever dreamed of attaining. Oh! to be borne on for ever over those rippling diamonds, thus companioned, soul linked to soul, heart bound to heart—looking up to heaven, seeing nothing but heaven, earth only a memory, something far off and separate—could there be a Paradise more holy and blissful?

"There is but one thing wanting to complete the magic of the scene," said Moreland, in a low voice, after they had gazed long and silently "on the moonlight flood," "and that is music. Sing one song or hymn, my Eulalia, such as I have heard you sing, where the shadow of the sycamore leaves played upon your brow."

Eulalia looked up and smiled, while the moisture gathered in her eyes. She was carried back to her native home; she was in the folding of a mother's arms; the fair locks of Dora fluttered against her cheek. She sang one of the sweet and simple songs of her New England village, and her nightingale voice floated over the waters and echoed from the vine-wreathed bluffs by which they were gliding. The passengers left the cabin and drew softly near to listen. The pilot leaned over the green railing to drink in a melody, liquid as the waves over which it flowed. Albert came and stood behind his master, his bright though dingy face lighted up with a rapturous expression, for the spirit of the negro is tuned to harmony, and is strung with chords which vibrate to the breath of music.

"Well, I never heard anything that could beat that," cried he, making a long and audible inhalation, after the songstress paused, blushing at the notice she had attracted. "Netty sings mighty sweet, but she can't come up to that, no way she can fix it!"

"And who is Netty?" asked Eulalia, not insensible to this tribute of admiration, however humble.

"It's a yellow girl, that waits in the house, mistress," replied Albert, with an air of consciousness, which brought a smile to his master's face. "She goes singing about her work like a bird, and we can all work better to hear her—and she, herself, too."

"You must know," said Moreland, "that Netty is the object of Albert's especial admiration. To pay her for her singing, he serenades her on the banjo, and sometimes puts in a flourish of the tambourine. I should not wonder if we had a wedding one of these days, and then you will see how finely we get up these things at the South."

"Now, Mars. Russell," exclaimed Albert, putting his red silk handkerchief to his face, "you know you say what you please. Miss Eulaly see for herself, bimeby."

"I shall be glad to see Netty and all the servants,"

said Eulalia, a shade of thought passing over her brow. Then turning to Moreland, she added—"I fear I shall make a poor, inefficient mistress. I shall look to you for instruction and guidance. Though timid and inexperienced, you will find me, I trust, teachable and willing to be instructed."

Albert, obeying his master's glance, retired, and was soon stretched on the hurricane deck, looking up steadfastly at the moon, and wondering if Netty were not looking at the same object.

"I have no misgivings for them," answered Moreland; "they will adore you as a mistress, and rejoice under your firm, yet gentle sway. You have every attribute to win their admiration, as well as their love The negro has an intense appreciation of beauty and grace, and feels the influence of mental superiority. I know you better than you know yourself, my too self-distrusting bride. There is a greal deal of latent energy reposing under those downy flakes of gentleness, and should occasion require, it will wake and astonish yourself by its power. I fear but one thing."

"And what is that?" asked Eulalia.

"Your own repugnance to the African race. You must struggle with this from the first, and it will surely be overcome. It is of unnatural birth—born of prejudice and circumstance. The few specimens you have seen of the negroes have been of the most repulsive kind. It is certainly a strong argument in favour of their condition at the South, that the free negro is generally far more degraded, more low in the scale of being, than the slave. The air of freedom, which gives luxuriant growth to his vices, does not foster his peculiar virtues. His social character degenerates. The philanthropists who interest themselves so much in his destiny at home, leave him to his own resources when brought within the sphere of their assistance. They will not hold social communion with one on whom God has affixed the seal of a darker dispensation. At a distance, they stretch out their arms, and call him brother, and exclaim, 'Are we not the children of the same Father?' but when near, they forget the ties of consanguinity, and stand back with a *holier than thou* written on their brows."

"My father doth not so," said Eulalia, with earnestness; "he took one of these wandering Parias by the hand, and, making no distinction of colour, treated him as a companion and friend. I tried to imitate his example, for I believed it my duty; but I cannot express the abhorrence I felt, the struggle of principle with inclination."

"And how was your father's kindness repaid?"

"I am sorry to say, with insolence and ingratitude. When we ascertained his true character, I was glad to believe that it was an instinctive horror of vice which I felt, instead of a loathing for his kind."

"My dear Eulalia, God never intended that you and

I should live on *equal* terms with the African. He has created a barrier between his race and ours, which no one can pass over without incurring the ban of society. The white woman who marries a negro, makes herself an outcast, a scorn, and a byword. The white man who marries a negress forfeits his position as a gentleman, and is excluded from the social privileges of his brethren. This is the result of an inherent principle of the human breast, entwined, like conscience, with our vitality, and inseparable from it. The most ultra Northern philanthropist dare not contradict this truth. He may advocate amalgamation with his lips, but in his heart, he recoils from it with horror. He would sooner see a son or daughter perish beneath the stroke of the assassin than wedded to the African, whom he professes to look upon as his equal and his friend. Nature has marked a dividing line, as distinct as that which separates the beasts of the field, the birds of the air, and the fishes of the sea. And why should any one wish to violate this great law of nature,—this principle of homogeneousness? The negro feels the attraction of his kind, and forms, like ourselves, congenial ties."

"But, alas!" exclaimed Eulalia, "how often are those ties broken by the rude hand of violence and oppression. How many heart-strings are bruised and torn by the stroke of the auctioneer's hammer. This is an evil which, kind and feeling as you are, you must deplore."

"I do; and it is one which good masters avert, in every possible manner. It is an evil which has never yet approached my plantation or household, and never shall, unless necessity lays its iron hand upon me."

"Ah! if all masters were like you, slavery would be robbed of its terrors and its gloom."

"I am no better than the majority, perhaps not as good. I know of some bad masters, and, what is still worse, bad mistresses; but public opinion brands them with its curse. Their character is considered as unnatural and execrable as the cruel and tyrannical parent of the North. There is no such thing as irresponsible power at the South. We are made responsible to man as well as to God, as our tribunals of justice can prove by abundant facts. But, my dear Eulalia, you will soon judge for yourself. You will see the negro, not as he is at the North, an isolated, degraded being, without caste or respectability,—a single black line running through a web of whiteness,—but surrounded with the socialities of life, and, though doomed to labour, yet free from the cares and anxieties that rest so heavily on us. You will compare the reality of their condition with the pictures drawn on your imagination, and make your own commentaries. And now let us change the subject, and think of the household joys that await us; let us talk of the home that is to be gladdened by your presence, and illumined by your love. Eulalia, I feel that I owe you a sacred debt, one that my whole life can never cancel. You have loved me in the face of opposition, prejudice, and reproach. You have given me a virgin's heart, and accepted in return one wounded and betrayed. You have confided in my power to make you happy, though so dark a cloud has rested on my home. You have assumed the cares of maternity, young and inexperienced as you are, under circumstances more painful than death creates. Let me go on, Eulalia, and enumerate your claims on my honour, devotion, and love, for you dream not of their existence, in the lowliness of your self-estimation."

"No, no—let us talk of your child. You know not how my heart yearns towards it; how I long to fulfil towards it a mother's duties!"

"I fear," said Moreland, and his eyes flashed up, then darkened, under his suddenly contracted brows,—"I fear you will find a father's as well as a mother's duties devolving on you. Think me not a wretch, Eulalia, but I cannot love my child. Though beautiful as a cherub, I shun its sight, and shrink involuntarily from its innocent caresses. I do not wonder you look at me so reproachfully, but it is in vain to endeavour to conceal what you will so soon discover. It has never lacked for tenderness, however, for my sister loves it as she does her own soul, and its black nurse feels for it more than love—worship and adoration."

"And you too shall love it," said Eulalia, her face lighted up with the holy expression of the Virgin Mother. "You shall love it for my sake, if not for its own. I shall make it a condition of my happiness and affection. This little cherub will be to me a younger, lovelier Dora, and I shall still retain my character of ister-mother."

"I believe you to be the most irresistible," replied Moreland, the dark expression passing from his countenance, and the smile of the bridegroom returning, "as I know you to be the most loveable of human beings. Yes, for your sake I would promise to love the whole universe. I would bind the North as well as the South in one common embrace. You have already been to me an angel of conciliation, softening the bitterness of my feelings when made to drink the wormwood and the gall distilled from the lips of rancorous prejudice. Oh! Eulalia! you and Ildegerte will love one another. You will find in her a dear and noble sister."

"Ildegerte!" repeated Eulalia, her voice lingering on the name—"that is a Scandinavian name. It has a peculiar sound."

"There is a noble romance in it, that suits well my sister's high-toned character. My mother found it, I believe, in some Runic legend, associated with the charm of poetry and love. But see, the silver mist curling along the shore. The river breeze wafts it in wreaths around us. I cannot trust you any longer in this moonlight, lovely as it is."

Eulalia felt as if she were in a different world, when immured once more in the close walls of the cabin; but her thoughts wandered to the world beyond—the Ultima Thule of her hopes and wishes—her beautiful Southern home.

CHAPTER IX.

THE residence of Mr. Moreland to which he first bore his Northern bride, was situated in the town of ——, and about two days' journey from his plantation. It was a large and handsome building, stuccoed and painted in imitation of marble, surrounded by a piazza, supported by massy pillars, which were covered with the same artificial porphyry. A wide passage ran through the centre of the house, opening into the garden through doors of green lattice-work, and making a channel through which waves of fresh air were constantly flowing. The yard in front was laid out in terraces, and semi-circular hedges of roses and cape jessamines enclosed two airy and vine-mantled summer-houses, on either side of the avenue. Two lofty oaks, whose gray trunks were twined with the dark green ivy, stood as sentinels over these domes of flowers, and gave an air of dignity to the tasteful elegance of the scene. A hedge of cedars, shaven on the top into a kind of table-land, on which the gossamer spread its silvery wed, margined the yard, and relieved by its deep, rich verdure, the white paling that surrounded it. As this dwelling faced the east, the cool evening shadows rested on the piazza, and made it a pleasant gathering place in the after part of the day.

It might be supposed, that dwelling in a more sultry clime, and warmed by the beams of a more burning sun, the children of a Southern latitude would sink in a lassitude and languor unknown at the North. But it is not so. It is true, during the noonday heat, when the very flowers bow their heads before the intensity of meridian glory, they yield to the pervading influence; but when the heat begins to assume a mellow, golden tint, they come out in the open air, that revels in their ample piazzas or airy verandahs, and their spirits acquire the freshness, elasticity, and buoyancy of the breeze that fans them.

At such an hour as this, we will introduce the members of the household, over which our Northern bride now presides.

Do you see that lady, seated by one of the pillars, with the vine-leaves which entwine it, resting like a chaplet on her black and shining hair? Her eyes, of the same colour as her hair, have the softness and richness of satin, though a spark in the centre, of quick, flashing light, shows that there is fire beneath that gentle brilliancy. Her figure is slender and pliant, and her hand, which plays with the green leaves that crown her, is dazzlingly fair. It is Ildegerte, the sister of Moreland; and that very pale, delicate, fair-haired, blue-eyed young man, seated near her, is her husband. A more striking contrast in personal appearance could scarcely be presented. She, radiant in blooming health, —he, pallid, drooping, languid, the victim of a constitutional malady. Of Northern birth, Richard Laurens brought to the South the germs of hereditary consumption, too deeply seated to admit of remedy or cure. Since his marriage, they have developed themselves with fatal rapidity, and every one but his young wife reads the doom that is written on his emaciated and altered features. She will not see it. The cough that racks his frame is the result of a cold,—nothing but a cold; his debility, the effect of the summer heat; his variable and fastidious appetite, caused by want of exercise and change of air. There is a well-spring of hope in her heart, inexhaustible as her love, and by both these unfailing fountains the wilting blossoms of her husband's life derive their chief renovation. He is a physician, and has commenced the practice of his profession under the most favourable auspices; but arrested by disease, he is obliged to turn himself to the healing art by which he had hoped to relieve the sufferings of humanity. Poor fellow! it is hard, with such brilliant prospects before him, with so much to endear and enrich life,—such a happy home, and, more than all, such a beautiful and loving wife,—it is hard to think of dying. He will not do it,—*he cannot.* He cannot give up existence with such strong ties to bind him to it. They are cable cords, and cannot be broken. On the morrow, accompanied by his wife, he is to commence a journey to the West. The physician with whom he studied resides in the Queen City of Ohio,—a man as highly distinguished for genius and virtue as professional skill. He is sure of finding restoration with him. Miracles, almost divine, might be expected from his touch. His only regret is, that he has not sought his saving influence sooner.

You recognise Eulalia. There needs no new description of her peculiar and spiritual loveliness. She looks at home in the midst of the refinements and elegancies which wealth only can command. Her new household dignity sits gracefully upon her. She is already familiar with her duties, and no longer blushes when addressed by the unwonted title of *mistress*. Even the name of *mamma*, lisped by the little fairy frolicking round her, has become a sweet and familiar sound to her ear. You have never seen that three-year-old child—the child of the misguided Claudia. The child whom the injured Moreland did not, could not love; because its mother's spirit flashed from its eyes of gipsy hue and brightness. But Eulalia says it has its father's smile, and that is

"All to love and her."

In the infantine face of little Effie, the features of both parents are singularly combined, giving her a twofold and varying expression. Sometimes she looks at you with a bold, mischievous, wicked glance, as if she mocked the very thought of restraint; then again, an exquisite softness will steal over her countenance, and a gentle, winning smile beam with hereditary sweetness. She is the spoiled child of indulgence, for Ildegerte never could attempt to discipline the little deserted orphan, and Aunt Kizzie, its black nurse and mammy, would as soon have thought of cutting off her head, as refuse to gratify its most unreasonable wishes. She is an elf, a sprite, a fairy, a cherub, a tricksy, wayward, fascinating little creature, that already gives its young stepmother a world of anxiety. She makes a charming picture, does she not, at this moment? She has been running about the yard, pulling off the most beautiful flowers (for hers are privileged fingers, and if the moon and stars were reachable, they would have been plucked long since for her gratification), and now, with her little white apron full and overflowing with blossoms, she has toiled up the steps and seated herself at the feet of Eulalia, her cheeks glowing with exercise and her jetty hair tossed back from her moistened brow. She stoops down and sticks the flowers in the binding of Eulalia's slippers; she throws them sportively in her face, then, clapping her hands, bursts into wild laughter, and, jumping up, scatters the broken and remnant leaves in a shower on the floor.

"Oh! Miss Effie! you so bad," cries Aunt Kizzie, waddling up behind her, her ebony face shining like the sun, and her thick African lips flattened in the broad smile that parts them; "you make such a litter you keep a body trotting arter you all day long. It mighty hard work to be picking up trash, tho' it ben't much to peak of."

Kizzie's audible grunt, as she stoops to gather up the trash, is an emphatic commentary on her words.

"Never mind, Aunt Kizzie," says Eulalia, "let her amuse herself. Netty can brush away the leaves."

"Bless your pretty face, mistress," exclaims the nurse, straightening herself with another demonstration. "You's got a heap of consideration. If it wer'n't for the 'flammatory rheumatiz that took me last winter, I wouldn't want Netty's help, no manner of way. But praise the Lord, I'm up and living, and able to see arter this blessed child. It never would let nobody do nothing for't but Aunt Kizzie. Would it, honey?"

Effie crooked her dimpled elbow, and raising it above her head, peeped at Kizzie through the triangular opening with a cunning, mischievous expression, as much as to say—"I make you do just what I please."

"Here, you Netty," said Kizzie, pointing with an air of authority to the floor, "wait on little missy."

Netty, a nice, trim-looking mulatto girl, with a yellow handkerchief twisted coquettishly round her crisped yet shining hair, was tripping across the passage, and immediately obeyed the mandate of her sub-mistress; for *nurse* is a person of great dignity, and speaks as one having authority over the other servants.

"Move, little missy—just a leetle bit," cried Netty, in a pleasant, coaxing voice, taking hold of her gently with her left hand, while she held in her right a large, mottled turkey wing.

"I won't," said Effie, pouting her red lips, and looking defiantly at the mulatto.

"Can't you let her be?" said Kizzie, reprovingly. "What need of pestering her?"

"But Effie, my darling," cried Eulalia, bending down and speaking in a low, gentle voice, "it is very wrong to say 'I won't.' If you do not like to do anything, you must say 'I had rather not.' Will you not repeat it after me?"

"I won't," exclaimed the child, still more emphatically, peering at her stepmother through her long black lashes, with her elfish, glittering eyes.

"Do you expect to make that little witch mind you?" exclaimed Ildegerte, bursting into a gay laugh. "I should not think of teaching children obedience before they were five years old."

"I should never expect it afterwards, if I had not required it before," replied Eulalia gravely. "As soon as a strong will is manifested, the discipline of the temper should commence."

"One would think, to hear you talk, that you were a grandmother Lois, if they did not look in your youthful face," cried Ildegerte, laughing still more heartily. "But pray make her say 'I had rather not.' It will be the most amusing scene in the world. Here comes brother to witness it."

Moreland, entering at the back door, came forward in a hunting dress of "Lincoln green," a rifle in his hand, an Indian pouch swinging over his shoulder, from the mouth of which protruded the brown heads of many a partridge, hanging from limber and rumpled necks; a beautiful white pointer, spotted with bright bistre colour, following his steps, with joyous bounds and a countenance sparkling with human intelligence.

"Down, Fido, down!" he exclaimed, as the dog leaped up and laid one of his quivering paws on his shoulder. "I only allowed you to come in and pay your respects to your mistress. Here, Eulalia, I lay my trophies at your feet."

"Really, I am very weary," added he, throwing himself carelessly on the upper step and casting his pouch at her feet; "but home seems doubly sweet, after roughing it awhile in the woods. What has given you such a beautiful colour, Eulalia?"

Eulalia was conscious of a bright glow on her cheeks, in consequence of Ildegerte's playful but satirical remarks. She did not wish them repeated to Moreland, knowing that he, too, believed a child of that age too young to be disciplined into obedience—and that he would naturally express that opinion in the hearing of

Effie, whose uncommon intelligence took in meanings they imagined above her comprehension.

"Your wife has been trying to make Effie obey her," said Ildegerte. "Don't you think she has a task before her?"

Moreland laughed, as Eulalia expected he would.

"Oh! you must leave all that to Kizzie for the present," said he. "Time enough, by and by, for you to trouble yourself with her waywardness. But, tell me, little despot," he cried to the child, who had been looking earnestly in Eulalia's face the last minute, "what have you been doing, to displease this gentle lady?"

"I—I—had rather not," cried Effie, a sweet, roguish smile dimpling her round cheeks; "I had rather not."

"A miracle!" exclaimed Ildegerte, clapping her hands. "Eulalia has triumphed. She must have the gift of magic."

"The Lord hear her!" cried Aunt Kizzie, who had retired into the background at the coming of her master. "Who'd a thought it, the little, knowing cherrup!"

While Ildegerte related, with sportive grace, to her brother, the scene we have described, Eulalia lifted the child in her arms, and covered her smiling face with kisses. She was equally astonished and enchanted at her docility, after witnessing so many instances of her waywardness and obstinacy to others. Of all things, she had a horror of a spoiled child—that tyrant of a household, more despotic than Nero, more formidable than an army with banners. That Moreland did not love the indulged and imperious little pet, whom Kizzie declared to be "the living military of its mother," she could not so much wonder; but she wanted to make him love her, to mould her into such moral loveliness that he would be constrained to love her. She hailed this incident as an omen of success, as a proof of her own influence and the child's attraction towards her; and again caressing her, she told her she was a dear, good, sweet child, and every one would love her better than they had done before.

"I had rather not," whispered Effie in her ear, apparently charmed with her new lesson, and repeating it like a little parrot.

Moreland watched them both, till the exceeding tenderness he felt for Eulalia diffused itself over the child she thus folded to her young and loving bosom. It seemed to lose its painful resemblance to its mother, and assimilate itself to her, who now filled that mother's forfeited place. He longed to clasp them both in his arms, and tell Eulalia the feelings with which his heart was swelling. He could not help rising and bending over the back of her chair, and saying, in those low tones she had so often heard under the sycamore boughs,

"Make her like yourself, Eulalia, all that is lovely and good, and I will forget she ever had another mother."

Eulalia bowed her head still lower over Effie's blooming face, to hide the tears that gushed into her eyes. She wondered she had ever thought herself happy before, so full was her content, so deep her gratitude. In the brief moment of silence that followed, she lived an age of thought. She travelled back to New England, and blessed her mother for her inculcations of wisdom and love. She travelled into the future, and saw herself surrounded by blessings that multiplied as she gazed. She looked up into eternity, and prayed that she might be true to the past and worthy of the future.

"What a sweet, lovely creature she is!" whispered Ildegerte to her husband. "Who would believe that the North gave birth to such an angel?"

"You forget that I was born at the North," replied her invalid husband, with a languid smile.

"Poor Richard!" said his wife, passing her hand caressingly over his fair, waving locks, the only youthful beauty which sickness had not dimmed and impaired. "You will be yourself again when Dr. Darley can prescribe for you. To-morrow, Richard, you know we start to-morrow. I wish we had gone long ago."

"I wish so too, Ildegerte. Heaven grant that it may not be too late. I sometimes think it is selfish in me to take you with me, and expose you to all the inconveniences of travelling with a sick husband,—you, who never knew what care or privation is. But, if I should die, all I pray is, that it may be in your arms."

"Don't talk so, Richard. You will not die! You will soon be as well as ever. You are so young, and naturally so healthy. Even now, what a fine rosy colour you have! We shall enjoy so much travelling together, and then the West is such a grand, magnificent region! You forget that Crissy is to go with me, the most faithful and attached creature in the world."

"We are going to a sad place to carry slaves," said Laurens, dejectedly. "They will leave no means untried to lure her from you. What a dreadful situation you would be in, if I should die, and you be left alone among strangers, many of whom are hostile to your best interests."

"For heaven's sake, don't talk so, Richard. I don't know what is the matter with you to-night. I never saw you so desponding before. Did not brother take Albert with him as far as Massachusetts? was he not beset by abolitionists on every side, and had one the power to shake his loyalty and attachment? I am sure that Crissy loves me, better even than Albert loves his master. She has a husband and children, too, whom she will leave behind, and to whom she will be anxious to return. I should as soon think of doubting your affection as hers, Richard."

After supper, instead of returning to the piazza as usual, they busied themselves in preparations for the morrow. Moreland looked forward to the journey with many hopes and many fears. He had heard so much of Dr. Darley, that, like Laurens, he sometimes thought he had omnipotent skill, and was invested, like the primitive disciples, with the healing touch. Under other circumstances, he would gladly have accompanied his sister; but he could not leave his Northern bride—a stranger in a strange land. Ildegerte did not ask or wish such a sacrifice. She was so full of health and hope and love, she saw no difficulties to deter them, no obstacles to impede the holy pilgrimage for which she was girding herself.

The trunks were packed, the little medicine chest carefully attended to, and all things placed in the passage, preparatory for the morning journey. Then a feeling of blankness and oppression, succeeding unusual bustle and excitement, settled coldly on the heart of Ildegerte. Her hopefulness seemed suddenly extinguished, and the future looked dark and threatening. All at once, she realized the precarious tenure of her husband's lease of life. If he should die in a land of strangers, what would become of her? Sitting down on her trunk, and leaning her head upon her hand, tears, which gushed before she was aware, rained upon her lap. She could hear his dry, continuous cough through the closed door of her room, and never had it sounded so dismal, so knell-like before. Poor Ildegerte! you should not have seated yourself on that trunk, all locked and strapped and labelled. It is a mournful seat, suggestive of separation, uncertainty, and unknown trials. "Dr. R. Laurens, Cincinnati, Ohio," written in large, black letters on the lid of the other trunk, looks very much like an inscription on a coffin. She tried to turn away from it, but her eyes would be drawn back to the obituary emblem.

"What is that, Crissy?" she asked, as a negro woman came in, with something dark swinging from her arm, something whose heavy flapping reminded her of a pall.

"Nothing but Mars. Richard's cloak, Miss Ilda. I 'fraid he miss it in the morning. Is that all, missus?"

"Yes. You had better go to bed, so as to wake bright and early. But stop a moment, Crissy. What makes you look so sober? Do you feel badly about going away?"

"I hates to leave my old man and the little children, just at the last pinch; but I ain't going to make a fuss, no how. You've got trouble enough of your own, missus, let alone being bothered with tother folks."

"I am sorry to take you from your family, Crissy, but we shall not be gone very long; and you know, Mammy will take as good care of your children as if they were her own. But I don't want you to go at all, Crissy, if you are not willing. I can take Netty, who has no husband nor children, and you can do her work in the house, if Mrs. Moreland will consent. I preferred you, because I know what a good, kind nurse you are, and you have always been used to waiting on me."

"Don't talk, Miss Ilda. Don't say nothing. It hurts me mighty bad to hear you talk 'bout Netty's going. She ain't fit for nothing but sweep house and ding her fol-de-rols, jist as if we're all ear, no hands, no feet, no nothing. No, no, Miss Ilda, I not gwine to give up to no 'rangement of that sort. I hain't waited on you this long to give my place to nobody—and you sich a 'dulgent missus. You go, I go; Mars. Richard sick, I nuss him; take care of you. Never mind Jim and the children. Leave 'em to Lord Almighty. He knows what's best."

"But, suppose they try to get you away from me, Crissy, as they did Albert from brother? Can I trust you? Will you promise to be faithful to me, whatever may betide? I cannot say, as brother did to Albert, 'go, if you will,' for I shall have nobody to depend upon but you."

Never before had Ildegerte acknowledged her dependence on a menial. She had always been kind and indulgent; but there was a certain loftiness and self-reliance about her that made her seem sufficient in herself for all things. But now, the strange oppression of her feelings made her lowly, and she leaned unconsciously on the sympathy and affection of the negro, whose faithful attachment was coeval with her existence. Crissy had not the young, bright, smart-looking appearance of Netty. She had a quiet, subdued air, and a pale, grayish tinge dimmed the blackness of her skin. She was thin, and had a slight cavity in her cheeks, which gave her somewhat of a melancholy cast of countenance. Unlike the negroes in general, she exhibited no fondness for gay colours, preferring drab to scarlet; her greatest finery consisting of a white apron and gold ear-rings. The fine dresses and ornaments which Ildegerte lavished upon her she loved to hoard, and every Sunday she had a grand review of her treasures, which had an hebdomadal increase. The negro is generally prodigal, having no need of forethought or care for the supply of the morrow's wants. If he has money (and he always does have money), he spends it; if fine clothes are given to him, he wears them, certain of a future supply. But Crissy was an exception to the general rule. She did love to hoard, and her chest, always carefully locked, and covered with a spread of white dimity, fringed with tasselled netting, was sacred to her as the ark of the covenant to the children of Israel. Netty—the gay, coquettish, warbling Netty—called her a "stingy old thing," and teased her about her clothes mouldering to pieces, stuck away in a musty chest. She declared everything Crissy wore had a mouldy smell and a moth-eaten look, and that her money was gangrened, it had been put away so long. In consequence of this hoarding propensity, which is always linked with selfishness, Crissy was not a favourite with the other servants; but she was invaluable in the household, for her neatness, industry, and fidelity. She was endeared to Ildegerte by long habit, and her extreme kindness in sickness. She was associated with all the comforts of her childhood and the enjoyments of her youth. She had another quality, remarkable in one of her colour, wakefulness. The negro's sleep is deep and sound as a magnetic slumber. He can sleep anywhere and everywhere,—reclining, sitting, standing, even walking. He can sleep, we verily believe, on the ridge-pole of a house, or the apex of a church-dome; but Crissy seemed a stranger to this soporific influence. She was never caught napping or nodding in the daytime, and the lowest sound of Ildegerte's voice awakened her at night. This was probably owing to her unusual prudence and forethought, anxious watchers by the bed of the white man, but strangers to the couch of the African.

Ildegerte inhaled the inspiration of hope with the morning breeze. Richard had had such a quiet night, such refreshing slumbers, was so brightened and encouraged himself, that she was quite ashamed of the despondency of the preceding evening. They were to travel the first day's journey in their own carriage, Moreland accompanying them on horseback, so it seemed more like an excursion of pleasure than the commencement of a long and weary pilgrimage.

The travellers were seated in the carriage, Moreland

mounted ready to escort them, Eulalia standing by one of the lofty gate-posts, in the shade of a coral honey-suckle, that climbing to its summit tossed its glowing wreaths to the gale, so near him that her hand could play with the horse's shining mane; Kizzie, in all her well-fed rotundity and consequential dignity, on the other side, holding little Effie in her arms, who frisked from shoulder to shoulder, not forgetting an occasional vault to the top of her head, in her wild, elfish pranks; and a row of household negroes, gathered in a body-guard round the carriage. But where was Crissy? Every-thing was ready but Crissy. A messenger was des-patched to hasten her movements, when she appeared with a large bundle on her head, while Jim toiled on after her with a tremendous box on *his* head, so large and heavy it seemed to flatten it on the top into a pan-cake form.

"What are you going to do with that box, Jim?" inquired his master.

"Don't know, massa. It's Crissy's plunder. She tell me to tote it to the carriage."

"That box! that big, heavy, clumsy thing!" ex-claimed Ildegerte, impatiently. "Why, Crissy, you must be crazy, to think we could carry that. It can never go in the world. And here you have kept us waiting half an hour already."

"I'm obleeged to take my clothes, missus. Hain't got nothing else to put 'em in."

"You might have had that small trunk in my dressing closet. Why didn't you tell me before?" cried Ildegerte, laughing in spite of herself at Crissy's rueful countenance. "Go, this minute, and put what you need in that. Make haste. We ought to have been gone an hour ago."

"Ain't you 'shamed to entertain your missus in this way?" said Kizzie, removing Effie's foot from her mouth, who was now frolicking all round her head. "Go 'long. What you want to carry them duds to look over every Sunday for? Nobody wants to steal 'em. Hi—smell too musty for me."

"Come 'long, Jim," said Crissy, giving a jerk to the arm of her obedient Benedick, who went toiling back, receiving as he went innumerable directions about taking care of her property during her absence, and keeping the moths from her woollen things.

"You had better go in, Eulalia," said Moreland, dismounting, and coming to her side. "You will be weary standing here. This is a specimen of the way our servants *entertain* us, as Aunt Kizzie says. Now, I think, in spite of the dreadful stories they tell of us, we are a marvellously patient people."

"I think so too," cried Ildegerte, leaning from the carriage-window, and pushing back the thick, shining black tresses that fell over her forehead (for her bonnet lay carelessly in her lap). "Tell me, my dear, sweet Northern sister, do your servants at home take greater liberties than ours? Are your Northern masters and mistresses more enduring than this brother of mine, or his very meek and forbearing sister? Did you not expect to see him spring from his horse and make Jim and Crissy dance a gallopade through the yard to the music of his whip?"

"No, indeed," answered Eulalia, smiling, though blushing at the recollection of what she would have expected a few months ago. "I expected no such thing. Neither did I expect to see you bear the delay with so much grace and good-humour."

"Russell says I am the most impatient creature in the world; but don't believe him, sweet Eulalia. I want you to think most kindly and lovingly of me while I am gone, and imagine me all that is gentle and lovely and of good report. As you have robbed me of the first place in my brother's heart," she added, smiling through the tears that gathered into her brilliant eyes, "it is no more than just that you should indemnify me, in some way."

"The place *she* occupies was never given to another," replied Moreland, looking from Ildegerte to Eulalia, with the tenderness of the brother and the love of the husband beaming in his eyes. "It is one set apart, and holy for an angel's residence."

"That's the way Richard used to talk," said she, turning to the pale, fair-haired young man at her side; "but he knows now that a woman is a better nurse than an angel would be. They can't make jellies and custards as well as we can, though they may be smarter in other respects."

The reappearance of Jim and Crissy checked the conversation. Jim looked as if he had sadly dwindled with his diminished head-piece, and Crissy, as if she had parted with her last friend, in the capacious box.

"Good by, Jim," said she, to her anxious spouse, who was drawing his left hand briskly under his nose, while he shook hands with her with his right; "mind what I tell you, and the children too."

"Now, Crissy, you 'member, you not to run away," cried Jim, in a meek, snivelling voice; "if you do, you 'pent in saccloth and ashes."

"No danger!" exclaimed Albert, laughing; "she'll be glad enough to come back, you see if she ain't. May be they set her scrubbing too hard," continued Albert, rubbing his elbows and knees, with a comical expression. "Give my respects to Mistress Grimby, Crissy, may be you see her."

As the carriage-wheels rolled down the green slope which led up to the house, Eulalia's tearful glance followed their evolutions. Alas! how much she feared that those fair locks would lie low beneath the green-sward of the West, and the sparkling light of Ildegerte's eyes be quenched in the tears of widowhood. But her last gaze was fixed upon the horseman, who ever and anon turned and bowed his head and kissed his hand in token of farewell. A sudden winding in the road took them from her sight. It was the first time she had been parted from Moreland, and it seemed to her a cloud rested on the landscape. He was to return on the morrow; but what a long, long day was before her! She stood, for a moment, leaning against the gate-post, drawing a wreath of the honeysuckle before her eyes, as a veil to her emotion, thinking of the possibility of her having to endure such a trial as Ildegerte seemed doomed to bear. Could *she* bear it, and live? Could she see the pale shadows of the grave slowly, slowly stealing over that countenance, whose light was now the glory of her soul, as well as the warmth,—the vitality of her heart,—and live? Oh! no. Why does she call up a vision so dark and sad? God in mercy spare her such a blow!

"You've got a mighty tender heart, missus," said Aunt Kizzie, in the same soothing, affectionate tone in which a mother would address a child. She would speak in a domineering manner to the servants, but her language and manner were gentle as a lamb's to Eulalia and Effie. She adored her master; and, when he introduced his Northern bride to the assembled household, in all her beauty, sweetness, and timidity, distinguishing *her* as a faithful friend of the family and the kind nurse of his child, she was so proud, so happy, so full of admiration and delight, she could scarcely restrain from hugging them both in her ample arms. She had disliked, nay, even hated Claudia, who had either kept her at a haughty distance, very unusual in a Southern mistress, or tyrannized over her with the most capricious despotism, and whom, with a true perception of character, she believed unworthy of the love of her noble young master.

"You've got a might tender heart, honey," repeated she, setting down the restless Effie, who, scampering off, lighted like a butterfly among the roses; "the Lord keep it from rough handling. And you've got a good husband, if there ever was one. He's a gentleman, a raal gentleman. 'Tain't no sham, nuther. It's sound, clean through. Black folks knows it as well as white folks. There ain't a nigger a hundred miles round but what'll take off his hat as soon as Mars. Russell come in sight. Bless a Lord for good massa. Bless a Lord for good missus, too. Oh! you get along, Kizzie; you nothing but big baby, no how."

The tears were fairly dropping down her black shiny cheeks, as she concluded her hosannas, and Eulalia's heart felt drawn towards her with strong and tender chords. The praises of Moreland were music to her ears. How she wished her father could hear them from the lips of the Africans themselves, with all those demonstrations of sensibility which proved their sincerity and truth. How grieved and indignant she felt at the recollection of the injustice and wrong her husband had suffered, in consequence of the prejudices and misconstruction he encountered from her father's partisans at the North! How she honoured him for his Christian forbearance; and how deep was her gratitude for the love which, overlooking all this, had chosen her from all others, made her the presiding Queen of his princely home, and was crowning her with daily blessings! Gratitude! who would not smile at the idea of her feeling gratitude for the love of any one? Of her, who was the incarnation of all that is pure and good and lovely in woman? But nothing is so lowly and self-depreciating as true love. In proportion as it exalts another it humbles itself. It places its idol on a throne high as the heavens, and bows, a trembling worshipper, below.

Eulalia could not help feeling slightly embarrassed at finding herself alone, for the first time, saving the little Effie, with the negro members of the household. It was a mystery to her how they could all find employment in so small a family, yet it was astonishing how much they found to do. There was the cook, who had an under vassal to pick up chips, tote water from the spring, &c.; the washwomen, who had nothing to do but wash and iron and scrub floors; Aunt Kizzie, the nurse and plain seamstress—that is, she cut and made the other negroes' clothes, hemmed tea-towels, sheets, &c.; Netty, the chambermaid and fine seamstress, the maker of her master's shirts and Effie's wardrobe; Albert, the valet de chambre and gentleman at large; the coachman, who was also the gardener; and Jim, who did a little of everything and not much of anything, pottering about the grounds, mending a broken paling, sawing off a dried branch, making the kitchen fires, and airing Crissy's clothes. Then, there was Kizzie's mother, an infirm old woman, who had a nice little cabin of her own, where she sat with a white handkerchief pinned under her chin, not much whiter than her wool, knitting or patching, or holding the baby, if there happened to be one in the establishment. She was a kind of *elect lady*, to whom all paid respect and reverence. She was a simple-hearted, pious old soul, who had been favoured with marvellous revelations from the other world, and thus acquired the influence of a prophetess among her people. She had seen three white doves sitting one moonlight night at the head of her old mistress's grave; she had heard a voice from heaven, telling her "that her sins were forgiven;" and once, when she was praying and asked the Lord to give her a token that her prayer was heard, a piece of white paper flew into the window, and rested right on the top of her head. It would have been cruel to have wrested from old Dicey her unquestioning faith in these miracles, it made her so happy. The horse-shoe suspended over her door did no harm to others, and a great deal of fancied good to herself. The vial filled with a decoction of bitter herbs, which was deposited under the threshold, hurt nobody, and was a charm of great power in her estimation. If any one could find any poor, old, infirm woman at the North, happier than Dicey, more kindly treated, more amply provided for, living in a more nicely furnished cabin, and more comfortably clothed, we should like to see them and congratulate them on their favoured destiny. Did you ever see a whiter counterpane than that spread as smooth as glass over Dicey's bed? Look at her pillow-slips, all luxuriating in broad, flaunting ruffles. Sleep must come down in state when such royal accommodations await it. But that counterpane, and those pillow-slips, were not intended for the dark unseeing night. They were taken off when bedtime arrived, and more plebeian ones substituted. There is nothing in which the negress prides herself so much as a nice bed. She saves all the feathers she can get held of, till they form a mass large enough to be diffused with generous thickness over the given surface, and then makes a bed which she is for ever sunning and adorning. It is true they can roll themselves in a blanket and sleep as soundly on the bare floor, but they must have the bed to look at and admire. We have been more particular in describing this little cabin, because an old Aunt Dicey is found in almost every large household establishment at the South. The old family nurse, often the tutelary genius of three generations, the faithful servant, who has devoted the vigour of her youth and the energies of her womanhood to her master's interests, and to his children's service, and dandling his children's children on her aged knees, looks upon them with worshipping tenderness, and dreams that the babes of Paradise are cradled in her dusky arms. Dicey had been the nurse of Moreland's mother, she had been his own nurse, and now in gratitude and affection he drew around the evening twilight of her existence the curtain of repose, that she might wait in quietude and peace the dawning of an eternal morning.

It may be said that this is a remarkable instance, but it is not so. Cruel indeed is the master or mistress who imposes a hard task on an aged slave, or leaves them to neglect and suffering; and the ban of society rests upon them. We have seen a whole family drowned in tears by the death-bed of a slave: the head of the strong man bowed on his breast in wordless sorrow, while woman's softer soul

"in woe dissolved aloud."

We will pause a moment in our story, to relate an incident which occurred when we were a guest of the household, and eye and ear-witness of its truth. Perhaps it may add force to the illustration, if we say that *our hero* belonged to the governor of the state, whose body-servant and coachman he had been for many years.

It was a bright, clear, winter's morning, when Lem harnessed his master's fine black horses—a span very precious to the governor's heart—to the wagon, and drove them into the woods for a load of pine. In felling a tree, the trunk fell upon his own body and one of the noble horses, which was killed instantaneously by the crash. A young son or nephew of the governor, who was riding about the woods on horseback, witnessed the accident, heard the groans of Lem, who lay mangled and bruised under the gray, old, crushing trunk, and, flying homeward in grief and terror, told the story of his danger and sufferings. His mistress wept unrestrainedly; the children burst forth into audible demonstrations of sorrow.

"Father!" said the boy who brought the tidings, "it is your best horse that is killed, your blackest and strongest."

"I don't care," exclaimed the governor, wringing his hands, "if both horses are killed, if poor Lem is spared. Give me that horse directly. Take another, and go after Dr. H*****. Ride like a streak of lightning, and tell him to meet me in the woods. Wife, have a bed sent to spread in the bottom of the wagon."

It was a sad and touching scene when Lem was brought home, half-fainting from excessive agony. Yet amidst the sadness one could hardly forbear smiling at the strange manner in which his wife expressed her grief. She was one of the pillars of the African church; but her husband, though faithful, honest, temperate, industrious, and of irreproachable morality, had never made a profession of religion.

"Oh, marcy! Lord a marcy!" she cried in piteous and bewailing accents; "I wouldn't mind it so much, 'cause the Lord a mighty done it; but Lem is sich a sinner, sich an awful sinner. He ain't fit to die. Oh! oh! how awful I'll feel way up in heaven, singing the praises of the kingdom, when I see Lem way down in the great black pit. Lord have marcy, and make him 'pent of his 'niquity."

"Hush," said the eldest boy, in indignant tones; "if Lem don't get to heaven you won't, nor any of the rest of us."

"We must have a light elastic mattress," cried the Doctor, "to lay him on. This is too hard."

"Take mine," exclaimed his mistress; "it is the best in the house."

Immediately, with her own hands, she bared her bed of its covering, and sent her new, unsoiled mattress to be placed under the negro's bleeding limbs. She sent him two sheets of soft, fine linen, that he might have every appliance that luxury could furnish to soothe his sufferings. His thigh-bone was broken, his limbs mangled and torn, and it was thought he had received some internal injury that might prove fatal. Never have we seen a sick person more carefully, tenderly watched.

"If I was the Gubenor hisself," said he, tears of gratitude streaming from his eyes, "I couldn't hab no more done for me. I most willing to die, eberybody so good to poor Lem."

After months of anxious and unwearied care and watching, he recovered the use of his limbs, and then gradually his strength returned; and to the inexpressible joy of his better half professed the religion whose influences had long been acting on his heart. In a letter written by his mistress, some time after, she thus affectingly alludes to the death of his wife:—

"We are all in deep affliction for the loss of Charity, our old and faithfully attached servant and friend. She belonged to my mother, and loved me, and my children after me, as if we were her own children. She was so much beloved by us all, that it seems as if the void made in our household can never be filled. I have been dreading this event, but it is hard to be reconciled to it."

Why cannot those who speak and write bitter things of the South, record such incidents as these, when they are far, far more frequent than the dark scenes which they seem to take a strange delight in depicting in the blackest, most revolting colours? Why do they pass over everything that is fair and pleasant to the moral sense, and gather every shadow, which, darkening under their touch, rolls into a mass of gloom and horror, oppressive and sickening to the soul? Why are they ready to believe the most awful tales of the abuse of the slave which imagination can conceive and calumny invent, and turn a deaf ear to the history of the master's kindness, humanity, and benevolence Why, with frantic zeal, do they light the brand of discord, and throw it blazing into the already burning heart of a community, when the stars of the Union may be quenched in the smoking, and the American eagle flap its wings in blood?

Would it not be well to pause and think of the consequences of all this? Can you sever the interests of the North and the South without lifting a fratricidal hand? Sir, perhaps you have a son, who, finding no outlet for his energies, no field of enterprise in a New England clime, has come an adventurer to the South, and made a fortune from its rich resources. He has married one of its dark-eyed daughters, and the blood of the North and the South mingles in the veins of their children. Woman! it may be that you have a daughter or a sister wedded to one of the sons of the South, whose interests and affections are so closely entwined with his, that the stroke aimed at one must cut the life-chords of the other. Man! you have a friend, the friend and brother of your youth, whom you once loved as your own soul, whose path of life diverging from your own has led him to seek a home beneath a Southern sky. Here he lives prosperous and happy, and the fragrant gale that fans his brow whispers to him sweet memories of his early days, and the friends who then made the sunshine of his life. It whispers to him of you, whom he left on your native granite hills, and his heart throbs over the reminiscences of childhood.

Sir, if through your instrumentality the fires of insurrection are kindled in the land, and the knife sharpened in the hand of the assassin, the blood of your son may cry to you from the ground; your daughter, clasping her innocent babes to her bosom, may lift her dying eyes to heaven, feeling the conviction, keener than her last death-pang, that a father's hand guided the blow of which she is the victim. Your sister, your brother, your friend may rise up in judgment against you, when their accusing spirits meet you at the bar of God! Have you not said, have you not written, that it was the duty of the slave to plunge the steel in the bosom of his master, rather than submit the vassal of his will?—that it would be right to roll a fiery wave of insurgency over his sleeping dwelling, and leave only the "blackness of ashes to mark where it stood!"

England, too, lifts her coroneted brow, and stretches out her jewelled hands over the waters to loosen the fetters of the African, and pour the vials of avenging wrath on the tyrants who enthral him.

Thou! on whose magnificent empire the sun never casts its setting ray, turn thy glorious eye to the slaves whose life-blood thou art draining at the threshold of thy own doors. See that pale and ghastly and multitudinous band of females imprisoned within close and narrow walls, most of them in the springtime of life; but, oh! what a cold, blighted, barren spring!

"With fingers weary and worn,
With eyelids heavy and red,
These women sit, in unwomanly rags,
Plying their needle and thread."

And it is "*stitch, stitch, stitch,*" from the chill gray morning twilight, to the dim gray evening twilight, and then, by the light of a dripping candle, they "*stitch, stitch, stitch,*" till the long, long midnight hour; nay, more, till one, two, three o'clock of another day, then, crawling into some miserable, crowded, airless hole, lie down to a few feverish, restless, unrefreshing dreams. And so it goes on for weeks, months, and years, till the needle drops from their poor wasted fingers, and they lie in a deeper, colder, but scarcely darker bed. You may say that this mode of existence is voluntary on their part; that they are free, and freedom is sufficient of itself to enrich the most abject and miserable of human beings. It is false. They are not free. Poverty, with a scourge of iron and a scorpion lash, stands behind them and urges on the life-consuming task. Starvation, with grim, skeleton features, and wild, hollow eyes, stares them in the face, and shame and dishonour stand on either side, weaving a winding sheet for their souls. They have no choice left. They must work or starve; work or die; work or sell themselves to the demon of temptation. Freedom! God of the white man, as well as the black, if this is freedom, give us bondage and chains instead. Where, in all the broad lands of the South, is a negro doomed to work for eighteen or twenty hours out of the twenty-four, in silence and hopelessness and anguish that passeth show? Do songs ever gush from those bloodless, pallid lips? Do those weary feet ever spring in the light and joyous dance? Alas! no! The breath of life comes struggling from the weak and wasting lungs, and every step is impeded by the dull, heavy, leaden weight of despair.

Imperial England! Island-queen of the ocean! There are thousands of these pallid slaves, whose bleeding hearts are bound in iron chains to the chariot wheels of thy wealth and power; whose sufferings the African may well pity, rejoicing in his happier lot. And yet one gem from your royal diadem would scatter plenty mid these starving throngs. Bring forth your *mountain of light*, whose focal splendours illuminated the crystal walls that enclosed a congregated world—bring it forth, fuse it (perchance the chemic miracle may be performed) in the flaming forge of human suffering, and pour it in dazzling streams through the dry, deep channels of poverty and want Bring forth your glittering diamonds, your costly pearls, your jewels and precious stones, for the relief of your famishing vassals, and then talk of philanthropy, and justice, and compassion. In the great day of revelation, when the earth and the ocean shall give up their dead, and the different races of men stand before the judgment bar of God, think you no cry for vengeance on the oppressed will be heard, save from the dusky lips of the African? that no scars of suffering will be seen on any soul but his? Methinks, on that day, when the motives of every act, the spring of every thought will be visible in the full blaze of eternity, the judgments of God will be found very different from those of man, and many a spirit on whom the curse of public opinion has fallen with withering power, will be exalted to the right hand of glory, and crowned with immortal honours. There will be many a grateful Lem, whose tears of gratitude have been preserved in the vials of the saints; many a good old Dicey, who will bless the humane master, who made her declining years serene as an autumn sunset.

And hark! a voice as of many meeting waters, comes from the excellent glory—

"I will say to the North, give up, and to the South, keep not back: bring my sons from far, and my daughters from the ends of the earth.

"Even every one that is called by my name, for I have created him for my glory. I have formed him. Yea, I have made him.

"Bring forth the blind that have eyes, and the deaf that have ears.

"Let all the nations be gathered together, and let the people be assembled. Who among them can declare this, and shew us former things? Let them bring forth their witnesses, that they may be justified; or let them hear, and say—It is truth."*

* Benjamin Walker, Esq., of Jamaica, writing to his brother in Charleston, S. C., uses the subjoined language. He is an Englishman, who has resided in the island for many years, and, after a personal investigation of the abolition operations of his own government,

says—"I hope and trust you will never be imbued with anti-slavery doctrines: and if many could witness the ruin of interest, both moral and material, the misery of families, and the desolation of all which I now see around me, occasioned by the emancipation of the negroes, there would be less agitation in your country on that much-vexed question. I hope the people of the South 'will hold their own. Emancipation means confiscation and misery to both races. Let people come to Jamaica and judge for themselves, and witness the white race driven from their hearth and home by the destructive policy of the mother country. An Exodus of the white race has already commenced, and I am preparing to join in the stream, and abandon a worthless and ruined country."

CHAPTER X.

WE break, for the first time, the unity of our story, to follow Ildegerte and her invalid husband to the Western city. We leave Eulalia, for a while, happy beyond the charter of her sex, receiving new and bright impressions, and transmitting them with added brightness to her Northern kindred. There is scarcely a ripple now on the smooth wave on which she is borne,—no cloud on the blue heaven that bends over her, in sunny or in starry love; but, by and by, there may be darkness for brightness, and angry billows for smoothness, and the storm-gale of the North sweep cold and blighting over her Southern bower. Rejoice, in thy happiness, sweet Eulalia! gather up the manna that falls in a honey-shower upon thy path, but forget not to garner a portion for the day when none may fall.

Richard Laurens appeared to acquire new life and vigour as the distance widened between him and his Southern home, and, just in proportion, the spirits of Ildegerte sparkled and bounded in their original brilliancy and elasticity. Crissy remained taciturn and rather sullen for some time, brooding over the remembrance of the goods and chattels she was compelled to leave behind; but gradually her gloom dispersed before he generous promises of Ildegerte, who pledged herself to reward her a hundredfold for every sacrifice she had required. Everything was novel and therefore exciting to the young and ardent Southerner. She had never before left the boundaries of her native state, having been educated at a Southern college, and she carried the freshness, brightness, and impulsiveness of a child into scenes where she was to learn some of the bitterest experiences of the life of woman.

When borne upon the Mississippi's deep, majestic stream, margined by such grandeur and luxuriancy, she was filled with the most enthusiastic admiration; and when gliding on the silver bosom of its gentler tributary, Ohio, she was equally enchanted.

The weather was delightful, having the mild, uniform temperature of departing summer. Everything seemed to favour the travellers, and Ildegerte declared her determination to travel every year in the warm season.

"Next summer, Richard, we will go to Saratoga and Niagara; the summer after, to Europe. Russell and Eulalia will go too—and what a charming family party we shall make! There is so much to see and admire in the world, it is a shame to stay in one place all the time, looking at the same things."

"If I live, Ildegerte."

"But you are so much better, Richard. You get better every day. Indeed, you are almost well. I *thought* it was only a long protracted cold that had weakened your lungs. I will not hear that cold and doubting *if*. Is he not a thousand times better, Crissy, than when we left home?"

"I think Mars. Richard does look a heap better than he did. I 'spect he go back right fat and peart."

Ildegerte and Richard both laughed at his prospective obesity, for in his most robust days he had more of the slender grace of the stripling than the vigorous proportions of the man.

"There is room for improvement in you too, Crissy," said she, playfully touching the sink-holes in her grayish-black cheeks. "You are something of Pharaoh's lean kine order. I am afraid the people will think we don't use you well. You must tell them you get a plenty to eat and drink—and wear too, if I have doomed you to a small trunk in travelling. You must look smart and bright, Crissy, and put off that *down* way of yours."

"I wants to see Jim and the children, missus."

"And the big chest, Crissy. Never mind. You will see them all soon. Don't *I* want to see my brother, and his sweet wife, and that dear little witch of an Effie? And don't I wan't to see old Dicey, and Aunt Kizzie, and all the precious darkies?"

"You have got *him* by you, you loves best of all, missus. 'Spose he way off—'spose you never see him no more—'spect you wouldn't feel funny, missus, like you do now?"

"And do you really love Jim so much, Crissy? had an idea that you thought him inferior to you; that you didn't think him very smart or genteel. I am glad you are such an affectionate wife."

There was a merry sparkle in Ildegerte's eye, that illumined the meaning of her words.

"I knows Jim ain't none of the smartest," said Crissy, with a conscious expression; "but he's the willingest creatur and the best conditioned that ever was. It 'pears now like I never sot as much by him as I oughter."

"We never appreciate the blessings within our reach," said Ildegerte; "but oh! Richard,"—turning to her husband, who was listening to the voice of the dashing wavelets—"when you are restored to perfect health I will always prize the blessing, and be the most contented and grateful of human beings."

"For your sake, more than my own, I pray for returning health," he replied, gratefully pressing the beautiful white hand that was laid gently on his arm. "I sometimes think I have been very selfish in taking you with me, when you *may* be left alone in a land of strangers. I blame myself, too, for not taking Albert, whom your brother pressed so earnestly upon me; but I thought it would be an admission of weakness and helplessness on my part, which I shrunk from acknowledging. It seemed so unnecessary, such a superfluous expense. You will have Crissy, however, whatever may happen, on whose attachment and fidelity you can rely with implicit confidence."

The white hand was pressed upon his lips, while she called his attention to the flowering vines that hung trailing from tree to tree, and festooned the shore with rich and gaudy wreaths. She would not allow him to give utterance to one gloomy thought, one sad misgiving. If every cloud has a silver lining, that which hung over *them* was fringed by her with a golden edging too.

As they approached the city to which they were bound, which rose like a Queen above the stream that rolled in majesty at its feet, they gazed with rapture at the beautiful panorama presented to the view. Crowning the gradually ascending shore, Cincinnati looked down in its loftiness, across the severing river, on the green plains of Kentucky, that stretched out before it. Its spires and domes were defined on a misty blue background of swelling hills. These beautiful hills were enriched by cultivation; and many a lordly mansion and elegant cottage seemed climbing their verdant heights, or reigned enthroned on their brows. They arrived at an appropriate hour; for all the pomp of closing day was gathering in the West to gild and beautify its Queen. The blue, misty hills put on a drapery of golden purple; golden arrows, tipped with fire, shot up from the roofs and turrets and fanes; the dark blue river changed to glowing saffron and rippling crimson; and the emerald fields of Kentucky sparkled with the gleam of the topaz. The dark eyes of Ildegerte reflected the radiance, and even the pale blue orbs of Richard were lighted up with their wonted lustre.

"Beautiful? beautiful!" exclaimed Ildegerte. "Is not this glorious sun-burst an omen of joy, Richard? I hail it as such."

"And I too, am catching the inspiration of your hopes," cried Richard, a bright colour kindling in his face. "This city of refuge," continued he, quoting the language of Scripture, "let me reach it, and my soul shall live!"

"Beautiful!" repeated Ildegerte. "Is it not, Crissy?"

She pitied the lonely Crissy—without any companion of her own colour—and was constantly encouraging her to express her thoughts and feelings to her.

"La, missus, it goes up like a big corn-hill. Is this where the niggers is all free?"

"Yes, Crissy, but I don't believe one of them is half as well off as you are. Do you?"

"Don't know, missus; don't know nothing 'bout *them*. I'm mighty well satisfied; got nothing to complain of. Don't see what a body want more."

Crissy never was demonstrative, like Kizzie. Their manner differed as much as the warm, shining black skin of the one, from the cold, grayish darkness of the other.

"I don't want to see none of 'em, while I stay," she added, after looking up earnestly into the streets of the city, and turning up her nose with an expression of contempt. "I 'spise the free niggers as much as I do poor white folks."

"But you should not despise poverty, Crissy, nor negroes, either, because they are free. If I die before you, I am going to set you free. Would not you like that?"

"Don't want to be free, Miss Ilda; heap rather live with you and Mars. Richard. Don't know how to take care of myself, no how. Jim 'most a fool. What'll I do with the childen? Lord bless you, missus! don't say nothing more 'bout that. Wish I was at home agin. 'Pears like I been gone a year."

With such sentiments as these, Crissy followed her mistress to the hotel, which was to be her temporary home, wondering what it was that made people free there more than in any other place. She had heard so much talk about the free States, she expected to see an entirely different aspect of nature. She expected to breathe a different atmosphere, and to see a set of people looking very different from any she had seen before. She glanced from one side to the other, with a vague dread of being pounced upon and carried off, where she would never see her mistress, or Jim, or her hoarded possessions any more. She watched the servants at the hotel very narrowly, and thought they did not look any happier than her fellow-labourers at home, nay, not half as happy, and she was sure they had to work a great deal harder.

Richard, who had despatched a note to Dr. Darley soon after his arrival, waited his coming with mingled hope and fear. He thought he could ascertain, from one glance of his penetrating and truth-beaming eye, the reality of his condition. When the servant announced that he was below, he turned excessively pale, and sunk back in his chair, trembling with agitation.

"I will go and meet him," exclaimed Ildegerte, "and bring him here. In the mean time, pray get composed, Richard. He will think you a great deal more sick than you really are, and then you will be discouraged."

Ildegerte hastened to meet the doctor, in the confidence of finding a friend as well as physician; one on whose kindness and sympathy she could trustingly rely, on whose wisdom she could lean for counsel and guidance, whose skill, she had been led to believe, was almost supernatural. She had strong reasons of her own for wishing to see him first; and, without hesitation or embarrassment, she introduced herself as Mrs. Laurens, the wife of his former student. The doctor rose at her entrance, and, making at first a very deep and rather fonnal bow, advanced with extended hand and smiling eye to greet her.

"Is this Dr. Darley?" was Ildegerte's first thought. "I expected to have seen a much older-looking man."

And this was the expectation of almost every one, who, being familiar with his wide-spread reputation, associated his image with the venerable characteristics of age. He was past the meridian of his days, but youth lingered in the short, crisped curls of his brown hair, undimmed by a single touch of frostiness; youth sparkled in the bright, intense, smiling glance of his grayish eye, and the earnest, animated expression of his whole countenance. Intellect, in all its youthful freshness and vigour, beamed upon his features, and, what to Ildegerte was far more attractive, a generous, noble heart, in all its young warmth of feeling, unchilled by contact with a cold and selfish world, imparted fervour and interest to his whole face.

The doctor, who had a keen perception and pure love of the beautiful, gazed with affectionate admiration on the young and handsome woman, who seemed to his poetic imagination a rich tropic flower, transplanted to a colder clime. Excitement had given the brilliant bloom of the brunette to her cheeks and lips, and her eyes had that velvet blackness so seldom seen, but so inexpressibly bewitching.

"Is your husband very ill?" he asked, in a tone which struck her as grave and solemn, in contrast with his smiling eye.

"No, sir. I think he is convalescent now. He has

been much more sick, and all our friends feared that he was in danger of consumption. I believe, now, that his cough is the result of a severe cold. He has such unbounded confidence in you, he feels sure that if he has any serious malady, you can heal it. I wanted to see you first, doctor, to tell you that you cannot judge to-night how he really is. He is weary, excited, and agitated. Do not let him think he is ill. Do not discourage him—he will be so much better to-morrow."

"Is he easily discouraged? is he prone to despondency?" inquired the doctor.

"No, not much,—that is, not often; but he is not near as hopeful as I am."

"Are you alone with him? Did no friends accompany you?"

"No one but a faithful black woman. She is a host in herself. We need no other assistance."

"This is a very dangerous place to bring a slave," said the doctor. "I wish you had brought a white servant instead. Living, as we do, on the very borders of slavery, our city is the resort of runaway negroes; and, what is still worse, those who are making every effort to swell their number. I advise you to keep your woman as constantly with you as possible."

"Oh! sir, I have no fears for Crissy. No temptation, I am assured, would induce her to leave us. She is fidelity itself, and is very strongly attached to our family. No, no, I feel very easy on that subject. But

Richard, I know, feels very impatient to see you, and will think I am encroaching on his rights."

Leading the way, with a light step, to the upper apartment, appropriated to them, she ushered in the doctor, watching his countenance, as he addressed her husband, as if her own life depended upon its expression.

"Why, Laurens," cried he, giving his dry and feverish hand a long and affectionate pressure, "is this the way you commence your professional career? I taught you to heal others, not to be sick yourself."

"I have come to you for invigoration, doctor," replied the young man, with a languid smile. "I already feel the inspiration of your presence. I feel so much better than I did when I left home, I fear you will think me foolish, to come. Yet I can never regret meeting you again, and feeling once more the kindly pressure of your guiding hand."

He looked earnestly, thrillingly in his face as he spoke, while the fever-spot burned brightly on his own. The hand which had pressed his so affectionately, now lingered on his wrist, and he knew that its quick pulsations were being counted with professional accuracy. Agitated by this consciousness, he began to cough. It was a short, dry, hacking cough. It always made Ildegerte gasp for breath, and press her hand on her heart, when she heard it. It was an involuntary motion, but her heart literally ached, and she could not help pressing it. Yet she would not acknowledge that it was an alarming cough,—it was only an obstinate one, and so she told the doctor. As he suffered the pale hand which he had been holding to slide gently from his, she caught his quick and quickly receding glance. It seemed to her that the bright, merry spark that burned there, was quenched in moisture. There was an expression of unutterable sympathy, compassion, and tenderness, transient as lightning, but as intense too. Ildegerte, who stood a little behind Richard's chair, turned pale, and cold and sick. She felt as if his death-warrant had been pronounced, and that hope had indeed bidden the world farewell.

"Come," said the doctor, in a cheerful tone, "what you need to-night is rest. Your nerves are excited. Your pulse quickened at my touch like a love-sick girl's. We must cultivate more composure. Recline on this sofa and put yourself perfectly at ease, while I make myself acquainted with Mrs. Laurens."

Ildegerte's freezing veins thawed in the kindly warmth of his manner. She must have mistaken his glance. How foolish, how childish she was! What a baby he would think her! She would show herself more worthy of his respect! She soon found that no effort was necessary to feel interested in the conversation he commenced with her, while Richard, obedient to his counsel, assumed a recumbent position, and was soon folded in tranquil slumbers. There was something so fresh, so sparkling, so original in his ideas, it seemed as if every word he uttered was sprinkled with morning dew. There was a vein of poetry and romance, too, pervading his mind, like golden ore imbedded in the solid rock. He told her something of his own early history; of the death of his wife, whom he had lost in the bloom and beauty of her womanhood; of his belief in the constancy, the eternity of love; that it was only its germ that was planted on earth; that it was reserved for the gales of Paradise to fan it into blossom.

"I do not feel separated from my wife," he said, his countenance kindling into rapturous emotion. "She is still associated with all my hopes and my joys. I never read the works of genius and sensibility without feeling the participation of her sympathy. I never listen to the sweet strains of music without being conscious of the presence of her listening spirit. So positive to me is this intimate and divine communion, that I should no more think of wedding another than if she were living and breathing at my side. I am called an enthusiast. Perhaps I am one; but I would not relinquish this abiding, inextinguishable sense of her continuing love, for all else the world can offer. Death does not really divorce us from the object of our affection. It only destroys the material tie—the spiritual, the immortal still remains."

"But it takes from us the form we love," said Ildegerte, shivering; "it lays it in the cold grave. Everything else seems so shadowy, so unreal. For my part, I would have no wish to survive the friend I loved best on earth. One coffin, one grave, would be my soul's prayer."

"We should pray rather for faith to sustain, for patience to endure, and for submission and resignation. The silver chords which bind earthly hearts together must be broken. If they writhe and struggle under the loosening hand, they may bleed and suffer in every vein and fibre, but they will nevertheless be torn asunder. It is better to lie still and be gently parted."

"*We* are not to be parted, are we?" asked she, in a very low voice, impelled by an irresistible impulse, as her eye rested on the reclining figure of Richard, who lay with one cheek supported by his hand and his fair locks partly shading the other. There was a boyish grace in his attitude, which combined with the hectic bloom of his complexion to throw the illusion of health around him.

"God alone can answer that question," he answered, with gentle solemnity. "The issues of life and death are with Him. I trust, my dear young lady, you have learned to look to him as a Father, as well as a God."

Ildegerte bowed her head, but the tears she could not suppress glittered in the lamplight. Yes! he was preparing her—she knew it, she felt it—for the coming blow. Once more her elastic spirits sunk, and a cold shadow flitted over her.

"You will come early in the morning, doctor," she said, when he rose to take leave, "will you not?"

"Certainly; 'Richard will be himself' then, I hope."

Strange, what magic there may be in a few little words! This old, old quotation,—she had heard it repeated a hundred times, and yet how reviving it sounded! Poor Ildegerte!—to what an alternation of hope and fear was she doomed, as day followed day, without fulfilling her constant, unwearied prophecy, "He will be better to-morrow." As for him, he had read his doom in Dr. Darley's undeceiving eye. He knew that he must die; and, with that pliancy with which the finite will bows to the Infinite, when the inevitable fiat is gone forth, he yielded, without a murmur. But he could not tell Ildegerte the terrible truth, —he could not rend all hope from her bosom. Often and often, had Dr. Darley resolved to inform her of the hopelessness of his condition; but she had a strange, elusive power that baffled his intentions. Since the first night, when the question "*We* are not to be parted?" was forced irresistibly from her lips, she had never asked him his opinion of his patient; and when he began to express it, unasked, she would turn the conversation at once into a different channel, find an excuse for leaving the room, or for being occupied with something present.

In the mean time, Crissy was forming new acquaintances and acquiring new ideas. Ildegerte had her meals brought to her own room, and saw nothing of the other boarders; while Crissy ate hers in the kitchen with the servants, and as she was a stranger, and a slave, she was an object of peculiar attention to them. By attention, we do not mean respect, but observation, curiosity. They evidently thought her far beneath them in position; and Crissy as evidently demeaned herself as a being of superior order. If they turned up their noses at her, she turned up hers at them, till there was a kind of nasal warfare between them. There was one free black woman, who occupied the place of an underling, whose freedom consisted in doing the greatest part of the drudgery of the kitchen, and in the privilege of being called "a good-for-nothing nigger" by the *high-life-below-stairs* Irish gentry. Her name was Judy, an unpardonable offence to one of the Irish women, whose name was also Judy, and who henceforth denominated herself Julia. Judy must have had a lower extraction than Crissy, for she did not express herself with half the elegance, saying "dis and dat," and "gwine," and "high and ki," and all those phrases which characterize the corn-field negro. Crissy pretended she had never heard such gibberish, and the Irish brogue, which was much less familiar to her ears, she pronounced a horrible jargon. There were three distinct classes in the kitchen. The Irish and German servants constituted one class; Judy, the free negress, a second: and Crissy, the slave, a third. So many incongruous elements could not fail at times to produce a discord, particularly as the first class were constantly changing their forms,—the black-haired cook of one day being a red-haired one the next. That is, there was a constant ebbing and flowing in the white population. For the slightest cause of dissatisfaction they would relinquish their office, leaving the vacancy to be supplied by other servants till another supplied the place. As it was a large establishment, they were frequently obliged to employ raw, unpractised hands, whose ignorance was the cause of blunders equally provoking and amusing.

One day one of the *raw material* was cooking her first dinner. She had recommended herself as a "suparior cook," who understood all the mysteries of the culinary department, but Crissy watched her movements with contemptuous wonder.

"Why don't you pluck out them are pin feathers?" cried Crissy, "and you ain't going to put 'em in the oven with their legs sprawling and kicking every which way!"

"I'm going to do just as I plase, you impertinent cratur," answered indignant Erin. "I should like you to show me a pin in the feathers. And don't the legs look gracefuller loose, than tethered like a slave, as you ba yourself?"

With that, she gave the oven a tremendous ding, right in the midst of a blazing fire, hot as that in which

Shadrach, Meshach, and Abednego were cast, where the devoted twins scorched and blackened and shrivelled, till they appeared the most wretched, spindle-shanked pair that ever were seen side by side.

"Why don't you drudge and baste them chickens?" exclaimed Crissy, quite scandalized at her ignorance and self-conceit. "Who ever seen potry done dry afore, and burnt all to cinders besides?"

"Do you call me a drudge and a baste, you mane, black, woolly-headed thing?" cried cook, her face in as great a blaze as the fire; "say it again, and I'll bate you across the back with this poker. What are you but a slave, I want to know? Can't you demane yourself better to your supariors?"

"I don't see as I'm more a slave than the rest on ye," said Crissy, shrugging her shoulders till they touched the tip of her ears. "You all have to work a heap harder than I do, and don't get much thanks, nuther."

"But we get wages for our work, and I'd like you to show me the blessed copper you ever got for yourn."

"I wouldn't touch a copper, leave 'em to poor folks," said Crissy. "I got a heap of money at home—all in silver,—more than you'll ever lay by, I 'spect. We don't have no coppers where we come from. We 'spises em."

"A hape of silver! Och! I'd like to spake to it,

and ask who it belonged to. And you've got any number of silks and satins, hav'n't you?"

"I've got more fine dresses than you know how to count—or any other buckra. I don't wear 'em tho', 'cept 'mong quality folks."

"Oh! you spake up for the quality, do you? Won't the craturs lie still?"

She was trying to compose the burnt and sprawling limbs of the chicken on an elliptical dish, but their feet would kick up in the air, in the second and fifth position.

"I never saw such an unaven dish," she muttered. "I like to have the convaniences where I cook. What you got in this stewpan?"

"It's Mars. Richard's broth. He won't taste of a drop but what I makes for him."

"Mars. Richard! Och! before I'd call a man or woman my master, I'd ate my tongue betwane my teeth."

Just then an exclamation of horror was heard behind them, so sudden and piercing that Erin jumped at least two feet in the air, in her consternation and affright. The mistress of the hotel, finding the dinner hour arrived, without the warning bell, had entered the premises, and, beholding the specimens of cookery surrounding the fire, a shriek of astonishment burst forth from her lips.

"Is tnat your cooking?" she cried, pointing to the fire.

"To be shure it's mine."

"Didn't you tell me that you understood all kinds of cooking, that you were an experienced, first-rate hand?"

"Well, indade, ain't I exparienced, I should like to know?" said Erin, flaring up like a candle in the wind. 'May I be spacheless if I didn't cook for Miss Wallis a wake and sixteen days over. And didn't she tell me to roast the bafe brown and crisp?" pointing to a stately sirloin, covered with a dry, black crust, that looked more like a chunk of charcoal wood than meat.

"And here's my dinner spoiled—not one thing fit to eat, and the boarders pouring in as fast as they can! It is enough to provoke a saint. If there was such a thing as keeping a steady cook—but as soon as one has a good one, they take a miff at nothing at all, and off they go. I have had three different cooks in the last three weeks, and I shall have another to-morrow! Take your things and march, miss; and never let me see your face again in this part of the world. Cook, indeed! Why I should think you had just taken a shovel of coals and dashed over the dishes."

The lady was not a scolding lady, but certainly her patience was put to a severe test. Erin was not the only one who had spoiled a dinner, and made the most awful and ridiculous mistakes. An incident which had occurred a few weeks before, rose fresh in her memory.

A girl, whom she had hired to wait in the dining-room, and who professed to be *au fait* in her line, was told to put seasoning in the castors.

"What sasoning, if you plase, ma'am?"

"Why, pepper, and vinegar, and mustard, and catsup, to be sure."

The girl did not know what castors were, but, ashamed of her ignorance, she would not acknowledge it. But hearing some one tell the servant, who was rolling a table back against the wall, not to let the castors catch in the carpet, indicating the little brass wheels with his index, she exulted in having acquired the desired information without exposing herself to ridicule, though what good in the world *sasoning* would do to them, she could not tell. Nevertheless, faithful to her instructions, she got down on her knees under the table, and plastered them with mustard, sprinkled them with pepper, and bathed them with vinegar. Not knowing what was meant by catsup, she ventured to omit that ingredient, much to the benefit of the carpet, already saturated with vinegar. These occasional misfortunes were caused by the necessity of employing emigrants, fresh from some mud-walled cabin or chimneyless roof. They may serve as sources of amusement in the retrospect, but in the moment of endurance require a Spartan spirit to bear.

"I wonder what that is, if it ain't having a missus," thought Crissy, as Erin, gathering up bundle, bonnet, and shawl, marched towards the door with the air of one who owned the whole establishment. "She needn't brag over me, the Lord knows."

"You'd better take *her* for a cook," exclaimed Erin,

in a scornful tone, as she closed the door. "Interfaring with me all the time, and nothing but a born slave."

"Do you know how to cook, girl?" asked the lady, when the wrathful figure of the Irish woman disappeared.

"I b'lieve I does, missus; tho' it ain't my rig'lar business."

"I have a great mind to hire you and try you for a while."

"La, missus! I couldn't hire my time to nobody. I belongs to Miss Ilda, and couldn't leave her no way."

"That's all nonsense," replied the lady. "You are as free as she is, if you only knew it. She has no more right to your services than I have, and you are a fool to work for nothing, when you might be getting good wages. I would not stay with her another day if I was in your place."

"When Mars. Richard so sick and she feel so bad, way off from all her kinfolk! Oh! missus, I couldn't do that. Somethin' *here* keep me from it. She bin mighty good to me, and it would be ugly to turn my back on her, when she in trouble. 'Sides, I don't see freedom what it's cracked up to be. It does mighty well for rich folks: but poor, working folks can't be free any way. Long as I got to work I'll work for my own master and missus, 'cause they cares for me."

"Poor, foolish, ignorant creature!" said the lady, in a tone of mingled compassion and contempt. "Look at Judy here—how much better off she is. She has all she earns, and does what she pleases with it."

"I'd a heap ruther be in my place than Judy's," said Crissy, looking down at her own neat, genteel apparel, and then casting a furtive glance at Judy's coarse and slovenly dress. "If I don't get reg'lar wages, I gets everything I needs without the 'sponsibility. I'm willing to help you when I've time, missus, for nothing, but don't say nothing more 'bout my leaving Miss Ilda, for I ain't a going do it."

That night after supper, when the servants had a respite from their labours, Judy was sitting on the threshold of the back kitchen door, her elbows resting on her knees, and her head resting on her hands.

"Let me go by," said Crissy. "You needn't get up, only don't spread yourself out like a fodder stack."

"You jist sit down, one minnit, Crissy, and let me say someting ben on my mind dis long time. 'Spose you ask your massa to buy me?" She uttered this in a low voice in Crissy's ear, who had seated herself at her request, pressing her clothes close to herself, to avoid the contact of Judy's soiled garments.

"You!" cried Crissy in astonishment; "I thought you free!"

"So I be—dat is, dey call me so; but dat don't make me so. I run way from old massa, 'cause he treat me bad. He live way over de river, in old Kentuck. I thought if I got among free folks I'd be de fine lady, equal to de white folks; but I'm noting but a nigger, arter all—noting but poor Judy. That ain't my name tho'. They call me Judy for short, but the Lord named me Julia. What o' dat?—no matter. You got good massa and missus—wish *I* had—den I'd have somebody to take care of me. Don't know how to take care of myself—folks 'pose on me. White folks call us niggers brudders and sisters way off; but when dey close to us dey find out we noting but niggers. Please ask your massa to buy me, and say noting 'bout it."

"He's no use for you; he's got plenty now," said Crissy; "and Mars. Russell don't approve of buying or selling. He jist keeps what he's born to, and won't have nothing to do with speculators. You'd better staid at home, and not run away. The last words Jim ses to me, 'Crissy,' ses he, 'don't you run off. You'll 'pent of it, long as you live.'"

"I tell you what, Crissy, when de nigger have good massa and good missis, dey well off. When dey have bad massa and missis, dey bad off. Talk 'bout us being on a 'quality with white folks, no such ting. De Lord never made us look like dem. We mustn't be angry wid de Lord, for all dat; He knows best, I 'spose. Look a' me, black as de chimney back,—dey, white as snow; what great, big, thick, ugly lips I got,—dere's look jist like roses. Den dis black sheep head, what de Lord make dat for? Dey got putey, soft, long hair, jist like de silk ribbons. Now look at dat big, long heel, will you?" added Judy, putting out her bare foot in the moonshine, giggling and shaking; "who ever saw de white lady with sich a heel as dat? I do wonder what the Lord made us nigger for? I 'spect de white dust gin out, and he had to take de black."*

"I wouldn't talk 'bout myself in that way," said Crissy, whose personal pride was quite wounded by the association; "all the coloured people ain't black. I ain't black myself."

"I'd heap sooner see 'em black, dan gray or yellow. It's more 'spectable. La sus! how my bones does ache. I've scrubbed de house from top to de bottom. Dat my Saturday work. Bless a Lord! I rest some to-morrow."

All that occurred in the kitchen department only made Crissy more contented with her own lot, and rather confirmed than shook her fidelity and loyalty. But she was assailed by a more dangerous influence, which, gradually winding round her, found where she was most vulnerable, and fastened on the weak spot.

There was a gentleman and lady boarding at the hotel, bearing the somewhat peculiar name of Softly. Their appearance and manner corresponded so well with their name, it seemed to have been made on purpose for them. Mrs. Softly had the softest voice in the world, and the softest step. She seemed shod with

* The very description a negress gave of herself, in our own family, in comparing the negro race with the white.

velvet, like a cat, and stole along the passages, leaving no echo of her footfalls, giving no warning of her approach. She had very light hair, and very light eyes, almost white, with no perceptible eyebrows or eyelashes, and having altogether a most crude and unfinished look. Her husband was the softened image of herself, having, if possible, still lighter hair and eyes,—and, if possible, still more indefinite brows. Like her, he had a soft, doughy, sodden appearance; and they both dressed with Quaker-like precision and neatness. Mrs. Softly had called on Ildegerte, and Ildegerte had returned the call; but she did not seek to conceal the feeling of repulsion she experienced in her presence. She was too impulsive for policy, too careless of the opinion of others, to affect an interest which she did not feel. Her coldness and indifference probably gave offence to Mrs. Softly, for she discontinued her visits, and spoke of her as very proud and haughty.

Crissy had to pass her room in going up and down stairs. The door was often left open, and Mrs. Softly generally had a soft, pleasant word for Crissy, and sometimes she asked her to come in and take a seat. Crissy was not insensible to this kindness and attention, and thought her one of the nicest and best ladies she had ever seen. Mr. Softly, too, always reflected his wife's courtesies, and talked to Crissy in a condescending, patronizing way, that was quite irresistible. By and by, it seemed to be a matter of course to drop in as she passed, and before she knew it she had related everything concerning the family of Moreland, going back to the first generation. Sometimes she heard them talking about her, for their soft voices would glide into the passage in a marvellous manner.

"Poor thing!" Mrs. Softly would say, "how I pity her! How melancholy and subdued she looks! No spirit left in her. How hollow her cheeks are! Such a nice, lady-like person, too!"

"Yes," responded Mr. Softly, "if she were only free, what a respectable member of society she would make! We must exert our influence upon her, and not suffer her to remain in bondage and degradation."

At first Crissy resisted with respectful firmness all the arguments which her new friends urged upon her understanding; but there was one temptation held out, which became gradually stronger and stronger. She could make a great fortune, all her own. She could do it in a hundred ways, with her smartness and industry. Then she could buy her husband and children, and they could all live together in a fine house, and hold up their heads as high as anybody. Moreover, she was living in sin and shame and misery and degradation, and when the means of deliverance were held out to her she would never be forgiven by the Almighty if she refused to accept them.

Crissy's weak point was a love of money—a love of gain. It was on this the incision was made, which reached at length to the heart's core. The fine house, fine furniture, and fine ladyism loomed up in her imagination, like the spires and domes of a distant city. She began to think that if she had been happy and contented before, it was only because she didn't know any better. She began to think that she had been abused without knowing it, and that her master and mistress, whom she had been silly enough to believe kind and liberal, were cruel and tyrannical, and the worst enemies she had in the world.

"If Massa Richard wan't sick," she said, "I wouldn't mind it."

"Can't she hire as many servants and nurses as she likes?" asked Mrs. Softly. "Is not she rich and independent? She can fill your place in a moment; but you, if you let this opportunity slip, will never have another."

"Never," echoed Mr. Softly.

"But where shall I go?" exclaimed Crissy, bewildered and agitated, as the crisis of her destiny approached.

"We will direct you. Leave everything to us. There is a nice place, where you can conceal yourself a while, and where you will be treated like a lady, not a slave."

Thus beset, day after day, poor Crissy grew weak and impotent, till she became a passive tool in their soft, insinuating hands. She stayed now as little time as possible in the room of her mistress, whose confiding trust in her fidelity and attachment was a dagger to her faithless and alienated heart. Ildegerte unconsciously favoured the designs of her enemies, by allowing her to be away from her more than she had been accustomed to be. Dr. Darley, who was a real philanthropist, conversed a great deal on the sectional difficulties of the country, and she thought it best that Crissy should not hear all that was said. He was pained and distressed by the fierce and bitter feelings, the fiery fanaticism, the frantic zeal, which, reckless of all consequences, was spreading through the land. His far-reaching mind beheld the inevitable consequences of these, and he lifted up his voice in public as well as private, endeavouring to arrest the burning tide of prejudice and intolerance. His piercing intellect, and large, generous heart, took in the whole, instead of a part of the social system, the interests and rights of the white race as well as the black. He believed that both would be injured and destroyed by coercive measures, unsanctioned by law, and unauthorized, above all things, by the great golden law written on the tablet of every human heart.

CHAPTER XI.

"AND must he die?" she exclaimed, clasping her hands passionately together, and looking wildly upward. "Oh! Dr. Darley, must he die? Is there, indeed, no hope?"

"Has no voice told you this before?" asked he, in grave and solemn tenderness. "Has not its whisper come to you lately with every rising sun? have you not heard it as you watched its setting beam? He asked me to tell you, but you knew it all before."

"I feared, doctor, but still I hoped. Take not hope away from me, or my heart will break. Why did he bring me here, if you cannot save him? Why have you stopped the remedies from which we hoped so much?"

She spoke wildly, and knew not that her language was upbraiding.

"Because all medicines are unavailing," he replied, with gentleness; "we can only smooth his passage to the grave. The arm of an archangel could not snatch him from it now, how much less my bounded skill, or your human love! My dear Mrs. Laurens," added he, unclasping her clenched hands, and pressing them kindly in his own, "by the great love you bear him,—by your belief in the sovereignty of God,—and by your faith in a crucified Redeemer, I entreat you to submit, with meekness and resignation, to a doom common to all the sons and daughters of Adam. Wrestle not, in impatient despair, with the mighty hand of God! I pity you, from my soul, I pity you; but what can I do for him or you that has not been done already?"

"You have been kind, more than kind—heaven bless you for all your goodness! but oh, doctor, it is so hard—you do not know what it is!"

"I know what it is to see the flower of one's life languish and fade away, leaving nothing but a waste and howling wilderness. I know what it is to watch the glimmering spark one would gladly feed with their own vitality, go out, leaving nothing but the blackness of darkness. I have travelled the same thorny path you are now treading, with bleeding feet and sinking frame. *I know what it is.* I found no hope, no comfort, no support, but in God. Neither will *you.* There is but one refuge from the life-storms which, sooner or later, sweep over every human heart, and that is, the cleft Rock of Ages."

The wild despair of Ildegerte's countenance yielded to a softer expression, as the Christian physician thus solemnly and affectionately addressed her. Bending her head till the loosened darkness of her hair wove itself into a veil for her sorrow and her tears, she wept and sobbed like a gentle, heart-broken child. The doctor did not attempt to check these gushing tears; he knew they would have a relieving influence. He was going away from the city, to be absent days, perhaps weeks, on professional business that could not be deferred. He regretted this circumstance, for though his skill in this instance was impotent to save, his sympathy and friendship were powerful to sustain.

"You are going to leave us, doctor," she said, as, with slow steps, they turned towards the chamber of the invalid, "and we have no friend but you."

"You are wrong there. You are surrounded by friends whose kind offices would be proffered the moment you required them. Then your black woman is the best nurse in the world. You must not forget her."

"Poor Crissy! yes, I am ungrateful. She is a faithful friend, who never will forsake me. What could I do without her? But, oh! Richard—"

Another burst of grief; another struggle for composure; a mighty effort to keep back the welling waters, and to roll the stone against the door of the fountain. Poor Ildegerte! she thought her cup of bitterness was brimming; but there was another drop of gall to be infused into it, of which she little dreamed.

That night, after the doctor had bidden them farewell, with a cheerful voice, but moistened and averted eye, promising to return at the earliest possible moment. Ildegerte sat in silence by her husband's couch, on which the pale and solemn moonlight fell in silvery glory. There was no other light in the room, the lamp having been removed to the passsage; and it seemed as if every lunar beam clustered round that pale and fading form, leaving the remainder of the apartment in deep shadow. As the light of life grew dim in Richard's eye, he loved more and more the benignant and holy lustre of the moon. He would have his couch wheeled to the window, through which it looked in all its calm and heavenly beauty, and there he would lie in silence, gazing upward into the deep, deep dome, where that glorious chandelier was hung. His lungs were so weak, his breath came so quick and short, and then that terrible racking cough, ready to seize him on the slightest exertion, that he seldom talked now. He was gentle, quiet, patient, and childlike, repaying every tender care with a glance of unutterable gratitude and love. "Dear, dear Ildegerte!" he would say,—then followed the upward, prayful look, and she knew he was commending her to the mercy of Him in whose presence he was shortly to be.

The deep silence of the hour was interrupted by the entrance of Crissy, who came in softly and stood beside her mistress. She stood silently gazing on her master's pallid and illuminated face,—on the burning flame-spot on either cheek,—on the paly gold locks that fell lifelessly on the pillow,—till something rose swelling and choking in her throat, and she turned to her mistress as if to avoid a sight too harrowing. But Ildegerte's dark, melancholy eyes met hers with such a wistful, desolate expression,—her face looked so pale and sorrowful, with her black hair all loose and dishevelled, making such a thick, mournful drapery,—she could not bear to see it. The choking in her throat grew worse.

"Is Mars. Richard worse to-night?" she at length asked.

Ildegerte shook her head, she could not speak. Richard did seem better, more quiet and composed than he had for many nights.

"I'll go out a little while, if missus don't want me just now," said the negro, trying to clear her swelling throat.

Ildegerte merely bowed her head in token of assent, then making a painful effort, for a dull lethargy was succeeding her late stormy emotions, she said,—

"Don't stay long, Crissy. What makes you look at me so hard, Crissy?—how strange you look! What is the matter?"

"Nothing, missus; I was just thinking of you and Mars. Richard."

Richard held out his feeble hand, as Crissy turned to the door, and taking her dusky palm in his, said, in a low, husky voice,

"God bless you, Crissy! be faithful to her when I am gone."

"God bless you, Mars. Richard!—oh! master, God bless you and missus too!" cried Crissy, bursting into a passion of tears, and sinking on her knees by the couch. "Oh! master, I poor, sinful creatur; pray forgive poor Crissy!"

"Don't, Crissy, don't!" said Ildegerte, trying to raise her from the ground, where she lay actually writhing. "You hurt him; you'll make him cough. Pray go, quick!"

Crissy partly raised herself, but not before she had kissed again and again the hem of Ildegerte's dress, and then she kissed the white hand extended to lift her, and wet it with her tears.

"Oh! Miss Ilda, God bless you and make master well! I feel like I could die for you and Mars. Richard."

Overcome by her own feelings and Crissy's impassioned sympathy, the more affecting for being in contrast with her usual calmness, Ildegerte threw her arms round her dark neck, and weeping on her bosom, exclaimed,—

"Oh, Crissy! Crissy! I shall soon have no friend left but you. You will never forsake me,—no, no!" she repeated, "you will never forsake me!"

"I can't stand that, missis!—oh, Lord! I can't

breathe! I 'most dead! I wish I was dead,—I wish I dead this minnit!"

"Go, Crissy!" said a faint voice from the couch. "I would sleep, if it were quiet."

Crissy gave a quick, spasmodic spring, and vanished Tossing her hands above her head, and flying through the long passage, she rushed into Mrs. Softly's room, more like a maniac than a sane person.

"I can't go to-night. I can't never go. I can't leave Miss Ilda. I can't leave master, I love 'em too much. I'll die fust. Wish I could die this minnit."

Mrs. Softly looked at Mr. Softly and Mr. Softly looked at Mrs. Softly as if they were in extremity, straining their white invisible eyebrows as they looked.

This was the night selected for Crissy's exodus. They had arranged everything themselves, very nicely and carefully. She was not to have any trouble in the world. Mr. Softly was to take her to a particular friend of his, whose house, situated about ten miles below the city, near the banks of the river, was a kind of negro caravansary. He was to take her in a boat, and they were to have a charming sail in the depths of the moonlight night. She was to remain there awhile, till the excitement of her flight was over, and then return to the city and commence making the fortune that was to elevate her so high in the scale of being. And after all these preparations, so benevolent and disinterested on the part of her new friends, the weak, foolish, ungrateful creature comes weeping and wringing her hands, declaring she will die rather than leave her master and mistress!

It is no wonder that they were astonished and indignant, that they upbraided her for her perfidy and ingratitude, that they placed before her in the strongest colours, the enormity of her offences, and the consequences of her transgressions. It is no wonder that the poor bewildered creature again yielded herself to their influence, and promised to be guided passively by their will.

Why did this man and woman, who had enrolled themselves under the banner whose angel-inscribed motto is "peace and good will to *all* men," thus labour and travail to rend asunder the bonds of affection and gratitude which united this faithful heart to the master and mistress she so fondly loved? They saw her contented, perfectly unconscious that servitude was a burden, without one wish to exchange situations with the hirelings, who had the liberty of going from place to place and serving many masters instead of one. Why were they not willing to leave her so? What had that sad young wife done to them, that they thus toiled to deprive her of her chief comfort and stay in the night-time of her sorrow and despair? Had they no compassion for that pale, patient, gentle, dying stranger, that they thus stole from him his attendant and nurse, at the very moment when the death-dew is falling beneath the silver moon?

What motive, we ask, in the name of all that is kind, and Christian, and holy, could have actuated them in the present instance? What, but the carrying out of a fixed, inflexible purpose, at any cost, at any sacrifice; the triumph of an indomitable will; the gratification of prejudice and intolerance? No matter what flowers are in the pathway, trample them down, though they be sweet as the blossoms of Paradise. You have marked out your course, and must not turn to the right or to the left. No matter if hearts lie palpitating and bleeding below, let the chariot wheels roll on, crushing and mangling them. You have mounted your car—you have sworn to rush on, with a sword in one hand and a torch in the other; and, though blood and flame may gurgle and crackle around you, your purpose must be accomplished, your mission fulfilled.

That night the midnight moon looked down on the bosom of the Ohio, as a small batteau glided swiftly over its glittering surface. A stout black man sat at one end, propelling it over the water; a white man occupied the centre, folded carefully in a cloak, for the river-damp might be dangerous at such an hour; while a negro woman crouched at the other end, with her head bowed on her knees, and dull and heavy in her ears was the sound of the dipping oar. She had no outer covering to shield her from the night-damps,—her guardian and protector had not thought of that; why should he? and, in her trepidation, remorse, and anguish, she had forgotten to wrap her shawl round her. After a while, she lifted her head and looked about her, with a wild, frightened countenance. She looked at the banks, with their dark fringe-work of swaying boughs, and shuddered,—it seemed so like the sweeping of Ildegerte's long black hair. She looked down into the river,—the deep, rippling, shining river,—and looking right up to her, through the quivering brightness; she could see her master's large, languishing blue eyes, and his long fair hair curling in the water. She looked up, and right over her head, distinctly seen in the dark-blue of the sky, she could still see those languishing eyes fixed mournfully and reproachfully on her.

She heard voices, too, calling to her from the dark places on shore. Sometimes it was the voice of Jim, saying, "Crissy, Crissy, I told you neber to run away. You'll neber see poor Jim no more!" Sometimes they were the voices of little children, crying, "Mammy, mammy, ain't you neber coming agin?" She could see their little black faces and woolly heads peeping at her through the thick, rustling foliage. Sometimes she saw something long and whitish in the distance,—it was the large wooden chest, the ark of her wealth, the garner of her gifts and treasures; and then, all at once, they all vanished, and she could see nothing but the figure seated directly in front,—stiff and perpendicular with its cold, doughy, indefinite face, and lank white hair. Splash went the oar!—on went the boat!—more and more chill blew the river breeze! Where were they bearing her to? She did not know. What was she going to do? She did not know. She only knew that she had left all she loved behind, and that a cold, dark, uncertain future was before her.

The midnight moon looked down on another scene. Ah, midnight is a solemn and mysterious hour! It was at midnight that the destroying angel flapped its raven wings over the Assyrian camp, and the dead lay in thousands beneath its folds. It was at midnight that the same commissioned angel passed over the thresholds of Egypt, and slew the first-born of Pharaoh that sat upon the throne, and the first-born of the maid-servant that was behind the mill. It is the hour when the cry of new-born life is oftenest heard in the household,—when the wail over the dying is borne on the still and dewy air.

Ildegerte sat by the couch of her husband, who, soon after the departure of Crissy, had fallen into a deep and tranquil sleep. She watched for a while his unusually gentle breathing, then, exhausted by weeping, her own eyes closed, and she too slept, with her head reclining on the arm of her chair and one hand clasping Richard's. She had seen nothing in the unwonted agitation of Crissy but deep sympathy and affection, and the last feeling of which she was conscious before falling asleep was gratitude for the possession of this humble and faithful friend. She was awakened, she scarcely knew how, but starting from her chair she uttered a piercing shriek. Richard's head was slightly raised on his left hand. There was a gurgling sound in his throat, and a red stream flowing from his mouth on the pillow, the sheet, and her own white dress. The moon was still shining, though it was higher in the heavens and did not gleam directly on the couch. She could see it all though—the drooping head, the flowing blood, the white, white face, where the hectic fire was all extinguished; and in agony and terror that baffles description she looked wildly round for Crissy—for Crissy at that moment gliding away on the shining river. She flew to the door and shrieked her name;—no answer. Her own voice echoed mournfully in the winding passage.

"Oh! Richard!" she cried, coming back and throwing herself on her knees by his side, "speak to me, look at me, tell me that you will not die and leave me here alone!"

He opened his eyes and gave her *such a look*—but he spoke not, and the red stream still kept flowing on, till the folds of her dress were all dabbled and stained.

"Oh! God!" she cried, "he *is* dying, and I am alone! What shall I do! Oh! brother, brother, would to God you were near! I *must* find somebody! He must not perish so!"

The wire which communicated with the bell in her room was broken, so that she could not ring it. The only way was to go for help herself, and leave him bleeding, dying there. Rushing through the passage, she knocked vehemently at Mrs. Softly's door, under which a light was glimmering, and opened it without waiting for admission. The lady had not retired to bed, having sacrificed sleep on the altar of benevolence and mercy. She was just about to say her prayers, with a feeling of unusual self-complacency, when the loud knocking came thunderingly to her door, it was burst open, and Ildegerte stood before her, pale as a corpse, her black hair sweeping wildly back from her brow, and her white dress crimsoned with blood.

"Mercy! mercy!" screamed Mrs. Softly, recoiling as from an avenging spirit, and spreading both hands before her face.

"For God's sake, come and help me!" cried Ildegerte, seizing her frantically by the arm and dragging her towards the door. "Richard is dying—bleeding to death! I can't find Crissy! Have you seen her? Do you know where she is? I must have her with me! I can't do without her! Dr. Darley is gone! I am all alone! Oh! my God! is there nobody to help him?"

Thus wildly ejaculating, she kept her hold on the frightened, shrinking woman, dragging her along with her into the room where Richard lay, all ghastly in his blood.

Ildegerte snatched up the lamp from the passage floor and held it over the couch. As she held it, her trembling hand grew steady, as if clenched with iron fingers. She realized at once that she was in the presence of that mighty power whose coming she had so long dreaded, and a sudden, instantaneous, awful calmness ettled on the wild tossings of her soul. She felt as one might, who, borne on the rushing wings of a whirlwind to the mountain top, looks down upon a waveless, boundless sea of glass. Her spirit was preternaturally illuminated; and, above the darkness and stillness and fearfulness, there appeared to her a glory like the body of heaven in its clearness.

"Richard! Richard!" she cried, stretching her arms upwards as if he were already ascending. "The Lord is coming. He is coming to bear thee away."

The eyes which she had thought for ever closed, opened for one moment and looked steadfastly upon her. Through the glaze and mistiness of death, a ray of heavenly joy and love flashed, quivered, and was gone. Every nerve of Ildegerte's frame thrilled, as if unsheathed, beneath that last intense, burning ray of life. Her own soul seemed leaving her body and mingling with his.

"Yes," she said faintly, "oh, yes!" and falling forward, she lay as cold and insensible as the form her failing arms vainly attempted to enfold.

When consciousness returned, the whole scene was changed. She was in another room, lying on a strange bed, and faces that looked strange and dim were looking at her through the curtains. There was a strong odour of camphor and hartshorn, and when she put up her hand to shade back the hair from her brow, she found it heavy and wet.

"Oh! it is blood!" she murmurred. "I remember it now."

Rising on her elbow, she sent her glance piercingly round the room, in search of an object which she could not find.

"What have you done with him?" she shrieked, trying to spring from the bed. "I will not be separated from him! Take me back—Crissy will take me! Where is she? Why does she stay away so long?"

Mrs. Softly, in whose bed she was laid, shrunk from the keen questioning of those wild, dark eyes. More than once during the night had her self-complacency been disturbed; and Ildegerte's imploring cry for Crissy sounded like anything but music in her ears.

"What have you done with Crissy?" repeated Ildegerte, with delirious earnestness. "Tell me, have you sent her away?"

"Mercy on me!" cried Mrs. Softly, with a kind of hysterical spasm. "What have I to do with Crissy? How should I know? I am sure I am not her mistress."

Ildegerte lay still a moment, then suddenly exclaimed—

"Where is Mr. Softly? Is he gone too?"

This abrupt and startling question entirely destroyed

the equilibrium of Mrs. Softly. Blushing and stammering, her fringeless eyes, incapable of hiding themselves, rolled from side to side as if in search of escape. Her embarrassment and evasion, the strange absence of Crissy, the absence of Mr. Softly, also, a thousand little circumstances, unnoticed before, but rising up with vividness and distinctness now, all told the story of desertion and wrong. Husband, servant, friend—all taken, and she left desolate and alone. Were God and man leagued against her? Gone was the supernatural illumination; gone the glory-vision that gilded the solemn death-hour. Gone, too, the crushing sense that followed the brief apocalypse of being under the awful pressure of God's almighty hand. It was man with whom she had now to contend—man in his littleness and spite, and all the scorn and indignation of her soul flashed up and mingled with the fast-kindling fires of delirium that gleamed in her eyes.

"*You*, *you* have done me this foul wrong!" she cried; "and may God avenge me in his own good time! When Richard and I stand with you before the judgment-seat of Christ, oh! may He remember the bitter anguish of this hour!"

Another fainting fit followed this paroxysm of agony, and thus the night waned away. The morning star—one of that glorious company that sang for joy at the birth of creation—shone in between the parted curtains, through which the moonbeams lately stole. But its voice of music was now hushed. It looked in sadness on a cold, still, shrouded form, with folded arms and moveless feet, and divinely placid brow. The lips, from which the life-stream was so lately flowing, were composed with an angelic smile, and all the charm and tenderness of youth, which disease and suffering had impaired and partially obliterated, were restored to the calm, reposing features.

Shine on, thou beauteous star! type of the bright and morning star, that rose upon a sin-darkened world. Star of the manger!—star of the cross! shine upon the night-shades of sorrow and death, and usher in the day-spring from on high!

Ildegerte lay for weeks on a sick-bed. Though her own nurse had been decoyed from her, she did not want for kindness and sympathy. Dr. Darley, who had returned, took her under his parental care, and every one lavished upon her the tenderest attention. Mr. and Mrs. Softly had left the house, suddenly discovering a deficiency in their accommodations which they had not noticed before,—and every one seemed rejoiced at their departure.

As no proof existed, but the coincident absence of Mr. Softly, that he or his wife had any agency in the flight of Crissy, nothing could be done to convict them. Indeed, the circumstance of negroes being bribed to leave their masters, was too common to excite more than a passing remark.

Ildegerte, on whose bruised and wounded heart the gentle courtesies of strangers fell softly and balmily, silent, patient, and mournful, came slowly back to life and health. Dr. Darley had written to her brother immediately on his return. He had seen the body of Richard deposited in the stranger's vault, ready to be removed where it could mingle with Southern dust. He had ministered to the young and sorely stricken widow, as physician, friend, comforter, and father.

She had another devoted friend, of whose sympathy she for some time took little heed; but, as her perceptions quickened, she was conscious that a dark form often lingered in her apartment at night, and sometimes when she awakened it was shading her pillow. At first, she would start, and utter the name of Crissy, but she soon learned to distinguish its lineaments from hers. They were very ugly, but there was a redeeming expression of honesty and sincerity, which prevented them from being altogether repulsive. It was nobody but Judy, who, after having accomplished her daily work, would put on her cleanest clothes, and steal up into the room where Crissy's young mistress lay, and watch by her, as if she were a little child.

"You are very good," said Ildegerte, one night, when she was left alone with Judy; and, forgetting that she was in a free state, she added, "To whom do you belong?"

"I belongs to a mighty mean missus, just now, honey

—dat's my own ugly, black self. I'm tired of being my own missus, dat I am. Wish you'd take me, missus—won't ask you one copper—only let me live wid you. I tells Crissy to beg you—tells her a heap of times how miserable I was—but she done run off herself, like de aggravatinest fool that ever was born."

"Poor Crissy!" said Ildegerte, gently. "I am not angry with her."

"Lord bless you, missus; if you ain't an angel, there ain't none in de kingdom come. Crissy was great big fool, dat she was; but dem white-eyed, no-account people—dey wan't no quality folks, missus—sorter bewitched her and made her uneasy and uncontented. She neber run away of her own cospiracy. Hunded times she say to me—'Judy,' ses she, 'I've got the best missus and massa in de whole universe. Dey neber gin me one single stripe, scarce eber speak de cross word or gin de cross look.' 'Crissy,' ses I, 'tank de Lord for his goodness. Good massa de great blessing. If de Lord had gin 'em me I neber run away in de life.'"

"And did you run away, poor creature, from a cruel master?" asked Ildegerte, compassionately.

"Yes, honey. He mighty bad man. Eberybody 'spise him, black and white. He treated his wife awfully. I do b'lieve she done dead of de broken heart. He got drunk and beat her, and left de black Satan mark on her bosom. No wonder he whip and beat de niggers, when he neber spare good missy. She neber 'buse us—she treat us mighty kind, but hi! didn't he make up for't, raring and taring and swearing like old Sam heself? Well, he kept on aggravating me, worse and worse, when one night he sent me tramping in de cornfield arter someting I neber left dere. I kept tinking 'bout de big riber and de free folks over de riber, and I come down to it jist as de boat gwine to cross, jist as de smoke go puff, puff in de air. Heap of folks gwine to cross. I steals in behind dem. Dat's de way I run off; but bless de heart, missus, I've seen sights since dat time. I go to white folks—ask for de work—dey say dey no use for de cornfield nigger like me. When I get work dey make me do all de drungery of de bus'ness. Den I get sick—nobody care—pay de doctor bill, pay de board. Wonder how much got left?"

Judy paused for breath, and drew the sleeve of her left arm across her face. Ildegerte felt very weary, and would gladly have been left to her own sad thoughts; but she pitied the poor, forlorn being, who knew so little how to appropriate the freedom she had won. She thought of Crissy and sighed—Crissy, who had been so tenderly cared for, now perhaps friendless and homeless.

"Won't missus let poor July wait on her? I'd go down, crawling all de way on he hands and knees, if you only let me go back to de South when you go."

At the mention of her Southern home, the vision of its sweet acacia groves, flowering vines, and bowers of roses, associated with the remembrances of her early love, rose bloomingly before her,—then she recollected her desolate widowhood, and burst into an agony of tears. To go back a widowed wife, a forsaken mistress! Oh! how sad!

"The Lord forgib me for dis!" cried Judy. "I no business to talk and make her cry—bless her tender little heart."

"Don't talk any more now," said Ildegerte, when she had subdued her emotion. "I will not forget you, and if I live to return, you shall go with me in place of poor, faithless Crissy."

It were vain to attempt a description of Judy's joy and gratitude. She laughed and cried at the same moment, then ran out of the room, that she could give more noisy vent to her feelings; then coming back immediately, rocked herself backwards and forwards, pressing the palms of her hands together and whispering "glory." Poor Judy had never known what real kindness and sympathy was, before. Under the dominion of a harsh and brutal man, the discipline of her life had developed but two traits—sullen endurance of wrong at one time, and a bitter, galling sense of them at another. Her master was cruel to her, cruel to all his negroes, but more cruel to his wife and children, because their hearts felt the wounds of his unkindness more keenly. But he was not *irresponsible* for all this. He was looked upon with the same detestation that the criminal is, who violates the immutable laws of God and man. Good men shunned his fellowship, and the social ban was on his brow.

After having gained her freedom, Judy knew not how to enjoy it. She always spoke of herself in such a depreciatory manner that people, judging her by her own estimate, thought her a "good-for-nothing nigger," and refused to employ her. When fortunate enough to obtain employment, the white servants looked upon her as an underling, and imposed upon her the most laborious and servile tasks. Crissy's description of her Southern home, of the contentment and comfort that reigned there, of the kindness of her mistress and master, and the many privileges she enjoyed, had excited an intense desire to belong to the same household. All the latent sensibilities of her nature were called forth by the sufferings of the beautiful young creature left so desolate, so lone; and she was perfectly sincere when she said that she was willing to crawl on her hands and knees, if she were only permitted to follow her, all the days of her life.

We would not depreciate the value of freedom. It is a glorious possession, but its glory depends upon the character of the nation or individual that owns it. Has it yet reflected glory or honour on the negro race? Let the voice of history answer. Turn to the islands where the emancipated slave revels in unmolested freedom. Turn to St. Domingo, where, more than sixty years since, it placed upon its brow a sable crown, and took into its hands an ebon sceptre, and abjured the dominion of the white man. Under the most propitious influences it commenced the exercise of its regal power. What aspect does its government and society now present? Lawlessness, rapine, and murder defy, with furious license, the laws of the first, and idleness, licentiousness, and blasphemy are the distinguishing features of the last. Too indolent to labour, too reckless to provide for future want, with scarcely energy enough to pluck the delicious productions of their rich tropic clime, the lords of this beautiful isle live like the brutes that perish; indulging in vices as exuberant as their vegetation, and fierce and desolating as the storms of the equinox.

Do the British West India Isles exhibit a nobler administration, a purer morality? Emancipation there has been the work of a later day, and yet the same dark scenes of violence and rapine destroy the brightness of these gems of the ocean, and change to the hue of blood their emerald dye. Unlicensed liberty riots amid the ruins of industry, order, and peace. Even the most awful visitations of heaven, to which these glowing regions are subject, have no power to check their crimes or to chasten their unhallowed spirits. Amid the convulsions of nature, the throes of the earthquake, the shrieks of the tempest, they indulge in the wildest excesses of sin, and commit the most fearful outrages. Has liberty proved a blessing to this lawless and degenerate people? Can the ark of freedom float secure over these turbid and billowy waves of passion, strife, and crime?

Could Great Britain have anticipated the result, when she lavished her hundred millions for the emancipation of these islands, so glorious in their beauty, so wondrous in their fertility, now in moral ruin and decay, would she not have appropriated it to the relief of her own starving children, of her nominally free, but literally and practically enslaved poor?

For thousands of years past, the Africans have existed in their own country as a separate people, free, as they came from the hands of God; yet what one solitary step have they taken in the great march of civilization, beneath whose majestic tramp the universe is resounding? While other nations, all around and about it, have been advancing with mighty strides, Africa has remained, *as a nation*, in the same low, degraded condition in which it pleased the Great Creator to place her. Surrounded by the gorgeous beauty and luxuriance of a tropic clime, with such magnificent materials ready for its use, can agriculture show one improvement made by its slothful hands? Do the mechanic arts owe it one invention? Does the music of manufacture echo over its rolling streams? No; in the depth and darkness of the ignorance, slothfulness, sensuality, and heathenism in which it was sunk nearly four thousand years ago, it still exists, and God has not laid bare his omnipotent arm to exalt it in the scale of being. As it was in the beginning, so it is now.

Why not arraign the Almighty with injustice and partiality, in creating one nation for glory and honour, and another for dishonour and degradation? Why not arraign Him, in whose sight all the nations of the earth are but as grasshoppers, and as a drop of water in the boundless ocean of infinitude? Him, who in the mighty work of creation, has exhibited a gradually widening and ascending glory, through all the vast range of inanimate and animated nature,—from the worm that writhes in the dust,

"To the rapt seraph that adores and burns."

Have you ever stood at the foot of the ladder, and then mounted, yea, from the lowest abyss of earth? The steps are at first muddy and slimy and loathsome, but as you go upward and upward they become golden rounds, and by and by, you can see the angels of God ascending and descending, as in the dream of the patriarch. Why this great graduated scale? Son of man, answer!—why?

But is Africa free, as a nation? Its negro population is estimated at sixty millions, and of this number, probably forty thousand are slaves,—slaves under a bondage of iron, a yoke of thorns.* The African master

* An African slave-trader had eight thousand of his countrymen in captivity, whom he was about to sell to the Portuguese and Spanish,

is indeed irresponsible; he has the power of life and death over his vassals; and when the infirmities of age throw them helpless and therefore useless on his hands, he crushes them as regardlessly as you would the reptile crawling in the dust. On the death of a king or a chief, whole hecatombs of slaves are slaughtered to bear him company in the grave, and bow to his sovereignty in the spirit-land,—thus extending their idea of servitude beyond the dividing line of time and eternity! Nor is this all; when once the thirst of blood is kindled by the sacrificial knife, they ofttimes keep the sword of massacre unsheathed till whole towns are bathed in the crimson tide! And most of these direful deeds are perpetrated in the name of religion, showing how dim and dark and awful are their ideas of God and futurity! how thick, how impenetrable the blackness that shrouds their moral and spiritual vision!

That Africa is not a fallen nation, degraded from its original position, is proved by abundant testimony. In no part of the continent, where the *native negro* exists, are there any remains of antiquity, any ruins or hieroglyphics, to prove a state of past civilization and refinement. He has left no more monuments than the beasts

whose slavers were then in port; but two English frigates, cruising along the coast, month after month, with unrelaxing vigilance, baffled his design. At length, in a fit of desperation and rage, he set fire to the building in which they were imprisoned, and all of the *eight thousand* human beings were burned to ashes. Not one escaped.

of the field, or the fowls of the air. Nature reigns there in all the grandeur and beauty of its virgin prime; but man has left no records of his plastic and improving hand. It is not so in other lands. Look at Asia,— o matter how low and degraded some of its regions may be, you will find the traces of ancient art and civilization. You will see the ruined temple, the deserted shrine, the dilapidated dwelling, telling of a once cultivated if now degenerate race. Even statuary and painting, the two most glorious handmaids of art, have left the print of their gilding footsteps, amid the desolation and gloom.

Look at our own continent. The Aborigines of America, with a few exceptions, were in as dark and savage condition as the native African. Yet, here were found similar ruins and evidences of ancient art. Indeed, wherever the white man and the bronze and red man exist, there is the indubitable stamp of present or ancient civilization; but no lingering ray of former genius or art, streaming on her night of darkness, tells that poor degraded Africa ever enjoyed a more exalted destiny.

At home, she is involved in shadows whose blackness, intense as the hue of her skin, is unrelieved by the brightness of the day-star of hope. In our own Southern land, amid lowliness and slavery, she has learned to lift up her hands unto God. Of her three million children dwelling in servitude here, more than *six hundred thousand* are the professed followers of Jesus Christ, and have enrolled their names with the sacramental host of God's elect.

Rejoice, benighted Africa! Is not He, who led the children of Israel through bondage and chains to the green borders of the promised land, leading thee also, in His own appointed way, to the glorious liberty of the children of God?

"I am the Lord and there is none else, there is no God besides me. I girded thee though thou hast not known me.

"That they may know from the rising of the sun, and from the west, that there is none beside me. I am the Lord, and there is none else.

"I form the light and create darkness; I make peace and create evil. I the Lord do all these things."

"Woe unto him that striveth with his Maker. Let the potsherd strive with the potsherds of the earth. Shall the clay say to him that fashioned it, What makest thou? or thy work, He hath no hands?"

CHAPTER XII

"WILL you go to the plantation with me to-morrow, Eulalia?" asked Moreland of his wife, a few days after the departure of Ildegerte.

"Oh, yes!" she answered with eagerness; "there is nothing I desire so much."

"As the season has advanced with uncommon rapidity," said he, "they have already commenced the picking of cotton, which will be something of a novelty to you. The fields are whitening for the harvest, and the labourers are gathering it in. But oh! my sweet Northern wife!" he added with a smile, "what a trial it will be of your love, to see your husband in the full exercise of his despotic power! You have only seen me in the household, and have thought me, perhaps, tolerably gentle. But what will you say when you see me driving the poor creatures through the cotton rows with a knotted lash, and making the white bolls red with their dripping blood? Can you love me still, and plead the force of custom in my behalf?"

"You speak mockingly. I fear no such test of the strength of my affection. You allude to what I once believed, to what so many of my Northern friends still believe; and I cannot wonder so much at the scornful smile that curls your lip. I know you too well now to credit such enormities. How I wish father were here, even for a little while! Cannot we induce him to come?"

"I hope so. I hope to see all your family, my Eulalia, gathered round your Southern home. Reuben is to be a lawyer. The professions are all crowded at the North; here he will have a wider scope and more abundant materials to work upon. Plenty of litigation here. I promised Dora to build her a bower of roses, and people it with canaries and mocking birds, expressly for her accommodation. Mark my prophecy, Eulalia. You will have all your family here, true-hearted Southerners, by and by."

"And Betsy with them?" said Eulalia, smiling.

"Oh, yes! I plighted my vows to Betsy, before our marriage, and I must not falsify them. She is an honest, industrious creature, worth a dozen of our pampered negroes. You must have perceived, even now, how much heavier the burthen of servitude is at the

North than here, where the labour is divided among so many."

"Yes! in the town; but I suppose on the plantations they must work very hard indeed, even when they have humane masters and overseers."

"You shall judge for yourself. They have their ap pointed tasks, and then, if they choose, they labour for themselves. There is one trait in the negro character of which you may not be conscious. You cannot make them work habitually beyond their strength. You can get a certain amount of labour out of them, and beyond that they will not go. Masters and overseers, having learned this fact from experience, seldom attempt to push them over this boundary. If they do, they meet with an obstinate resistance which coercion never can overcome. This peculiarity is one of the negro's greatest safeguards from the requirements of selfish power. The self-interest of his employer is enlisted on his side, and we all know what a powerful principle it is. A certain amount of labour is a blessing to every human being. That God willed it to be so, is proved by the withering curse of ennui, resting on the idler. You think, perhaps, it must be a curse to work under the burning sun of our sultry clime. It would be for me; it would be for the white man; but the negro, native of a tropic zone, and constitutionally adapted to its heat, luxuriates in the beams which would parch us with fever. I have studied him physiologically as well as mentally and morally, and I find some remarkable characteristics, perhaps unknown to you. In the first place, his skull has a hardness and thickness far greater than our own, which defy the arrowy sunbeams of the South. Then his skin, upon minute examination, is very different from ours, in other respects as well as colour. It secretes a far greater quantity of moisture, which, like dew, throws back the heat absorbed by us. I could mention many more peculiarities which prove his adaptedness to the situation he occupies, but I fear I weary you, Eulalia."

"Oh, no! I have heard the subject discussed since my earliest recollection, yet I acknowledge my profound ignorance. Every circumstance you mention is new to me."

"No man living," added Moreland, with a countenance of deep and earnest thought, "regards the negro with more kindness and sympathy than myself. I would sooner give my right hand to the flames than make it the instrument of cruelty and oppression to them. They are entwined with my affections as well as my interests. I was born and brought up in their midst, and they are as much incorporated with my being as the trees which have shaded my infancy and childhood, and the streams on whose banks I have been accustomed to wander. I never dreamed, when a boy, that it was possible to separate my existence from theirs, any more than I could flee from the shadows of night. How little do the people of the North reflect upon all this! How little do they understand the almost indissoluble ties that bind us to each other! And yet," he cried, excited to greater warmth as he proceeded, "strong as are these ties, and dear as are these interests, I can never look upon the negro as my equal in the scale of being. He has a heart as kind and affectionate as my own, a soul as immortal, and so far I claim him as my brother; but he is not my equal physically or mentally, and I do not degrade him or exalt myself by this admission. When Africa, as a nation, stands side by side with the other nations of the world in the arts and sciences, in literature and genius, by its own inherent energies and powers, then I will subscribe to this equality, but not till then. God has not made all men equal, though men wiser than God would have it so. Inequality is one of Nature's laws. The mountains and the valleys proclaim it. It is written on the firmament of heaven. It is felt in the social system, and always will be felt, in spite of the dreams of the enthusiast or the efforts of the reformer."

Moreland paused. The shadow of a great thought rested on his brow. Eulalia looked anxiously towards him. He smiled.

"You must not mind me when I fall into revery. It is my habit. But come, my Eulalia,"—there was inexpressible grace and tenderness in the manner in which he thus expressed his ownership—never had her name sounded so sweet, never had the possessive pronoun seemed so significant or appropriate—"sing me one of your own charming songs. I have heard a great deal of music, but never anything that thrilled my heart like the voice of the village chorister."

Eulalia looked at the superb piano that stood near, silent beneath its crimson cover, at the guitar swathed in green, leaning against the wall, instruments which the fingers of Claudia had once swept, and a blush rose to her cheeks. Moreland interpreted the glance and blush.

"Will my wife become a pupil, for my sake?" asked he, drawing her towards him. "Will she learn the use of those now silent keys and loosened chords?"

"Gladly, most gladly," she answered. "I have always sighed for such advantages, but I never expressed the wish. I knew my father toiled to supply us with the comforts of life. How could I be selfish enough to beg for its luxuries?"

"Well, as soon as we return from the plantation we will arrange our plans. You shall have the best of music masters, and I know you will make a marvellous pupil. But after all there is no instrument comparable to the God-tuned human voice!"

As soon as Eulalia began to sing, the little Effie came flying in, and nestling in her arms, listened, as if an angel were singing. She sat with her head thrown slightly back, her red lips parted, and her wildly brilliant eyes suffused with a glistening moisture.

"More!" she cried, when Eulalia paused. "Effie good girl, when mamma sing."

"*She* will make a musician," said Eulalia, turning o her husband, while she fondly caressed the child. "I never saw so young a child exhibit such a passionate love of music. Several times, when she has stubbornly resisted my authority, I have subdued her into the gentlest obedience, by singing a few simple strains."

"I do not wonder at it," said Moreland, gazing with passionate tenderness on the lovely young stepmother, cradling in her arms the brilliant little sprite, whom she was teaching him to love. "I am sure if I were in the wildest paroxysm of anger, your voice would soothe me into peace."

"But you never have such paroxysms," said she, with a smile; "so I shall have no opportunity of proving my power on you."

"You do not know me, my Eulalia. My bosom is the couchant lion's lair."

"I have never seen you angry. I think the lion must be very tame. I do not fear it."

"You need not," said he, looking fixedly upon he sweet, confiding, angelic countenance; "you could bind it with a silken thread. I remember, when a boy, reading about a holy virgin going on a pilgrimage through the wilderness, and the wild beasts hushed their howlings, and crouched submissively at her feet. The serpent that came hissing from the crevices of the rocks, curled in loving folds innnoxious in her path; and the birds flew down and nestled in her bosom. You have taught me the meaning of that allegory, my gentle wife."

He stooped down, kissed her, and left the room. He seemed moved, agitated. There was a world of sensibility in the darkening lustre of his eyes. She knew he had been thinking of Claudia, whose name had never been breathed between them since she had taken her place as the mistress of his home. A thousand times had it hovered on her lips, yet she had never dared to utter it; and the past seemed a sealed book to him. The servants had evidently been instructed not to talk of their former mistress; and Eulalia had too much delicacy to question them on a forbidden theme. Sometimes Kizzie would say, looking at Effie,

"Just see, ain't she the living military of her mother? —them black eyes, and that red, saucy mouth of hers. Bless your soul, Kizzie!" clapping her hand over her own broad lips, "what that you talking 'bout? What your Mars. Russell tell you? Poor master! he had a heap of trouble!—all over now, tho', bless a Lord!"

Eulalia well knew that Kizzie longed to relate all that she knew; and, had she questioned her, she would have considered herself bound to obey her mistress, even in opposition to her master's commands, for had he not told her himself, to obey her in all things? But Eulalia's respect for her husband equalled her love, and she considered his domestic misfortunes too sacred for curiosity. Yet the image of Claudia was for ever flitting before her. She would have given anything for one glimpse of the face, the haunting face, her imagination had drawn. It was not jealousy she felt, for she was sure of her husband's undivided love; but he had loved and wedded another, and death had not broken the nuptial bond. *She* lived!—where, how near, she knew not. She had a conviction that they must one day meet, and a thrill of indescribable emotion penetrated her, at the thought. She knew that, whatever were the circumstances of the separation, Moreland was not the offending party; but she also knew, by the dark expression that sometimes swept over his countenance, how much and deeply he must have suffered.

"Oh, never, never may he suffer through me!" was her soul's most fervent prayer; "let sorrow, danger, death come, if God will, but let our hearts still be one. Welcome any thing, every thing but estrangement from him!"

The next morning, at an early hour, they commenced their journey to the plantation. It was a two days' ride, and Kizzie made sumptuous preparations for their comfort. She packed up the greatest quantity of cake, biscuits, cold ham, and tongue, for their wayside luncheons, not forgetting the generous cordial and the sparkling wine.

"You must think, Kizzie, that your mistress and myself are blest with fine appetites," said Moreland, laughing.

"Ain't I going too, Mars. Russell, and ain't Miss Effie to be provided for? Besides, one likes to give a bit to the driver, you know, master."

"Is it your wish to take the child?" asked he, in some surprise, turning to Eulalia.

"Certainly—that is, if you have no objection."

"Oh, no! but will she not trouble you?"

"Even if she did, I would not like to leave her behind."

"Then I will go on horseback, as your escort. Kizzie will occupy a very comfortable space in the carriage, and Effie frisks about like a little monkey, wherever she is."

"Let us leave her by all means, then," said Eulalia. "I did not think of its depriving you of a seat. How inconsiderate I am!'

"Effie, my darling," added she, taking her up in her arms, "I am sorry we cannot take you; but Aunt Kizzie will be very good to you while we are gone. And *you* will be very good, will you not?"

"No! I won't be good! I'll go too!" cried the child, struggling and kicking like an angry kitten. "I won't stay! Kizzie sha'n't stay!"

The little creature's eyes actually blazed on her step-mother.

"Take her away, Kizzie," said her father; "she is a perfect little tigress. It is no wonder," muttered he, in a low voice, and with a reddening face.

"Wait a moment," said Eulalia, entreatingly; "you know you said I could tame the beasts of the field."

Then whispering in Effie's ear a few words which seemed to have the effect of magic, while she bent upon her her soft, serene, dark eyes; the child remained perfectly still a moment, while the angry crimson faded from its cheek, then, looking up with the gentleness of a lamb, lisped—

"I had rather not, mamma!"

"Well! you are certainly a female Van Amburg," said Moreland, wondering at the sudden transformation from passion to gentleness; "let her go, Eulalia. Keep her with you, by all means. I really prefer going on horseback; I do not feel half a man pent up in a carriage. Nothing but your company could reconcile me to it, and that I can enjoy through the open windows."

Effie, wild with delight, was perched upon the seat before the others were half ready, swinging her little gipsy straw hat by one string, till it looked like a twisted cord. It took a long time for Aunt Kizzie to deposit her "goodies," as she called them, to her own satisfaction, in the carriage-pockets and by-places; and it took her a long time to go up and down the steps of the carriage, as she had a good deal to carry besides her bundles and bottles. Albert, who stood near, holding his master's high-mettled and prancing steed, laughed at the audible grunt, by which she relieved her fatigue, every time she stooped. He laughed, too, to see little Effie punch her with her feet, as she tucked away the packages; but he laughed still more, when Kizzie sailed majestically by him, pretending to be angry and consequential, her face beaming with good-nature the whole time.

When Eulalia was about to take her place at Effie's side, she was astonished at seeing two nice pillows on the seat.

"Why are these here?" she asked. "I am no invalid, Aunt Kizzie, to require propping. Please take them out."

"Wait a little, missus, while I tells you the raal reason. When we stops at night, you won't find a pillow-slip fit to scrape your feet on, let alone your honey-sweet face. There ain't no quality folks at the stopping-places, and the piny-woods people have mighty curous ways of doing things, I tell you, missus."

"You had better let Kizzie arrange everything; you can rely on her judgment and experience,' said Moreland, mounting the beautiful horse, whose caracoling and prancing made Eulalia tremble for the fearless rider. "You are not familiar with the phases of backwoods life, Eulalia. They will at least have the freshness of novelty."

While the inspiring breeze of morn was blowing, and the dew yet glittered on the grass of the wayside, their ride was delightful and exhilarating. The bright-green tassels of the silver pine showered odours as they waved above them; the sturdy blackjack, the graceful willow oak, the shining-leaved magnolia, alternately shaded them from the sunshine, and thrust, here and there, a projecting bough into the carriage window as they passed. Eulalia's spirits were so elastic, she could have bounded, like Effie, to catch the festoons of hoary moss that hung in gray loops from the branches; and when the noon-day-heat made the sandy road burn under the horses' fetlocks, and flecks of foam whiten the rich, mahogany-coloured skin, and they all stopped near a beautiful spring, that gushed right out of a rock, and sat down on the mossy ground, while Kizzie fumbled after the *goodies*, and spread them out on a broad, flat stone, close to the spring, and put the bottles in the bubbling water to cool, Eulalia's rapture burst forth in joyous ejaculations. Moreland was charmed with her child-like enthusiasm, and dipping the silver cup, which the aristocratic Kizzie had not failed to bring, in the heart of the fountain, he drank sportively to the health of his Northern bride.

"Stay a moment," he said, tossing the silver cup on the grass. "I must teach you how to drink from a greenwood goblet."

Then gathering some large, fresh, glabrous oak leaves,

he wove them together in a mysterious manner, so as to form a rural cup. Eulalia declared she had never tasted a draught so delicious or food so refreshing; while Kizzie looked on with a comfortable, motherly, liberal expression of countenance, as if she had not only provided the feast, but the spring, the greenwood, and the covering heavens themselves, for their accommodation. An air of serene repose was diffused over every object, and every sound breathed of tranquillity. The water murmured and gurgled as sweetly and softly as if it feared to disturb the shadows that played upon its bosom. The trees dipped lightly their long, swaying branches in the fountain, and the low, musical buzz of insect life gave one the idea of an all-pervading, void-filling, infinite existence. The horses stood quietly feeding in the shade, wrinkling their glossy sides and flapping their tails, as the flies lit upon their moist hides; the driver reclined lazily near them, trailing his whip in the water with an occasional glance at the sun to see how late it was getting; and, fast asleep on the shady grass, with her little gipsy hat lying by her side, her cheek flushed with heat and moist with perspiration, Effie presented the anomalous picture of a noonday fairy. Moreland and Eulalia sat side by side, feeling that exquisite sense of heart-communion which silence only can express. They sat so still, so near, they could hear the beating of each other's hearts, and there was no need of any other language. Eulalia remembered the hour when she thus sat on the deck of the steamboat, in the hush of the moon-light, wishing she could glide on for ever over the shining river. Even so she wished she could sit for ever, indulging in that quiet dream of happiness in the midst of the languishing brightness of noon; but the journey was before them, and after a little bustle and considerable *Aunt Kizzieism*, they again started. After travelling a few miles they began to ascend a long, sandy, winding hill, and so slow was their progress, the wheels sometimes appeared to stand still. Moreland rode close to the carriage, keeping up a gay conversation with Eulalia, in which Aunt Kizzie occasionally joined with the freedom of a privileged member of the family, when they caught a glimpse of a carriage slowly descending, and Moreland turned his horse into a side path, to give the two carriages room to pass each other. Eulalia looked out with the interest one feels in meeting strangers on a solitary road, where the sight of a log-cabin is an event worth remembering, and even a grave-stone has a social aspect.

A lady sat lolling indolently on the back seat, with her arms folded in a drapery of black lace. She was young and handsome; but what chiefly distinguished her was a pair of large, brilliant black eyes, that glanced carelessly and haughtily towards the travellers she was about to meet. The moment Eulalia met that cold, bright, haughty glance, she started as if it had pierced her bosom, and leaned against the window side, keeping her own eyes fixed upon the stranger with an intense, magnetic gaze. She saw the brilliant, haughty orbs turn from her to Moreland and suddenly flash up like burning gas, while every feature expressed scorn, hatred and revenge. Never had she seen such an expression on woman's face, and her own turned pale as marble as she gazed. She looked at her husband; he was lividly pale, and his lips had the rigidness of stone. Again the scorching glance flashed back into the carriage and riveted itself on Eulalia with withering scrutiny. Effie, with the eager curiosity of childhood, stood up on tiptoe, and, leaning over Eulalia's lap, exclaimed in a clear, ringing, decided tone, peculiar to herself,

"Let *me* see, mamma."

At sight of the child, at the sound of its voice, an instantaneous change passed over the lady's countenance. The proud, scornful, defying lip quivered with sudden emotion; tenderness, anguish, and remorse swept in clouds over her haughty features. The arms so disdainfully, yet gracefully folded, opened as if to clasp her to her breast,—but, with one more revolution of the wheels, it all fled like a vision. Where the dark, bright, avenging angel or demon, whichever it was, appeared, there was empty space, with the white glare of the sand below.

When they reached the summit of the hill, the driver stopped the panting horses to give them breath, and Moreland approached the carriage; the shadow of the thunder-cloud yet lingered on his brow.

"Eulalia," he exclaimed, startled by her deadly paleness, "Are you ill? Are you faint?"

She shook her head, but so great was her agitation her lips faded to a pale ashy hue.

"Give her some wine, Kizzie! She *is* faint! She *will* faint! There is no water to be had!"

Kizzie fumbled in the pocket for the silver cup, declaring in her trepidation, that she believed "her fingers was all thumbs." Moreland, with a gesture of impatience, threw his bridle reins to the driver, and, jumping into the carriage, placed Effie in Kizzie's lap, seated himself by Eulalia and put his arm around her.

"It is all over now," she said, the cold, benumbing sensation passing away. "I am sorry to have troubled you so."

"Troubled!" he repeated. "Don't talk in that way, my Eulalia, when you know I would lay down my life at any moment to save you from suffering."

Yes! she knew he would—she had not one doubt of his exclusive devotion to herself,—then why the sick ening anguish she had just endured? Was it jealousy of the past or dread of the future? or were the mingling shades of both rolling darkly over her soul? She had been so happy a few moments before. Why had this woman come in her dark, splendid, terrible beauty, between her and her happiness? Yet, had she not yearned to behold her with strong, irrepressible desire? Yes! but now that desire was fulfilled, she would give anything to shut out the image of that flashing, passionate, haunting countenance. Ashamed of her want of self-possession, she raised her eyes and met those of her husband fixed so earnestly and sadly upon her, that every other feeling was swallowed up in sympathy for him. What untold agony *he* must have suffered, and yet he cared only for her, foolish, childish, selfish as he must think her! Sure it was *her* place to soothe and comfort him, and beguile him of the remembrance of his wrongs.

"I am better," said she, with a smile; "nay, I am quite well. You must not feel anxious if I do look pale now and then. You shall find that I am a heroine, for all that."

"I believe you," he replied, his grave, sad countenance lighting up in her smile. "Kizzie, supposing you take my seat on horseback and let me lounge in the carriage a while?"

"Oh, master, wouldn't I look funny on that are fine beast? Wouldn't young missus laugh till she done dead?"

"A merry laugh would do her no hurt;—but you ride like an Amazon, Kizzie. Come, I am not afraid to trust you!"

Eulalia thought him in jest, but Kizzie knew that he was in earnest, and prepared to obey with great good-nature. She had no objection to stretch her limbs and carry on a social chat with the driver. She had been brimming with indignation at the sight of Claudia, whose *evil eye* she had no doubt had made her young mistress sick, and she was bursting to have a talk with some body.

"Let me ride with mammy," exclaimed Effie, springing up with elfish lightness; "I so tired sitting here—I most sick!"

"Yes, Mars. Russell, let me have little missy right here," said Kizzie, who had mounted the spirited animal from the steps of the carriage with an agility that surprised Eulalia, considering her rheumatic affection. The next moment Effie lighted on the pommel of the saddle, like a bright-winged bird, and burst into wild, exulting laughter. Nor did she laugh alone—for Kizzie's figure did form an extraordinary contrast to her young master's. She looked very much like a large ball of India rubber, with a butterfly sticking to it; but the ball, though it seemed to roll about, this side and that, and threaten to tumble off, kept its place, as if it knew what it was about. It bounded up and down, when the horse pranced, as he always would when any one first mounted his back, but it settled in the right spot, and in spite of a quivering, jelly-like motion, maintained its equilibrium to the last.

"Laugh away, young missus," said she, "it does me good to hear you. Mars. Russell put me here purpose to make you laugh. What I going to do with this here strap? Can't get my big foot where master does his! Hi—see how Kizzie's long heel stick out!"

As she was not encumbered with long, flowing skirts, the form of her feet and ankles were liberally displayed. Eulalia could not help laughing, and the horse, turning his head entirely round and gazing at his new rider, seemed to enter into the spirit of the change, and twinkling his eyes merrily, jogged on, like a cornfield animal, accommodating itself to circumstances.

Moreland had accomplished his object. He had diverted the thoughts of Eulalia from the dark channel in which they were flowing, and he was left alone at her side. Then he opened to her his whole heart, and told her all the history of the past, without any reservation. From the perfect confidence of this hour, "that perfect love which casteth out fear" was born in Eulalia's bosom. She felt as one does, who, after gazing in quaking terror on the ghost which imagination has created, finds it, on approach, a mass of shadows or a bundle of moonbeams. The interdicted name, the forbidden subject, the deserted dwelling, are always invested with a dread charm, which vanishes with familiarity. While there is one forbidden theme to a husband and wife, it will rise between them a cold, icy barrier, freezing by slow degrees the living warmth of love. It was well that Moreland felt the truth of this in the morning glow of their wedded life, when the dew was on the flower and the freshness on the leaf and the glory in the sky. It kept off the mildew and the cloud. It kept away the tempest and the whirlwind.

"Is this where we are to rest for the night?" asked Eulalia, as they stopped about twilight at the door of a log-cabin, whose dark and dingy walls were unrelieved by a single pane of glass, the light and air being admitted through wooden shutters.

"Even so," answered her husband, as he assisted her to alight. "Are you sorry you came?"

"Oh, no! it makes me think a little of poor Nancy's cottage, only hers has glass windows."

"Are you very tired, Kizzie?" said she, hearing several expressive *grunts*, as she descended from the saddle, fearing she had purchased the happinesss of her husband's company at the expense of Kizzie's comfort.

"I does feel sorter bruised, missus, but not more than I can bear; you see I ain't used to master's saddle no how, and it makes me a little oneasy and discomforted. Never mind, missus; if you and Mars. Russell is satisfied, Kizzie won't complain."

Though it was a warm evening, a bright lightwood fire burned in the large tumble-down looking chimney. It was the lamp that lighted the cabin, and displayed, in its broad illumination, the persons of its occupants. A man, hard-favoured and sun-browned, who had evidently been at work in the field, sat in his shirt-sleeves, smoking a long pipe, in the back-door. A woman, nearly as brown as himself, dressed in the coarsest home-spun, stood looking out of the front window, while two girls, one about twelve, the other fifteen, with short, thick, coarse brown hair hanging in masses over their eyes, while dark calico sunbonnets covered their heads, were peeping over her shoulders. They all appeared very clean and tidy, though rough and uncouth. Their frocks were of a dark indigo colour, and they all wore dark-blue woollen mitts, with long points reaching over the backs of their hands. Why they were so careful of these members, which were of the hue of mahogany, was a mystery, especially the two girls, whose feet were bare as Eve's were in Paradise. Their costume gave Eulalia such an impression of warmth, that, combined with the bright blaze and long wreaths of blue smoke curling up round the warm, brown face in the back door, made her feel very sultry and uncomfortable. She was sure she would melt and suffocate; but she was very much amused, notwithstanding, with the rustic greeting that welcomed them. Her husband was received as a known guest, and evidently an honoured one. Aunt Kizzie was also recognised kindly; but on her, as the Squire's new lady, they bestowed most abundant attention. They came up to her, extending their hands in a straight line, while the long blue tongues on the back of their hands flapped up and down, and gave her the true, hearty, backwood gripe. Then the two girls walked around her, looking at her admiringly through their short, thick hair, and taking an inventory of her dress. The little Effie too received her due share of admiration, and, being a child, they ventured to approach her, as she sat enthroned on Aunt Kizzie's lap, and even slipped their fingers into her coal black ringlets. But the little lady was tired, sleepy, and consequently cross and inaccessible. Nothing could exceed the haughtiness with which she repelled their advances.

"Get away!" she cried, drawing up her right shoulder and pushing them with her feet; "you too ugly—you shan't touch me!"

"Shame, little missy," said Kizzie, gathering the offending feet in her black fingers—"Is that the way quality ladies talk?"

Eulalia, though shocked at the child's imperious rudeness, knew it was not the moment to correct it. She thought of the eyes, so full of pride, disdain, and vindictiveness—eyes that seemed burning on her still, and trembled to think that those dark passions might have been transmitted to the bosom of her offspring. Then she remembered the look of yearning anguish she had cast upon her child, the opening arms, the bending figure, and intense pity quenched her aversion.

"You had better put Effie to bed, Kizzie," said she, looking round the room, with a vague feeling of anxiety about their accommodations for the night. Moreland was watching her bewildered, half-frightened glance, and could not forbear smiling. There seemed to be but that one room in the whole house, for the rafters overhead indicated that there was no upper story. There were four beds in the room, one in each corner, two of them covered with white counterpanes, having a deep border of netting, and the two others with patchwork quilts. The corners occupied by the white beds were evidently considered the guest-chambers of the establishment, and in one of these Kizzie deposited the now sleeping Effie.

Eulalia had reason to thank the providing care of Kizzie, in having supplied them so liberally with home dainties, for she could taste nothing at supper but a cup of milk. Tumblers and goblets were unknown luxuries to this family of primitive habits. A large dish of bacon and greens, flanked by tremendous hoe-cakes, was the crowning glory of the table. A remnant of a cold sweet-potato pie, and some gingerbread cakes, as large as cheeses, were extra flourishes of gentility, introduced in honour of the guests. But what chiefly attracted Eulalia's admiration was the candlestick which dignified the centre of the table—a large gourd, with a tall, majestic handle, truncated to receive a dim compound of beeswax and tallow, stood upright and towering as Cleopatra's Needle, giving an occasional contemptuous sputter, and shooting upwards a long, fierce, fiery wick.

"Come, squire," said the lord of the feast, "set yourself convenient, and lay to and help yourself. We don't stand for ceremony in the piny woods—not a bit. Your lady there don't eat one mouthful. I 'spose she ain't used to such coarse vittles. She don't look as if she was. I tell you what, squire, you oughter leave her in the woods a while, and let her scuffle about with my gals a while. Then she'd have an appetite. See how brown and strong they look!"

"I do sometimes envy the labouring man his keen appetite and sound sleep," answered Moreland; "but we indulged in too late a luncheon to do justice to your hospitality."

"Well, squire, it's the truth," said the farmer, laying down his knife and fork, and using his sleeve for a napkin; "there's nothing like work to make a man contented. I wouldn't changes places with nobody—I wouldn't give a snap for a fine house. What's the use, I want to know, of so much paint and white-wash? It just shows the dirt. Who wants to sit on anything better than a good splint-bottomed chair? Not I. As for eating, I wouldn't give this bacon and greens for all your stuffed nonsense and made up-dishes. It's a great thing, squire, to know what you're eating. Here's my old woman and I hain't had a day's sickness, to speak of, since we was married, and the gals are as tough and healthy as all out doors."

"Do you never have chills and fevers?" asked Moreland.

"Pho! what's that? We don't call that sickness. Shake a little one day, up and smart as a pipestem the next. I mean your right down, regular, doctor-bill sickness, that takes all a man earns to pay for. There's only one thing I want, and that is, to give my gals an eddication. I am going to send them to school next year, if I have a good crop this. Eddication is a beautiful thing in a woman; it don't matter so much in a man, 'cause he's got more natteral smartness; but it does set a woman off mightily. My old woman, here, is a right good scholar. She can write as good a handwrite as anybody need want to see."

The good lady really blushed at this compliment from her husband, but was evidently pleased and grateful. Eulalia began to like her new acquaintances, for their homely good sense, contentment, and appreciation of each other. There was one fact that impressed her as very strange. The father spoke as if his daughters had their education yet to begin, though the eldest was fast approaching the years of womanhood. She thought of the superior advantages of the children of New England, where the blessings of education are as diffusive as the sunbeams of heaven, gilding the poor and lowly as well as the rich.

"Are you very weary?" asked Moreland of his wife, after the supper-table was removed and the farmer had smoked another pipe.

"No! I have been so much interested in studying character," she remarked in a low voice, "that I have quite forgotten my fatigue."

"Let us walk, then, awhile. The night is mild and starry, and the scenery around wild and picturesque."

Knowing the early habits of this class of people, he knew they would have an opportunity of retiring during their ramble, to their own peculiar corners, and that poor Eulalia would thus be saved from unspeakable embarrassment.

They extended their walk to a spring, whose gushings made soft music in the ear of night. The back-wood farmer always pitches his tent near some welling spring, where his horses and his cattle can be abundantly watered and his own thirst slaked at will. A beautiful grove of willow oaks surrounded it, and a sweet, low, quivering sound went through their branches.

"What a lonely life this family must lead!" said Eulalia; "no neighbours, no friends, no intercourse with society, save what the passing stranger permits them to enjoy. It seems like living in a wilderness."

"And so it is; and yet, you see, this life has its own peculiar enjoyments. You must recollect that it is comparatively but a few years since the red man was lord of these woods and plains, and the wild beast made its lair in their shades. This man, energetic and intelligent, is breaking in, as they say, a new portion of the country, and by and by the wild places will show the beauty of cultivation. He has already made money enough to purchase some negroes, who assist him in the field, he being chief workman, as well as overseer. His children, I doubt not, will be rich, and be associated with the magnates of the land. Our social system is like the tree now bending over you, Eulalia,—its roots, without grace or beauty, are hidden in the earth, from which they derive strength and support; its hardy trunk rises, without ornament, brown and substantial; then the branches extend, green with foliage, and the birds of the air make their nests among the leaflets. Hark! there is a mocking-bird singing now."

Yes! the nightingale of the South was just over their heads, and rills of melody, clear, silvery, liquid as the waters of the spring, came flowing down, and bubbled and sparkled around them. It sounded as if a whole orchestra of birds were practising their wild overtures and cavatinas for a great concert, so rich and varied were the notes. Surely such waves of music could not roll from one little, slender, feathered throat! Ah! the mocking-bird is the Jenny Lind of the wild-wood, and her single voice has echoed through the world!

A very different serenade greeted them when they returned into the cabin. A deep, sonorous bass was rising from under one of the patchwork bed-covers,—showing that the weary were resting from their labours. Every one was wrapped in profound slumber. Kizzie, whose pallet was spread upon the floor by the side of little Effie, was nodding in a chair to some invisible potentate, while waiting for her young mistress to retire. In spite of the novelty of her situation, and the loud, stentorian breathing within the room, Eulalia was soon wandering in the far-off land of dreams. When she awoke, the patchwork quilts were smoothly spread, the workman abroad in the field, his wife busy with her household duties, with the family poke on the top of her head; the girls, in their long-pointed blue mitts and dark calico sun-bonnets, seeming ready for any emergency; and Effie, bright as the morning, frolicking all over Aunt Kizzie. Moreland had gone out to meet the sun, whose coming was heralded by banners of crimson and gold unrolled in the East. Eulalia's toilet was soon completed, but when she looked round in perplexity for a ewer, that she might wash her face and hands, Kizzie made mysterious signs for her to come to the door.

"You see, missus," she whispered, "these is nobody but Georgia crackers; they just lives any which way; the way they washes, they pours water out of the gourd on their hands, and then scrubs their faces. I brought some towels, and if you'll just step down to the spring I'll bring 'em, and little missy, too,—there's where massa washed hisself."

Eulalia was quite delighted with Aunt Kizzie's arrangement, and felt the joy of childhood glowing in her heart, as she bathed her face in the cool, gurgling fountain, and moistened the soft waves of her dark-brown hair. It brought a pale but beautiful bloom to her cheek, which the master of the house complimented, by telling her she looked 'most as well as his gals did.

"You going to put me horseback to-day, Mars. Russell?" asked Kizzie, putting on a rueful look, when the horses and carriage were at the door.

"No, Kizzie. I think that would be too great a task."

"Lordy, master, I didn't mean that. I mean you going to ride in the carriage this time?"

"I believe I will ride in the open air this morning," he replied, to the great joy of Kizzie, who had an impression that she did not appear to particular advantage as an equestrian, and who was not partial to the exercise in general.

The parting benediction of the family was a cordial "wish you well" and "be sure and come agin;" and it probably had more heart in it than the graceful adieus and *au revoirs* of the fashionable world.

It was just before sunset when they arrived at the plantation, and Moreland welcomed Eulalia to her country home.

And now for the first time she realized that she was the wife of a Southern planter.

All around, far as the eye could reach, rich, rolling fields of cotton, bearing the downy wealth of the South, stretched out a boundless ocean of green, spotted with white, like the foam of the wave. Long rows of whitewashed cabins, extending back of the central building, whose superior style of architecture distinguished it as the master's mansion, exhibited some black sign at every door, to show the colour of the occupants. Though it wanted something of the usual time, as Moreland wished Eulalia to witness a true plantation scene before the duskiness of twilight, he ordered the bugle blast to sound which called the labourers home, and its echoes rolled ver the whitened plains with clear and sweet reverbera- ions. Soon, returning in grand march from the fields, came the negroes, poising on their heads immense baskets, brimming with the light and flaky cotton. Little children, looking very much like walking semicolons, toddled along, balancing their baskets also, with an air of self-importance and pride. Eulalia gazed with a kind of fascination on the dark procession, as one after another, men, women, and children, passed along to the gin house to deposit their burdens. It seemed as if she were watching the progress of a great eclipse, and that soon she would be enveloped in total darkness. She was a mere speck of light, in the midst of shadows. How easy it would be to extinguish her! She recollected all the horrible stories she had heard of negro insurrections, and thought what an awful thing it was to be at the mercy of so many slaves, on that lonely plantation. When she saw her husband going out among them, and they all closed round, shutting him in as with a thick cloud, she asked herself if he were really safe. Safe! Napoleon, in the noonday of his glory, surrounded by the national guard, was not more safe—more honoured or adored. They gathered round him, eager to get within reach of his hand, the sound of his voice, the glance of his kind, protecting, yet commanding eye. More like a father welcomed by his children than a king greeted by his subjects, he stood, the centre of that sable ring. Eulalia thought she had never seen him look so handsome, so noble, so good. She had never felt so proud of being his wife. An impression of his power, gently used, but still manifest, produced in her that feeling of awe, softened by tenderness, so delicious to the loving, trusting heart of woman. He appeared to her in a new character. She had known him as the fond, devoted bridegroom; now he was invested with the authority and responsibility of a master. And she must share that responsibility, assist him in his duties, and make the welfare, comfort, and happiness of these dependent beings the great object of her life. He had twined round her the roses of love, but she was not born to sit idly in a bower and do nothing for those who were toiling for her. He had adorned her with the gems of wealth, but she must not live in selfish indulgence while the wants of immortal souls were pressing upon her, while the solemn warning "Thou must give an account of thy stewardship" was ringing in her soul.

Never before had she made an elaborate comparison between the white and the black man. She had so often heard her father say that they were born equal—equal in mind, body, and soul, having only the accidental difference of colour to mark them—that she had believed it, and loathed herself for the feeling of superiority over them which she could not crush. But as she looked at her husband, standing in their midst, the representative of the fair sons of Japheth, wearing on his brow the signet of a loftier, nobler destiny, every lineament and feature expressive of intellect and power, and then at each of that dark, lowly throng, she felt a conviction that freedom, in its broadest latitude, education, with its most exalted privileges, could never make them equal to him.

Gradually they dispersed to their several cabins, and Moreland rejoined his wife.

"To-morrow, I will take you to their cabins," he said. "They are all anxious to see their young mistress."

"Why not now?"

"You are too weary."

"No, I am not. I have been watching their reception of you with such interest! Oh! my husband! I never dreamed that slavery could present an aspect so tender and affectionate! What a kind, indulgent master you must be, to inspire such warm attachment! Ah! I fear there are not many such!"

"Sceptic in all goodness but mine! That is not right, my Eulalia. I must not be complimented at the expense of my brethren. I am no better, perhaps not as good as the majority of masters, as you will find out, after having dwelt longer at the South. The cruel ones you will not see, as we have no fellowship with them. I would far sooner make the negro my social companion than the man who abuses him. Are not those cotton fields beautiful? Do you see the white blossoms blooming on the surface, some of them shaded with a pale golden tinge, others with rose colour, while the snow-white tufts are bursting from the bolls below? Did you ever see a Northern flower-garden half as beautiful? Do you say you are not tired? Let us go then to some of the cabins. I acknowledge I am impatient to introduce to them my sweet Northern bride."

We will not attempt to describe all the Aunt Dilsys and Dinahs and Venuses, the Patsys and Pollys, the Uncle Bills and Dicks and Jupiters and Vulcans—to whom Moreland presented his bashful, blushing wife. She really felt more trepidation in passing this ordeal than she would in attending one of the President's levees.

He carried her first to Aunt Dilsy's cabin, she being the most ancient and honourable matron of the establishment. There Miss Effie was sitting on a little piece of carpet, tossing up a large, scarlet pomegranate, with her lap full of all kind of *goodies*. Dilsy was not as old as Dicey, but her wool was profusely sprinkled with the ashes of age, and time had made many a groove on her face, where its shadows gathered. The locks of the white man grow gray as life wears on, but the negro's black skin, as well as his wool, assumes a dim and hoary aspect, as the dawn of a brighter day approaches.

"Bless you, for a sweet angel, as you be!" cried

Dilsy, whose salutation was a sample of the others, and whose dialect Eulalia at once observed differed from the household slaves;—"bless you, young missis, and make you de name and de praise of many generations, dat luv de Lord Jesus Christ. I didn't 'spec to see young missus 'fore I die; but, praise de Lord, she come,—and young massa look so happy. Well! he desarves it, de Lord knows. I've had him a baby in dese arms, and his moder before him. I've been praying my Hebenly Massa to send him good wife, good crishen wife, to be his 'zilary in 'nevolence and piety. Now poor Dilsy willing to lay down and neber wake up no more."

"I will try to deserve your blessing, and be a kind and faithful mistress," answered Eulalia, with unaffected humility, the tears trembling in her soft dark eyes, while she pressed the dry and wrinkled hand of the aged negro. Dilsy wept like a child, completely melted by such sweetness and condescension, and really believed that the Lord had sent an angel among them.

In one of the cabins, a young, bright-looking negro girl seemed quite beside herself with rapture, at the sight of her master's lovely young bride. She gazed upon her with distended eyes, showing every tooth of dazzling ivory, then threw herself on the floor, and rolled over several times, shaking with convulsive laughter.

"What is the matter with her?" asked Eulalia, timidly, fearing she had fallen in a fit.

"Oh! you're so putty, missus," said the girl, sitting up and rubbing her eyes,—"you're so putty, I can't help it. Oh, Luddy! I never seed any ting like it, since I ben born. I grate big fool, I know, but I can't help it."

Here she burst into a fresh peal of laughter, and covered her face with both her hands. Moreland, laughing at this hysterical tribute to his young wife's beauty, drew her away, to receive new testimonies of the personal magnetism, whose drawings *he* had felt when the choral strains first thrilled his soul, in the village church.

Eulalia, who had never seen the negro at the North, but as an isolated being, beheld him now in his domestic and social relations, and, it seemed to her, that he must be a great deal happier thus situated, bearing the name of a slave, than wandering about a nominal freeman, without the genial influences of home and friends. She had seen the Northern labourer return after a day of toil to the bosom of his family, feeling rest more grateful and refreshing because it was enjoyed there. So the negro returned to his cabin and sat down with his wife and children, and smoked his pipe, and ate his supper, and appeared to think himself very comfortable. But there is one difference. The Northern labourer has anxious thoughts for the morrow, fears that the daily bread for which he is toiling may be withheld, that sickness may paralyze his strong arm, and his children feel the pangs of destitution. The slave thinks not of the morrow, lays up nothing for the future, spends his money for the gratification of the present moment, and gives care and trouble to the winds. No matter how hard he has been at work, if it be a moonlight night, he steals off on a 'possum hunt, or a fishing frolic, or if he hears a violin, he is up and dancing the Virginia breakdown, or the Georgia rattlesnake. If he be one of the "settled ones," to use one of their favourite expressions, he may be heard singing the songs of Zion, in that plaintive, melodious voice peculiar to his race.

Do the spirits of the labourers in Northern factories ever rebound more lightly than this, after laying down the burden of toil? Do the two hundred thousand poor that throng the royal streets of London breathe forth a more gladdening strain, or lie down to rest with more contentment or gratitude? Do the hundreds and thousands buried in the black coal-pits and wretched dens of Great Britain, who have never heard, in their living graves, of the God who created, the Saviour who redeemed them, pass their sunless lives in greater comfort or fuller enjoyment? Are Russia's forty millions of slaves more free from care and sorrow? Can the victims of Austrian and Prussian despotism boast of greater privileges? Does the groan of oppression, rising above the vine hills of France, speak of joys more dear? Alas!

all these are forgotten, and the "bolt, red with uncommon wrath," is hurled at the devoted South; as if all the rest of the world were basking in a blaze of freedom, and slavery, condensed into the blackness of darkness, dwelt alone with her.

"Free! I wonder who is free?" exclaimed the Northern Betsy. We repeat the exclamation. We wonder who is really free in this great prison-house the world. One is bound to the Ixion wheel of habit, and dare not break the fetters that enthral him; another is the slave of circumstances, and writhes till the iron enters his soul. Bigotry stretches one on its Procrustes bed, dragging out the resisting muscles into torturing length, or mangling and mutilating the godlike proportions the Almighty has made. Fanaticism hurls another into an abyss of flame, and laughs over the burning agonies she has created. Poverty! most terrible of masters! We have tried already to depict some of the sufferings of its slaves. Let them pass here.

Ask that pale, majestic statesman, in whose travailing soul and toiling brain a nation's interests are wrought, who, month after month, is doomed to exchange the sweet atmosphere of home for the feverishness and strife of a political arena, whose sleepless nights are passed in the forge of intense and burning thought, and whose days in gladiatorial combats with warring intellects,—if he is free!

Ask him who sits in the White Palace, chief of this

great republic, filling the grandest station in the vast globe,—if he is free! Are you free? Are we? No! There is a long chain, winding round the whole human race, and though its links be sometimes made of silver and gold, nay, even twined with flowers, it is still chain, and if the spirit struggle for liberation, it will feel the galling and the laceration, as much as if the fetters were of brass or iron. For six thousand years the cry for *freedom* has been going up from the goaded heart of humanity—freedom from the bondage and mystery and necessity of life—and still it rends the heavens and echoes over the earth. And the answer has been, and now is, and ever will be—"Be still, and know that I am God."

CHAPTER XIII.

EULALIA was soon initiated in the mysteries of plantation life. With ever-increasing interest she studied the scenes around her, and the character of the community of whose dark circumference she was made the central light. Though possessing little skill or experience as a rider, she accompanied her husband to the bounds of his dominions, through cotton and cornfields, all along the beautiful hedges of Cherokee roses, that, instead of fences, divided the land. At first she only ventured to go on a gentle little pony; but soon, emboldened by practice, she was not afraid to mount the most spirited and high-mettled horse. She visited the saw-mill and grist-mill, built on the margin of a roaring stream; the blacksmith's shop, that, isolated from the other buildings, looked as if it were cooling its fiery forge in the fresh green expanse that surrounded it, and where the stalwart artisan, begrimed by nature, heeded not the black soot that settled on his dusky skin; the carpenter's shop, where all the furniture necessary for the negroes was made, even to "a right sharp bedstead or bureau," as the workman told her. She went to the weaving and spinning rooms, where cotton and woollen webs were manufactured for negro clothing, and counterpanes of curious devices. Everything necessary for comfort and use was of home-work, and everything was done with a neatness, order, and despatch that surprised the young mistress of the plantation. The cabins of the negroes, each with their own well-cultivated plot of ground, poultry yard, and melon patch, she loved to visit, for wherever she turned her eye she saw abundant proof of Moreland's considerate kindness and liberality. The watchful guardian providence of the whole establishment, he seemed to see and command everything at a single glance. The overseer was required to give an account of every transaction that occurred during his absence, and his presence was a signal for justice to ascend its throne, ready to weigh in its impartial balance every wrong or dubious act—while mercy knelt at its footstool pleading for the delinquent or offender, and softening its stern decree.

Eulalia admired the systematic arrangement of everything. The hours of labour were all regulated—the tasks for those hours appointed. For all labour beyond those tasks the negroes were paid an adequate remuneration. Their master purchased of them all the produce, the cotton and corn they had the privilege of raising for themselves, giving them the uttermost farthing. Thus they had an ample supply of spending money—

not being obliged to use one cent of it for the necessaries of life. One evening one of the men came in and asked his master to take care of his purse till Christmas, when he wanted to buy something fine for his wife. It was nothing but an old woollen mitten, but the contents were quite respectable, being fifty-five dollars.

"Have you earned all this, Cato?" asked his master.

"Sartain, massa, sartain—ebery cent. Hope massa don't think I steal it!"

"Oh, no, Cato! I know you are as honest as you are faithful and industrious. I must treat you as the Lord in Scripture did his servant, who brought him his five talents, to which he had added five talents more. I must give you your own with usury."

Taking out his own purse, he emptied the contents into Eulalia's hand, reserving a half-eagle which he left in the bottom. Then pouring the money from the old mitten into it, he tossed the fragment to the smiling negro.

"There, Cato, you deserve a better purse than that. You may make a present of it to your wife."

"Massa, you too good! Thank you, massa, twenty times over! May you and beautiful young missus live a tousand years, and a tousand arter, besides!"

"Pray, don't make wandering Jews of us, Cato, or at least save us from eternal old age."

Cato laughed and chuckled, as if he thought it an excellent joke which he did not quite understand, and went away with a jubilant spirit.

"What shall I do with this?" said Eulalia, blushingly clasping her fingers over the dripping money.

"Simple-hearted child! buy sugarplums or candy. How can you ask me how to dispose of such a trifle?"

"Trifle! I think it a great deal! At least, it is more than I ever had the disposal of before!"

Moreland smiled at her simplicity, and, clasping the hand which contained the money in his own, exclaimed—

"All that I have, and all that I am, is thine, my sweet Eulalia. Had I millions on millions, they should be at your command. Do with me and my fortune all that your pure and generous heart dictates. Have you no wish, my wife, that wealth can gratify, no friend whom your bounty can bless? Are there no poor in your native village, whose wants were forgotten when you left them? Would you not like to send some kind memento home?"

"I would like them to know how blest, how happy I am; how good, how noble you are!" cried Eulalia, for the first time throwing her timid arms round his neck; then, blushing at her boldness, would have withdrawn them, but he imprisoned them in his own, and retained her in willing bondage.

"There is a poor family," she said, falteringly, still feeling that it was presumptuous in her to suggest to him objects of charity, "whom my mother mentioned in her last letter, as having suffered much from protracted sickness. I thought, when I read of their distresses, how sweet it would be to relieve them. I intend d to tell you of their wants, but you gave so much to the poor of our village, I was ashamed to ask for more."

"Foolish, foolish Eulalia! your only fault is too great timidity, too much self-distrust. You must trust me, or I shall not think you love me. You must feel that I live for your happiness; that your slightest wish has the authority of a command—an authority second only to the canons of God. So perfect is my confidence in your purity and rectitude of principle, that I would hesitate as soon to execute the commission of an angel as I would yours. I have once been deceived, and I thought all confidence was wrenched from my bosom, but it is not so. My trust in you is as firm as that which rests upon the Rock of Ages."

"If I ever prove unworthy of that trust, may I forfeit the favour of my God!" cried Eulalia, awed by the deep tenderness of his voice and manner, and lifting her eyes of holy innocence to heaven.

"My confidence is based on your piety and truth, Eulalia," said he, after a pause, in which his mind went back to the past. "Your unhappy predecessor was destitute of this restraining influence, and became the slave of her own wild passions. Born of an Italian mother, and inheriting from her a warmth and vehemence of character that nothing but religion could control—but why do I speak of her now!—why recall her at this moment, sacred to joy and love!"

"There is one favour I would ask," said Eulalia, when the tone of their conversation was a little lowered; she was growing startlingly bold, it seems, in consequence of his excessive indulgence. "I want you to call me Eula. It was my name of endearment at home. It used to sound so sweet from the lips of Dora. I love it so much better than Eulalia."

"Eula, Eula!" repeated he; "well, henceforth and evermore be it Eula. I remember the first time I heard that name breathed by Dora's sweet lips, as I was following you out of church. I wanted to catch her up in my arms and kiss her, for teaching my heart the name it was throbbing to learn. But what will you call me? I don't believe you have ever addressed me by name yet?"

Eula, as she resolved to be called, blushed and smiled. She had often been perplexed how to address him, and was glad he had introduced the subject.

"Call me Russell, as Ildegerte does. It makes me feel like a boy to be called by my Christian name,—the name I received at the baptismal font."

"That would sound too familiar for me. I feel too much reverence to admit of it. I never could get accustomed to it."

"Anything then, but *Mr.* Moreland. I cannot consent

to that. What a pity I have not the dignity of a title; but, rife as they are in this country, I am neither colonel, major, or general: only a plain, unhonoured man."

"Moreland, then!" she repeated, in a low voice,—"that name is music to my ears."

This was a very trifling matter to arrange, and yet Eulalia (we will try to get into the habit of calling her Eula, thinking with her, it has a more home-endearing sound,) felt a little happier for it. It was one more link in the golden chain of love and confidence, wreathed round her heart.

She became so much pleased with plantation life, that, whenever her husband spoke of returning to town, she entreated him to remain, saying, she could do so much more good where she was. The injunction of her father, to be a missionary to the poor benighted slaves, often recurred to her; but she found the heralds of the gospel had preceded her, and that the ground on which she stood was consecrated by the footsteps of Christianity. Moreland had erected a chapel in the heart of the plantation, and though, like the cabins, it was constructed of logs, and the seats were only rustic benches, it was hallowed by as sincere devotion and childlike faith as ever filled with incense the heaven-dedicated dome. No proud, intellectual self-sufficiency,—no cold, questioning philosophy,—no God-defying strength of reason impeded, in their simple minds, the reception of evangelical truths.

Moreland paid a regular salary to an itinerant preacher for supplying this rustic pulpit on the Sabbath, and there was a black preacher besides, who, if he had not the learning, emulated the zeal of St. Paul. Eulalia was astonished at his knowledge of Scripture, and the occasional inspiration of his language. His name was Paul, and he was looked up to with as much veneration by the coloured people as if he were the great Apostle of the Gentiles. During the week they had prayer meetings at night, and their choral voices uniting in hymns of praise often rose in the stillness of the midnight hour. In the exercises of these meetings Aunt Dilsy took a conspicuous part. She was regarded as another daughter of Phanuel, who, by holy fastings and prayers, had become completely sanctified, and her exhortations were received as the oracles of truth and wisdom. She was a great singer; and though her once musical voice was untuned by age, no one was thought to sing with the *sperrit* as Aunt Dilsy did, or to shout hosannas of glory with such thrilling devotion.

Eulalia loved to witness their simple religious rites. Ofttimes, when she and her husband were walking out in the coolness of evening, in the path that led by the chapel, they heard their names as good massa and missus borne on the wings of prayer above the silent, listening stars; and they felt as if blessings came down upon them with the stilly dews. Sometimes they went in and united in spirit with the dark worshippers; and beautiful was the contrast of Eulalia's fair, ethereal face, with the black visages and coarse features of the Africans. And sometimes, moved by an irresistible impulse, she suffered her seraphic voice to mingle with theirs, and it had a tone of more than mortal sweetness.

One night she missed the old prophetess Dilsy in the evening assembly. This was such an unusual occurrence, she begged Moreland to accompany her to her cabin and see if she were ill. As they approached the door they heard low, monotonous, ejaculatory sounds issuing from within. They recognised the accents of prayer, and entered reverently. By a lamp glimmering on the hearth they distinguished the figure of Aunt Dilsy on the outside of the bed, looking so shrivelled and drawn up, it seemed to have lost half of its usual dimensions.

"Oh, massa! oh, missus!" she cried, in answer to their anxious inquiries—"I struck with death I know! Such a misery in my breast! 'Pears like a knife in dare! Poor old creetur!—time to go; ben long time cumberer of de ground! Thank de Lord, I'm willing to mind his blessed summons! I'm ready, 'cause he gin me de white wedding garment to put on, arter he wash it all over clean in his 'toning blood!"

Here a violent paroxysm of pain interrupted her utterance, and she lay panting and groaning, and her sunken eyes rolled upward with such an expression of mortal agony that Eulalia believed her soul was immediately departing. Her physical sufferings were relieved by some specific which Moreland applied, so that she was able to speak once more; but it was evident that the hour of her departure was arrived, and that the Son of Man was come. She wanted the negroes to be called in to receive her last farewell, and they were summoned. They stood in dark circles, one behind the other, gazing with unspeakable awe on the dying prophetess. Drawn by the mysterious and awful fascination of death, they pressed nearer and nearer, till Moreland was compelled to wave them back, lest every breath of air should be excluded from the expiring woman.

"Let 'em come, massa," she said, with a beckoning motion. "Can't hurt me now. Oh! brudders and sisters in de Lord Jesus! I most got home. I see de golden streets way up yonder. I see de grate house not made by hands, wid de door wide open, ready to let poor ole sinner in. Somebody, all shining like de sun, stand right in de door and say:—'Come in, Dilsy! Set down at de right hand of de Lord.'"

The most ecstatic expression it is possible to conceive lighted up her poor withered features. It seemed that a vision of glory, such as is never vouchsafed to any but the dying, was sweeping down upon her, wrapping her soul in folding sheets of splendour and bliss. Inexpressibly awed, Eulalia knelt by her bedside, clasping the hand of her husband, who stood reverently gazing on the aged negress, who, through nearly three generations, had been the faithful servant and humble friend of his family. Her children and her children's children were gathered round her; but as the vision gradually faded away, and her clouding eye turned wistfully to earthly objects, it was on the face of her master she gazed, with such an expression of affection, gratitude, and humility combined, that his answering glance was dimmed with tears.

"Good by, massa!" she cried, fumbling with the bed-cover, thinking it was his hand she was grasping. Perceiving her motion, he took hers in his. It was damp and cold as ice.

"Good by, massa! my Hebenly Massa has bought me wid his own precious blood, and he say I must leave you. You ben good, kind massa. I'll tell the Lord when I git home to glory, all you've done for de soul and body of poor nigger. Oh! massa! 'spose you don't know poor Dilsy when you git to heben, 'cause she'll be beautiful, white angel den; but you jist look hard at de hebenly throng, and de one dat lub you best of all, wid her new eyes—dat will be me."

"Dilsy," said her master, in a voice husky from emotion, "you have been a good and faithful friend to me and mine. You are going to receive the reward of your fidelity. You will hear the voice of God pronounce the glad sentence: 'Come, thou good and faithful servant, enter thou into the joy of thy Lord.' If I am ever admitted into the kingdom of heaven, I expect to meet and recognise you as an angel of light."

Amid the loud sobs that burst forth from the circling negroes, there went up a shout of "glory;" and several voices echoed it till the hosannas seemed too swelling for that little cabin. The sinking faculties of life gathered new energy from the jubilant sounds.

"Yes! brudders and sisters!" she cried, clapping her cold, feeble hands, "rejoice that ye eber hearn of de Lord Jesus and de blessed herarter. If we'd all staid in de heathen land, where all de black folks come from, we'd neber known noting 'bout heben, noting 'bout de hebenly 'deemer or de golden streets of de new Jerusalem. Tink of dat, if Satin eber tempt you to leave good massa and missus."

Looking at the weeping Eulalia, she said—

"Please, young missus, sing one of de songs of Zion. 'Pears like I'll go to glory on it. Someting 'bout Jesus and de Lamb."

Eulalia felt as if she had little voice to sing, but she could not refuse the last request of the departing Christian. Low and trembling she began, but the notes grew clearer and sweeter as she continued; sometimes low and soft, as if they came murmuring from the depths of ocean, then swelling in volume, they seemed to be rolling from the bosom of a cloud.

These were the words she sang,—

> "Jesus! lover of my soul
> Let me to thy bosom fly,
> While the nearer waters roll,—
> While the tempest still is high.
> Hide me, oh! my Saviour, hide,
> Till the storm of life is past,
> Safe into the haven guide,
> Oh! receive my soul at last."

She paused, but the half-closed eyes opened, and the gasping breath whispered "More, dear missus, more!"

Again she sang,—

> "Other refuge have I none;
> Hangs my helpless soul on thee;
> Leave, oh! leave me not alone
> Still support and comfort me.
> All my trust in thee is staid,—
> All my help from thee I bring;
> Cover my defenceless head
> With the shadow of thy wing."

As the last lines died on the ear, the shadow of the mighty wing of the death-angel visibly darkened the brow of the departing negress. There was an awful hush, for a few moments, and then an eager pressing forward, as if the eye could behold, in the rifted clay, where the struggling soul had rent its passage to eternity. Moreland drew Eulalia from the cabin, assuring her that every respect would be paid to the remains of the now enfranchised Dilsy.

All night the negroes watched by her body, singing, in choral strains, of the triumph of redeeming love. They even added another verse to the immemorial hymn of good old Daniel, enrolling Dilsy among the immortal worthies who have entered the promised land,—

> "Where now is good old Dilsy?
> Where now is good old Dilsy?
> Where now is good old Dilsy?
> Safely in de promised land.
> She went up from de bed o'er yonder,
> She went up from de bed o'er yonder,
> She went up from de bed o'er yonder,
> Safely in de promised land.

The next day, a little before sunset, Dilsy was laid in the green enclosure where some of her children already slept. It was the burying-ground of the plantation, surrounded by a neat, whitewashed paling, and shaded by evergreens and shrubbery. On some graves, flowers were growing, showing that the taste which loves to beautify the places of death is sometimes found in the bosom of the African. A long procession followed the body of the ancient matron, headed by the master whom she had loved in life, and blessed in death. He walked before them all, with folded arms and measured tread—stood, with uncovered head, while they lowered the coffin into the deep, dark, narrow cavity scooped to receive it; threw the first shovelful of earth on the hollow-sounding lid, and waited till the cold abyss was filled, and the damp clay heaved above it.

"Oh, God!" he silently ejaculated, lifting his eyes heavenward, "I have tried to do my duty to this poor dust committed to my care. I received it, as a part of my inheritance, as a trust for which I shall be responsible to thee, and thee alone. If I have failed, thou great Searcher of all human hearts, forgive me! and show me wherein my error lies. Here, by this solemn new-made grave, I renew the dedication of my soul to thy service, and the good of my fellow-beings."

Then, turning to the negroes who stood leaning on their shovels, looking down mournfully on the hillock they had made, he said—

"You heard the words of the dying Dilsy. You heard what she said to you and to me. She told you to be grateful that you were brought away from a land of darkness and the shadow of death, to regions where the light of the gospel shines upon your souls, where you are taught that the grave is a passage to glory and happiness, where you are prepared to meet, in faith and hope, the dark hour through which she has just safely passed. Did you believe her words? Do you think she would deceive you, when her gasping breath was about leaving her body?"

"No, massa!" answered Paul, the preacher; "sartain she wouldn't! We know she spoke the truth."

"Then you would not think freedom without a God,

freedom without a Saviour, without hope of a hereafter, without the promises of eternal life, a blessing?"

"No, massa! not a bit, not a bit."

"Would you think freedom a blessing, if I should scatter you all at this moment to the four winds of heaven, give up all care and guardianship of you and your children, suffer you to go where you please, leaving you to provide for the necessities of the morrow and all future wants?"*

"No, massa, no!" burst forth simultaneously from the funeral band.

"You heard," added Moreland, with solemnity, "her dying blessing upon your master. You heard what she said she would repeat before God and his angels. Do you believe her words were true? Have I been kind and just to all? Or do you look on me as a tyrant, from whose dominion you long to be free?"

Here the denial was still more earnest and emphatic. Tears were streaming down the cheeks of those around the grave, and sobs were heard in the back-ground.

"Then," said Moreland, "let us make a new covenant together, and let this grave be a witness between us all,

* A free negro, who resides at St. Andrew's Bay, had amasse money enough to build him a comfortable house. He supporte himself and family by boat-building. In one of those storms which often desolate the coast, his house was swept away. He came to many gentlemen, entreating them to purchase himself and family, saying he was tired of the responsibility of their support. He had known what slavery and freedom were, and he preferred the first.

that we do it in sincerity and truth. I call upon you all to renew your promises of fidelity and obedience. I pledge myself anew to watch over your best interests for time and eternity. If I ever forget my vow, if I ever become unjust, unkind, or tyrannical, you may lead me to this clay-cold bed and remind me of my broken faith. And now, Paul," turning to the weeping preacher, whose sensibilities were all melting and flowing from his eyes, "let us all kneel together, while you consecrate this burial spot by the breath of prayer."

Just as the last words of Paul's devout and eloquent prayer, the ascription of praise and thanksgiving, was uttered, the setting sun, which had been curtained by a cloud parallel with the horizon, so that all thought the twilight was begun, suddenly gleamed forth, sending out innumerable radii of crimson and gold, from its red and glowing disk. It gilded the pale and earnest countenance of Moreland with a kind of supernatural radiance, bronzed the crisped wool and black glossy skin of the negroes, and gave a tinge of ruddiness to the cedar's dark green foliage. Was it a token from heaven? Was it fire from above descending on the altar of the heart, showing that the sacrifice was accepted? So thought Paul, the preacher. So thought all the Africans; and they were as sure, ever afterwards, that Dilsy was in glory, as if they had seen her with victorious palms in her right hand and a golden lyre in her left.

It was not till several weeks afterwards that her

"funeral was preached," as the negroes say, and then the slaves from adjoining plantations came to do honour to the memory of this sable mother in Israel. It was some time before the solemnity caused by her death passed away. No music was heard at night but choral hymns; and the step of the dancer was still. But the banjo's monotonous thrumming at length was heard, rather faintly at first, then giving out a bolder strain, and then the violin's melodious scraping called out the little darkies from their nooks and crannies to *jump Georgia motion* with their India-rubber toes.

It was with reluctance that Eulalia left the plantation. All her fears and repugnance of the black race were gone, leaving, in their stead, the sincerest attachment and the deepest interest. She wrote to her parents the most enthusiastic description of the life she had witnessed; and, while she made her mother the almoner of her husband's bounty to the poor, dwelt upon all his excellent and noble qualities with fond and eloquent diffuseness. "Happy!—do you ask if I am happy?" she added. "I tremble at the excess of my felicity, knowing that it cannot be always thus. On the blue and cloudless firmament I watch for the rising cloud."

Poor Eulalia!—the cloud was near at hand. A letter from Dr. Darley was awaiting their return, involving the necessity of Moreland's immediate departure. It was written after the death of Richard, and the abduction of Crissy, while Ildegerte was languishing on a sick-bed. The moment the letter was given into his hands, Eulalia knew that it was the messenger of sad tidings, for she caught a glimpse of the black seal; but she did not anticipate the extent of Ildegerte's sorrow. She watched her husband's countenance as he read. At first it was sad, very mournful, but gently so. The grief that shaded it was of that nature which sympathy might soothe, and she drew near, that he might feel her readiness to participate in all his sorrows, and laid her hand, with soft, unobtrusive motion, on his shoulder; when suddenly starting up, shaking it unconsciously from his arm, he knit his brows fiercely, while angry lightning flashed from his eyes.

"Mean, cowardly, cruel!" he exclaimed, clenching the letter with such force that he shivered and rent it in his grasp. "When God afflicts, it is easy to submit; but when the blow comes from man,—comes in the dark, with the cruelty of an assassin, and the baseness of a robber,—by Heaven, it is hard to bear!"

Eulalia trembled and turned pale. She had never before seen her husband angry, and there was something terrible in the wrath of that usually serene and beaming countenance. She dared not question him, save with her beseeching eyes. Crushing, as it were, his vehement emotion as suddenly as he had done the letter, he said, in a more subdued but still indignant tone,

"Forgive my violence; I did not mean to alarm you. Richard is dead!—God took him,—it is well. Crissy is gone!—lured from her mistress, in the hour of her bitterest agony,—miserable dupe that she is! Let her go,—let her go! But Ildegerte lies on a sick-bed,—no friend but Dr. Darley by her. Eulalia,—Eula, I must go to her. I must leave you for a while. *You* would not wish me to stay."

"Oh, no!" she exclaimed, bursting into tears, "she needs you more than I. Alone among strangers; with a broken heart!—how sad! How could Crissy leave her, when she seemed to love her so dearly, and promised so faithfully to abide by her!"

"Blame not her," said Moreland; "poor, ignorant, deluded creature! She was probably assailed by arts which her simplicity was powerless to baffle. I feel only pity for her. But for those who inflicted this wrong on my unoffending sister, whose situation should have inspired the deepest sympathy and commiseration, I have no words to express my indignation. Give me the foe that braves me face to face in the blaze of noonday; but shame on the coward who skulks in ambush, with the smiling lip and the assassin hand! Had they broken into Ildegerte's room, rifled her of her gold and her raiment, the act would have been less unprincipled, for her *heart* would not have suffered. They have stolen from her a *friend*, in the hour of her extremest need, and added dreariness and anguish to the desolation of widowhood! Great God! what will the end of these things be! What will be the end of unprovoked attack, injustice, and aggression on one side, and exasperated feeling, wounded honour, and disregarded brotherhood on the other! Oh! my wife! my dear wife! if it were not for *thee*, I would rather rend asunder, with one mighty effort, the ties which bind the South and the North, than live with this burning under-current accumulating strength from a thousand sources, and undermining our institutions, our prosperity and happiness! Perish the body, if the spirit be wanting there! Madness to talk of union, with bitterness and rancour and every evil passion rankling in the heart's core!"

Moreland was excited beyond the power of self-control. What could Eulalia say? Was not her own father a leader in the party whose influence he deprecated with such indignant vehemence? But every thought was soon swallowed in the idea of approaching separation. He was to leave her on the morrow, to be gone she knew not how long; he was going on a sad errand—to bring back a widowed sister, accompanied by the lifeless body of her husband. In the contemplation of Ildegerte's sorrows she tried to forget her own; but she felt that absence was the shadow of death, and it hung dark and chill over her soul.

Moreland was anxious that she should invite some female companion to cheer her solitude, but she shrunk from the suggestion. She would a thousand times rather be alone, or with no companion but little Effie, who was becoming every hour more dear to her affections. In instructing Effie's heart, and through her heart finding the avenue to her understanding; in her music lessons, books, letters; the care of her servants, the superintendence of her household, she would pass the dreary hours of absence and wait his return.

Early in the morning he took his departure. Eulalia did not stand under the blossoming wreaths of the now fading honeysuckle to witness his going, as she had done once before. Her face was buried in the window curtain of her chamber. She had not the courage to look upon his departing figure. Just as he was leaving the gate, poor Jim detained him to repeat once more the injunction not to come back without Crissy. He seemed quite broken-hearted by her desertion, and could not speak of her without tears. There was no place for resentment in his soft, uxorious heart.

"Tell her, massa, I done forgive her. 'Tain't none of her doings, no how; but her things will spile sure as she be alive. Tell her I got no heart to air 'em no more. Don't care if they drop to pieces!"

Notwithstanding this assertion, Jim pored over the contents of the big chest with increasing devotion, and early on many a bright sunny morning a long line of parti-coloured garments rejoiced in the freshening breeze.

CHAPTER XIV.

A VERY unexpected visiter interrupted the monotony of Eulalia's life, during the absence of Moreland.

She was sitting one morning alone, in the parlour, practising her last music lesson with all the assiduity of a school-girl, wishing to surprise her husband with her proficiency, on his return, when the door opened and a lady entered, unannounced. The music drowned the sound of her entrance, and Eulalia's first consciousness of her presence was so startling that it made her spring from her seat, as if penetrated by an electric shock. She heard no step, and yet, an inexplicable sensation induced her to turn, and close to the instrument she beheld the haughty, yet graceful figure, whose lineaments, once seen, could never be forgotten. There were the large, black, resplendent, yet repelling eyes, that were for ever haunting her,—the red lips of scorn, the pale olive cheek, the bold, yet classic brow—all the features daguerreotyped on her memory.

They stood for several moments without speaking, gazing at each other,—the repudiated wife and Northern bride of Moreland,—two of the most striking images that womanhood can present, of material beauty and spiritual loveliness. They were both young, both beautiful, but evil passions had darkened and marred the brilliant face of the one, while purity, goodness, truth, and love had imparted to the other an almost celestial charm.

"And *you* are now mistress here!" exclaimed the lady, sweeping her proud, bright glance round the apartment, her lip curling and quivering with undefinable emotion.

"I am," replied Eulalia, her self-possession returning as the voice of the stranger broke the spell which seemed thrown around them both. Her tone was cold and unnatural. She paused, as if waiting an explanation of this unexpected and unwelcome visit. Then, her native courtesy and gentleness, mingled with compassion for the unhappy woman before her, induced her to add—

"Will you be seated, madam?"

Claudia threw herself on a sofa, in an attitude of careless independence. The crimson velvet of the covering brought out, in strong relief, the handsome, but bold outlines of her figure, which swelled through the dark mistiness of a black lace drapery. She sat, wrapping this drapery round her exquisitely white hands, all glittering with rings, then, suddenly untying the strings of her bonnet, she tossed it down by her side, and shook her raven black hair back from her brow. Her air of proud assurance, the careless home-attitude she assumed, as if she had come to dispossess the sweet young creature before her of the throne she deemed still her right to occupy, roused all the woman in Eulalia's breast. The colour came warm and bright to her cheek and brow.

"To what am I indebted for a call as unlooked for as undesired?" she asked with dignity, without resuming her seat.

"To any motive you please," replied the lady, with a deriding smile. "I presume I am not the first lady who has called to pay their respects to the new Mrs. Moreland. Is it a Northern custom to ask one's guests the reason of their coming, the very moment of their arrival, too?"

"At the North, as well as the South," said Eulalia, her mild eyes flashing with unwonted fire, "the woman who has forfeited her position as a wife and mother is excluded from the social privileges she has wantonly abused. She may be an object of charity, pity, kindness; but of friendship and esteem, never!"

"Do you dare say this to me?" exclaimed Claudia, starting to her feet, with a look that threatened annihilation.

"Yes, madam, and far more!" cried Eulalia, emboldened to candour by the insolence of her visiter. "Were you in want, I would most willingly relieve you; were you in suffering, either in body or mind, I would gladly administer succour and consolation; were you bowed down by remorse and sorrow, I would kneel at your side, praying the Saviour of sinners to have mercy on your soul! But when you come with haughty defiance, glorying in your shame, to the home you once desecrated, placing yourself on an equality with the virtuous and pure, I am constrained to say, that your presence is unwelcome and intrusive."

Grave, serene, and holy, in her youthful purity and sanctity, stood Eulalia, before her predecessor, as stood the angel before transgressing Eve.

"And you believe *his* story!" exclaimed Claudia, bursting into a scornful laugh. "You believe I am really the vile thing he represents me to be. Yes!—*he* believes it, too. I wanted him to. I would not undeceive him. I trampled him in the dust of humiliation, —willing to endure obloquy and disgrace myself, since shame and dishonour rested on him!"

"Impossible!—impossible!" cried Eulalia; "woman never sunk so low!"

She recoiled from her, as if she were a serpent or a demon. Could it be, that the man whom she so idolatrously loved, had inspired such bitter hatred and revenge!

"Yes!" continued Claudia,—walking backwards and forwards, with the fierce grace of a leopardess,—"I hated him so intensely, that I was willing to destroy myself, provided I involved him in ruin. I was fool enough to think I loved him when I married. Yes, I was the fool then you are now! I thought I married a lover! he turned into my master, my tyrant!—he wanted me to cringe to his will, like the slaves in the kitchen, and I spurned his authority!—I defied his power! He expected me to *obey* him,—me, who never obeyed my own mother! He refused me the liberty of choosing my own friends, of receiving them in my own house! He even had the audacity to command me to shut the doors upon my mother's face! Did he tell you of that? If he did not, I do!"

She paused for breath, panting from angry excitement. Eulalia beheld a faint specimen of that irascible and indomitable temper which, resisting every moral and religious influence, had made its wretched possessor an alien and an outcast.

"He did tell me. Shall I repeat the cause?" said Eulalia.

"No! I will not hear it; it is slander,—the vilest slander! Because my mother was a foreigner, they accused her of all that was evil, and forbid me to associate with her. But, I can tell you, the spirit of the Italian is resilient, and will not be held down. You!—the daughter of a Northern clime, without impulse or passion, cold as your wintry snows,—may wear the yoke without feeling it, and yield the will without knowing it. You are wondrously happy, are you not?"

Eulalia felt a quick, sharp pang at her heart, at the

sudden storm of passion rising and surging within. She knew not before that such powerful elements were slumbering in her breast. At every scornful and mocking word, dashed, as it were, in her face, answering scorn sent its flash to her eye and its bitter taunt to her lip. But the flash went out, the taunt died away without utterance. The angel of consideration did not forsake her, but she could have wept at the introspective view that moment of passion had given her. Without trusting herself to speak, fearing she would say something which she would hereafter regret, she turned away, wondering how this strange and harrowing scene would terminate.

Claudia made no movement of departure. She was restless, nervous, constantly looking towards the door, sometimes walking with impatient gesture, then throwing herself back on the sofa, and squeezing the crimson cushion with clenching fingers. Once she sat down at the piano, and running her fingers over the keys, produced a wild, passionate burst of harmony, in which a minor note of wailing softness strangely mingled, then, dashing into a gay, reckless strain, the ivory seemed to sparkle under her touch.

At this moment the door suddenly opened, and Effie, running in, exclaimed—

"See, mamma, what a beautiful necklace. Netty made it!"

The child held up a string of wild scarlet berries that encircled her neck and also passed round her waist.

Claudia sprang towards the child so suddenly, that the little creature, trembling and terrified, ran to Eulalia, leaped into her lap, and locked her hands tightly round her neck.

"Give me the child!" cried Claudia, with a vehemence that increased Effie's terror, and made her cling still more closely to Eulalia's throbbing bosom. "She is mine! I will not give her up! Has not the mother a right to her own child? Look at me, Effie! Speak to me, Effie! I am your mamma! Come and go with me!"

"No, you ain't my mamma!" answered the child, making a repelling motion with her foot, still keeping her arms tightly folded round her stepmother's neck. "This is my mamma—my sweet, pretty mamma! I love her! I won't leave her! Go 'way! I don't want you to look at me so hard!"

An expression of unutterable anguish passed over the features of Claudia, and she pressed her hand upon her bosom, as if it were closing over a wound. Then Eulalia pitied her, pitied her from the bottom of her heart. Over the wreck of all womanly charities and graces and sensibilities, maternal love cast a ray of redeeming lustre. Like a plume dropped from the wing of a departed angel, it was a token of vanished glory.

For a moment the young stepmother doubted her

CLAUDIA AND EULALIA.

right to resist the pleadings of nature. Had not the mother purchased her child by the pains and sorrows of maternity, and could any legal decision annul the great law of God, which makes the child a mother's almost life-bought property?

"She isn't my mamma, is she?" whispered Effie, glancing obliquely at Claudia through her long, curling black lashes. "Make her go away—I don't love her!"

Eulalia clasped the child closer to her bosom, feeling still more intensely for the unhappy mother. What answer could she give to this direct question? Moreland had insisted that Effie should never know of the existence of her own mother; that her name should never be uttered in her hearing; that to Eulalia alone her filial thoughts should be directed, her filial obedience paid. Could she, knowing this prohibition in all its length and breadth, say to the child that the woman, from whose large, black, wildly-beaming eyes she was shrinking in terror and repugnance, was indeed her mother?

"Is she my mamma?" repeated Effie, impatient at Eulalia's silence.

"Answer her!" cried Claudia, sternly; "answer her! Tell her no, at the peril of your soul's salvation!"

"Why—why have you come hither, to bring confusion and sorrow into a home no longer yours!" answered Eulalia, the purity and strength of her moral principles conquering the softness and tenderness of her nature.

"This child is *mine*—committed to my guardianship by the father, who has abjured your maternal right! The conduct by which you forfeited your position as a wife, made you unworthy to fulfil a mother's duties! Even if virtually innocent, as you declare yourself to be, and you have allowed disgrace and shame to rest upon you through hatred and revenge, you are guilty of blacker, more deliberate sin, than if you were the victim of passion and temptation! Go!—this child is mine! I never will resign her! Go!—your presence makes me very unhappy! The air is oppressive! I cannot breathe freely!"

She looked very pale, and really panted for breath. Little Effie was half-suffocating her with her clinging arms; and the eyes of Claudia, so dark and sultry, like the lurid dog-star, seemed surrounded by a hot, stifling atmosphere.

"I *will* have the child! By Heaven! I'll not return without her!" exclaimed Claudia, snatching Effie with frantic violence from her arms and rushing to the door. With a shriek that rung through the house, Eulalia sprang after her, but Claudia had gained the outer door, smothering the cries of Effie by pressing her hand tightly on her mouth. She there met an unexpected impediment in the ample person of Aunt Kizzie; and right behind her were Albert and Netty, all drawn by that one piercing shriek. Claudia struggled to pass them, commanding them to give way, with the authority of a queen, and the look of a lioness fighting for her young.

"What you doing with little missy, I want to know?" cried Kizzie, holding out her strong arms to the child, who was writhing and coiling herself up so that it was almost impossible to hold her. "Give her here!—you got nothing to do with her now! Putty story to tell master when he come back home! Don't cry, honey, mammy got you, sure enough! Folks as wants to carry you off better look sharp—see if Kizzie ain't somewhere 'bout! Good morning, missus;" making a mocking curtsy—"won't keep you standing!"

Claudia, baffled and insulted by the very vassals she once tried to trample under her feet, turned furiously upon Kizzie, and struck at her with frantic rage. Kizzie dodged her head at the exact moment, and Claudia's hand came down upon the door frame with such force that the blood gushed from her fingers. Albert and Netty both laughed. They were revenging themselves for her former haughtiness and insolence. Infuriated by this fresh insult, she again lifted her hand to strike, but the sight of her bleeding fingers suddenly arrested her. Perhaps she realized for the first time the impotence of her passion, the disgrace she was bringing on herself Gathering the rich drapery of lace that was falling from her shoulders, and folding it round her arms with such a quick, passionate gesture, the delicate meshes were rent like a cobweb, she flew down the steps, entered the carriage, and was driven rapidly away. Eulalia, who stood faint and trembling in the inner doorway, saw her put her head from the carriage just as it rolled away, and gaze at the house and its surroundings, with a wild, lingering glance, such as was once turned upon the forfeited bowers of Paradise by earth's first tempted and exiled.

It was long before Eulalia recovered from the shock of this interview. She was afraid to have Effie absent from her sight one moment. She did not feel safe herself from the violence of this fearful woman. She was numiliated by the knowledge of such deep depravity in one of womankind. It was exquisitely painful to her to think that Moreland had ever loved such a being. It seemed to detract from the purity, the dignity of his love for her. True, it was a boyish passion, caused by a fascination such as the serpent exercises on its victim, but she would have given worlds if it had never existed. Then she reflected that she knew this before she married, that Moreland had never deceived her, and that whatever his feelings had once been for Claudia, *she herself* now reigned sole mistress of his reclaimed affections. It was weak, it was sinful in her to indulge in these morbid regrets. Who was she, that, of all the daughters of humanity, she should gather the roses of joy, and find no thorns beneath, that she should quaff the sparkling wine, and find no lees in the cup? Had not her husband far more to regret than she? For her sake he had borne with injustice, misconstruction, and prejudice; he had bowed his pride and subdued his will, and sacrificed all personal feeling.

Her next emotion was unalloyed compassion for the erring Claudia. Had *she* been good and true, the village maiden of the North would never have been the Southern planter's bride.

We said in the beginning of this history, we should say no more of Moreland's past life than was necessary for a clear understanding of passing events. We will only say a few words here, to vindicate him from the charges brought against him by the unhappy Claudia. She was the daughter of Italian parents, who trained her from childhood for public exhibition in the song and the dance. They themselves were itinerant minstrels, wandering through the American cities, leading a kind of wild, gipsy life, satisfied if the wants of the present moment were supplied. The little Claudia, dressed in fantastic and gaudy attire, attracted the admiration of all by her singular and brilliant beauty, and her wild, elfin graces. It was to her the silver was tossed, which she caught as lightly and gracefully as the wind catches the blossom from the trees, and every act of bounty was acknowledged by a fairy-like curtsy and a kiss wafted by the tiny hand to the delighted donor.

Once they stopped in front of a stately mansion in a Southern city; a widow lady of wealth and high standing was the occupant. She had no children of her own; and, as she looked from her curtained window on the beautiful child, doomed to such a reckless, vagabond life, her heart yearned towards her, and she resolved to rescue her from the degradation in which she would inevitably plunge. She took the child, exacting a promise from the parents to relinquish all claim to and intercourse with her, which they willingly gave, for the sake of the gold she so liberally bestowed upon them. Claudia gave a great deal of trouble to her benefactress, by her wilful, passionate temper, which had never known correction or management; but she was so beautiful, graceful, and intelligent,—was so much caressed and admired by all her visiters,—that it was an easy task to forgive her childish offences. She grew up with every advantage of education that wealth could impart; and, as the adopted daughter of Mrs. ———, took her position at the head of fashionable life. When Moreland was in the first glow of manhood, he met her in the ball-room, where the airy graces she had cultivated in childhood hung round her, like gay and flowering festoons, giving a wild charm to her beauty that rendered it irresistible. Moreland was young, handsome, and rich. This was all that Claudia asked in a husband. They seemed drawn by a mutual attraction,—nay, it *was* mutual, for Claudia then felt for Moreland all the love her vain and selfish heart was capable of feeling. Soon after their marriage, her benefactress died. A great restraining influence was thus unfortunately removed;

and Claudia began to display those violent and passionate traits of character she had cunningly concealed from the lover she had wished to charm. The slightest opposition to her wishes, the mildest admonition or reproof, created such a storm of passion in her, he often turned from her in consternation and dismay, almost believing he had been the victim of an evil spirit, who, assuming the form of a beautiful woman, had ensnared his heart, and was seeking the destruction of his soul. Another source of misery and contention was the reappearance of her mother, claiming to be received into their household. Her husband was dead; and as the adopted mother of Claudia was no more, she was released from the promise which bound her to her. This was a bitter trial to Moreland, but he could not refuse admittance to the mother of his wife. But when he discovered that she had been leading an abandoned life,—that, even then, she was introducing her unprincipled companions into his household during his absence, and making his home a scene of midnight revelry,—he commanded her to depart, promising, at the same time, to provide liberally for her future wants. We will not attempt to describe the frantic violence of Claudia at this just decree. Not that she loved her mother much, but she loved the associations of the wild lawlessness of her early life, awakened by her presence; and she had more fellowship of feeling with the gay, unprincipled men, who had lately frequented the house, than with her noble and highminded husband. She was now a mother, and Moreland dealt very tenderly with her on that account. He endeavoured to win her by gentleness and love to a wife's duty,—a mother's holy cares. But with all this tenderness and gentleness, he never forgot his own dignity and self-respect. There was one of her countrymen whom she welcomed as a visiter, whom he knew to be unworthy and unprincipled. He forbade her to associate with him. She laughed at the prohibition, continued to meet him at every opportunity abroad, and received him clandestinely at home. Arrested by detection in her mad career, she justly forfeited her reputation, her position, and her name. The fortune bequeathed to her by her adopted mother was still her own, Moreland had settled it upon her at the time of their marriage; so, in all the glory of independence, she launched anew into the world; but found, by fatal experience, that neither wealth, nor accomplishments, nor beauty, can give a passport in society to the woman whose fame is clouded by suspicion, or stained by ignominy.

It was about two years after his legal emancipation from these unhallowed bonds, that Moreland travelled in New England, and first met Eulalia Hastings in the village church. Was it a mysterious magnetism that drew him towards her, after having abjured the love of woman? Was it not, rather, the divine sweetness of her voice, the heavenly serenity of her countenance, the simplicity and tranquillity of her manners, presenting so striking a contrast to the stormy electrical splendour of Claudia's beauty, her impassioned gestures, and wild paroxysms of mirth or anger?

Is not the truth of God, proclaimed mid the thunders and lightnings of Sinai, and written with the burning finger of Almighty justice there, "that the sins of the fathers should be visited on the children, even unto the third or fourth generation," fearfully shown by instances like these? Evil qualities, like physical diseases, are often hereditary, and descend, like the leprosy, a clinging, withering curse, ineradicable and incurable. The taint was in Claudia's blood. Education, precept, and example kept down, for a while, her natural propensities, but when circumstances favoured their growth, they displayed a rankness and luxuriance that could proceed only from the strongest vitality. She had transmitted to her child her passionate and wilful temper, but Effie also inherited her father's heart, and heaven gave her into Eulalia's keeping. Happy influences, in her case, neutralized the transmitted curse, or rather, converted it into a blessing. But it is not always so. Let the man who, infatuated by passion, is about to marry a woman taken originally from the dregs of social life, beware, lest he entail upon his offspring the awful judgment pronounced by a jealous God.

CHAPTER XV.

Does any one wish to know what became of Crissy, whom we left floating on the moonlighted bosom of the Ohio?

When she awoke the morning after her flight, she looked round her with bewildered gaze. She sat up on her pallet, and rubbing her eyes very hard, endeavoured to realize where she was and how she came there. The room was unplastered, not even lathed, and when she looked up she knew by the slanting rafters overhead that she had been sleeping in a garret. She was conscious of having overslept herself, for the roof was already radiating upon her the rays of the morning sun. The air was very close and oppressive, there being but two small windows at each end, too high for the ventilation of anything but the angle of the roof. There was no furniture in the room but old chests and boxes, and large bags, and a pile of feather beds, with the hot down oozing through the worn tick, jammed under the eaves. Crissy felt as sultry and uncomfortable as if one of those gushing feather beds were pressed upon her breast. She got up and tried to look out of the window, but it was too high for her reach. Then she was conscious of a soreness and aching in her limbs, a heaviness and weight upon the brain, that made her want to lean against something for support. The chill damp night-air in which she had been bathed, followed by the stifling heat of the garret, had brought on a malady from which she had sometimes suffered in her Southern home. She began to feel deadly cold. Chill, shivering sensations went creeping up and down her back, while hot water seemed splashing on her face. Her hands were like ice, and the blood settled, in purplish darkness, under her nails. Presently her teeth began to chatter like a windmill, and, throwing herself back on the pallet, she delivered herself up to all the horrors of a shaking ague. She had felt them before, but then she had somebody to take care of her. Old Dicey would have her brought to her room, and see that all kinds of warm possets were made for her relief. Jim always fussed and pottered about her, bringing the supreme remedy, red pepper tea; and if it chanced to be Sunday, he would stand by her bedside all day, smothering her with blankets when the process of congelation was going on, or fanning her when the fever fit was on her. Ildegerte too—how kind and sympathizing she was in sickness! How often her soft, white hand, had bathed the negro's aching brow, or swathed her head with cloths saturated with camphor and cologne! Crissy remembered all these things in her lonely garret, with an acuteness of anguish she had never felt before. Then she began to recollect how she came in that garret; how Mr. Softly landed her at night at the door of a large, tall, dark-looking house; how he talked a long time with a large, somewhat rough-looking man, while she stood weary and frightened at a little distance, not knowing what they said, but certain that they were talking about her. Then she recollected that a sullen-looking negro woman came with a light and told her to follow her, and that she went climbing and climbing after her, till she reached her present altitude. Mr. Softly had returned immediately in the boat, so she had no opportunity of appealing to him, as she would gladly have done, for permission to return to her deserted mistress. He had taken every precaution to prevent such a contingency. He had brought her by water, so that she could not trace her path backward. He had given particular instructions to the master of the house not to allow her any facilities for departure, advising him to take charge of her money, of which he was assured she had a tolerable supply.

It was very strange that Mr. Softly should have taken so much trouble about this woman, that he should have carried her off so far, when she could have been secreted so easily in some of the by-lanes and corners of a large city. But no matter how secure was her retreat there, she could at any time wend her way back, if she found her first draught of freedom dashed with bitterness. Mr. Softly had no idea of allowing any such thing. She must be free! She should be free! It was *her* duty to be so, whether she desired it or not. It was *his* duty to make her so, in spite of her resistance and remorseful scruples. If she was such a fool as to wish to remain in bonds because she had a pleasant home and kind mistress and security against future want, it did not lessen the responsibility that rested on him. He was a liberator, and his system must be carried out, let circumstances be what they might. Opposition only gave energy to his purpose and fuel to his zeal. The very fact of Crissy's being content with her lot and unwilling to change it, showed the depth of her misery and degradation. It was that morbid insensibility, more frightful than the extremity of suffering. So Mr. Softly said, and Mrs. Softly said, for it was a shocking thing to them, that a person should presume to be happy in a situation in which they had resolved she should be wretched. It was an unpardonable insult to their judgment, an insolent defiance of their will.

Crissy seemed to have risen above the recollection of the inmates of the house, for no one approached her lofty attic, though the morning was rapidly advancing. The cold stage of her disease had passed, and the burning and restlessness of fever commenced. She would have given worlds for a drop of water, but there was none near. Unable to endure the tortures of this unquenched thirst, she sat up, dressed herself as well as she could, and fumbled down the narrow stairway to a broad landing place, and there, several diverging paths seemed open to her through various doors, but she was afraid of going wrong, and stood looking on this side and that, trembling and irresolute. At length one of the doors opened, and a pale, interesting, anxious looking young woman appeared, poising a baby on her left hip, as if to rest her weary arms. She stopped at the sight of Crissy, and rested herself against the broom-handle which she held in her right hand, while the baby, with four fingers and a thumb buried in its mouth, fixed on the stranger its round, speculating eyes.

"Please, missus," said Crissy, in a querulous, distressed tone, "please tell me where I can get some water. I most done dead with fever."

"Are you the runaway negro who came in the night?" asked the woman, with so compassionate an expression of countenance that Crissy felt drawn towards her at once. Yet she resented being called a runaway negro, and answered indignantly, that she was no runaway, "she came in a boat."

"Well, what did you come here for?" asked the young woman.

Crissy stared upon her as if she did not know what she meant, then stammered—

"Come here for, missus! To be free, I 'spose.

Mars. Softly brought me. Don't know nothing about the place."

"You had better have stayed where you were, I suspect. Mr. Softly might be in better business than filling our house with fugitive slaves. What a poor sickly creature you seem! What in the world do you expect to do?"

"I ain't sickly!" replied Crissy. "I only cotched a chill by being out on the river at night. I'm smart as anybody when I'm well. I just wants water, missus, to quench the fever."

"Poor creature!" again repeated the young woman, "how hollow your cheeks are!" adding with a sigh, while she led the way down another flight of stairs, "you must have been dreadfully treated and abused, I know!"

The baby was transferred to the other side by this time, and had another set of fingers in its mouth, and all the way down stairs it kept throwing its head back and rolling its round eyes up to Crissy, to whose sore and wounded pride even the baby's scrutiny was painful. She had lost all her self-respect, and felt lowered in the scale of being. To be called a runaway, a fugitive slave, a poor, miserable, sickly creature, was an indignity she never expected to meet. What made it harder to bear, was, that the young woman spoke compassion ately, and had no intention of insulting her. Her hol low cheeks! just the way Mr. and Mrs. Softly talked

When she was at home, where everybody was used to her, they never twitted her with her hollow cheeks. She mentally resolved, that, before she started out to make the great fortune which was hers in reversion, she would stuff them with cotton, and take away the reproach of past unkindness on the part of her mistress.

She was conducted to the kitchen, where the negro woman who had shown her the way to the garret was making a clatter among the pots and kettles, preparatory for dinner. Poor Crissy half emptied the water bucket, in her burning thirst, then seated herself by the door, where the air could refresh her aching and feverish frame.

"Could you hold the baby for me, a few moments?" said the young woman, pressing her hand wearily against her side. "She won't cry or pester you!"

Crissy held out her arms for the child, who sprang rejoicingly into them, glad to have a position where the balance of gravity could be preserved with less difficulty. Crissy, as the little creature looked up innocently in her face and smiled, thought of her own forsaken children, and the tears rolled, one after another, in big drops down her dusky cheeks. The cook glanced obliquely upon her from her iron battery, muttering something about the kitchen being no place for lazy folks, whose room was better than their company.

"She's sick, Holly!" said the young woman; "let

her be. You must not speak cross to her. There's enough beside you to do that."

"Are you tired?" said she to Crissy; "I will come back soon."

"No, no; I love to hold it. It takes away the lonesomeness from my heart," answered Crissy, looking wistfully in the face of the young woman as she left the kitchen,—a face which, though pale and faded, had the traces of beauty and symmetry. It was a face of sickly interest, and told of early disappointment, sorrow, and debility.

"Is that your missus?" asked she of the cook.

"No—that she ain't. I hain't got no mistress. I'm my own mistress. Her daddy hires me—Mr. Springer. That's young Miss Springer—his son's wife. Her husband killed a man in a quarrel, and had to run off to Texas. That's what makes her look so down in the mouth."

Crissy felt a sensation of unspeakable relief in knowing the name of the people to whom she was transferred. She learned, moreover, that Mr. Springer was an architect, a master builder, who had a great many workmen under him, and that everybody round and about him had to work. There were two women down at the spring washing, but, as Holly said, "they couldn't begin to get through," and Crissy was to help them wash and iron.

"Mr. Springer gets a heap of work out of runaways,'

said Holly, with an air of conscious superiority; "he's willing enough to let 'em come and stay a while, 'cause of the help they be to him. But hi!—the way they have to work!"

"He gives 'em wages, sure enough?" cried Crissy, whose heart sank lower and lower with every word of Holly, till it felt heavy as the weight of a clock.

"That he don't—not to the runaways. He just gives 'em a home and their vittles. Now such as me won't work without wages. I ain't going to stay much longer, though. The place is too hard. Heap ruther work for quality folks than mechanics: ain't half as hard to please."

Crissy, who had been brought up in the house as a waiting-maid, had never known what hard work was. Her constitution was naturally slender, and had never been hardened by labour or exposure. She was a neat seamstress, a nice, handy attendant, and excellent nurse; but as for cooking, except dainties for the sick, it had never been required of her, and washing and ironing had always been considered too laborious for her.

"I was never used to hard work," said Crissy, groaning at the prospect before her.

"What did you run away for?" asked Holly. "I 'spose they abused you. You look as if you had seen hard times—and you ain't got through, either!"

"Nobody never had a better massa and missus, in the world," exclaimed Crissy, with a burst of feeling she could not repress. "They never gin me a cross word, let alone anything worse. No, no: nobody shall say nothing against them!"

"Well, if you ain't the biggest fool I ever did see!" cried Holly, elevating her tongs in the air, as if she were going to seize her by the nose; "what in the world did you run off for?"

"Mr. Softly made me. He and she both beset me, and said it was an awful sin to live as I did, and that I'd make a great big fortin', and live like a fine lady, and buy Jim and the children! Oh, Lord! 'spose I never see 'em no more!"

Crissy squeezed the baby to her breast, and wept and sobbed outright. Where were her golden castles now? All melted away, leaving the dross of disappointment, the ashes of remorse. Where was the exulting sense of freedom, that was to bear her up, as on the wings of an eagle, while the chains of bondage dropped clanking below? A more helpless, forlorn, dispirited creature never existed than Crissy was at this moment!

"If you'd had a cruel master and mistress, that threatened to sell you and take away your children, I wouldn't blame you for leaving 'em," said Holly, with another flourish of her tongs; "but I could tell you that freedom for poor black folks ain't what it is to the rich white people. Some of us has to scuffle mighty hard to get along, I can tell you. My master set me free when he died; but I've seen a heap harder times since than I ever done afore. I earn enough to git my vittles and clothes, and them was gin me at home."

Unable to endure any longer the burning restlessness of fever, increased by the agony of her mind, Crissy begged for a place where she could lie down,—anywhere but that dreadful, lonely garret. Holly, who seemed to have more kindness than her sullen countenance promised, pointed to a little room adjoining the kitchen, where she said she could find a bed.

Such was Crissy's introduction to the new home which Mr. Softly's philanthropy had procured for her. But this was only the beginning of sorrows. The chill she had caught on the river was the precursor of a bilious fever, which prostrated her for many weeks, making her a burden on the strangers, who had received her for the benefit of her labour. Mr. Springer, a hard-working, industrious man himself, who had everybody up and doing at the dawn of day, and who estimated every one according to their capacity for labour, was exceedingly angry at Crissy for being sick, and at Mr. Softly for imposing upon him such a good-for-nothing, no-account creature. He had trial enough already, in a sickly, moping daughter-in-law. Sickness was, with him, an unpardonable sin. He had never known a day's illness in his life, and thought, if every one was as industrious as he was, they would have the same immunity from suffering. As day after day, and week after week, Crissy lingered on her sick-bed without showing symptoms of amendment, he became more and more incensed, and declared that as soon as she was able to walk she should tramp, as he had no idea of having his house turned into a lazar-house.

Elizabeth Springer, whose own sorrows and waning health had taught her sympathy and compassion, and whose heart was naturally gentle and kind, did all she could to alleviate the sufferings of Crissy, and to shield her from the harshness of her father-in-law. She had a pallet made for her in her own room; and, when she felt well enough, the baby would sit by her, and play with her woolly locks, or stick its chubby fingers in the cavities of her cheeks. Crissy conceived for Elizabeth a grateful, enthusiastic attachment, second only to what she felt for Ildegerte. As soon as she was able to sit up, she insisted upon taking charge of the baby, and relieving the young mother of a care she was too feeble to sustain. But this was an arrangement Mr. Springer had no thought of sanctioning. If she was able to sit up, she was able to work,—and work she must, or go away from there. Things had come to a pretty pass, if it took two women to take care of one baby.

"She is too feeble to work, yet," said Elizabeth, in a mild, deprecating tone.

"Well, let her take her choice, either to put herself to work to-morrow, or to take herself off. She is as well and strong as anybody, if she has a mind to think so."

Crissy's only desire was to return to her forsaken mistress, and throw herself upon her forgiving love. Her image, weeping, despairing, hanging over her dying master, was for ever before her, a reproachful, haunting remembrance. She would describe her to Elizabeth again and again, whose countenance expressed the most vivid sympathy with her sorrows.

"There's something worse than that," said the young woman, sighing; "something worse than death. If I could weep over the grave of my husband, it seems as if it would take away the dull, leaden feeling from my heart; but to know that he's alive, and yet dead to me, suffering for other people's sins (for it was to save his own life he took another's), yet talked about as if he were a criminal. Oh! this is a heavy cross to bear!"

Elizabeth was one of those sensitive, gentle beings, who, if placed in a genial atmosphere, bloom with the ragrance and delicacy of the lily, but if exposed to unkindly influences, droop and wither, with an untimely blight. Hers was a sad and dreary home, without sympathy or love, without one flower of sentiment or beam of joy. She had no female companion or friend on whom she could lean her weary heart, and to whom she could unburden its bitterness and grief. Perhaps this was best. It reconciled her to the prospect of an early grave. The wilted blossom falls of itself to the earth. It requires not to be wrenched from the stem.

Elizabeth has been drawn into our story by the stream

of events, like a twig cast into the water and drifted on its foam. We shall shortly leave her, and of her after-history know nothing; but no one could look upon her pale, sad, and once beautiful countenance, without feeling drawn towards her as Crissy was, pitying her as a wanderer from her proper sphere.

The next morning Crissy, summoning all the strength and resolution of which she was mistress, went to Mr. Springer, and told him, as she was too weakly to do hard work, she was going back to her mistress, and asked him to please give her the money he had taken care of.

The money! had not she spent that, and far more, for her board and medicine? Had not she been a cost and a trouble, and then to have the impudence to come to him for money! It is no wonder that he was angry, but Crissy had never thought of herself as a boarder. She had been so accustomed to being taken care of, she forgot she had no claims on a stranger's bounty. No matter! she could beg her way back to the city. It was only ten miles. Beg! there would be no need of begging. Elizabeth would give her food enough to last her, and she could inquire from house to house the direction she must take. No one would deny her the privilege of resting awhile, when she was too weary to go on.

So, with her bundle on her head, and a little money, which Elizabeth insisted upon her taking, in her pocket, Crissy, like the returning prodigal, prepared to leave the husks she had been chewing, and seek again the wheaten bread she had thrown away. She wept in parting from the sad, gentle Elizabeth, and her innocent, smiling baby; even to Holly she felt grateful, and of Mr. Springer's harshness she had no right to complain. Very meek and humble and subdued was poor Crissy, when she started on her backward pilgrimage, convinced, by her own experience, that, however glorious freedom was in itself, it had proved to her the only slavery she had ever known.

Her trials were far from being ended; for, enfeebled by long sickness, after walking a few miles, she could hardly drag one weary foot after another. She was obliged to stop and beg permission to rest,—and the rest proved long. She was unable to resume her journey that day; the next found her too ill to rise; and though she was fortunately thrown on the kindness of Christian people, who administered to her necessities, she still felt the soreness and loneliness of the stranger's heart; she still felt the humiliation of being the recipient of favours to which she had no legitimate right. She overheard herself spoken of as a poor runaway; and, as formerly, her master and mistress had to bear the reproach of her thin, unhappy appearance.

At last the wanderer reached the city, and crawled towards the hotel where she had left her master and mistress. Would she find them both? Would she find either? These fearful questions had been pressing upon her, forcibly and painfully, as she came nearer and nearer her journey's end. Ashamed of being seen by the servants in her present altered and forlorn condition, she entered the front door, and was gliding up the stairs to the apartment of her mistress, when her eye was arrested by the figure of Dr. Darley, walking up and down the passage. He saw her, and, calling her by name, approached the place where she stood, clinging to the banisters, a cold dew oozing from her forehead.

"You need not go up," said he, sternly; "your mistress is not there."

Crissy tried to speak, but she only gasped for breath. The doctor, seeing the agonized expression of her countenance, added, more mildly,

"You have come back too late. Your master has been dead many weeks. Your mistress has gone back to her home; her brother came for her. Judy, your fellow-servant, filled your vacant place."

Crissy felt as if a dart were shot right through her heart. Gone, and she left! Gone, and Judy with her!

Throwing up her hands, with a wild cry of despair, she fell forward with her face on the stairs, perfectly insensible.

Yes! Ildegerte was gone, and, faithful to her promise, took with her the ugly and despised Judy. Moreland had made every endeavour to find the fugitive,—not with any intention of forcing her to return, but to give her the opportunity, which he had no doubt she by that time desired, of being restored to her mistress, her husband, and her children. Being unsuccessful in his search, he commended her to the kindness of Dr. Darley, should she happen to cross the path of the benevolent physician.

"Tell her," said Ildegerte,—her large, melancholy, but still lustrous eyes suffusing with tears,—"tell her that I forgive her. I have not one bitter feeling towards her. If she has found a happier home than I could give her, I rejoice. I only wish I knew, so that I could tell her husband and children that she is happy. Poor Crissy! she never could endure much hardship."

The doctor promised to be faithful to the trust imparted, and he promised, moreover, that in his professional rides in the vicinity of the city he would bear the fugitive in mind, and endeavour to trace her footsteps.

"Do not, I pray you, my dear sir," said he to Moreland, just before parting—"do not go away believing our city is made up of Mr. and Mrs. Softlys. I assure you we have as high-minded and noble-hearted citizens dwelling in our midst as can be found on the face of the earth."

"Believe me, doctor," answered Moreland, with earnestness and warmth, "one Dr. Darley would outweigh in influence a thousand Softlys. I wish you would come and see us, come and dwell among us, that we might have constant, daily communion. To me it would be a source of immeasurable benefit, as well as happiness."

"Thank you—I do intend to visit you. I am studying the diseases indigenous to the South, and my path will lead me through the regions which you inhabit. I have travelled much in the South; and being a native of the North, and a dweller in the West, it may be presumed that I could make fair comparisons and draw rational deductions. The subject of slavery has been only secondary in my mind, and I have constantly compared what I have heard with what I have seen. I heard that your slaves slept like cattle, in hovels destitute of floors, with nothing but a blanket to protect them from the damp, mouldy earth, being deprived of the comfort of beds. I found them the tenants of as comfortable cabins as our respectable poor occupy, and almost every one adorned with a very ambitious-looking bed. I heard they were half-fed, half-clothed, miserable creatures, in the most abject condition it is possible for imagination to conceive. I saw them fat, sleek, good-natured, well clothed, and above all contented with their lot. I cannot say but that there were some exceptions; but I speak of the general aspect of things. I do not believe I ever encountered a misanthropist among the negroes. Now, it is my deliberately formed opinion, that those who sow the seeds of discontent and disaffection in their midst; who would deprive them of the comforts which they really enjoy, without offering them an equivalent, are, under the garb of friends, their most dangerous enemies. And the master who, actuated like yourself by Christian principles, regards them as members of his family, dependants on his care, considering himself responsible for their physical and moral well-being, is their best and truest friend. Forgive me for giving you a long and tedious homily, instead of the friendly farewell that my heart urges me to utter. I have got a habit of lecturing, and I do it unconsciously. God bless you, sir, and you too, dear young lady. May the roses of the South once more bloom upon your cheek! We have had many, many talks together. I do not expect you will remember them all; but if you have gathered a few grains of wheat, in the midst of much chaff, may they bring forth in memory a golden harvest."

Dr. Darley *would* make rather long speeches, but no one thought them too long while listening, and meeting the kind, smiling glance of his intellectual beaming eye.

Ildegerte did not attempt to speak the gratitude that filled her heart to overflowing. The tears, however, which she abundantly shed, were more eloquent than words.

We will not describe the homeward journey. It was sad; for they were accompanied by one silent, voiceless traveller, who diffused around him a cold, mournful atmosphere.

It was the request of Richard Laurens that he might be borne back to the beautiful groves of the South, and buried in their fragrant shades. Then, when his wife was ready for the last deep, quiet sleep, she could come and lie down at his side, and the same green covering would envelop them both.

So, in a triple coffin, the body of the young husband was carried to the scenes of his short-lived wedded happiness. And all the way the widowed Ildegerte could see with the spirit glance, the marble face, shaded by pale, golden hair, concealed by the dark coffin lid.

CHAPTER XVI.

We come to a new era in our history, and a new character, whose influence will be felt during the remainder of these pages.

A stranger, in a very plain, unpretending Jersey wagon, stopped at the gate of a noble, pillared mansion. As it was a warm summer evening, the family, as is usual at the South, were gathered in the portico, which, being elevated by a long flight of granite steps, looked down upon the street, like the gallery of an amphitheatre. It was a beautiful family group, and might justify the long and earnest gaze of the stranger, while fastening his horse, preparatory to entrance. As the individuals who composed the group were all old friends but *one*, we will speak of them by name, as, with mingled curiosity and surprise, they waited the approach of the stranger who had come in so humble an equipage.

"Does not that remind you of New England, Eula?" asked Moreland, with a smile.

"The Jersey wagon? Oh, yes!" she answered, the quick colour rising to her cheek. Perhaps he was a messenger from her own home. Did he come the herald of joy, or of woe? The bare thought of the last turned to the whiteness of marble the dawning rose-hue.

Kizzie, who was walking the portico with a beautiful babe in her arms, while Effie gambolled at her side, glanced contemptuously at the humble vehicle, and muttered to herself—"He's no quality people. They don't ride in that style. I 'spect he's a pedlar."

Ildegerte, pale and statue-like in her black robes of widowhood, manifested not the slightest interest or emotion. Her large, pensive black eyes passed beyond the advancing figure, and rested on the golden clouds that lay cradled near the setting sun. They looked as if they might be the throne of angels, and she imagined she could trace, in their dazzling outline, one form reclining on a couch of downy gold, whose pale amber hair made a crown of glory on his brow. But there was one, who stood behind Ildegerte, who watched with suspicious glances the meek stranger, who had now reached the lower step, which led up to the portico. Are we mistaken, or is it indeed our old friend, Crissy, come back, like a wandering sheep, to the fold? If it is, we verily believe she has stuffed her cheeks with cotton, they look so much fuller and rounder than we have ever seen them before. She must have been feasting on the fatted calf of welcome, and revelling in the joys of restoration.

Moreland met the stranger at the foot of the steps, and conducted him forward with that courtesy which is the distinguishing grace of the Southern gentleman. The stranger took a letter from his pocket, and handed it to Moreland with an air of humility and meekness. Holding his hat in his left hand, he smoothed back his long darkish hair behind his ears with his right, while his eyes, riveted upon the floor, seemed to think themselves unauthorized to gaze on the beautiful women before him, until permitted by the master of the mansion.

"You are welcome, sir," said Moreland, after perusing the letter. "The Rev. Mr. Brainard, from the North," added he, introducing him to his wife and the other members of the family. A bow of the deepest reverence and humility acknowledged this hospitable greeting. Eula, whose heart warmed towards any one from her own Northern regions, gave him her hand, and expressed her pleasure in meeting one whom she could claim as a countryman. Perhaps he knew her father? Yes! he had the pleasure of knowing Mr. Hastings. He had once been his guest since her departure from home, and had heard most affectionate allusions made to the absent daughter and sister. He had seen her excellent mother, her studious, high-spirited brother, and the little chattering Dora. This was sufficient to insure him the reception of a friend, and his clerical profession was, of itself, a passport to respect.

In a few moments Albert was seen mounted in state in the little wagon, whirling it off to the stable with greater rapidity than it had ever known before. The minister seemed somewhat shocked at the unministerial gait of his horse, and looked anxiously after the animal, when, suddenly starting, he exclaimed—

"My trunk, if you please, sir! I would like to have my trunk carried to my room. I have very valuable papers in it—at least to me. To us poor labourers in our Master's vineyard, notes and heads of discourses are more precious than bank bills."

The voice of the minister was very sweet-toned, and now that he had summoned courage to raise his eyes and exhibit their colour, they were observed to be of a clear, soft blue. There was something deprecating and appealing in their expression, which excited the kind of interest which woman inspires. Moreland assured him that his trunk should be cared for immediately, and begged him to feel perfectly at home while he remained his guest.

"Oh! how grateful to the weary stranger is a welcome like this!" he exclaimed, lifting his soft, blue eyes with devout gratitude to heaven. "Thanks be to God for his unspeakable goodness! When I approached this magnificent mansion, I did not expect its princely owners would receive so kindly the wayfarer who entered their gate. I have heard of Southern hospitality, but now I begin to experience its soul-cheering warmth."

Aunt Kizzie, who had an unbounded veneration for

preachers, no sooner discovered that the stranger belonged to the sacred order, than her contempt for the Jersey wagon was forgotten. And when he stretched out his arms towards the infant she so proudly carried, and asked Eula, "if that beautiful babe were hers?" he was beginning to storm the citadel of her heart. Yes! the crowning grace of maternity had humanized the celestial loveliness of Eula. The infant boy, whom the minister now cradled very gently and lovingly in his arms, was her own child, the first male heir in the family of Moreland, the darling of the household, and the especial idol of its father. Though not more than five or six months of age, a finer specimen of baby humanity could rarely be exhibited, than the little Russell Moreland, and he possessed one of those serene and lovely temperaments which transform infants into cherubs. With the innocent pride of a young and doting mother, Eula watched her child as it perused with its pure hazel eyes the face of Mr. Brainard, with the intentness of a physiognomist, and twisted its waxen fingers in his ministerial locks.

"Blessed art thou among women, and blessed be thy offspring!" said he, raising the infant aloft, as if to bring it nearer the heaven he was invoking. Then, giving it back to the exulting Kizzie, he stooped down to the black-haired fairy, seated, for a wonder, quietly on the floor. She seemed engaged, like her little brother, in physiognomical investigations, for her black eyes were sparkling on him through her thick curls, like glow-worms in a thicket.

"Is this little girl also yours?" he asked, lifting Effie to his knee, who made herself wondrously heavy, by sinking downward in proportion as he elevated her. "It is not possible."

"It is Mr. Moreland's child by a former marriage," replied Eula; and, in spite of her efforts to prevent it, her whole face crimsoned.

"Ah!" said Mr. Brainard, "its mother is dead, then! but it will never know the want of a mother's care."

Eula looked at her husband, but they both remained silent.

"I am very fond of children," said he, trying to smooth back her rippling hair, while she shook her head waywardly from side to side; "you and I must be better acquainted, little lady."

"I don't want to," cried Effie. "I don't like you."

"And why, my darling, don't you like me? I have a little girl at home, who loves me very much."

"Your chin is too sharp, and your eyes are sleepy," said the child, sliding from his arms, which involuntarily relaxed. "You are not like my papa, and we can't be friends."

The face of the minister grew very red at the little girl's criticism of his features; but he smiled very pleasantly, and said he liked her candour. Eula was shocked at Effie's rudeness; but there was an undaunted frankness about the child, which she had vainly endeavoured to bring under the discipline of politeness. As Mr. Brainard's profile happened to be in a line with her eye, she was struck with the truth of Effie's remark, for his chin *was* sharp and projecting, and he had a manner of half-closing his eyes when he talked, which did not please the bright, wide-awake child.

At supper, when he asked the customary blessing on the board, he included, in an especial manner, all the coloured members of the household,—a circumstance which did not escape the appreciating ears of Aunt Kizzie. He seemed oppressed by the attentions of the servants, received them with an apologetical look, and an air of meek endurance, like one submitting his will to the bondage of custom.

"Have you become reconciled to the South, Mrs. Moreland?" he asked of Eula, whose fair face at that moment was relieved by the yellow countenances of Albert and Netty, which shone on either side of her.

"Far more than reconciled,—strongly attached," she replied.

"Do you prefer it to your native North?"

"That is rather a hard question; but I do prefer the lovely climate, that makes the rigours of a Northern winter seem a cold dream. Then there is so much bloom and beauty around me,—"

"And wealth and luxury," he added, glancing, with a smile, at the richly furnished apartment,—at the table, with its tea-service of the most delicate porcelain, set off by accompaniments of massy, glittering silver; and then, more expressively still, at the negroes in close attendance.

"Yes," said Eula, looking gratefully at her husband, I am not insensible to the superior advantages of my present position. In the simplicity of my native home I was content, and I trust I should have remained so; but I have had many, many sources of enjoyment opened since, of which I never dreamed then.

The vision of a dark, polished walnut table, set out with old-fashioned china,—of an antique silver urn,—of a mother's mild, dignified countenance, reflected from its mirror, passed before her, and moistened the dark, drooping lashes that shaded her cheek.

"It is astonishing," said Mr. Brainard, laying down his silver fork with mathematical precision across his plate, "how soon one gets weaned from old habits and associations. One would suppose," he added, turning to Moreland, "that my fair countrywoman here had been born and bred at the South, instead of a simple New England village."

"She is filling the place for which she was expressly created," cried Moreland, "therefore she falls easily and gracefully in it. She is at home *now*."

"I shall visit her parents when I return, and tell them how happy she is."

"I have told them so a thousand times already, with

my pen," exclaimed Eula. "I believe I have written volumes; and I believe, also, I have removed already, prejudices which were once thought insurmountable."

The minister shook his head.

"Your father's prejudices," said he, "are too deep-seated to be removed. They are his principles, and their roots strike deep as life."

Moreland seemed anxious to change the conversation, and started topics of general interest. He did not know yet whether Mr. Brainard was the friend or enemy of the South, by his ambiguous expressions.

After supper was over, and Eula retired with the children, the gentlemen again took their seats in the piazza, and Moreland drew his guest into an expression of his object in coming among them.

"I have come," said Mr. Brainard, after a long and confidential interview—"I have come hither as an humble missionary, in the cause of my divine Master. The sphere I have chosen is a lowly one, but I leave the mountain path to the high and mighty. The narrowest by-path of the valley, so that I can trace there the print of my Saviour's feet, is lofty enough for me. I have ever felt the deepest interest in the poor benighted African. When I was a boy, I longed to plunge at once into the wildernesses of Ethiopia and drag out some of the perishing wretches who were doomed to the rayless darkness of heathenism. I made a vow, that when I grew to manhood I would devote my whole life to labours of love for them. As I have told you, it seems to me that I can be most useful by preaching to those who have become civilized and partly Christianized by slavery. It is true you have preachers in your midst, who give them religious instruction; but it is a secondary object with them. They have white congregations who have the first claims to their labours. If they preach in the morning to their own people, and in the evening to the blacks, they do not carry to them the freshness and earnestness of a first effort. They do not give them the firstling of the flock. Whereas, a man who, like myself, devotes himself exclusively to them, must feel a more burning zeal, a more concentrated desire for their salvation. If he have but one duty to perform, he must do it more faithfully and conscientiously than when his energies are turned into innumerable channels."

"There is much truth in your assertions, sir," replied Moreland; "but we Southerners are justified in preferring preachers educated among us to those raised at the North. We do not wish to expose our institutions to the undermining influences which you are well aware are at work against us. We are obliged to be cautious, sir; for the agents of fanaticism are scattered over the length and breadth of the land, and in the name of the living God endeavouring to destroy our liberties and rights."

The lamp suspended in the passage threw long streams

of radiance across the portico, and lighted up the place where the minister sat, making a halo round his chair. He did not speak immediately, but lifted his eyes upwards in silent appeal to Heaven. Moreland saw this, and his conscience upbraided him for his suspicions.

"I am not naturally suspicious," said he; "no man has more unlimited trust in my fellow men than myself; but our dearest interests are at stake, and what is still more, the union which the blood of our forefathers has for ever hallowed."

"Far be it from me," said Mr. Brainard,—and his low musical voice dropped with silver cadence on the ear of night—"far be it from me to encroach on your rights, or to interfere with your peculiar institutions. All my desire is to preach Jesus Christ, and Him crucified; to address the coloured race as sinners, not as slaves. I think I have been blessed in my preaching to them. I think God anointed me with his Holy Spirit for that one purpose. I came to you with letters of introduction, in the hope of finding aid and encouragement from you. I was told you were a Christian, and would eagerly embrace an opportunity of improving the religious condition of a race, excluded by circumstances from the usual privileges of education. Having wedded a Northern lady, I dared to think you would welcome, for her sake, a brother from the New England States. You *have* welcomed me, and I am grateful; but I want still more—your earnest, Christian co-operation."

"You shall have it," exclaimed Moreland, ashamed of his weak misgivings. "I will introduce you to-morrow to some of the most influential religious persons in the city, and I do not doubt you will find a cordial greeting. There is a very fine church, belonging exclusively to the Africans, situated on a beautiful common, quite aloof from all other buildings. There are also houses appropriated to negro worship, near the churches of the various religious denominations. The Methodist, however, is the predominant sect."

"I am a Methodist, sir," said the minister, meekly.

"I thought so," replied Moreland; "but that makes no difference, in my estimation. I am an Episcopalian; my wife a Presbyterian. I have no sectarian feelings. George Whitfield and John Wesley are great and glorious names. I honour them. Besides, I think your peculiar style of preaching is better adapted than any other for their warm and simple hearts. The demonstrations of enthusiasm, which a colder formula represses, constitute the joy of their religion. They all expect to go to heaven with shouts of glory and songs of victory, or never reach there at all. There is no silent path for them."

In the mean time the kitchen cabinet discussed the merits of the stranger guest.

Netty, who was young and giddy, and much given to

worldly vanities, was disposed to cavil at his ministerial peculiarities, and indulge in witticisms at his expense.

"I thought I should have died a laughing," said she, winking at Albert, her professed admirer, "to hear Miss Effie tell him 'bout his sharp chin and sleepy eyes. I had to pinch myself hard as ever I could to keep from busting out. I never noticed afore, but 'tis as sharp as any razor, and turns up like the peak of Albert's old boot yonder."

"Ain't you 'shamed, Netty," cried Kizzie, in a tone of solemn rebuke, "to speak so unrespectably of the Lord's anointed? Miss Effie's a child, and don't know no better; but for grown folks there's no manner of excuse. He's a godly man and of beautiful countenance, according to my appearance, and seems to have a great respect for us coloured people. I tell you preachers is not to be lightly spoken of. The Lord set the wild bears on the children, once, that mocked at their blessed heads."

"He's got a fine carriage, hain't he?" said Albert, throwing a roguish glance at Netty over Aunt Kizzie's shoulder, "and a most beautiful horse—I expect it can go at least a mile an hour! His trunk that he's so choice of, looks a thousand years old, and the back of his coat shines like Aunt Kizzie's forehead. I mean to ask master to let me give him one of my cast-off ones. 'Spose I do?"

"Saucy boy!" exclaimed Kizzie, slapping him on the

back, laughing, in spite of herself, at his good-natured insolence; "you knows you're a favourite, or you wouldn't presume the way you do. You'd better hush up among you. This gentleman's come a purpose to preach to us black people, all over the world. I hearn 'em tell massa so; and Mars. Russell say the doors of all the churches going to swing right open and let 'em in. You'd better mind what you say. He got the Lord on his side. You'll find it out."

"Hope he ain't no wolf in sheep-skin!" said Crissy. "I seen 'em 'fore now!"

Crissy quoted many a wise aphorism since her sojourn in the west.

"S'pose he come to make us all free!" said Albert; "how you like that, Crissy? When he asks you to tell your experience, give him a touch of Massa Softly, Crissy."

Crissy shrunk into herself, as she always did at Mr. Softly's name. It was associated in her remembrance with disgrace and sorrow, and had given her a taste for hard and harsh-sounding things.

There was one member of the kitchen cabinet who generally kept in the background, believing herself inferior to the rest—and that was Judy. At first she was looked upon rather as an interloper; but her love for Ildegerte, which fell little short of adoration, her willingness to bear the heat and burden of the day, and her humble appreciation of herself, soon removed all prejudice against her, and substituted in its stead a cordial good-will.

"Perhaps he come to tell us what de preacher did once in old Kentuck," said Judy, rapping the ashes from her pipe; "de corn-field preacher he was, and had de pulpit made out of de green pine boughs. 'Twas in de time of cotton picking, and we'd all been working mighty hard. I tell you—ses he,—'Niggers, if you're faithful to your masters and work to the top of your 'bility, neber lie, nor steal, nor run away, dare's a great big cotton field up yonder, where you'll pick to all etarnity and de basket neber git full. De field all white for de picking. De angels help pull off de bolls.' Tinks I to myself, I'll let de angels pick just as much as dey please for all Judy. She want to do someting else, if she eber get to heben. Plenty of cotton to pick in dis world. 'Spect to pick gold up yonder."

The silver tinkling of a little bell was heard, and Judy started to her feet.

"Dat's Miss Ilda's bell!" said she, eagerly; but before she could obey its summons, the lighter-footed Crissy was half-way up stairs.

"Dat's de way!" said Judy, taking up her pipe; "neber can keep up wid Crissy! Neber mind! She got de best right, I 'spose! Judy's too ugly to wait on de beautiful young ladies in dis house! better keep her place in de kitchen! tink dat de Paradise a'most!"

The evening of the following Sunday, Mr. Brainard

preached in the African church to an overflowing audience. The Northern stranger, passing through the city, would naturally ask what handsome brick building occupied so conspicuous and commanding a site on that smooth, grassy common. Green blinds protected its numerous windows from the sun, and formed a refreshing contrast with the pale red of the walls. The interior of the church was finished with great simplicity and neatness. The ceiling was of spotless whiteness, and the area around the pulpit handsomely carpeted. Astral lamps illuminated the altar, and shed a soft, moonlight radiance on the dusky faces, upturned with solemn reverence to the new messenger of salvation looking down upon them. Is that a congregation of slaves, that well-dressed, fashionably-attired audience? There is the rustle of tissues, the fluttering of muslins and laces, the waving of feathery fans, the glitter of jewelry, mingling with the white gleam of the ivory, seen through the dark, parted lips. Certainly, a more decorous, reverential, waiting, listening throng never gathered in a sanctuary, to witness the "stately steppings" of God's mighty spirit.

Moreland stood near the door, anxious to hear the first sermon of the Northern missionary. Never had he found it so difficult to form a decision upon the character of a stranger. At one moment he was strongly attracted, at another as strongly repelled. Sometimes he thought him one of those holy, self-sacrificing beings who, in the ancient days of persecution, would have gloried in the burning stake, the flaming crown, and shouted amid the agonies of martyrdom. Then, again, he imagined there was something sinister and insidious about him, and the soft closing of his blue eye reminded him of the slow sheathing of a shining weapon. Whenever he was conscious of such a feeling he would shake it from him, as he would a worm that crept stealthily over him, shocked that, for a moment, he could give admission to thoughts which he contemned and despised.

Now, as he looked upon him, with the length of the aisle between them, his countenance lighted up with the pale yet dazzling lustre of the mimic moonlight, and the sharp outline of his features thus softened and subdued, his long brown hair parted with an apostolic wave and flowing back from his temples, he seemed an admirable personification of the text—

"Beautiful on the mountains are the feet of him who bringeth good tidings, who saith unto Zion, Thy God reigneth."

He commenced in a low, clear, and sweet voice, and in a calm, dispassionate manner. He told them that he was a stranger, come among them to do them good,—that he had left the comforts and endearments of home for the love of their precious souls,—that he asked not for silver or gold, nor for praise nor fame; all he wanted was the willing spirit, the listening ear, and the believing heart. A faint groaning sound was the response to this exordium. Then gradually he kindled into deeper fervour, and made those startling appeals to the imagination which the negro never hears unmoved. Had little Effie been present, she would not have accused him of looking *sleepy* then. His eyes flashed like the lightnings of heaven; his voice deepened into its thunders, and his arms swayed at the bidding of his stormy eloquence. The negroes began to shout and clap their hands in an ecstasy of ungovernable emotion. Many of them prostrated themselves at the foot of the altar, and grovelled there in tears; others shrieked "Glory! glory!" till the walls resounded with the hosannas, and they rolled forth on the breezes of night.

Moreland scarcely recognised the meek, humble traveller of the Jersey wagon, in the wildly splendid orator of the evening. Surely it was the inspiration of religion! It could be nothing else. He felt borne along himself upon the fiery waves of his eloquence. He did not wonder at the excitement of the congregation. By and by, the minister came down from the pulpit, and knelt by those prostrate and weeping at the altar. He addressed them in low soothing accents, ever and anon bursting forth into snatches of sacred melody, and gushes of holy song. He went down the aisles and grasped the sable hands eagerly extended towards him, giving a fervent "God bless you, my brother!"—"Joy be with you, my sister!" as he passed along.

There were many white men present that night who

went away deeply impressed with the eloquence of the preacher. He received the most urgent invitations to address his white brethren, also; but he quietly, though firmly refused. He had marked out his line of duty, and would not swerve from it. In consequence of this refusal, the African church was crowded almost to suffocation whenever he preached, till at length he was compelled to come forth under the canopy of heaven, and beneath the moon and the stars, and the stilly, falling dews, to scatter the fiery sparks of his eloquence, till the multitude kindled and glowed like a blazing prairie.

Peculiarly susceptible as are the Africans to religious impressions, it is not strange that a general revival was the result of Mr. Brainard's exertions. Even Albert and Netty were prostrated before him, in the depths of humiliation,—believing that he held the golden keys of Paradise in one hand, and in the other the iron ones that open the gates of despair. No more laughter and light talking about the old horse, and the shining coat, and the worn-out trunk. Indeed, the coat was replaced by a handsome new broadcloth one, the gift of Moreland; and, when he rode abroad, Moreland's elegant carriage and fine horses were at his disposal. Well might he say that his lines had fallen in pleasant places.

It was not, however, in a city well supplied with ministers, that Mr. Brainard wished to locate himself. It was on the plantations that he thought he should find the most abundant field for his labours, where the privileges of religion were less abundantly enjoyed. The preacher whom Moreland and an adjoining planter jointly employed was at this time disabled by sickness from fulfilling his duties, and Moreland offered the situation to Brainard, in whose piety he had now the most implicit confidence. The offer was gladly accepted, and in a short time he was to be installed in his new office.

It was astonishing how he had ingratiated himself with every member of the household. He seemed to have found the avenue to every heart but Effie's, who experienced one of those instinctive dislikes which children sometimes conceive, and for which they cannot account. In vain he coaxed and caressed her, offered her sugar-plums and candy; she would shake her elfin locks, pout her red lips, and elude his detaining arms.

"You are very wrong, Effie," Eula would say; "Mr. Brainard is very kind, and takes a great deal of notice of you, for a little girl. It is not lady-like, either."

"I don't want to be a lady, mamma," the child persisted in replying; "and I don't want Mr. Brainard to love me. I don't want him to touch me, and I can't help it."

He had completely won the heart of the young mother by his devotion to her beautiful boy. He would dandle it by the hour, sing it sweet lullabys, or toss it in his arms till its infant laughter rung like silvery bells on the air. He dwelt on the pride and delight with which she would exhibit her infant to her parents and Northern friends, in her contemplated visit home. He expatiated on the noble and generous qualities of her husband; on his humanity as a master, his devotion as a friend, on his manly, Christian graces, till her heart glowed, like the disciples at Emmaus, when their master was talking.

To the widowed and sorrow-stricken Ildegerte he was an angel of consolation. He conversed with her of her departed husband, of his present glorified state, of the divine communion she was to enjoy with him hereafter, in terms of such sweet, exalted rapture, his breath seemed to fan the drooping wings of her spirit, and winnow fragrance from the fluttering plumes.

One day while he was sitting with Eula in the parlour, and Effie was playing in the passage—

"That child," said he, looking at her through the open door, "is a very remarkable one. She requires the most watchful and tender guardianship, as well as the firmest and most unshaken discipline. Happy is it for her, since death has deprived her of a mother's care, that the void has been filled by one so fond to cherish, so faithful to watch over her as yourself."

"She was not deprived of her mother by death,' replied Eula, with burning cheeks. She felt a strange reluctance to allude to the unhappy circumstances of her husband's first marriage, but her reverence for truth was paramount to it.

"Ah!" he exclaimed, in an accent of surprise. "Indeed!" he repeated. "It must have been, then, by something still more sad—by sin!"

Eula bowed her head, oppressed by the humiliation of another. Mr. Brainard seemed grieved, shocked beyond expression. He walked up and down the room with agitated steps. His emotion appeared so much greater than the occasion justified, that Eula looked at him with surprised and questioning glance

"My sister," said he, addressing her with the affectionate freedom customary with the disciples of Wesley, "forgive me for exhibiting feelings which are perhaps unwarrantable; but I am so pained, so distressed at this disclosure, I cannot conceal my anguish. Is it, can it be true that you have married one who has been *divorced?*"

Eula, struck with consternation at the stern emphasis on the word *divorced*, turned of ashy paleness. She felt all that it implied, and a cold, sickening sensation crept slowly over her. But immediately her pure, womanly feelings, deeply wounded, came to her aid, and enabled her to lift her eyes to the face of the minister.

"I know not why you express such horror at thi communication," she said, with dignity. "It certainly is not an unexampled case. I married with the sanction of my parents, sir. One of the best and holiest of men, a minister of God, with the full knowledge of every circumstance, pronounced over me the nuptial benediction. I cannot say but what it has been to me a source of regret and sorrow; but I expect some thorns in a path clustering with roses. Why do you speak as if I had committed sacrilege? I do not like to be the object of such exaggerated emotion."

She rose and was about to leave the room, when Brainard interposed himself between her and the door.

"I cannot suffer you to depart in anger, my sister," said he, in the gentlest and most persuasive tones. "The expression was involuntary, and cannot be recalled. I have very peculiar views on that subject. I understand my Bible differently from most men. I have never, in my sacred office, admitted such an union; and hence my start of irrepressible surprise. But far be it from me to question the authority of those whose sanction you quote. I am a man like them, of frail and fallible judgment, and I may be wrong. In my deep interest for your happiness I may have overstepped the bounds of propriety. Forgive me; forgive a too ardent, too impulsive nature!"

"I have nothing to forgive," said Eula, "though much to regret. If your peculiar views implicate in the slightest degree the honour of my husband, whose irreproachable life is known to all; if they would sacrifice his happiness to a false and shadowy idea, there can be no congeniality in our sentiments, no Christian fellowship or sympathy. I wish to be alone, that I may recover the great shock you have given me."

MR. RRAINARD AND EULALIA.

"Alas!" exclaimed the minister, clasping his hands and looking upwards; "by overmuch zeal I have offended. What have I done! and what can I do to atone for my indiscretion?"

"Think no more of it," said Eula, touched by his sorrow, and ashamed of her resentment; "I will try to forget this painful interview, and remember only our previous acquaintance."

"You will not speak of it to your husband?" asked he, anxiously. "I would not for the world have him suppose I encroached on his hospitality by interfering with the sacred privacy of his domestic relations. He might consider it unpardonable; and his displeasure would be a millstone in the way of my duties."

Eula promised silence and left him, bearing an arrow in her bosom, which she tried in vain to draw out. The idea that any act of her life should cause a Christian minister such ineffable grief and horror, however involuntary its expression, was agonizing. Perhaps others felt the same, though politeness or hypocrisy led them to concealment.

We do not like the hackneyed expression of angel, as applied to woman. In the common acceptation of the term it means nothing; and yet there are some beings so different from the grosser multitude, so apparently etherealized from the alloy of earth, we must distinguish them by some epithet, indicating a higher degree of purity and refinement than usually belongs to womankind. The word *seraph* would better express their heavenly attributes. No one could look upon Eula without feeling he was in the presence of one of these pure and holy intelligences, which, though clothed in humanity, receives from it no pollution, but rather imparts to it its own celestial nature. Her eyes, like stars shining in deep waters, brought down heaven to earth, and discoursed of celestial things. Though a wife and mother, she retained the expression of child-like, virgin innocence, which gave her the similitude of a vestal in the white-robed village choir; and this expression was the mirror of her soul. Eula was still a child in heart, in simplicity, purity, innocence, and confiding faith in the goodness and truth of those around her.

If Brainard had studied her character for years, and studied too a refined and subtle poison, that would prey slowly and surely on its sensitiveness and delicacy, he could not have applied it more successfully. What a pity that the godly man, in his too fastidious piety, should have inflicted as keen a pang as the utmost art of malice could have invented! She cherished no resentment against him; it had died away with the breath that expressed it; but the look, the start, the shudder were never forgotten. She was too artless, too ingenuous to be able to disguise all that she felt; and when she met her husband he noticed the shadow on her brow, though the smile trembled on her lips.

"Are you not well, my Eula?" he asked, with anxious tenderness.

"Perfectly so," she replied, and the colour rose at once to confirm the truth of her words.

"Something has happened to disturb you. Som little pebble has ruffled the sunny lake. Have the servants troubled you? Has Effie been unusually wayward?"

"Oh, no!"

"Perhaps you sigh for your Northern home; a little while, my dear wife, and we will behold it once more. Next summer it will be three years since I transplanted you to our Southern bowers. Then you shall revisit your native scenes, and carry our beautiful boy, as one of the noblest specimens of the products of our sunny clime."

He took the smiling infant in his arms, and caressed it with all a father's fondness.

Effie, who had glided in unperceived, for her motions were as quick and noiseless as a bird's, wrapped her little arms round his knees, and said, in that sweet, endearing tone which contrasted so bewitchingly with her wild waywardness,

"You don't love me, papa, as well as you do little brother."

The truth of this artless reproach struck home to the heart of Moreland. He never could forget that Effie was the child of Claudia, her resemblance to her was too painfully striking; and, though he struggled with the feelings awakened by this association, they still existed, and the child knew it. But his boy-baby, Eula's infant, came to him a cherub from the gardens of the blest,—pure from all unhallowed remembrances, fresh with promises of future joy. How could he help loving it better than the only remaining pledge of his first unhappy love? At this moment, however, the doors of his heart seemed to swing open suddenly, to take in the little fascinating being clinging to him with such childish earnestness, and looking up to him with such a bright, begging look. Bending down, he took her up with one arm, and the two children were cradled in one embrace. Eula was touched by this scene. She had made use of every effort to equalize his affection for his children; but the dread canon of the Almighty would be obeyed. The sin of the mother was visited upon her offspring, and the outraged husband became inevitably the alienated father. Eula remembered this in her interview with Mr. Brainard, and it barbed the arrow his words winged into her bosom.

Her own affection for Effie was very deep and strong. The surprising alternations she exhibited, the dark shades, the brilliant lights, kept her in a constant state of solicitude and interest. Then her quick intelligence, her eager, thirsting desire for knowledge, her reaching after things unknown, her grasping at the invisible links that bind matter and soul together, furnished an unfailing subject for her mind and heart. In trying to teach Effie something of the great mystery of life, of the nature of the Deity and her solemn relationship to Him, she learned much that seemed unknown before, and was drawn by this child of clay to more intimate communion with the Glory of Glories, whose ineffable essence she daily sought to explain.

"This is as it should be, my husband," said she, gazing on the charming family-picture before her, with moist, approving eyes; "never again justify a reproach like that."

"We will take Effie with us on our Northern tour," said he, "and show them an embryo daughter of the sun. Poor Nancy!—I would she were alive to welcome us. I have preserved the faded flowers she left upon my pillow, as a memento of her grateful affection."

"Poor Nancy!" repeated Eula, with a sigh,—"yes! she is gone, and her aged mother still lives. Yet why do I say, poor Nancy! Surely the bosom of her Saviour is a happier resting-place than her couch of suffering. Through poverty, sickness, and pain she has passed, I doubt not, into glory and bliss."

"How strange!" continued Eula, and she wandered in thought through her far native vale, "how strange and varied are our destinies! How little did I think, when I first met you in Nancy's cottage, that I should be your wife—that I should take, as it were, the wings of the morning, and fly to this distant clime! And I have left those behind who will probably never see the sun set beyond their native horizon, and the same trees which shaded their cradle of infancy will bend over their graves. Those lilac bushes near Nancy's window! Do you remember them? Methinks their sweet oppressive odour weighs upon my senses now!"

"Our magnolias are sweeter still," said Moreland. "You do not regret being borne away on those morning wings—do you?"

"Regret!" repeated she, "never—even if—" she stopped, hesitated, and turn pale.

"Even if what, Eula?"

"Nothing," said she, hastily; "but of one thing be assured, if all my future life were dark and dreary, I could not regret the unutterable happiness that has once been mine."

Moreland looked at his wife earnestly, and the conviction that she concealed some feeling from him, that she had some latent source of disquietude, pained him. There had always been such perfect confidence, such a transparency of thought between them, that a film, light as the gossamer's web, was distinctly seen.

"Perhaps," thought he, "it is one of those faint clouds that often arise between the soul and God. Brainard has been sounding the depths of our hearts, and stirring the stagnant waters. She has been brought by self-examination into close communion with her Maker, and even she, pure and holy as she is, must shrink before Him, into whose presence the archangels come with veiling wings."

Thus he explained her thoughtful, pensive mood. Suspicion might glance in his breast, but, like the dart from tempered steel, it turned aside without entering.

In the evening, just about twilight, when the family were gathering in the portico, Eula looked round for Effie, who generally came bounding up the steps at that hour, either tricked out with flowers, or bearing them in her apron, making flowery litter in her way.

"Where is Effie?" asked she, of Kizzie, who, since the advent of young Master Russell, had relaxed a good deal in her surveillance of little missy.

"I saw her in the garden about an hour ago," was the reply; "you know, missus, she e'ena'most lives there."

This statement was corroborated by Netty, who was sent immediately into the garden, where the shrubbery was high and dense enough for a host of children to hide in.

"She is playing hide and go seek with the butterflies, I dare say," said Moreland. "She is the most fearless child I ever saw, and would willingly walk abroad at midnight, were she permitted."

The return of Netty without Effie excited some surprise, but not much alarm; but, when a general search was instituted through the house, kitchen, negro cabins, when voices had become hoarse calling upon her name, and ears ached with the intensity of listening in vain for a reply, then apprehension grew into torture, and the wildest, most painful conjectures were formed. She was not in the habit of running into the neighbouring houses, yet messengers were despatched to all, to return without tidings of the missing one.

Moreland, who, for the first time that very morning, had allowed his parental feelings to gush forth towards the child in a full, unobstructed stream of tenderness, was distracted with anxiety. It was now dark, and every place had been searched but *one*,—that was the deep well in the back yard, scooped out in the shadow of a giant oak. There was a deep curb around it—so high that Effie's raven ringlets could just drip over the mossy edge. Moreland snatched a torch from one of the negroes, who were rushing about the yard with blazing lightwood flambeaux, exploring every nook and corner, and bent over the dark abyss, but he saw nothing save a spot of inky blackness in the centre, that seemed at an interminable distance, and narrowed almost to a point. The water was very low, so that, by descending, the bottom could easily be sounded.

"Hold your torches over the well, and light me as I descend!" he exclaimed, throwing off his coat as he spoke, and tossing it on the arm of Albert.

"My God!" cried Eula, who was looking down into the same fearful chasm—"Oh! my husband, what are you about to do!"

"Hinder me not, Eula, for God's sake! There is no danger: look at this triple chain!"

"Let me entreat you, Mr. Moreland," said Brainard, "not to do anything so rash. If the child has fallen in, she must be drowned by this time. It is too late to save her!"

"If she is drowned, she shall not be left weltering there!" cried the father, springing into the inside of the curb, and placing one foot on the edge of the bucket, while he grasped the massy chain with both hands. "Let me down slowly, steadily, Albert. Brainard, give him your help. Eula, turn away, if you love me!"

"Oh! master, don't—don't go down!—for Lord Almighty's sake—for dear missus' sake—don't!" cried Albert, clinging to the arm he could reach with frantic gestures. "Oh! dear master, let me go! I heap rather go than see you!"

"Hush, my boy!" exclaimed Moreland; "take hold of this chain firmly and steadily: now let me go!"

The negroes were half-frantic at the idea of their master's danger; but when they saw his pale, resolute countenance slowly sinking below them, they pressed in a dark ring round the well, and held their breaths, in awful apprehension. Eula spoke not, moved not; but stood looking down, down, into that deep cold grave—for such it seemed to her—and every time the windlass turned and creaked and groaned, her heartstrings would strain and quiver and twist themselves in agony on the wheel. Lower and lower he went down. The gleam of the red torchlight played a moment on his dark hair, but the shadows extinguished that; then it played on his white shirt-sleeves, which were at length all that could be distinguished in the chill obscurity of the cavern.

Slowly, steadily, Albert! Take care; the chain gives a sudden jerk, a horrible clank, and the bucket rebounds against the rocky walls! It swings from side to side; it rights itself at last! Now strain every sinew: thy master committed his safety into thy hands—and such a master!

Hark! hear that splashing sound! He has reached the water; he is searching in its cold wave for his drowned child, but he finds her not! He gives the signal for ascending. And now the wheel makes more rapid evolutions, in spite of the weight that impedes its motions. The windlass creaks and groans, but the sound is less doleful. The red torchlight gleams once more on a mass of dark-waving hair; a pale countenance receives the ruddy illumination. At length the whole form is visible, behind the massy glittering chain, which the white-clad arms are wreathed around.

"Eula!" he exclaimed, springing from the curb, and throwing his cold, dripping arms round his wife, "Thank God, she is not there!"

Eula gave a short, quick gasp, and fell forward on his bosom. She had fainted.

The mysterious disappearance of the child, the danger to which the father had exposed himself, the sudden fainting of Eula, circumstances so exciting in themselves, were sufficient when combined to create indescribable confusion and dismay. The negroes were perfectly beside themselves; tossed from one billow of emotion to another with such frightful rapidity. Their mingled ejaculations of "Oh! little missy!" "Oh! my massa!" and "Oh! missus!" accompanied by sobs and wringing of hands, were quite heart-rending. Even old Dicey came tottering from her cabin to join in the general bewailing. Ildegerte, the moment she saw her brother spring upon the well-curb, had rushed into the house, and throwing herself upon her knees, awaited in loneliness and silence the issue of the awful moment.

"Oh! let me not look on death again!" she cried,—burying her face in her hands, as if to shut the appalling vision from her view,—"I've seen it all terribly dyed in blood,—terrible must it be, in the dark, whelming waters!"

She was not, however, doomed to look on death; but its semblance, in the pallid face and insensible form of Eula, which Moreland bore into the hall. The swoon, however, was of short continuance,—Eula recovered to mourn for the lost and rejoice over the spared. Little Effie was almost forgotten, while the lives of Moreland and Eula were endangered; but now her claims to remembrance asserted themselves with new power. There was no clue to thread the labyrinth of conjecture, in which thought was lost. Had Claudia been in the vicinity, it might be supposed that she had stolen her from her home; but she had been absent during the past year,—gone to Italy, her mother's native country,—and, it was said, never to return. When silence had settled down on the stormy emotions of the household, and they were all gathered in the hall, where Eula lay extended on a couch, the low, sweet voice of Brainard uttered the simple, solemn words,

"Let us pray."

With a simultaneous movement they all knelt, while Brainard poured out his soul in the fervour of intense devotion. Like frankincense rising from a golden censer, his prayer arose, and the air seemed perfumed with the odours of heaven. He prayed to Him who was once a babe in the manger, who took little children in his arms and blessed them, to watch over the missing lamb, and bring it back in safety to the fold. Every one was comforted, and, though no trace of Effie was discovered, they looked forward with hope to the morrow.

The morrow came, but not the lost one. Messengers were despatched into the country, far and near; advertisements inserted in every paper, with offers of munificent reward; placards were put up in the most conspicuous parts of the city, but no tidings came of the lost child. The last time she was seen, like the lovely Proserpine ın the vale of Enna, when borne off by the terrible Pluto, she was gathering flowers, and twining them in garlands, probably for her sweet mamma, as she always called her lovely stepmother. The withered wreaths were found trailing in the garden walks, as if suddenly thrown down. Eula bedewed them with her tears. Wherever she turned, she saw something that reminded her of the pet, the fairy, the darling of the household. There was a waxen doll, lying on one side, with one arm amputated, and one blue eye fearfully gouged, witness of Effie's destructive propensity,—and, on the other, innumerable gilded playthings, scattered in glittering profusion, and mingled with fadcd blossoms.

Had the child sickened and died,—had they laid her down in the quiet grave, and seen the green turf heaved up over her clay-cold breast, they would have wept, it is true; but submission would have arisen from the dread certainty of death. But the fearful incertitude of her fate caused a gloom deeper than the dark flapping of the funeral pall.

One day, Albert came in with Effie's little white muslin sun-bonnet in his hand, no longer white, and all torn with thorns and stained with green; yet, still it was recognised as hers. He had found it swinging from the bough of a low tree, in the woods skirting the road that led to the plantation, several miles from town.

Here was fresh food for conjecture. The child could not have wandered so far by herself. The Indians no longer lurked in ambush, among the deep pines, for the capture of helpless innocence. The wild beasts of the forest no longer prowled in the wilderness to seek whom they might devour. There was a half-crazy, half-idiot negro in the city—but this was a thought too horrible—it was crushed in the birth. The plantation had already been searched; indeed, everything possible had been done, yet no gleam of light had illuminated the obscurity that shrouded her fate.

"Would you be reconciled to her loss if her own mother had claimed her—supposing an impossible case?" asked Brainard of Eula.

"No!" replied she, shuddering at the recollection of Claudia's ungovernable temper and stormy passions. "I believe her death would cause me less sorrow. If dead, she is in the arms of her Saviour,—but with such a mother, such an example, she would live alone for misery and sin."

"And yet," said Brainard, thoughtfully, "nothing can cancel a mother's claims to her child. She has bought it by sufferings known only to her God, and no human laws can annul her sacred rights. The beasts of the fields and the fowls of the air vindicate the demands of maternity with the most terrible ferocity,—and shall we deny to human affection what we yield to the instinct of brutes?"

"Do you think it wrong, under any circumstances, to withhold a child from its mother?" asked Eula, remembering Claudia's agonizing supplications for her child, which she had resisted with such a painful effort.

"I do!" replied the minister. "I am sorry you asked me the question, for the answer may wound your feelings; but truth is omnipotent. I have told you that my views do not conform to the common code of laws and morals. I think I can see the hand of God stretched out in retribution, in snatching this idol from your arms. It was not yours. You had no legitimate claim to it, and He who gave it to the bosom that yearned over it, with nature's strong desirings, has taken it to Himself, that He may confirm His immutable justice and sovereign will."

Again Eula felt the barb of the arrow, and she pressed her hand involuntarily on her bosom.

"Forgive me, my dear sister!" said he, kindly and soothingly. "You are too sensitive. I would not for the world accuse you of voluntary wrong. You have been the victim of circumstances, and your affections have triumphed over the decisions of judgment. My object is not to give you pain, but to reconcile you to a just and irrevocable decree."

Eula spoke not to her husband of this conversation with Brainard. Judging of his feelings by her own, she knew it would give him pain, and probably excite his displeasure against the minister, whose opinions condemned his conduct.

It was singular, but, with all her reverence for Brainard's talents, zeal, and piety, she never entered his presence without an uncomfortable and oppressive feeling. She was dissatisfied with herself for her coldness and inward recoiling. She did not like to meet the glance of his soft blue eyes, which always fell instantaneously before the beam of hers, neither did she like to see them raised, as they so often were, in silent appeal to heaven. She hated herself for all this, but she could no more help it than the instinctive throbbing of her heart. Ever since his arrival (and he had been domesticated with them several weeks), the household seemed changed. The servants, carried away by their religious enthusiasm, hurried over their duties, or performed them with a less willing spirit. She could hardly refer to any particular violation of obedience or respect, yet she felt a change. But, as usual, she blamed herself, rather than others. Perhaps she was becoming selfish and exacting. She would watch herself more closely, and beware of self-indulgence and captiousness.

One evening, after supper was over, and she had, as usual, retired to the nursery, she found the baby restless, and, as she imagined, feverish and unwell. She did not feel well herself, and waited, in some anxiety, the coming of Kizzie from her supper. When she entered, the clean, starched white apron and bright headkerchief denoted a preparation for going out. Brainard was to preach; but he did so every evening, and Eula thought it would be imposing no hardship on Kizzie to detain her at home, especially as Moreland was absent.

"Did you think of going to church to-night, Kizzie?" he asked. "Little Russell is so unwell I would rather you would not leave me. I have a bad headache myself, also."

"La, missus! there is nothing the matter with him, just wakeful; that's all. He'll go to sleep directly."

"I do not feel able to take care of him to-night, Kizzie. I want you to stay."

"Won't Netty do, missus? I 'specially anxious to go this time. Mars. Brainard going to the plantation soon. There's to be great preaching to-night. Every 'vidual will be there but me."

"Netty has no experience, and I am sure the child is sick; but you may go if you cannot willingly remain I will try to take care of him."

Her heart swelled and choked her words. She was not willing that Kizzie should see how much she was wounded by her reluctance to fulfil a positive duty. She might have commanded her to stay; but her natural gentleness restrained the exercise of just authority. Pressing her baby to her breast, she bent her cheek to its velvet one, and tried to hush its unwonted cries. Her lip quivered, and a tear dropped on the infant's warm temples. She was very childish—but Kizzie had always seemed so self-sacrificing, so devotedly attached to her and the child, she could not help feeling distressed.

"If you insist on my staying, missus," said Kizzie, folding her fat fingers over her waist, without offering to take the child, "of course I'll give up the preaching. But maybe it'll cost me my soul, missus. I feel kinder awful to-night. The Sperrit tells me I oughtn't to stay, when I might git the blessing."

"Go, then, Kizzie, and say no more about it."

"I'll send Netty."

"I don't wish Netty. I had rather be alone."

She spoke falteringly, impatiently, and Kizzie turned to the door. She laid her hand lingeringly on the latch, hesitated a moment, then opened and closed the door, and Eula was left alone with her infant.

"What is the reason," thought she, walking backward and forward the length of her chamber, for she was too much agitated to sit still, "what is the reason, that ever since this man has been here, I have felt my happiness insensibly diminish? What is the silent, invisible influence he is exerting, that is so fatal to my peace? He has gradually assumed the empire of the household, and making us secondary agents in it. Would he had never come among us! And yet, how wicked I am to breathe such a wish! Surely he is a man of God! What motive but pure, evangelical religion could induce him to devote his splendid talents to such a lowly cause? The very incident which has so deeply wounded me, is only a proof of his Christian influence! How selfish I am, to grudge poor Kizzie this little gratification! Oh! how often has my own dear mother rocked me, a weeping infant, in her arms, when there was no one near to relieve her of the burden of care. Lie still, my darling baby; hush, my own little Russell!"

But the little Russell would not lie still; he writhed in her embracing arms; and the more she caressed the more bitterly he cried. At length, very weary with her vain efforts to soothe him, she seated herself in a rocking-chair, and began to sing that sweet cradle hymn, that holy lullaby, which has been so often breathed over the couch of infancy:

"Hush, my dear, lie still and slumber,
Holy angels guard thy bed;
Heavenly blessings without number
Gently fall upon thy head."

As the charming voice of the young mother warbled in the ear of the child, its moanings ceased, and looking up in her face, it smiled with that heavenly sweetness of expression never seen save on the lip of infant innocence. Ah! where is the mother who is not repaid for a thousand pangs by one such angelic smile? It passed away, however, as quick as a sunbeam, and was succeeded by a feverish restlessness that defied all her soothing arts. Never had Eula spent so weary an evening. She would not call on Ildegerte for aid. She had the natural pride of wishing to bear her own peculiar trials. She wanted Kizzie to see, when she returned, how much trouble she had caused. She wanted her to feel sorry for having left her.

By and by, when her arms drooped with their burden, and refused to sustain it any longer, she laid the child in the cradle, and kneeling by it, continued to sing another verse of the divine song—

"Soft and easy is thy cradle;
Coarse and hard thy Saviour lay—
For his birth-place was a stable,
And his softest bed was hay."

Again that heavenly smile. Then the beautiful, innocent eyes gently closed, and, like stars withdrawing behind a white, fleecy cloud, grew dim in slumber. Eula, fearful of disturbing him by rising, slid from her knees in a reclining position on the floor, and still keeping one arm around him, lay with her head bending over him, watching his gentle breathing. In this attitude she unconsciously fell asleep herself; and thus Moreland found her when, having transacted the business that called him away, he returned to his home.

He paused by the cradle to contemplate the beautiful picture, so dear to a husband's and father's heart. The light, subdued by its crystal shade, fell with moonlight softness on the slumbering pair. The cheeks of the infant were flushed with a deep rose bloom; the mother's as fair and spotless as the petals of the lily. The hair of Eula hung loose and floating over the side of the cradle, and swept the floor in bright hazel waves. Her attitude was the perfection of reposing grace, though it expressed weariness and self-abandonment. He thought of the virgin mother and the infant Jesus; and holding his breath as he gazed, continued to drink in their beauty, till his whole soul was steeped in tenderness and delight. Then he wondered at finding her thus alone with the child, evidently overcome with watching and fatigue; and kneeling down by her, he put his arms round her, and raised her from her recumbent position.

"Eulalia, my Eula," he cried, "why do I find you thus? You should not recline on the floor, with the night-air flowing in on every side."

It was some time before she could rouse herself to a consciousness of her situation; then she smiled, and explained the cause of her uneasiness.

"You should not have permitted Kizzie to leave you," said he. "I shall not allow this to happen again. I fear they are all taking advantage of your mildness and indulgence. But I shall prevent any future encroachment."

"Do not blame Kizzie. I told her she might go. It is my fault entirely. If the baby had slept, I should not have missed her. Mr. Brainard is going away, you know, and the same temptation will not occur again."

"Yes, he goes to-morrow, I believe, and I do not regret it. I would not like to have this excitement continue much longer. The imagination of the negro is so powerful, that when it once gains the ascendancy, it is almost impossible for reason to exercise the least sway. I have no doubt that Kizzie believed her soul would be endangered by staying away from that meeting to-night. Brainard is really a wonderful man. He has flights of eloquence that bear the soul up to heaven itself. I do not wonder at all at the hold he has taken of the susceptible and believing Africans. And yet, Eula, strange as it may seem to you, I do not like the man. I feel a sensation of relief in thinking of his approaching departure. I feel what our poor little lost Effie so innocently, yet rudely expressed. I am conscious of an antagonism, for which I cannot account."

"Is it indeed so?" said Eula. "It is thus I feel, and reproach myself bitterly for want of Christian sympathy and regard."

"Well! it is strange; but as we feel alike, there must be some inexplicable cause. Perhaps the attraction which draws him to the negroes, proves a repulsion to us. I think he will do a great deal of good on the plantation; and as they are just now destitute of a preacher, I could not possibly refuse his offered services. He says he does not wish any remuneration; but of course I shall liberally reward him. There is one thing of which I am assured: he has very just views of slavery, and looks upon it, as it now exists, rather as a dispensation of Providence than as an institution established by ourselves. He deprecates the mad zeal which would involve by premature efforts our country in ruin, and condemns, without reservation, the insidious attacks of those who endeavour to undermine what they cannot openly destroy."

"I have one consolation," said Eula: "whatever are my father's sentiments, he glories in their avowal. If he be an opponent, he comes forth to battle in the noonday. He never seeks the midnight shade."

"You are right, Eula; your father is a manly enemy and a sincere one; an unprejudiced one, I cannot say he is. It is one of the rarest things in the world, to see a man who looks upon the differing phases of the social system with an impartial eye. Dr. Darley is one. What a head, what a soul, what a heart he has! I never think of him, without feeling my respect and admiration for mankind exalted. Just as strongly as I was repelled by Brainard, at first sight, was I attracted to Dr. Darley. It seemed as if my being became incorporated with his."

"He is, indeed, a fascinating and remarkable man," replied Eula. "How kind it was in him to take charge of Crissy, when he travelled South this spring; and how very kind it was in him to find her a good and comfortable home during her stay in the West! Then, what a friend to Ildegerte! I do not wonder that her reverence for his character approaches to worship."

Moreland and Eulalia were right. There are few such men as Dr. Darley; but, for the honour and glory of humanity, there are a few such, who, even while walking through the Sardis of this world, defile not the whiteness of their garments with the slime of prejudice or the dark stains of passion.

CHAPTER XVII.

We return to the plantation, where the missionary, Brainard, is now established in the full plenitude of his ministerial power.

Nothing could exceed the enthusiasm which he inspired in the simple-hearted community in which he was introduced. He told them that he had come all the way from the North, actuated by love for their poor, despised race; that he had given up home and friends, fame, wealth, and honourable position, to claim brotherhood with them, and preach to them of the riches of redeeming love. He told them that he loved his white brethren; but far better he loved the dark and lowly African,—loved him, because, like his Saviour, he was despised and rejected of men, and there was no comeliness in him that men should desire him; that he had come to distil the dews of divine love on the root of a dry ground, and make it a green and blossoming plant, whose leaflets should reach into heaven. The negroes listened, and thought an angel was before them, sent by the Almighty, for the ransom of their souls. Every night the log chapel was crowded, and the meeting kept up beyond the midnight hour. The minister seemed incapable of fatigue. He rose with the dawn of day, and, long after the negroes had retired to their cabins, his lamp glimmered through the windows, or his figure was seen gliding beneath the shadows of the trees.

The overseer, fatigued with the labours of the day, usually retired to rest at an early hour, while Brainard assumed the responsibility of seeing order and quietude established in the negro quarters. As he was invested with the sanctity of a minister of the Gospel, and the authority of a man employed and recommended by the master, he did not hesitate to confide in him with implicit trust.

Brainard stood on an elevated platform, reminding one of a picture where a figure is seen rising above a mass of dark-rolling clouds, he, the only point of light in that black assembly. An unusual solemnity pervaded the audience. He had promised them a sermon adapted to their own condition. He had promised to tell them of an ancient people, whose lot resembled their own. Opening the Bible, he read, in a voice of plaintive melody, the one hundredth and thirty-seventh psalm:—

"'By the rivers of Babylon, there we sat down and wept, yea, we wept when we remembered Zion.

"'We hanged our harps upon the willows in the midst thereof.

"'For there, they that carried us away captive required of us a song; and they that wasted us required of us mirth; saying, Sing us one of the songs of Zion.

"'How shall we sing the Lord's song in a strange land?

"'Oh! daughter of Babylon, who art to be destroyed; happy shall he be that rewardeth thee, as thou hast served us!'"

Closing the book and looking earnestly on the serious, upturned faces before him, he began to describe, in simple, but expressive language, the sorrows of captivity, the sad doom of the exile. He described the Babylonish slave, weeping beneath the willow's weeping boughs, while his neglected harp-strings responded only to the mournful gale. He painted him as writhing under the scourge of him who carried him into captivity, and who, in mockery of his despair, called for songs of joy and mirth, in the midst of desolation and woe. Having wrought up their susceptible feelings, by an eloquence which they only partly understood, he changed the scene to their native Africa, and carried them in imagination to the green banks of the Niger, where the shadow of the lofty palm tree is reflected in its clear dark waters. He painted the negro, not degraded, benighted, and imbruted as he really is, in his native land, plunged in the lowest depths of sensuality and heathenism, but wandering in all the glory of freedom, in his beautiful tropic regions, the lord and king of all the boundless wealth of nature spread out around him. Then he drew a thrilling sketch of his being torn from his country and home, deprived of his glorious privileges and lofty inheritance by the hand of rapine, and doomed to a life of slavery and wretchedness. He paused not till he had created the wildest excitement and confusion. Groans mingled with shouts, and sobs with loud hosannas. Uncle Paul, who sat near the pulpit, though he made no boisterous exhibition of his feelings, took in every word with breathless attention. He arose and drew as near as possible to the platform. He seemed to be magnetised by the preacher. Every time Brainard waved his arm in the energy of speaking, Uncle Paul waved his in response. If he bowed his head to give emphasis to his words, Uncle Paul would bow his likewise. The negro preacher was tall and brawny, and his large, swelling muscles heaved visibly under his checked cotton shirt. His collar was left unbuttoned, displaying the working sinews of his neck, and the grizzly beard that bristled round his chin. His head was covered with a thick fleece of coal-black wool, white as snow on the surface, but, whenever it parted, showing the hue of ink. His forehead retreated under this woolly thatch, like the slanting roof of a building, while the flattened nose, large, spreading nostrils, ash-coloured and protruding lips, opening on rows of strong, unbroken ivory, proclaimed the legitimate son of Africa.

When the congregation was dismissed, they gathered in knots round the door, to talk about the wonderful sermon, and ask each other what it meant, and what was going to follow.

Paul stood just where he was in front of the preacher, gazing in his face and waiting his every motion. When he descended from the pulpit, Paul walked by his side to the door of the chapel. They went out together and walked in silence, till they left the enclosure bounded by the cabins, and entered a path that led into the woods.

"Massa preacher," said Paul, as soon as he thought they were out of the hearing of the rest, "I want to talk with you. I can't go to sleep till I hear you 'xplain some of the difficulties of my comprehension."

"Wait, my brother, till we reach a more convenient place than this," answered Brainard; "follow me, and I will make every difficult place easy, and every rough one smooth."

He threaded the wild-wood path, dark with the shadows of a moonless night, till they came to a small opening, where the blacksmith's shop stood, isolated from the other buildings of the plantation. Just behind it, a gnarled and blasted oak, twisted off near its base by the whirlwind's breath, lay upon the earth. Brainard seated himself on the rough, knotted trunk, and motioned Paul to take a seat by his side."

"No, massa," said the negro. "If you please, I'll stand just where I be. I want you to tell me more 'bout that sermon, that's tingling in my ears as if someting had stung 'em. I never hearn afore Africa such a great country. I thought this a heap better."

"My poor fellow!" exclaimed Brainard, "you have been brought up in ignorance and deception. You know nothing beyond your master's fields, which you enrich by the sweat of your brow. Born in bondage, fettered, manacled, and enslaved, you are made to drag out a hopeless, joyless existence, ten thousand times more degraded than the beasts of the field, for the birthright of immortality is not theirs. Are you a man, and willing to submit to this disgrace and shame; this outrage to humanity; this robbery of your dearest, most sacred rights?"

"Now, massa," said Paul, after a short pause, in which he could see the blue eyes of Brainard glittering like burnished steel in the clear starlight, "I thought I mighty well off till I hearn you say I ain't. I got a kind, good massa, that neber said a thing he oughtn't to, nor did a thing he oughtn't to. He neber made me work harder than my conscience telled me was right. He gives me good clothes, good vittles, and never spited me in no manner of ways. When he was a leetle boy he larned me how to read the Bible; and though he ben't a preacher, he can talk beautifully from Scripter. He neber made me a slave; he neber bought me; he neber will sell me. I was born on his grandfather's plantation. I belonged to his father, and so slipped through God's hands into hisn."

"That you have believed all this I cannot wonder," said the minister, in a commiserating tone; "but the time is come when you must learn greater, better things; when you must realize what you are, what you may be, and what you ought to be. I am come, commissioned by the Almighty, to teach you how to rend asunder the iron chains of servitude, and secure the glorious privileges of freemen. I appeal to you, because I see well that you are the most intelligent of the number I see around me, and better capable of understanding me. If you choose you can be free—you can make all your brethren free. Instead of being slaves, you can be men. You have but to will it; the means are certain. You have friends at the North ready to assist you, and place you upon perfect equality with themselves. I have been labouring in your behalf, wherever I have been. I have been sowing broadcast the seeds of freedom, that you may reap a golden harvest. Will you not put in your sickle and reap, or will you lie, like a coward, on your back, and let the ploughshare cut through your vitals?"

"Oh, massa, you talk mighty grand, and I know you means right, and we ought to be much obleeged for your thoughts and obligation of us; but 'spose, massa, we get way off North, who's gwine to take care of us and our wives and children?"

"Take care of you!" repeated Brainard, scornfully; "are you not a man, and cannot you take care of yourself? Who takes care of *us?* Who takes care of *me*, I want to know, in the name of the God who made me?"

"Ah! but you got the head-piece, massa," touching a forehead that indeed showed the absence of intellectual power. "God don't make everybody alike. He make some for one thing, some for anoder. If he make massa to take care of me, and me to work for him, why ain't that good? If I be satisfied, why not go to heaven the way I started?—got halfway there 'ready, massa!"

Brainard made a gesture of impatience, and crushed the dry twigs beneath his feet. Then, with admirable patience and consummate eloquence, he continued to enforce his arguments, and to stir up the quiet pool of contentment in the negro's mind, into the troubled billows of disaffection. He talked till the midnight stars flashed through the deepening blue of heaven,—till the wakeful mocking-bird was hushed to silence; and Paul listened, like one awaking from a dream, wondering how he could have lived so long, without knowing what a wretched being he was before. It was not the policy of Brainard to startle him at first, by unveiling all his designs; but he had taken the first step, and all succeeding ones would be comparatively easy. He had been strewing a gunpowder train the length and breadth of his journey, and waited the favourable moment to apply the kindling spark and let the blazing track be seen,—a fiery serpent winding through the land!

"And now, Paul," said he, rising from the gnarled trunk, and taking a Bible from his bosom, "you believe in this holy book of God?"

"Sartain, sartain!—blessed be the Lord!—I do."

"Swear, then, over this sacred volume, never to speak of what I have this night revealed to you, without my permission. By and by we will take others in our counsel; but you and I must have many talks together, before we understand each other; but, as sure as you are a man, you were created to be the instrument of deliverance to your brethren, and a light to them that sit in darkness and the shadow of death. Ages hence shall hear of Uncle Paul, and the sons and daughters of regenerated Africa shall arise up and call him blessed! Here, take this volume in your hand, and swear that death itself shall not wrest from you the secret of this hour."

The bewildered and awe-struck negro took the book, and reverently kissing it, mechanically obeyed the bidding of the master-will, acting upon him with such iron force.

They then separated, and returned by different paths to their respective dwelling-places. Uncle Paul was so absorbed by new and momentous thoughts, he did not think that he was approaching the graveyard, till he saw the white paling glimmering in the darkness, and he felt the cold, fearful proximity of the dead.

"Wouldn't go by there this time for all the universe," said he; "didn't I tell massa, right over Dilsy's grave, I didn't want to be free? and ain't it the old sarpent that's beguiling me? Wish I'd neber known I so bad off; wish 'twant a sin to be satisfied with myself; wonder if the Lord did send Massa Brainard, sure enuff?"

Turning round abruptly, he retraced his steps, and circumambulated the woods, to avoid the grave of Dilsy. He felt restless, unhappy,—he could not sleep. The next day he could not work. Every few moments he would stick his spade in the ground, and resting his brawny hands on the top of the handle, look fixedly on the earth, as if trying to solve some great problem. Then he would rouse himself, shake his head, as much as to say, "It won't do,"—and, renewing his labour, make the earth fly under his plunging utensil. But at night, he was again under the magnetic influence of Brainard, who at last found a spot in the negro's yielding heart where he could place the lever of his strong will, and move him to his purpose. The blacksmith,—a man black as his coals, and endowed with the strength and nerve of Hercules, was next admitted to their midnight deliberations—another and then another,—till, fed by numbers and inflamed by the mystery of their nocturnal meetings, the elements of insurrection began to roar, in sullen murmurs, like subterranean fires.

That a man, gifted with the eloquence of Whitfield, the will of Napoleon, and the perseverance of Peter the Great, should exercise a resistless influence over the simple and credulous beings thrown so completely in his power, it is not strange. The overseer suspected nothing, because *religion* was the watchword of all their meetings, *religion* the cloak that mantled all their designs. But he perceived a spirit of insubordination gradually stealing over the plantation. There was sullenness and gloom, where, formerly, cheerfulness and good-humour enlivened the labours of the field; and the merry laugh, the spontaneous song no longer were heard in the evening twilight.

In less than a fortnight after Brainard's first unwitnessed meeting with Uncle Paul, a dusky form could be seen travailing by the burning forge, in the hush of the midnight hour, with closed shutters, to exclude the ruddy beams from flashing on the darkness of night. Rude swords and murderous weapons were shaped by the swarthy artisan, from whose reeking brow the sweat-drops rolled upon the hot metal, hissing as they evaporated. Then, by and by, the black Vulcan would steal forth, and, removing a pile of dried underbrush and moss, crawl on his hands and feet under the building, and deposit the hastily-wrought instruments in a dark cavity, dug out, deep and narrow, beneath the forge.

Some old planks covered the aperture, and the moss and underbrush concealed the place of entrance. Sometimes a white face gleamed stealthily through the cautiously-opened door, and a low, sweet-toned voice invoked the blessing of heaven on the sable workman.

"Toil on, my brother—toil on, and faint not, for the day of redemption is at hand! Think of Him who said 'I come not to bring peace on earth, but a sword.' Think of Him who came in dyed garments from Bozrah, travelling in the greatness of his strength, whose raiments were sprinkled with blood, who said 'The day of vengeance is in my heart, and the year of my redeemed is come.'"

It was thus, with burning words, more powerful because partially unintelligible to the hearer, he set the negro's excitable imagination into a blaze of enthusiasm, who went on toiling with ten-fold zeal, while his large eyes glowed by the flaming forge, like balls of living fire.

It is not to be supposed that Moreland's plantation was the only scene of the labours of the indefatigable Brainard. There was one about eight miles distant, where he preached on alternate Sundays, and where the same dark scenes were enacting. He had runners employed in travelling secretly from place to place, giving constant information of all that was passing—shuttles of the loom of abolition, weaving a web which should be the winding-sheet of the South. It was now autumn, and the Christmas holidays were to witness the fruition of his labours. He had ample time to work in, ample materials to work with, and opportunity smiled most benignantly on his plans.

Shall we look into the secret chambers of his heart, and try to discover the moving spring of the complicated machinery at work there? Is he really one of God's anointed ministers, or has he assumed the sacred name, as a passport with a hospitable and unsuspecting people? Has he borrowed the snowy fleece of the sheep, to clothe the gaunt limbs and hide the gnashing fangs of the wolf? Has Moreland ever injured him, that he should come stealing and coiling himself secretly and insidiously into the heart of his household, and endeavour to sting the bosom that has warmed him? that he should throw the brand of discord in his peaceful plantation, and abuse the sacred trust committed to his keeping? Has the *South* ever injured him, that he should seek to make its blossoming fields and fragrant bowers, *Aceldemas* and *Golgothas*, furrowed with the ploughshare of ruin? Does he really think, with Saul of Tarsus, when breathing fire and persecution against the Christians, that he is really doing God and man service? We should like to ask him if he has no home, wife or child of his own, no household gods to defend, no domestic penetralia to keep sacred from intrusion. We think he talked to Eula of his fondness for his children—of his own smiling offspring. We should like to ask him if he would teach the hand of the assassin, where the life-veins were wan dering in the bosom of his wife, or his bloody fingers to twist in the shining ringlets of his child?

Is he the leader of a confederated band, or a mere tool, a machine moved by the will of others?

Look at him! He is alone now in the room appropriated to his accommodation. It is nearly three o'clock in the morning, and yet he is still awake,—seated at a little table, and poring over the pages of that Bible, on which, with Judas kiss, Paul had sworn to betray his kind and once beloved master. Ah! he must be a good man, or he would not read his Bible so earnestly.

But, perhaps he is studying passages to give sanctity and effect to his incendiary addresses. Like Belshazzar, he may be purloining the golden vessels from God's temple, to gratify his own unhallowed passions.

There is one passage of Scripture on which his eye glances; then he hastily turns over the leaf. We wonder he does not commit it to memory, for it is a most eloquent denunciation. The arrows of divine indignation are quivering in every word.

"Woe unto you, Pharisees! for ye tithe mint, and rue, and all manner of herbs, and pass over judgment and the love of God: these ought ye to have done, and not leave the other undone.

"Woe unto you, Scribes and Pharisees, hypocrites! for ye are as graves which appear not, and the men that walk over them are not aware of them."

Years ago, in one of the Eastern States, there was a boy, a very young boy, the son of obscure and indigent parents, who, being convicted of theft, was immured in the walls of a penitentiary. In consequence of his extreme youth, and the remarkable talents he had exhibited at school, a petition, signed by some of the most influential gentlemen in town, was sent to the governor, to mitigate his sentence; and after one year's imprisonment he was released, with the felon's brand on his youthful reputation. But the benevolent gentlemen who had manifested so deep an interest in his fate, resolved to rescue him from the disgraceful consequences of his first transgression, by giving him those advantages of education necessary for the development of his uncommon genius. They sent him to college, defrayed all his expenses, and exulted in the bright promise of his future eminence. But the dark spot, for a time concealed, but never effaced, began to spread. His sole ambition seemed to consist in deceiving and mocking the judgment of those who had known him as a transgressing boy. Possessed of a graceful carriage, a voice of rare and winning power, he never failed to ingratiate himself with strangers, on whose credulity he wished to impose. Under different names, he went from place to place, exciting admiration and commanding attention even from the magnates of the land. Now he was a lawyer, keen in debate, clenching in argument, eloquent in speech; now a young Esculapius, armed with power to crush the Python, disease, in all its hideous convolu tions; again a minister of God, with the dew of Hermon on his lips, and the music of David's harp flowing from his tongue. He seemed to glory in detection, exulting over the dupes he had made. As adroit to escape the consequences of his deception as he was skilful to deceive, he flashed, a brilliant *ignis-fatuus*, here and there, the wonder and shame of his native regions. Destitute of principle, ready to lend himself to any party, provided his momentary interests were advanced, always anxious to enter on a new field of action, since it afforded a larger development of his Machiavellian powers, would it be incredible if this felon boy, this artful, unprincipled young man, and Thomas Brainard, now in the full meridian of manhood, should prove identical? Who could be better fitted as an agent of the powers of darkness, than one who had served so long an apprenticeship to its Satanic Prince?

CHAPTER XVIII.

It was a bleak, dull, cloudy, autumnal day. Moreland was travelling alone, a dismal, solitary road. The oak leaves were brown and sere, partly strewed and drifted on the ground, and partly quivering on the half-naked boughs. The pines still wore their hue of perennial green; but the wind roared through their rustling branches, like the voice of the surging waves, in melancholy gusts. The road was one bed of sand, in which the horses' feet plunged to the fetlocks, throwing up a cloud of dust at every step. Moreland was going on a sad errand, and felt more than usually susceptible of the depressing influences of the lonely scene and the withering season.

He had received an unexpected summons that morning, before the breaking day. The messenger was from the unhappy Claudia, whom he believed still in her mother's native land. She had returned, was ill, the physician had pronounced her malady incurable,—she wished to see him, if it were but one moment, before she died; she entreated him to hasten his coming, lest it might be too late. Could any one turn a deaf ear to such an appeal?—and, least of all, could Moreland?

It was terrible, to be compelled to plough through those drifts of sand, when his agitated and impatient spirit urged him on with lightning speed; but, perhaps it was well that he had leisure for reflection. In reviewing his past life, he blamed himself so much for having slighted the warnings of experience, and yielding to the impulse of passion, that he felt only compassion for the wrongs he had once believed beyond the reach of forgiveness. He felt how long and how bitterly one might rue the consequences of one rash act. It was true, that he was legally freed from the disgraceful connexion; but the scars, where the chain had galled and corroded, would for ever remain on the heart. To exasperate and humiliate him, she had remained where her influence could still be felt, her appearance awaken in full force the memories of the past. He knew that Eulalia never thought of her without anguish, as having made less honourable and holy the name of wife,—of his wife. But she was dying now; and he could meet her as a fellow-sinner, whose only reliance, like himself, must be on the mercy of the Son of God.

Suddenly the sand disappeared, and the hardened soil assumed a deep red hue, that contrasted richly with the dark-green pines. He proceeded with accelerated velocity; but it was not until the close of the second day's journey that he reached the place of his destination.

It was a lonely dwelling, situated at some distance from the main road, and densely shaded in summer with the sweet-blossomed acacia, and the graceful China tree. Now the only shade was a large and spreading live-oak, hung with festoons of gray moss, that swept over Moreland's head, as he passed under it, in long, weeping garlands. Had they been wreaths of blooming roses, they would have had a funereal seeming, at that gloomy moment.

A light, subdued by muslin curtains closely drawn, indicated the chamber of Claudia. Was that light shining on the struggles of departing life, or glimmering on the cold, still couch of death? With an agitated hand he lifted the knocker, which was muffled, then without suffering it to fall, he gently let it go, and entered the house without calling a servant to the door. There was a light streaming from the parlour, the doors of which were thrown widely open, showing it to be unoccupied. Glad of an opportunity of composing his thoughts, he entered, and throwing himself on a sofa, waited the coming footstep which he was sure would soon approach. The reckless character of the mistress seemed stamped on everything around him. The furniture was rich and showy, but its polish was dimmed with dust, and the flies had left innumerable traces on the large gilded mirrors, hanging on opposite walls. A harp, with broken strings dangling on the carpet, stood in one corner; a guitar, in the same neglected plight, was thrown carelessly in another. A piano, with uncovered keys, and burdened with music books, confusedly piled together, stood between two windows, whose curtains, gathered back into gilded shafts, contained volumes of dust in their sweeping folds. Splendidly bound books, with the backs loose and broken, lay scattered on a marble centre table, around a costly Etruscan vase, filled with faded and shrivelled flowers. No well trained, neat, and considerate servant, thoughtful of the reputation and comfort of her mistress, presided in that neglected household. Moreland sighed bitterly, while the image of his lovely wife, surrounded by an elegance and purity, which was but a reflection of inward refinement and innocence, rose before him, rebuking the tawdry splendour on which he was gazing.

The sound of footsteps was heard in the passage, and voices speaking in quick, passionate tones met his ear.

"You *shall* go to bed, missy!"—it was the voice of a negro, harsh and imperious. "I'm not going to be bothered with you up arter supper, gracious knows! Come along, this minnit!"

"I won't!—you ugly, cross old thing!" exclaimed a pair of very juvenile lips,—and Moreland started from the sofa, with a sudden bound, while the pulsations of his heart were wildly quickened. "I won't go to bed till I'm sleepy! Let go of me, and hush your big mouth!"

Oh! Effie, is it indeed you, uttering this coarse, violent language?—you, in whose little bosom Eulalia had transfused a portion of her own angelic sweetness? Is it the cherub, whose loss she has so wept and bewailed, transformed into the miniature vixen, who is now rushing by the door?

"Effie, Effie!" Hark!—whose voice was that? With a galvanic spring, she leaped forward, and, uttering a loud, shrill cry, fell into the arms opened to embrace her.

"Papa, papa!" she cried—bursting into hysterical laughter, mingled with tears—"oh! papa, have you come for me?"

She clung to him with passionate affection, and the eyes that so lately flashed with defiance were swimming in liquid softness. Moreland's heart yearned over his restored child, with indescribable tenderness. In the rude burst of passion, which had shocked and pained him, he perceived the influence of her unhappy mother, and he pitied far more than he blamed. Her person was neglected and changed. Her dress was soiled, and carelessly put on; her thick, clustering curls tangled, and devoid of lustre. What would Kizzie say, to see her darling thus?

"Is your mistress better?" he asked of the negress, who stood staring in at the door, with a sullen, dogged expression of countenance.

"Just as bad as can be!" was the uncourteous reply.

"Tell her Mr. Moreland is here," said he, and the girl turned from the door.

Effie's quick, glancing eyes followed her movements. The moment she was out of sight, she said,

"Take me home, papa; I don't love to stay here! Take me to my dear, sweet, other mamma! How came I to have two mammas?" she added,—knitting her brows, and looking earnestly in his face,—"when I don't love and don't want but one?"

"We have been very unhappy about you," said he,—without answering her last perplexing question,—"we feared we should never see you again. I little thought to find you here."

At the return of the black girl, Effie drew back with such instinctive repugnance, Moreland was convinced she must have been very harshly if not cruelly treated by her. He could not help frowning, as he rose to follow her.

"Mistress says you mustn't come," said she to Effie, who immediately began to make a show of resistance; "she says you must mind me, and go to bed, right off."

"You *must*, Effie," said her father, in a tone of authority, which subdued her at once, for, sliding from his arms, she stood with an air of submission by his side. Lightning is not quicker in its flash than the transitions of feeling in the breast of Effie. "Speak another harsh, insolent word to this child at your peril," he added, in a low but distinct voice to the girl, when they reached the door of Claudia's apartment. "Leave me."

He paused a moment on the threshold, while Effie walked quietly away with her surly conductress, looking back wistfully at every step; then opening the door with noiseless touch, he found himself in the presence of her who had once been his wife. She lay on a low couch, in a half-reclining position, supported by pillows, not more colourless than her face. How ghastly white it looked, gleaming from amid the purplish blackness of her hair! Her eyes, so large, so black, so wildly, painfully brilliant, were riveted upon him with such burning intensity, they seemed to scorch while they gazed. He was not prepared for such a fearful change. He felt cold, faint, dizzy, and his face turned nearly as pallid as her own.

"You have come; yes, you have come," said she in a quick, panting, husky tone. "I ought to thank you, but I have no time for idle words. You see I am dying. I have often prayed for death; but I did not know what it was,—no, no, I did not know what it was!"

"Oh! Claudia!" he exclaimed, with a burst of irrepressible emotion. It was all he could utter. He seemed hurled back, with a violent wrench, over th chasm of years, to the moment when, in the splendour of her girlish bloom and beauty, she had fascinated his young imagination. He saw that radiant, graceful figure, the goddess of the ball-room, side by side with the pale, emaciated, reclining shadow—the sad mockery of life; and he shuddered and groaned at the contrast.

"I don't want you to pity me," said she, a softer expression nevertheless passing over her face; "it will do no good. An ocean of tears could not save me now from the grave that yawns black and cold before me. I did not send for you because I wanted your compassion, or even your forgiveness. I have suffered you to believe a lie. After I am dead, I do not wish you to think of me as worse than I really am. The crimes imputed I would not deny, because they reflected shame and misery on you. In my hatred and revenge, I felt willing to sink down to the lowest abyss myself, provided I dragged you with me, the sharer of my disgrace. But, on the word of a dying woman, the accusations brought against me were false. For my after career, I am responsible to no one. I make no confessions: I ask no absolution."

Moreland was too much shocked to reply. Whatever joy he might feel at the avowal of her innocence, was deadened by the knowledge of the bitter and revengeful motives which had so long withheld it.

"You do not speak to me! You do not believe me!" she cried, in an impatient, yet exhausted tone, a dark fire kindling in her eyes.

"Yes, Claudia, I do believe you; but let the past be forgotten in the contemplation of the future. Time is nothing to you—eternity, everything. You do not want *my* forgiveness; but there is One whose forgiveness you *must* obtain, or the doors of mercy will be for ever closed."

"It is too late to think of such things—too late!" said she, sinking back on her pillow. "I am going; but whether into the blackness of annihilation, or—" She stopped, with a spasmodic shudder, and added with rapid utterance—"Oh! if you knew what I have suffered!—such agonies of pain! I have died ten thousand deaths already! Oh! surely there is expiation in this! Tell me, if there is not! Sin must be burnt out in the flames of suffering like mine!"

"There is One who bore the burden of our sins, and the agonies of our sufferings," said Moreland, with inexpressible earnestness and solemnity. "His alone are expiatory. To Him only can the living look for happiness; the dying for hope and consolation. Oh! Claudia, by the love we once bore each other; by the child in whose heart our own life is throbbing; by the eternity to which we both are hastening; and by your soul and mine, which the Son of God died to redeem, I beseech you to cast yourself, lost and helpless as you are, into His arms of love, and breathe out your life in prayers for pardon! It is not too late! Dare not limit the mercy of the Omnipotent!"

"Where is He?" asked she faintly, raising herself on one elbow, and looking wildly upward. "Where are the arms open to receive me? I see them not! I feel them not! No, no, no! There is no Saviour for me! I cannot pray—and they tell me prayer alone can open the gates of heaven!"

With an involuntary motion, Moreland knelt by her bedside and breathed forth one of the most solemn, fervent, thrilling prayers that ever gushed from mortal lips. A soul shrouded in almost heathen darkness, trembling on the threshold of eternity, seemed pleading through him, in agonies of supplication, from the depths of penitence and remorse.

Claudia lay with closed eyes, and hands tightly clasped over her bosom. The silence of death reigned in the chamber long after his voice ceased, and Moreland thought she slept, when, suddenly, low sobs, that threatened her with suffocation, convulsed her frame, and she burst into a passion of tears, such as seldom flow but from the eyes of childhood. The more Moreland endeavoured to soothe, the more bitterly she wept. Deeply affected, he raised her head on his arm, and put back the damp, matted locks that fell blinding over her temples.

"I don't deserve this," she said. "You ought to curse me. Oh! I have been walking in darkness all my life, and light dawns just as my eyes are about to close for ever. How kind, how good, how just you have been, and I knew it not till now! Oh! Moreland! if the living could know how the dying feel!"

We will not attempt to describe all that passed in

this hour of awful reconciliation. Several times she was seized with paroxysms of agony terrible to behold, but she would not allow him to ring for assistance.

"The anodyne you have given me is the only thing that gives me the slightest relief," she said, in the inter val of her sufferings. "I cannot bear the sight of those horrible negroes. I can bear pain better than their insolence."

Moreland might have told her that no tyrants are so despotic as those who have once been tyrannized over themselves; that they were revenging themselves while she lay helpless on the bed of sickness, for the wrongs they had endured from her in her day of power. He might have upbraided her for tearing away her child from the gracious influences which were blessing her childhood, and exposing her to the harshness and insolence she had brought in judgment on herself; but he came to pour oil, not vinegar, on the wounded heart of the humiliated victim of her own unmastered passions.

"Why are you here without friends?" he asked; "at the mercy of menials, so destitute of comfort, so lonely and desolate? Why did you not send for me sooner, that I might relieve your sufferings and administer to your necessities?"

"I felt a sullen pride in suffering alone and unpitied," she answered. "I dreamed there was atonement for sin in such unknown anguish. Friend! I have no friend. You are the only friend I ever had in the world. Friend—lover—husband once," she slowly repeated, "now for ever lost to me. Yes! I had one more friend—my adopted mother. Thank heaven! she died without knowing how utterly unworthy I proved of her guardian love. My God! It was in this very room she died! perhaps on this very pillow!"

"Would that Eulalia were with me!" exclaimed Moreland; "she would prove to you an angel of consolation. Let me send for her. You may linger yet for days and weeks. You may yet be restored to health and life."

"Never! the talons of the vulture are here," laying her hand on her breast. "It is more than a year since I have known that I have an incurable malady, and I have seen death coming slowly and surely, nearer and nearer, dark, cold, and inexorable, with a burning dart in his hand, ready to transfix my writhing heart. They wanted me to stay in Italy and die, but I would not. I could not die without seeing you once more. I went to your door, almost, but dared not enter. Sickness had made me a coward. I saw my child playing among the flowers, and there was no one near to guard her. I stole softly behind her, threw my mantle round her head to stifle her cries, and fled. Poor child! I wish I had not done it. I had better left her with your Eulalia. I cannot make her love me."

After another pause, in which her thoughts seemed flowing in a more tranquil stream, she added—

"You must not bring her hither. We ought not to breath the same atmosphere. She is too pure, too holy. I should envy her even in my death-gasp. As I have lived without the friendship, I can die without the sympathy of woman."

Moreland could not realize that death was so rapidly approaching—she spoke with such occasional energy, and such jets of fire issued from the dark fountains of her eyes. But when unnatural excitement subsided into lethargy, and the dark-veined lids closed over the large sunken orbs, while a deeper pallor settled on her altered and sharpened features, he could see but too plainly the mark of the skeleton fingers, whose grasp was tightening over her heart. There was nothing left but the embers of life, which a breath might reduce to a cold heap of ashes. Sad and mournful were his vigils. The melancholy winds of autumn swept with a sighing, wailing sound against the windows, and sometimes the dry leaves came in a drift against the panes, rustling and crackling as they fell. The stars gleamed faintly through gray, rifted clouds, and the roar of a distant waterfall, with a monotony more dreary than silence, murmured on the ear. Oh, woman! how dreadful, even in this world, is the retribution that follows thy aberration from rectitude and duty! Canst thou gather grapes of thorns, or roses from the barren sand? Canst thou put thy hand in the cockatrice's den, without feeling the sting and venom of his fangs? Canst thou wrap thyself body and soul in the sheet-lightning of passion, without being scorched and shrivelled, furrowed and scarred? A wife, without the protection or name of her husband,—a mother, disowned by her child,—a mistress, the vassal of her slaves,—an accountable being, awakened to the responsibilities of life at the very moment when they are sliding from the grasp; an eternal soul, trembling, shivering, groping in darkness illimitable, for something to sustain it, even if it be but the wind-shaken reed! Wasted hours, perverted gifts, lost, lost treasures behind, an unfathomable abyss below, a consuming God above—oh! is not this retribution? These thoughts swelled high in the breast of Moreland, as he sat watching the death-like slumbers that hung, like a heavy mist, over the couch of Claudia. The wind rose higher, and swelled into loud and stormy gusts, before which the dark cloud-racks scudded, unpiloted barks of a dim and boundless sea. Moreland rose and looked out through the curtains, feeling a gloomy pleasure in the apparent sympathy of nature. Dreariness without, desolation within. He was glad the moon was not shining down, with cold, sickly effulgence; he was glad the stars were hiding their twinkling faces under a cloud-veil, whose edges, torn by the wind, seemed to flap as he gazed; and, when lightning came darting in zigzag leaps, high up from the zenith, and plunged hot and fiery into the bowels of the earth, he felt congenial electricity burning in his soul.

He waited for the thunder, and it came muttering and roaring, like the startled lion from his lair, mingling with the howling wind and the drifting rain. It was one of those wild, terrific storms, peculiar to a Southern latitude, which destroy, in a few moments, the growth of years. The shallow roots of the China trees were torn up, and lay heaving and quivering on the earth; the broken branches of the acacias went hurrying through the air like birds of rapine; and every drop of rain seemed to bear upon its bosom a rent and twisted leaf.

Claudia slept in the midst of this elemental war, for her senses were steeped in lethargy by the powerful drug of the East. She slept, but she began to moan in her slumbers, and toss her arms with delirious gesture—those poor, emaciated arms, once so round and fair, and glittering with gems.

"Oh! thou who ridest upon the wings of the wind, who makest darkness thy pavilion," cried Moreland, turning from the dim-lighted couch to the darkened heavens, "come not in judgment, but mercy! Have pity on the frail and erring creatures thou hast made! Thou knowest our frames: thou rememberest that we are but dust! Oh! it is a fearful thing, this rending of the immortal from the mortal—fearful to witness, but, alas! more dread to bear!"

At this moment, a large branch of the live oak came tumbling, crashing against the house, bursting in the casement, and shivering into splinters the crystal panes.

The house rocked, and every article of furniture vibrated with the concussion. The shock, the crash, roused Claudia from the stupor in which her senses were steeped. She opened her eyes with a look of indescribable terror.

"The destroying angel is come!" she ejaculated, in a hollow, trembling voice. "I hear the rushing of his terrible wings!"

"The Lord is in the whirlwind, as well as the still small voice, Claudia," said Moreland; but even as he spoke an awful change came over her countenance, and violent paroxysms convulsed her features. Moreland, believing that the last struggle had indeed begun, roused the servants, who, awakened by the storm, came hurrying into the room, incapacitated by terror from rendering the services required. Effie glided in after them. She looked with awe and dread on the pale, writhing form her father was supporting in his arms; but she manifested no alarm at the wild storm-gusts raging abroad.

Moreland would have sent for a physician, but it was impossible to brave the fury of the tempest; and he knew the skill of man was vain. That chill, gray tint, never to be mistaken, that shows the tide of life has all ebbed, leaving the sands dry and bare, was stealing, like twilight, over every feature, with a gradually deepening shade.

Moreland hung over her in unspeakable agony. He

would have given worlds for one assurance from her dying lips of submission to her God, of hope in her Saviour's mercy. He felt a portion of that divine love in his heart, which threw its halo of light round Calvary's blood-stained brow. He would willingly have offered up his life for the peace of that departing soul.

"Speak to me, Claudia," he cried, "and tell me if the hope of pardon has taken the sting from death, the victory from the grave! Look at me, if speech is denied! Give me one glance, in token that a forgiving God is found!"

She could not speak, but she lifted her eyes, where all that remained of vitality was concentrated in one burning spark, and fixed them steadfastly on his. Never, never did he forget that glance. It haunted him years afterwards. He saw it in the blaze of noonday—the darkness of midnight. It haunted him till his dying day.

The morning sunbeams shone clear and bright on the wreck of the midnight storm—on the uprooted trees, the splintered limbs, the drifted leaves, the torn and dripping moss garlands. The morning sunbeams stole, with stealthy rays, through a rifted curtain on the ruins of life,—the cold, white face, the shrouded eyes, and folded hands; on the chillness, the stillness, the mystery of death. They glimmered on triple bars of dust, stretching across the apartment, and gave them the appearance of gauzy gold. The glittering particles sunk lower and lower, till they seemed to float like a shroud over the body of the dead.

Even in death was the hand of retribution visible. No white blossoms, emblematical of purity, were scattered over the couch,—no fragrant jessamine or roses, overpowering, with their sweetness, the deadly odour of mortality. The fair, perishing tokens of love and memory with which Southern custom beautifies the shroud and the coffin, were wanting here.

Moreland and his little daughter followed her to her lonely grave. He was spared the pain of a public funeral by the isolation of the dwelling. It was the country-seat of Claudia's adopted mother, remarkable for the beauty of its situation, and once distinguished for its elegance and taste. Now, however, everything wore a neglected, dilapidated appearance. The vines and shrubbery which the former mistress had so carefully trained had grown to rank luxuriance, the former trailing in the dust, the latter covered with dingy cobwebs and defaced by the caterpillars' nests.

A new care now rested on Moreland. Effie, by her mother's death, became the heiress of her property. He would gladly have been released from this additional responsibility, for the negroes, left so long without proper discipline, were exceedingly difficult to manage. He resolved to break up the establishment and take them to his own plantation, which was under such excellent regulations, and where the influence of example would be more powerful than precept or reproof.

Little did he dream of the subterranean fires sullenly roaring under the apparent quietude of the surface. Little did he dream that Lucifer, in the garb of an angel of light, concealing the cunning of the serpent under the dissembled innocence of the dove, was plotting rebellion, bloodshed, and ruin.

There was peace and happiness, however, in reserve, in the home doubly endeared by contrast with the harrowing scenes through which he had lately passed. And yet the remembrance of Claudia, her sufferings and her death, long brooded in sadness on his heart. That last glance, so earnestly sought as a token of peace, and received as a sign of unutterable agony, often awakened him suddenly from the dreams of midnight, and seemed to be accompanied by a wailing cry that rang through the household, and left its mournful echoes in his soul. Eula wept over her fate. Not all her joy at the restoration of the lost Effie could remove the sad impression of her mother's melancholy death—and it was long before the Effie who was taken from them reappeared. The little wilful being, whose childish prattle was vulgarized by African phrases, learned by constant association with the negroes, was not the child of Eula's tender, restraining care. She had to begin anew her labours of love. New tares were to be uprooted, new thorns extracted, and choking stones removed, before the lately neglected plant could receive, in blessing, the sunshine and the dew of culture.

But Eula, with unexampled sweetness of temper and constancy of purpose, applied herself to the task, in the hope of final success. She had another cause of anxiety, of which she never complained, but which her natural sensitiveness and timidity made her shrink from analyzing. She missed the respectful, affectionate, spontaneous obedience which had made the relation of mistress and servants hitherto so delightful. Albert seemed less changed than the others, but there was something, even in him, which she felt, without being able to explain.

"The Ides of March! The Ides of March!" Will a darker spirit than that which crimsoned the Roman Capitol with blood, be suffered to consummate its fell designs?

CHAPTER XIX.

THE jailer's wife sat alone in a little room adjoining the prisoners' cells. Her husband was absent, and had committed to her care the keys of the prison-house, which she most faithfully guarded. The new jail, a handsome, massy brick building, had been burned down a short time previous (whether by accident or design, no one had been able to discover), and the dismal walls of the old wooden one once more showed signs of occupancy. The partition that separated the cells from each other were so thin, the shrunken boards exhibiting many a chink and crevice, that voices could easily penetrate the barrier. Thus the prisoners, though nominally divided, could hold occasional intercourse with each other, when they believed themselves safe from vigilant and listening ears.

The jailer's wife was an energetic and industrious woman, who frequently sat up beyond the midnight hour, plying her busy needle. It was a nice, quiet time to sew, when the children were asleep, and the prisoners at rest on their pallets of straw.

The only present occupants of the jail were two negro men, who had been arrested in the act of breaking into the bank. They belonged to different masters, and had previously sustained honest and respectable characters. The name of one was Jerry, the other, Jack.

Mrs. Wood, the jailer's wife, was seated by a comfortable fire, for it was a chilly, wintry night; and, as she heard the low whistling of the wind under the doors and windows, she thought of their cold, lonely cells, and wished she could communicate to them some of the genial warmth she was enjoying alone. She was a kind-hearted woman, and many a heart had blessed her, in going forth from those prison walls.

She was startled by the sound of voices in the cells, where she knew the prisoners were in solitary confinement. Laying down her needle-work, and stepping to the door on tiptoe, she put her ear to the key-hole, and held her breath to listen. She heard distinctly the voice of Jerry talking to Jack through the chinks of the partition; and, gathering the import of their preceding conversation from the words which met her ear, she stood paralyzed with amazement and horror.

"Hush!" said Jack, "you talk too loud. 'Spose somebody hear what you say? Put your mouth close to this crack. Now, just talk easy. How long, you think, 'fore Christmas?"

"'Bout two weeks, or so; 'spect it's most by," answered Jerry. "The Lord Harry! ain't we gwinter have a merry Christmas, this time? White folks laugh wrong side of the mouth, won't they?"

"'Spose they find us out, Jerry!—wonder how merry we'll be then? 'Most wish I'd never had nothing to do with it, no how! If the Lord all on our side, as *he* tell us, wonder what he let 'em catch us and shut us up here for? He said the Lord gwine to fight for us, with great big flaming sword! Don't see it! Don't much believe he got any!"

"You're fit for nothing but a coward, Jack! If it hadn't bin for you being afeard, we shouldn't bin cotched in the fust place! I tell you 'twill all come right. The patrole never stays out arter twelve,—they're too lazy to keep out of bed more than they can help!"

"Wonder if they warn't up when they poked us in this here ole dark hole?"

"The niggers 'll be too mighty for 'em *this* time, I tell you! Ain't they coming from all the plantations? And what good, I want to know, is the patrole gwine to be, when the bridge set afire, go splash in the water, and white folks got nowhere to go?"

"How we gwine to get out, wonder?" said the mis giving Jack.

"You great big black fool of a nigger," cried Jerry, in a contemptuous tone, "think they won't set fire to the old jail fust of all? Can't get 'long without Jerry, I know!"

"Look a here, Jerry—wish I'd never had nothing to do with this business. Hain't had no peace of mind since it was sot a going. 'Tain't right, killing and burning folks in the dark—folks as done well by a body, too. Don't think we gwine to better ourselves, arter all."

"There's no use in talking to a fool," cried the lordly Jerry; "but you better mind! If you let out on it, one syllable, you'll swing up by that black neck of yourn, way up yonder on the pine tree! Don't you know what the preacher said?"

"Shouldn't think the Lord would send that sort of preacher. Well! he know best, sure enough. Tell you what, Jerry—I'm gwine to sleep. Bimeby you'll find out what a raal fool means. 'Spect you think you my massa aready—hi!"

"Shut your mouth and go to sleep," said Jerry, who, though he addressed such imperious language to his brother prisoner, uttered it in a tone of good-natured contempt, as if he were more in jest than earnest. Silence followed this last injunction, which was soon interrupted by a snoring sound, implying that the order was obeyed.

The jailer's wife turned from the door and walked softly back to the fire, shivering in every limb. Leaning her elbows on her knees, and her head upon her hands, she revolved in her mind the startling hints she had just heard, and the best course of conduct for her to pursue. As we said before, she was a woman of great energy of character; and though horror-stricken at the plot just unfolded, she was not intimidated. The idea that Providence had made her the instrument of discovering a conspiracy so dark and deadly, gave her a moral courage and determination appropriate to the emergency. Her husband being absent, she resolved to act on her own responsibility. Not being able to sleep, she watched with impatience the dawning day, thinking the morning twilight had never lingered half so long.

After having sent the prisoners their usual breakfast, she filled a plate with nice things from her own table, and went to the grate of Jerry's cell. His was the master spirit, and the one she was resolved to bring under her influence.

"Here, Jerry," said she, "if you didn't sleep more than I did last night, I thought you might feel poorly this morning, and would relish a mouthful of my breakfast."

"Missus mighty good," answered Jerry, gloating over the plate with eager, devouring eyes; "but what make her think I didn't sleep? Slept like a top all night long. Wonder what made missus keep awake!"

"I'll tell you presently," said she; "but I want to ask you one question before I begin. Have I not been kind to you, Jerry? Have I not done all I could for you and Jack, and treated you just as well as if you were white?"

"Yes, that you have, missus; but what make you ax

me that now?" The eyes of the negro glanced from one side to the other, without looking towards her, and the muscles about his mouth began to twitch.

"Have you a cruel master, Jerry, and a bad mistress?"

"No, missus, not as I know of: got nothing to complain of. Never worked at home much—work out by the job. Pay so much to massa; all I make over, keep myself."

"Have you had hard times getting work? Do the people cheat you out of your money?"

"No, missus! good work, good pay, or Jerry wouldn't have nothing to do with it. Always got 'long mighty well 'bout money."

"Then, Jerry," said she, fixing her eyes resolutely on his face, and speaking in a calm deliberate tone, "what do you want to kill me for, if I am your friend? and your master and mistress, if they have been good to you? and the white people, if they have never abused you? What put such a thing as that in your head?"

So quietly and coolly she questioned him, one might have supposed she was asking him how he liked the breakfast she had brought him. The negro winced under her steadfast gaze, and his hands trembled so that the plate dropped into his lap.

"Don't know what you talking 'bout," said he, putting both hands to his head and rubbing his wool till it stood up fierce and grim all round his temples. "Sure enough missus must be crazy!"

"No, Jerry! I'm in my right mind, thank God! and you soon will find it out. I heard all that you and Jack said last night, and if you don't tell me the whole plot, from beginning to end, you shall both swing from the scaffold into flames hotter than your Christmas bonfires."

"Oh, missus!" cried Jerry, every feature working and convulsed, while his eye-balls glowed like burning coals. "I just talking in my sleep—knows I was. Don't know nothing what you mean. Hain't got nothing 'gin white folks—never did have."

"There's no use in lying to me, Jerry. It won't do. Your only safety now is in speaking the truth, and the whole truth, and nothing but the truth. On no other terms can you have one hope of pardon. I am going to a magistrate, to tell him all I have discovered; and you will just as surely be hung upon the scaffold as you are sitting on that bed of straw."

Here groans and ejaculations from the next cell came gushing through the chinks. Jack could not hold in any longer.

"Oh, Lord a'mercy! Lord a'mercy!" exclaimed Jack; "wish this nigger had never been born!"

"Hush, Jack!" said the jailer's wife; "hush that noise! I'm coming to you presently. Make up your mind, Jerry. Tell everything you know, and get a good chance for life, or choose chains, the rope, and the scaffold."

In consequence of the quiet behaviour of the negroes and the entreaties of Mrs. Wood, their manacles had ,een knocked off, and their limbs were now free as her wn.

Jerry sprang to his feet, shaking himself as the shaggy mastiff does, when the fierce, animal nature is roused within him. He looked wild and desperate, and a timid woman would have fled trembling from that grated window. But the jailer's wife stood her ground with undaunted mien, and kept her intrepid eye on the black, ignited face before her.

"I am not afraid of you, Jerry," said she; "you would not lift a finger against me to save your life. You have not a bad heart. You have been set on by others, who would destroy you, body and soul, if you would let them. Well! I am going. There is no time to be lost."

"Stop, missus!" exclaimed the negro. "I made up my mind."

"'Twon't do no good if you hain't," cried Jack, through the chink. "I'll make a clean breast, if I be hanged for't."

The plot, as related by Jerry, with occasional episodes from Jack, was cunningly devised and deeply laid. During the Christmas holidays there was to be a general insurrection in the surrounding country, and the rallying spot was the city, of which they were to take possession by fire and sword. Quantities of ammunition, brought in by night, by secret agents, were concealed under the African church and in the old cellars of houses occupied by negroes, who hired their own time of their masters. A false key was to open the doors of the arsenal; the bridge was to be set on fire; the strongholds of wealth and power to be broken up. And who was the master spirit that raised the whirlwind, and was to direct the storm? What power had lashed the peaceful waters into wrathful foam, and was rolling them on in waves of insurgency over the land?

It was he, who, clothing himself with the authority of a divine mission, and gifted with an eloquence passing that of the sons of men, had wrapped his influence, like a mantle of fire, round his superstitious victims, and every struggle but drew the burning folds tighter and tighter. When prostrate at the altar, where his terrible representations of Almighty wrath had driven them, he first breathed into their ears his insidious designs. He told them he was the agent of the Almighty, and that whoever betrayed his counsel would be doomed to everlasting punishment. He promised them riches, honours, and happiness in this world, and crowns of glory in the next, if they yielded themselves to his will, in faith and trust. The robbery of the bank was a step towards the kingdom of heaven. The money was needed to carry on the Lord's work, and he who stretched forward the boldest hand would be accounted the most faithful and profitable servant.

The next step taken by this firm and resolute woman, was to go for a magistrate, to whom the statement was repeated, and taken down in writing. He enjoined upon her perfect secrecy, till the authorities of the city had decided upon the proper measures to be taken in an affair of such vital importance.

That evening Moreland was called away, and remained till a late hour. When he returned, Eula noticed at the first glance that something unusual had occurred. He was very pale, his eyes seemed to wear a darker hue, and there was no love-smile as usual, responding to the greeting smile of his wife.

"Where is Albert?" he asked; and never had Eula heard his voice sound so stern and unnatural.

"I suppose he is in the kitchen," answered Eula. "I have not seen him during the evening."

Moreland rung the bell with such force that a quick, startling peal rung echoing through the house. Becoming more and more alarmed, Eula's fears, winged by natural affection, flew to her native home, and imagined a thousand ills, whose tidings had just reached him, and which he would fain conceal from her.

"Oh, Moreland, tell me what has happened!" she asked, in tremulous accents. "Have letters from the North arrived? Do they contain evil for me?"

"The North!" repeated he, almost fiercely. "No,

Eula! Would to Heaven—" He paused, and added in an altered accent—"Do not question me, my dear wife. I am hardly master of myself; but be assured, that as far as I know, your Northern friends are well You have no cause for apprehension, believe me. Al-b rt," said he to the mulatto as he opened the door, "put the black horse in the buggy directly, and bring it round to the gate. I am going to start for the plantation, and you must go with me."

"To-night!" exclaimed Eula. "Oh! not to-night! The sky is dark and lowering! You will not go to-night!"

"I must, my Eula; there is no alternative. I wish I were not obliged to leave you and my children. Albert, why don't you obey me? Must I repeat my commands a second time?"

"Oh, master, don't go to the plantation! Don't leave mistress and the children here!" cried Albert, his golden complexion changing to a gray, ashen hue, and his eyes expressing the very agony of supplication.

"And why should I not go?" demanded he, sternly. "Do you know of any evil threatening me there that you keep back from my knowledge? Have *you* turned traitor to the master who has so loved and trusted you, Albert?"

"No, dear master," cried he, throwing himself at his feet, and winding his arms round his knees, "I wouldn't harm you or mistress for a thousand worlds; but there's them that will! Don't go to the plantation, master! That preacher you sent there—oh! Mars. Russell—he made me swear on the Bible not to tell what he was going to say, or I'd told on him long ago. I wouldn't have nothing to do with it, and they never let me know nothing since. He says I'll lose my soul for a false oath; but I'll lose body and soul 'fore I see harm happen to you and mistress. Oh! Mars. Russell, don't go to the plantation!—don't go where Mars. Brainard is! Don't think Albert would turn against you!—no, he die first!"

The mulatto wept bitterly, as he lay grovelling at his master's feet, entreating his forgiveness, and imploring him to take care of himself and "Miss Eula."

"Rise, Albert," said his master. "I am glad you have told me this, but I knew it all before. I can no longer trust, though I may forgive. My wife, there is no cause for these pale cheeks, this trembling frame. There is no danger, for everything is discovered. The moment there is a suspicion of a plot, there is safety. Every one is on the watch. A strong patrole will guard the city every night, and all the night. You are surrounded by friends, under whose guardianship you will be as safe as at this moment, in my enfolding arms. Would to heaven I were not compelled to leave you! but the serpent is spreading his venom among my poor deluded people, and I must go and save them from his fangs!"

"Let me go with you!" cried Eula, clinging to him,

with passionate entreaty;—"let us take our children, and go together. If there is no danger for you, there is none for me. I fear not for myself; but, oh! let me not be separated from you, in these dark and troubled moments! Let me go, my husband; I will not trouble you with one weak, womanish fear!"

Moreland looked at her with an irresolute, troubled countenance, and clasped her closer to his breast.

"Was it for scenes like these," he cried, in tones of mingled bitterness and sorrow, "that I took you from your peaceful village and quiet home? But, oh! my Eulalia, the spoiler came from your Northern region; and, under the sheltering banner of the Cross, has been working the deeds of hell! His birth-place was his passport,—his holy calling his protection from suspicion. Am I to blame, for being so blindly duped, so basely deceived?"

"No, no!—but let me go with you. I shall die if you leave me behind! With you, I fear nothing, not even death itself!"

"I know not what to do!" cried Moreland, his heart yielding to the pleadings of his wife, while his judgment condemned its weakness; "it is agony to leave you,—seems madness to take you! And Ildegerte,—poor Ildegerte!"—

"Take her with us. She will think and feel as I do. Husband and brother, as well as master, listen to our pleading hearts!"

"If I did not know that you would be as safe there as in this drawing-room," said Moreland, "I never would consent. But it is only in my absence the tempter can have any power. I know my own influence. The moment I am in their midst, they will return to their allegiance, ashamed of their transient dereliction. Well, be it so, then; but prepare as quickly as Josephine did, when she followed Napoleon in his midnight tours. Go, Albert, and have the carriage ordered as well as the buggy,—a saddle-horse besides."

Eula, who felt as if she had had a reprieve from death, in permission to depart, flew to Ildegerte, and told her in as few words as possible all that had transpired. To the crushed heart of the young widow, everything short of the one great sorrow that had darkened her life seemed a minor consideration. Like Moreland, too, she felt such perfect confidence in the attachment of their slaves,—she believed his presence only was necessary to insure their obedience and returning loyalty.

It was astonishing with what celerity and ease everything was accomplished. Kizzie, though bewildered and half-terrified at the summons, took the sleeping Effie in her arms, while Eula cradled the infant Russell in her own. All necessary garments were previously packed; and, when the carriages came to the door, the whole party were in readiness.

A threatened insurrection! Eulalia well remembered

the horror she had felt, even as a child, at the bare idea. She remembered, too, that her father had justified the act, and said that were he near the scene of action, he should think it his duty to abet and assist the insurgent party. Brainard had announced himself as her father's friend. He had sat down at his board, been warmed at his fireside, and admitted into the most intimate social communion with him. Could he be aware of his secret designs? Was he willing to sacrifice his daughter, with more than Roman stoicism, to the fierce spirit of *philanthropy*, embodied in the reckless, cruel, and insidious Brainard? She could not, would not believe it; but the possibility of her father's being in collusion with this agent of darkness, gave her unutterable anguish. Strange! she did not tremble, now she was brought face to face with a reality, whose phantom had so often chilled her in her Northern home. Her courage rose with the occasion; and since she was permitted to remain at her husband's side, she felt that whatever trials were in reserve for him, she could not only share them with the devotion of a wife, but endure them with the spirit of a martyr. Gentleness, sensitiveness, and delicacy, flowers of life's sunshine, had always blossomed in her heart. Fortitude, heroism, and self-renunciation, stars of the night-shade of existence, now illuminated with deepening lustre the darkness of her spirit. And now she recalled the manner in which he had spoken of her marriage, and of Claudia's right to her child, and his words lost their sting, since she understood the spirit which gave them utterance,—envy, malice, and all uncharitableness, and a fiendish love of inflicting pain.

As they approached the plantation, Moreland became silent and abstracted. The dependencies which hung upon him were heavier than the chains of slavery, and more galling. He had a double task before him,—to unmask the *holy* traitor, who had so basely requited his hospitality and his confidence, and unwind his coils from the necks of his deluded victims. He felt, in all its venomed power, the sting of ingratitude and treachery. He had fulfilled the duties of a master so faithfully and conscientiously, bearing them not only on his mind, but his heart; had laboured so assiduously for the moral improvement, as well as happiness of his slaves, and felt towards them so tenderly and affectionately, that he could not think of their disaffection and alienation without bitterness and sorrow. Yet it was in compassion, rather than anger, that he regarded them, for he well knew the arts which had seduced them, and the eloquence which had swayed.

Had he received no intimation of the conspiracy, he would have known from the countenances of the negroes that an under-current, black as their skins, was flowing beneath the smooth surface of their welcome. Had they been thunder-stricken, they could hardly have appeared more smitten than by the unexpected arrival of their master and his family.

Moreland's first inquiry was for Brainard. He had just left for the other plantation. How long since? About ten minutes. Aha! he must have seen their coming, as they wound round the hill, which looked down on the cultivated fields and smiling plain, which Moreland had never before greeted without an emotion of pleasure. He had a warrant, given him by the city authorities, to arrest the villain, whom he expected to find in the comfortable quarters he had assigned him. For one moment he felt an impulse to pursue the traitor, whose flight was sufficient proof of his cowardice and perfidy; but the next he dismissed the thought. He could not leave his family unprotected. Let him go,—the emissaries of justice were now abroad in the land, and would, sooner or later, circumvent his path. Let him go,—"Vengeance is mine, I will repay," saith the Lord.

CHAPTER XX.

A LONG, winding blast of the bugle-horn summoned the labourers from the field, the carpenter and blacksmith from their shops, the spinsters from their wheels, the weaver from her loom, and emptied, as if by magic, the white-washed cabins. The negroes, one and all, had been told to attend their master's call, expressed by that sounding blast. It was just before the sunset hour,—one of those mild, glowing days, that so often diffuse over the aspect of a Southern winter the blandness of summer and the haziness of autumn. Eulalia and Ildegerte stood in the portico, spectatresses of a scene which made their hearts throb high in their bosoms. Ildegerte's eyes flashed with excitement. Eulalia's cheek was the bed of its coming and vanishing roses. She saw her husband standing, as she had seen him once before, the centre of a dark ring, but she gazed with far different emotions. It could not be said that she feared for him. His superiority was so manifest, that it suggested, at once, the idea of triumph—the triumph of mind over matter. He seemed to her an angel of light surrounded by the spirits of darkness, and, knowing that he was defended by the breastplate of righteousness, she was assured of his safety as well as his power.

Moreland waited till they had all gathered, and they came with halting, lingering steps, very unlike thei former cheerful alacrity; then, telling them to follow him, he led the way to the grave of the old prophetess, Dilsy, at whose burial he had made with them a solemn covenant, which *he* had kept inviolate. It was long since any of them had approached the burying-ground. In all their nightly meetings they had avoided passing it, fearing that the spirits of the dead would sweep their cold wings in their faces, or seize them with their stiff and icy fingers, or shriek in their ear some unearthly denunciation. As they walked through the place of graves, the long, dry yellow grass broke and crumpled under their steps, and the brambles twisted round their ankles. They had neglected their dead. The autumn leaves lay thick, damp, and rotting on the sods that covered them, choking the vines and plants, which, in happier hours, had been cultured there

Moreland stopped by the headstone, which his own hand had placed at Dilsy's grave, and indicated by a commanding gesture the places they were to assume. Paul, the preacher, stood nearest to him, his arms folded on his brawny chest, and his hoary locks of wool bent so low they seemed scattering their powder on the ground. Vulcan, the blacksmith, black and sullen as a thunder-cloud, stood on his left. The women, who had most of them been excluded from the secret deliberations, hung timidly in the rear, curiosity and apprehension struggling in them for mastery. And beyond the edge of the burying-ground, the two children of Moreland,—the one holding the hand, the other borne in the arms of Kizzie, shone in the innocence of infancy and beauty of childhood, on the gloom and duskiness of the scene.

"More than two years have passed," said Moreland, his eyes glancing from face to face, calmly and gravely, as he spoke, "since I stood on this spot, on which the grave-clods had just been thrown, and you all stood around me then, just as you are gathered now. At that hour, I renewed the vows of protection and kindness to you which I uttered, when a boy, in the ear of a dying mother. I told you, if I ever proved unkind, unjust, and tyrannical, if I ever forgot my duties to you as a master and a friend, to meet me here, in this solemn enclosure, and remind me of what I then said. You all promised then, to continue faithful, trustworthy, and obedient, and, judging of the future by the past, I believed you. And yet," he added, his voice deepening into sternness and his eye kindling with indignation, "you have basely deceived me; you have been listening to a traitor and a villain, and plotting against your master and your friend. Under pretence of worshipping God, you have been engaged in the service of Satan, and doing the work of devils. I know all your horrible plans. I know what holiday frolics you are preparing. Which of you has a word to say in his defence? Which of you can look me in the face and say he does not deserve the severest punishment, for treachery and ingratitude to a master as kind and forbearing as I have ever been? Paul, you have taken upon you the office of a preacher of the gospel of peace, who, on all occasions, are the voice of your brethren; look up, speak, and if you have one word to say in your justification and theirs, let us hear it, and hear it quickly."

"No, massa!" cried Paul, slowly raising his head, without lifting his eyes; "got noting to say—noting—only Massa Brainard."

"Poor, deluded creatures!" said Moreland, "poor, blind tools of an artful, selfish, false, and cold-hearted hypocrite, who cares no more for you than the grass you are trampling under your feet. I pity you; for I sent the wretch in your midst, believing him to be a man of God. He has beguiled you with promises of freedom. What is the freedom he can offer you? Nothing but poverty, degradation, and sorrow. If you could compare your condition with those of the free coloured people at the North, you would shudder to think of all that you have escaped. Listen! You are slaves, and I am free; but I neither made you slaves nor myself a free man. We are all in the condition in which we were born. You are black, and I am white; but I did not give you those sable skins, nor myself this fairer complexion. You and I are as God Almighty made us, and, as I expect to give an account of the manner in which I fulfil my duties as a master, so you will be judged according to your fidelity, honesty, and uprightness as servants. The Bible says—'Can the Ethiopian change his skin?' No, he cannot! but there is no reason why he should have a black heart, because his skin is black. Free! how willingly would I make you free this moment, if, by so doing, I could make you better and happier! Free! I would to heaven you were all free,—then I, too, should be free from a burden made intolerable by your treachery and ingratitude! I would rather, ten thousand times, cultivate these broad fields myself, than be served by faithless hands and false, hollow hearts. I have hands that can work. I would do it cheerfully, if labour was the portion God had assigned me in this world. Better, far better, the toiling limbs, than the aching heart!"

He paused a moment in indescribable emotion. Among those who were looking earnestly in his face, and drinking in his words with countenances expressive of shame, remorse, and returning devotion, were some who had been the playmates of his childhood, and others in whose arms he had been dandled and caressed when a little boy, and others, again, mere boys now, whom he had made the playthings of his youthful years. He remembered sitting, many and many a time, in the lap of Paul, under an old tree, teaching him to read, while the negro would twist his dark fingers in his childish locks, and pray God Almighty to bless him and make him a blessing to mankind. A sable filament was twisted in every cord that bound him to the past. The associations of bygone years rose above the painful and gloomy present, and it was far more in sorrow than in anger, that he regarded the large family whom the most consummate art had alienated from him.

"Paul," said he, turning to the preacher, whose head was drooping still lower on his breast, and whose cheeks were marked by a wet, shining streak, where silent tears were travelling, "Paul, do you remember Davy, to whom my father gave his freedom many years ago, and who afterwards bought his wife and settled in the State of New York?"

"Yes, massa!"

"Here is a letter, which I received from him a few days since. I will read it. I want you all to listen to it."*

Moreland took a letter from his pocket-book and read as follows:—

"DEAR YOUNG MASTER:—I hope you have not forgotten Davy, though you was a little boy when I came

* This is a genuine fact, and the gentleman to whom the letter was addressed complied with the request it contained. He arrived just in time, to receive the legacy so solemnly bequeathed, and to comfort, with his presence, the dying negro.

away. I'm very sick; the doctor says I can't live long. I'm willing to die; but there's one great care on my mind. I don't want to leave my wife and children here. I've made a considerable property, so they wouldn't be in want; but that ain't all a person wants, master. If I had life before me again, I'd come back myself, for I've never been as happy, or as respectable, as when I lived with old Master. I heard so much talk about the white people at the North being such friends to the blacks, I thought we'd be on perfect equality; but it's no such thing. They won't associate with us; and I never want my wife and children to put themselves on a level with the free negroes I see here,—they are a low, miserable set, and folks that respect themselves won't have anything to do with them. My dear young master, please come on, or, if you can't come yourself, send somebody to take back my wife and children,—I have but two daughters, if they were boys I would not care so much. I give them to you, just as if they had never been free. I bequeath you all my property too, and wish it was more. Oh! happy should I be, could I live to see the son of my dear old master before I die,—but the will of God be done. I've got somebody to write this letter for me, for I am too weak to sit up; but I'll put my name to it, that you may know it comes from

DAVY.

"If you can't come or send directly, please write a line, just to ease my dying thoughts."

"This letter," said Moreland, "was dictated by one who has tasted the joys of freedom, as it exists among the black people at the North. His condition is far better than the majority, for he has acquired property, while most of them are miserably poor. Listen to me, sons and daughters of Africa! If I thought freedom would be a blessing to you, it should be yours. East, West, or North, anywhere, everywhere, you might go, and I would bid you God speed; but I would as soon send those poor sheep on the hill-side, among ravening wolves, as cast you amid such friends as this pretended minister of God represents! Which of you wants to trust him now? Which of you wants to leave your master and follow him? Tell me, for I will have no Judas in the field, ready to betray his too kind and trusting master!"

"Oh, massa!" exclaimed Paul,—completely subdued and melted, and sinking down on his knees, right on the grave of Dilsy,—"forgive us! Don't send us away! Trust us once more! We've ben 'ceived by Satan, and didn't know what we were doing!"

The moment Paul prostrated himself before his master, all but *one* followed his example, entreating for pardon, and imploring with tears and sobs not to be sent away from him. Vulcan, the blacksmith, stood firm and unmoved as the anvil in his forge. All his dark and angry passions had been whetted on the edge of the murderous weapons hidden beneath his shop, and made red not by the flames of the midnight furnace. His stubborn knees refused to bend, and a sullen cloud added luridness to his raven-black face.

Moreland and he stood side by side ;—all the rest were kneeling. The beams of the departing sun played in golden glory round the brow of Moreland; the negro seemed to absorb the rays,—he looked of more intense, inky blackness.

"Vulcan!" said his master, "if you expect my forgiveness, ask it. Dare to resist me, and you shall feel the full weight of my indignation."

"I'm my own master," cried the blacksmith, in a morose, defying tone. "I ain't a gwine to let no man set his feet on my neck. If the rest are a mind to be fools, let 'em!" and he shook his iron hand over the throng, and rolled his bloodshot eyes, like a tiger ready to spring from its lair.

The face of Moreland turned pale as marble, and lightnings kindled in his eyes. To brute force and passion he had nothing to oppose but moral courage and undaunted will; but he paused not to measure his strength with the muscles swelling out, like twisting serpents, in the negro's brandished arm. Laying his right hand commandingly on his shoulder, he exclaimed:—

"There is but one master here. Submit to his authority, or tremble for the consequences!"

Suddenly wrenching his shoulder from the hand that

grasped it, the blacksmith leaped forward, and seizing his master in his gigantic arms, was about to hurl him to the ground, when a tremendous blow on the back of his head laid him prostrate and stunned at Moreland's feet. So sudden had been the attack, so instantaneous the release, that Moreland was hardly conscious how it had been effected, till the sight of Paul, standing with dilated nostrils and panting chest over the fallen giant, and brandishing with both hands a massy rail, which had been lying at the foot of the grave, made him aware who his deliverer was.

"Let me kill 'em, massa—let me kill 'em," cried Paul, swinging the rail above his head, and planting his foot on the broad breast of the rebel.

"Stop!" cried Moreland; "in the name of God, stop! He may be dead already! Let him be carried to the guard-house and there taken care of. Give him in charge to the overseer."

Four of the stoutest negroes sprang forward, eager to show their recovered zeal and loyalty, and lifted up the heavy mass of insensible flesh, which they would have beaten to jelly in their indignation, so powerful was the reaction of their feelings.

"Paul," said Moreland, holding out his hand, "true and faithful servant yet! Let the past be forgotten, or remembered only to forgive!"

"Oh! dear massa!" cried Paul, dropping the rail, and throwing his arms round Moreland's shoulders, he wept and sobbed like a child,—"you're safe and alive yet! Bless a Lord Almighty! Paul's heart always was right, but he got a mighty poor head of hisn."

When Moreland seemed under the ruffian grasp of Vulcan, the women uttered the most terrible screams; but wilder and more piercing than all the rest was the shriek that issued from the portico, that commanded a full view of the scene. Eulalia and Ildegerte, who were standing with arms interlaced, gazing on what to them was an exciting pantomime, for they could not hear one syllable of what was uttered, beheld the giant leaping on his master, and believed it the signal of death. How they reached there they knew not, for the place was at some distance from the house,—but they found themselves forcing their way through the ring just as Paul was weeping on his master's shoulder.

"All is safe!" cried Moreland, as they threw themselves into his arms, clinging to him in an agony of emotion—"all is well! Look up, my Eula! Sister, be not afraid; it is all over! Here is Paul, who is ready to die in my defence."

"Me too, master!" cried Albert, with glistening eyes; "Paul struck 'fore I got a chance, or I would have killed him!"

The little golden-brown head of the infant Russell was seen peeping behind the ring, like a sunbeam playing on the cloud-edge. Kizzie, nearly distracted, had pressed as close as possible to the scene of action, after the terrible rebel was secured; and the infant, excited by the tumult, clapped its cherub hands, and glanced its beautiful hazel eyes from face to face with innoceut curiosity.

"Bring that child here," said Moreland; and Albert, springing forward, bore it in triumph over the woolly heads between, to his master's extended arms.

"This child," said he, raising it aloft in its smiling beauty, "is your future master. With its first lessons of obedience to his parents and love to his God, he shall be taught his duties to you, and yours to him. Born and brought up in your midst, he will learn to regard you as a part of his own life and soul. I trust, with the blessing of God, he will live to be a better, wiser, kinder master than I have ever been, and watch over your children's interests when I am laid low in the grave."

The infant, delighted with its elevated position, laughed in its glee, while the negroes gazed upon both father and child as beings of a superior world.

The admiration, love, and devotion which the negro feels for the children of a beloved master, is one of the strongest, most unselfish passions the human heart is capable of cherishing. The partition wall of colour is broken down. The sable arms are privileged to wreathe the neck of snow, the dusky lips to press soft kisses on the cheek of living roses. And, though, in after years, the child feels the barrier of distinction drawn by the

Creator's hand, in infancy it clings with instinctive affection to the dark bosom that nurses it, and sees only the loving heart through the black and sooty skin. If such are the feelings which infancy usually inspires, it is not strange that the child of such a master as Moreland should be an object of idolatry, for, notwithstanding they had been tempted from their allegiance by the irresistible arts of Brainard, the principles of strong affection and undying loyalty existed in their hearts, and now throbbed with renovated vitality—with the exception of the fierce and rebellious artisan. His was one of those animal natures which, having had a scent of blood in the breeze, snuffed it with savage delight, and, being baffled of its prey, revenged itself for its unslaked thirst in roars of defiance and deeds of violence. He was now, however, incapable of inflicting farther injury. The well-aimed blow of Paul, though not mortal, had caused a terrible concussion in his system, from which he was likely long to suffer; and he was also strongly guarded.

That night the deepest tranquillity brooded over the plantation. The stormy elements were hushed; the late troubled waters subsided into a peaceful yet tremulous expanse. Eula, exhausted by the agitation of the several preceding days, slept as quietly as the babe that rested on her bosom. But no sleep visited the wakeful eyes of Moreland. He went abroad into the stillness, the solemnity and loneliness of night, and beyond the clear and illimitable moonlight, he looked into the darkening future. The clouds of the preceding night were all swept away, and the moon glided, slowly, majestically, radiantly over the blue and boundless firmament, a solitary bark of silver navigating the unfathomable ocean of ether. Moreland walked through the long rows of cabins, whose whitewashed walls reflected, with intense brightness, the light that illumined them, and envied the repose of the occupants. The signs of the times were dark, and portentous of disunion and ruin. The lightnings might be sheathed, but they were ready, at any moment, to rend the cloud and dart their fiery bolts around. Supposing, for one moment, the full triumph of fanaticism, how fearful would be the result! The emancipation of brute force; the reign of animal passion and power; the wisdom of eighteen centuries buried under waves of barbarism, rolling back upon the world; the beautiful cotton-fields of the South left neglected and overgrown with weeds; the looms of the North idle for want of the downy fleece, and England, in all her pride and might, bleeding from the wound her own hands had inflicted. None but the native of a tropic zone, physically constructed to endure the heat of a Southern clime, can cultivate its soil and raise its staple products. That the African, *unguided by the white man's influence*, would suffer the fairest portions of God's earth to become uncultivated wildernesses, let St.

Domingo, Jamaica, and the emancipated islands bear witness. Suppose the triumph of fanaticism, agriculture would inevitably languish and die ; the negro, as well as the white man, would not only sink into an abyss of poverty and ruin, but the withered energies, the decaying commerce, and expiring manufactures of the North would show the interests of the two different sections of our common country to be connected by as vital a ligament as that which unites the twin-born brothers of Siam. Let the death-stroke pierce the bosom of one, the other must soon become a livid and putrifying corpse.

If it be God's will that our country, so long the boast and glory of the ge, should become its byword and reproach; if the Genius of America is to be driven from her mountain heights into the dens and caves of earth, weeping over her banner insulted, its stars extinguished, its stripes rent asunder, with none left to vindicate its rights; if the beauty, order, and moral discipline of society are to be resolved into the gloom and darkness of chaos, the silver chords of brotherhood snapped asunder, and the golden bowl of union for ever broken:—if it be God's will, let man lay his hand upon his mouth, and his mouth in the dust, and say,

"It is good!"

But let him beware of mistaking the traces of human weakness and passion for the stately footprints of the

Almighty, lest the Lord come in judgment and avenge his insulted majesty!

Such were the thoughts that banished sleep from the eyes of Moreland, and sent him abroad, a nocturnal wanderer, in the holy splendour of the night. His feet involuntarily turned to the blacksmith's shop. It was a lonely path that led to it, and, just before it reached the building, a dense thicket of pines made an impervious shade, black and heavy by contrast with the beams beyond. While he was passing through the shadows, and about to emerge into the light, he saw the figure of a man stealing cautiously round the shop and approaching the door. A low, distinct knock was heard, repeated at intervals. He was sure, from the outline, that it was the form of Brainard, and he could see that it was the face of a white man. His first impulse was to rush forward and seize him,—his next, to watch his farther motions. Stepping very cautiously, and looking round at every step, the figure went to the pile of brushwood we described in a former chapter, and removed it from the excavation. Stooping down and groping his way under, he disappeared, while Moreland, accelerating his steps, reached the spot before he had time to emerge again into the light. He could hear distinctly the clinking of steel under the house, and wondered if the man had engaged some subterranean knight in conflict. An old door, broken from its hinges, lay upon the ground. Moreland raised it as noiselessly as possible, and putting it up against the opening, planted his foot firmly against it,—thus making the man, whoever he was, his prisoner. The sudden darkening of the moonlight, which streamed in under the building, made the intruder aware of his situation, and he came rushing against the barrier with headlong force; the planks vibrated and cracked, but Moreland stood his ground, firm as a rock.

"Vulcan, Vulcan! is it you? For God's sake, let me out! It is I! Don't you know my voice?" It was the voice of Brainard,—not the sweet music he was accustomed to breathe from the pulpit, but the sharp, quick, startled accents of fear.

"Excuse me, Mr. Brainard," said Moreland; and a proud smile curled his lip at the ridiculous and humiliating position of his enemy. "I hope you do not find yourself uncomfortable! I was not aware that you had lodgings there before; but I believe you are fond of subterranean works!"

"Mr. Moreland," exclaimed Brainard, "it is not possible that it is you who are opposing my egress? Is this the treatment that one gentleman has a right to expect from another?"

"Gentleman!" repeated Moreland, in an accent of withering sarcasm; "coward! traitor! knave! too vile for indignation, too low for contempt! Come forth, and meet me face to face, if you dare! Rise, if you are not too grovelling to assume the attitude of a man!"

Removing his foot from the door, it fell forward, and

the moon again shining into the aperture, revealed the prone and abject form of the pretended minister. Crawling a few steps on his hands and knees, he rose slowly, for his limbs were cramped and stiff, and shook the earth-soil from his garments. His face was now directly opposite Moreland; and from his blue, half-closed eyes, the unsheathing daggers of hatred and revenge were furtively gleaming.

"What are you doing here?" asked Moreland, sternly, "stealing round my premises at the midnight hour, burrowing like a wild beast in the earth, after having fled like a coward at my approach, to avoid the consequences of detected perfidy?"

"I have been on my Master's business," he answered, looking upward. "I am not accountable to any man, being amenable to a higher law."

"Hypocrite!" exclaimed Moreland, his dark eyes flashing with indignation, "away with this vile cant! Throw aside the cloak with which you have tried in vain to cover your iniquitous plots! Everything is discovered. If you were seen now in the city whose hospitality you have so wantonly abused, you would fall a sacrifice to the vengeance of an incensed community We are safe, thank Heaven, from your incendiary purposes; but what can save you, bare and exposed as you are, from the hands of an outraged public?"

Brainard was in such a position that it was impossible for him to escape. On one side was a jutting beam, an abutment of the building; on the other, the pile of brushwood he had thrown aside; before him, the proud, resolute form, and commanding glance of the man he had deceived and attempted to destroy. By what subterfuge could he now elude the doom he had brought upon himself?

"Mr. Moreland," said he, "I have sat at your board, slept in your bed, and broken bread at your table. Even the wild Arab will protect the stranger who has partaken of his hospitality. Will you, a Christian, do less than he?"

"Yes; you have done all this," replied his host. "I know it but too well. You have slept in my bed that you might strew it with thorns. You have broken my bread that you might infuse into it poison and death. It is my duty as a Christian to incapacitate you for the perpetration of new crimes."

"I may have been carried farther than I intended," said he, in an humble, adjuring tone; "but it was not for myself I was labouring. I have been made the agent of others, whose cause I embraced with premature ardour. I have been misled by false misrepresentations, to adopt a course which I now sincerely regret. A candid man, Mr. Moreland, would require no other apology."

"False as cowardly!" answered Moreland. "If you are the tool of a party, it only aggravates your meanness. There may be those who are degraded enough to employ a wretch like you, as an instrument to work the downfall of the South; but, if so, they must be the lowest dregs of society. There may be men, and women too, for I have heard of such,—but I do not believe there is a respectable town or village in the Northern States that would not consider itself disgraced by your conduct, and blush for the opprobrium which you have brought upon their name. I have travelled in the North,—I know the spirit of the times; but I know, too, that there is a conservative principle there, that would protect us from aggression, and itself from ignominy."

"It matters not whose agent I am," said Brainard, bitterly. "I see I am at your mercy. Yet, if you will suffer me to depart in peace, I will pledge my solemn word to leave this part of the country, immediately and for ever."

"What faith can be put in promises like yours? No, sir! The day of blind confidence is past. I arrest you by virtue of a warrant which I bear about me. Come with me, till better accommodations are provided for you at the public expense."

Even while speaking these words, Moreland was conscious of great perplexity, for he knew of no place of security but the guard-house, where Vulcan was already imprisoned, where he could put the arch-traitor. It is true, Vulcan was now in no situation to be influenced by his insidious arts, but he did not like their juxtaposition. Another thing, it was considerably distant from the blacksmith's shop, and it would be no easy task to conduct a desperate and infuriated man to that place of confinement. Still, he must not be suffered to escape, so, laying a firm hand on his shoulder, he commanded him to follow him. Quick as a flash of thought, Brainard drew a bowie knife from his bosom with his free right hand, and made a plunge at Moreland's breast. Moreland saw the steel glittering in the moonlight, and the next moment might have been his last, but, throwing his assailant back with a violent jerk, the stroke glanced in the air. This was the commencement of a life-struggle, fierce and bloodthirsty on one side, bold, firm, and unrelaxing on the other. One could hear the gritting of Brainard's grinding teeth, as he tried to release himself from the clenching grasp of his antagonist. Moreland was armed, for, at this time of threatened insurrection, every man was provided with defensive weapons, but, instead of drawing his own, his object was to get possession of Brainard's knife. Had he released his hold one second, his life might have been the sacrifice. Once or twice he felt the sharp steel gashing his left arm, but he heeded it not, and once, in warding off a deadly blow at his heart, he turned the point of the knife and it plunged in Brainard's right arm—the arm which wielded the destructive weapon. Moreland, after the first moment of exasperation and excitement, did not want to kill him, but to defend himself, and incapacitate him from further mischief. The knife dropped from Brainard's powerless hand, and the blood spouted from the wound. Moreland, well knowing it was not a mortal stroke, and that his left hand still had power, snatched the knife from the ground an sheathed it in the folds of his vest. The blood was flowing from his own wounds, but, without heeding it, he bound his handkerchief round Brainard's arm, who had reeled as if fainting, against the walls of the shop. He looked very pale, but Moreland could plainly see that it was not the death-like paleness preceding a swoon. Still, he did not like to drag him, in that situation to the guard-house, and, enfeebled as he was, he believed he could leave him in the shop with safety, while he went to rouse the overseer and some of the strongest hands, to assist in guarding him, and he himself obtained proper materials to dress his wound. The door of the shop was usually locked at this hour, but, in consequence of Vulcan's arrest, who had the charge of it, the key was left hanging in the padlock—a circumstance fortunate for Moreland's design. The wooden windows were barred inside, and Vulcan, while prosecuting his midnight labours, had added iron staples, as a greater security from intrusion. Had Brainard not been disabled by his wound, Moreland would not have dared to have enclosed him, even for a brief time, in a place where the weapons of deliverance might be found in the massy iron tools of the blacksmith; but he well knew that the arm, whose reeking blood had already dyed his handkerchief, could not wield the ponderous sledge-hammer or the iron bars.

"Come," said he, taking him by the left arm, "come into the shop, while I go for linen and balsam to dress your wound. I presume it is not the first time that you have found shelter in its walls."

"Bring none of your linen and balsam for me," he answered, "I'll none of it. Put me where you please, it makes no difference; I scorn and defy your power!"

Though he spoke in a faint voice, it was expressive of malignity and revenge. He no longer resisted, however, and Moreland, drawing rather than leading him round to the front side of the shop, opened the door, sprang upon the threshold with his prisoner, then releasing him suddenly, he sprang back, closed and locked the door, and returning to the rear of the building, examined the shutters on the outside.—It would not do to leave them without some barrier, for Brainard might remove the inner bar with his left hand, and leap from the window. There were two large posts lying on the ground, which seemed left there for his peculiar purpose, and though it required an exertion of strength to lift them, with his left arm weakened and painful as it was, he did it with astonishing celerity, and steadying the lower ends against the old fallen tree, suffered the upper ones to fall heavily upon the shutters, just below the jutting of the wood-piece nailed across them, and in this position every effort to open the windows would only make the posts more firm in their resistance.

"That will do," said Moreland, turning away, and directing his steps towards the overseer's dwelling-house. With an involuntary impulse, he drew forth the knife concealed in his bosom, and suffered the moonlight to gleam upon it. Half of it was stained with blood, the other half shone cold and blue, with deadly lustre, in the serene glory of the night. He shuddered at the temptation he had momentarily felt, to bury it in the false heart of Brainard, and blessed his guardian angel for covering the edge of the weapon with his interposing wings.

The chivalry of his nature had received a painful wound. He had discharged an imperative duty, but in a manner revolting to the magnanimity of his character. He had felt his cheek burn, while turning the key of that black sooty prison on a wounded enemy. Had he known that Brainard was familiar with even more gloomy walls, that, even when a boy, he had made his bed on the dungeon's floor, and worn the felon's badge of ignominy, he would have been less fastidious with regard to his accommodations.

Having awakened the overseer, and told him to rouse immediately several of the stoutest negroes, including Uncle Paul, and repair to the shop, which they were to guard during the remainder of the night; he began to feel the necessity of having his own wounds attended to,—

though not deep, the flowing of the unstanched blood, and the straining of the muscles in barricading the shutters, made him feel weak and nerveless. He therefore commissioned the overseer to act as leech, as well as guard, and sought his own dwelling.

Fearing to awake his wife, and alarm her by th sight of his blood-stained garments, he entered with noiseless steps, and the faint, soft, regular breathing that met his ear gave him a sensation of exquisite repose. Eulalia still slept, and the babe still slumbered on her bosom. Again the image of the virgin mother and the infant Jesus rose before him, as when he had knelt by her, when reclining over the cradle of her son. And once more he knelt, but without awakening her, and commended them both to the God of the South as well as the North,—"to the Monarch, and Maker, and Saviour of all!"

"Ah, my sweet wife!" thought he, when, rising from his knees, he looked down upon her with unutterable tenderness, "you are paying a sad penalty for the love that lured you from your quiet village home. Better had it been for you had I left you near the shadow of that temple where your seraph voice first waked the slumbering music of my heart."

For a moment he had forgotten his arm, and the blood-stains on his dress; but a stiff, painful feeling reminded him of the past conflict, and, with the same noiseless steps with which he had entered, he left his own room, and, seeking the one where Albert slept, committed himself to his healing hands.

In the mean time Brainard was not idle. When left by Moreland in the grim retreat with which he had made himself so familiar, he stood at first perfectly still, in the centre of the shop, where the momentum given by Moreland's releasing arm had sent him. It was not utterly dark, for silvers of moonshine penetrated the chinks of the boards, and fell on the blackened planks. He looked round him, straightened himself up to his full height, and shook his left arm in defiance, as if facing an invisible enemy.

"Fool!" he muttered. "He did not know he was dealing with an ambidextrous man. There is as much cunning in this hand as in that. Does he think these drops of blood have weakened me so that I cannot burst these bars and free myself from his power? Ha, ha! I played the part of a fainting man to put him off his guard; but I have strength enough yet to perform a good night's work. These shutters are nothing but old boards. I'll soon shiver them. I'll hurl them into fragments. Yes, yes! if the morning find me a prisoner here, may I hang from the gibbet, and the fowls of heaven feed upon my carcass!"

Guided by the light of the silver bars on the floor, he seized the sledgehammer with his left hand, and, swinging it high in air, brought it down upon the shutter with a tremendous blow. There was a jarring and rattling of boards, and a cloud of black dust, but Moreland's strong barrier resisted the effort.

"Death and fury!" he exclaimed; "are the boards lignum vitæ? I'll try the door. If I cannot break that open, I'll spill my own brains on these planks!"

Swinging the huge hammer once more, he hurled i against the door with maniac force. Ha! it does begin to yield. Bravo! strike again. They hear your blows, to be sure, but they think the horses are pounding and kicking in the stable, as they are wont to do. Strike again; a desperate man can do anything. No matter if every stroke makes the blood ooze from your wounded veins, and the sultry sweat-drops gush from your pores. There! don't you see the hinges strain, tug, crack, and at length give way with a sudden crash. Jump through! the avengers are coming. Make haste! they are in the dark path now. Remember *you* are in the moonlight.

Yes! Brainard did remember all this, and he leaped through the opening with supernatural agility, flew, rather than ran to the stable, mounted the fleetest horse, and cut the air like the arrow. He was seen, just as he reached the stable, by the party appointed to be his guard. Paul, who seemed to have the vigour and fire of youth miraculously restored, shouted till the thicket reverberated the sound, and rushed after him, his long limbs sweeping over the ground like forked lightning. The overseer and other negroes followed, but they could not begin to keep up with the streaking steps of Paul As he reached the stable Brainard leaped into the road. Paul was on the back of Swiftsure, one of his master's strongest, fleetest horses, with the quickness of thought, and away he went in pursuit of the fugitive.

"Good Lord!" cried Paul, "let me only catch 'em! Just let massa know what Paul can do for him! Go it, go it, Swiftshur!—wide awake! wide awake!—keep a eye open!—stretch a feet apart!—that the way to go!"

Paul lay almost horizontally on the barebacked animal, grasping his mane for a bridle, his body thrown up and down by the violence of the motion. Brainard had saddle and bridle, for he was on the same horse which had been caparisoned to bear him from the plantation, just before Moreland's arrival. The odds were in his favour, and he knew it. His scornful laugh was driven back into Paul's face, like a dash of cold water. Once he reeled in the saddle, and his speed perceptibly slackened, and the shadow of his pursuer appeared to be leaping on his back; but just as Paul stretched out his long arm, thinking him within reach, he shot ahead, with dizzying velocity, and Paul grasped a handful of moonbeams. It was all in vain. As he told his master the next day—"The devil was in him, and one might as well try to catch hold of a streak of lightning."

All the time Brainard was winging his way, thought, swifter than his flight, was darting in his mind, bringing messages from the future, that lit up his countenance with vindictive joy.

"Oh! I have a glorious career before me," said he to himself, dashing his spurs into his horse's smoking flanks,—for he had equipped himself like a knight when he started on his midnight expedition. "I have planned it all—and when did I ever plan without executing? Who says I have failed? I tell you, you lie, sir. I have made a plenty of dupes. The flames I have kindled will not be quenched. They will burst out afresh, when people think they are gazing on ashes. Yes! I will go back to the North, and deliver such lectures on the South as will curdle the blood with horror. No matter what I say—I'll find fools to believe it all. If I pour falsehoods hot as molten lead down their throats, they will believe them all, and smack their lips with delight. Take care, Master Moreland! the devil shall be an angel of light compared to the foul demon I will represent you to be—you, and all your tribe. Thank Heaven for the gift of eloquence! Oh! I'll rave of blood-marked chains, of flesh torn from the body with red-hot pincers, of children roasted alive, of women burned at the stake! They'll believe it all! The more horrors I manufacture the more ecstasy they will feel! Curses on the arm that failed to pierce *his* heart's core! Curses on *him* for every drop of blood he has drawn! But I'll have my revenge!—a glorious revenge!—ha! ha!"

Away with him! Close the shutters of that workshop of Satan—his breast. We shudder at the glimpses revealed. Let him go, and fill up the measure of his iniquity: brimming as it now seems, it is not quite full. The crowning drop must be blacker than all.

CHAPTER XXI.

It cannot be said that Moreland regretted the flight of Brainard. Detected villany is no longer to be feared.

The threatened insurrection had been proclaimed trumpet-tongued through the state, and guards everywhere appointed to watch over the public safety. A minute description of his person was published in all the papers, so that none might unwittingly receive the traitor as a guest. Though Moreland was convinced that he was an impostor, he addressed letters to the Conference to which he professed to belong, making inquiries respecting his standing as a minister. The answer denied any knowledge of a person by the name of Brainard. There was no minister belonging to their Conference or denomination of that name. They did not hesitate to pronounce him a vile impostor.

Mr. Hastings also affirmed, in his letters, that he knew nothing of such an individual, relieving his daughter's mind of an unspeakable weight. He could not account for his familiarity with the names of his household, but by supposing he had passed through the village, and made himself acquainted, by report, with its principal inhabitants,—a supposition which was founded on truth. The agitation he had caused in the domestic circle and in the public mind gradually subsided, and the peace he had disturbed once more settled on the community. The negroes were pardoned, as their ringleader was white, but put under a stricter discipline. Having so shamefully abused their religious privileges, they were restricted in their nightly meetings, which were no longer allowed to be kept up beyond the ringing of the nine o'clock bell. The midnight hour, which was the scene of their unhallowed orgies, was constantly guarded, and no night passed without the scrutiny of the vigilant patrole within the walls of their cabins.

The domestic establishment of Moreland resumed its usual peaceful and cheerful aspect. Jim and Crissy were seen, as formerly, unfurling the contents of the big chest to the morning sunshine, and Kizzie's countenance rejoiced once more in its former expression of consequential good-nature. Eulalia began to look upon the past as a frightful dream, and to enjoy, without fear of molestation, the comforts of her Southern home. There was one circumstance which she considered a blessing; for she never could think of Vulcan, the blacksmith, without horror and dread. As soon as he had recovered from the effects of the blow, and, after humbling himself before his master, been released from imprisonment, he absconded, stealing, in imitation of his illustrious predecessor, one of his master's finest horses, and baffling the vigilance of pursuit.

"I am glad he is gone!" cried Moreland, when the tidings of his flight reached his ears; "for I never could have had any reliance on his fidelity, any confidence in his truth. He was an excellent workman, and, as far as labour is concerned, a great pecuniary loss to me, but he seemed to cast a dark shadow over the plantation, which I rejoice to have rolled away. I suspect he will soon be *lionized* at the North, as one of those poor, injured, persecuted beings, escaped from Southern tyranny to throw themselves in the expanded arms of Northern philanthropy. Brainard may become his keeper, and tell to a gaping multitude the story of his sufferings. When Vulcan was a little boy, a negro about his own age, who was playing with an axe, chopped off two of the fingers of his left hand, and he has the scar of a terrible burn on his shoulder. The mutilated hand may be shown as the mark by which a Southern planter identifies his slaves, and the scar as the brand of his cruelty. Mark my words, Eula, and see if I am not a true prophet."

Eula remembered her father's giant protegé and blushed.

Before we dismiss this era in our history, we ought, in justice to the intrepid wife of the jailer, to mention the manner in which the grateful public manifested their appreciation of her services. When told by a friend that she was to be presented with a splendid silver waiter, on which the prison scene, of which she was the heroine, was to be wrought in bas relief, she remarked, with her usual sound, practical good sense—

"I don't want them to give me anything, for I've done nothing but my duty—I would despise the woman that would do less—and least of all, a silver waiter. It would shame my homely furniture; and be as much out of place as if I should stick a crown on my head. If they would send my boy to a first-rate school, that would be something to be grateful for."

In consequence of this hint, the silver streams of knowledge were poured into the boy's mind, and his education continued at the public expense.

Eula hailed the opening spring with anticipations of delight. She was looking forward to a visit to her Northern home, and almost every thought and feeling had reference to that joyous event. She watched the unfolding charms of her beautiful boy with a jealous eye, fearing one infantile beauty might fleet, before the eyes of her parents could gaze upon its loveliness. She talked to Effie of her sweet little sister, Dora, as her playmate and companion, forgetting that three passing years had added considerable dignity to the five-year-old child, who used to call her sister-mother. She opened her casket of love-tokens, and spread them in fond review before her, thus reviving, in all their early freshness, the associations of her youth:—the faded flowers she had pressed; even the humble ironing-holder and modest comb-case, which had been carefully preserved; and, more precious than all, poor Nancy's heart-shaped breast-pin, containing a lock of her long raven hair.

"I fear I am selfish," said she to her husband, grateful for his animated sympathy in all her anticipations. "You can look forward with no such joy as mine. I fear even that the journey may be painful to you, from recent associations."

"You are mistaken," he replied. "I shall revisit with delight the beautiful village of your birth. I never can forget the kindness I received, as a stranger, when I was lying sick and apparently dying there. There was no cold Levite passing the other side: all were ministering Samaritans, whom I bless in remembrance. Your excellent pastor—how I long to clasp his venerable hand once more! that hand which I last saw placed so tenderly on the head of my kneeling bride! My friend, the bridge architect, I respect as a high-minded and most honourable gentleman; and good Mrs. Grimby will receive from me a most cordial greeting. You need not think of appropriating to yourself all the joy, leaving me nothing but self-sacrifice to console me. But there is one thing, my dear Eula, that we must not forget. You know we are going quite strong in number, and people are not accustomed, at the North, to visit in caravans, as we do. My sister, who will accompany us, has no claims on the hospitality of your home. Nay, let me finish my declamation. Our little Effie is another interloper. Then, two servants, my own inseparable shadow, and the nurse to the honourable heir of the house of Moreland, will make in addition a goodly company."

"I was thinking I had better not take a nurse," said Eula. "Ildegerte's experience has intimidated me."

"It should rather give you courage. There is no danger of any of them being induced to follow Crissy's example. Netty, who is now the wife of Albert, may go, in place of Kizzie, whose ample person is something of an encumbrance to a traveller. I do not intend that you shall endure the fatigue of a mother's cares unassisted, or that your parents shall be burdened with the expense of our family during our long summer visit. The fatted calf and golden ring of welcome will be ours; let this trifle" (putting a folded paper in Eula's hand) "be theirs. Coming from you as a filial offering, they will not shrink from receiving it. Do not blush, my Eula. Is not all mine thine, and all yours theirs, if occasion requires the appropriation? Had I millions to pour into their coffers, I never could repay them the countless debt I owe."

"Flatterer!" exclaimed Eula, smiling through glistening tears. "Is not mine the debt, and shall not my life repay it? How kindly, how generously and consi derately do you relieve me of every anxiety! I well know that my father's means are limited; and the fear of drawing too largely on his resources has been the only drawback to my joyous anticipations. How can I do justice to my grateful heart?"

"Hush, my wife; never, never speak of gratitude to me. If I could be angry with you, it would make me so."

Kizzie would have been greatly mortified at being superseded by the young and airy Netty, had not Eula told her most truly that she could not leave the care of the household in any other hands than hers. Dicey was too aged to take the superintendence; Crissy too delicate in health, and Judy entirely too ignorant. They had lately received a valuable addition to the household establishment. Moreland, in accordance with the dying wishes of Davy, had sent for his wife and daughters, by a gentleman who was then travelling to the North. They had arrived, and were now members of his family. He had offered to settle them in a dwelling of their own, where they could be entirely independent, but they pleaded so earnestly to remain with him, that he could not refuse. This was a perplexing circumstance to him; for, notwithstanding the husband's and father's legacy, he looked upon them as free, and resolved never to be personally benefited by their labours, or to appropriate to himself the property bequeathed to him. He could make no distinction in his treatment of them, however, and they seemed to desire none. Davy was now dead. His last injunction to them was, to place themselves under the protection of Master Moreland.

This is a remarkable fact, and, if placed in the scales of justice, might outweigh a thousand exaggerated statements of oppression and cruelty. But prejudice is stronger than iron, more heavy than lead, more sounding than brass,—opposed to its weight, the deeds of an angel would be as down in the balance; the ordinations of Heaven but as dust. Its trumpet-cry to the sons of men is, "Tekel, Tekel! thou art weighed in the balance and found wanting!" Is there no invisible handwriting on the walls of its conscience? Is there not a greater than Daniel to interpret the mystic characters?

At length the time appointed for the departure of the travellers arrived, and with it all the customary bustle and preparation. We have intimated before, that our good friend Kizzie was a very bustling body, and fond of creating a breeze wherever she moved. Now, when she was about to be left, with a charge scarcely inferior, in her estimation, to the seven churches of Asia, it is not strange that she should make her responsibilities known.

"Yes! mistress," said she,—enumerating a few of her duties to Eula, with emphatic gesticulations,—"I shall have a heap of things to see to; but you'll find I've taken an obligation of the whole. There'll be the pickles to make, the vegetables to be gathered, the peaches to dry, and the preserves, and jellies, and catchups to be put up; the watermillion rinds to be cut into citron; Master's winter clothes to be aired, so that the moths can't get in 'em, and your winter ones too, mistress; the linen aired, the carpets taken up, and the picter frames converted with muslin, to keep the fly-specs off. The curtains must be taken down, too, for they needn't be wasting themselves on nobody but niggers!"

"You will really have a hard time, Kizzie," said Eula, compassionately, while Moreland laughed at Kizzie's tremendous vocabulary.

"You had better let Jim and Crissy do the airing part," said he; "they understand it by this time."

"I tell you, mistress," said Kizzie,—after honouring her master's remark with a respectful laugh,—"the hardest part of all is to part with little master. I love little missy, but your baby has got the nighest place in my heart. It goes mighty hard, mistress, to gin him up. If anything should happen, and you never bring him back no more!—"

"Don't, Kizzie!—don't!"

"I can't help it, mistress!" cried she, beginning to sob, while she hugged the beautiful boy in her arms, and pressed her cheek on its silky hair; "things is so unsartin in this world, and children's lives are nothing but spiders' webs, any way! Lord Almighty bless you, honey sweet baby! and keep you a burning and a shining when Kizzie's candle done need no more snuffing!"

Eula could not help being affected by the grief of the demonstrative Kizzie; and the young Russell seemed to appreciate, in its fullest sense, the affection of his old nurse. He clung to her neck, refusing to unlock his loving hands, till Moreland, with gentle firmness, withdrew him from her arms, and gave him in charge to the waiting Netty.

"You must not forget me, either, mammy!" said Effie, blowing kisses to her from the carriage, where she had enthroned herself.

"Bless your little heart, no!" cried the tender-hearted nurse, sobbing afresh.

Ildegerte was very sad, for she remembered her last fruitless journey, and that she was lonely now; but the bright and beautiful morning, the air fragrant with the breath of opening roses, and the exhilaration of motion, soon produced a reaction in the spirits of the travellers, and Ildegerte's sadness became illuminated by the cheerfulness of her companions.

While the travellers are pursuing their way rejoicing, we will turn to the beautiful New England village, to which the reader was introduced in the early pages of this history.

How fresh and green and quiet it looks! Fresh as when baptized with the morning dew of creation, it first reflected its Maker's smile; green as when emerging from the waters of the deluge, the dove of the ark hovered over its bosom. It was fair and beautiful three years ago: it is fair and beautiful now. Scarcely one new building has been erected, one change made to remind one of the insensible lapse of time. Mr. Grimby's sign, having an eagle on one side, and Washington, prim and dim, on the other, swings majestically in the wind, and the beautiful bridge constructed by Mr. Brooks, spans with its graceful arch the river's azure volume. There stands the church, with its glittering vane, and leaden dome, and snowy pillars, "looking tranquillity;" yonder is the parsonage, embosomed in its consecrated shades; and here is the well-known mansion, rising mid its grove of sycamore and mountain ash. Methinks it looks younger and fairer than it did three years ago,—and well it may, for it has just put on a new robe of paint, and the old green blinds have been rejuvenated also. Let us peep in the inside, and see if it wears the same familiar aspect. The painter's brush has been there likewise,—the ceiling is dazzling in its fresh, unsoiled whitewash, and the walls papered and bordered anew. Everything is as fair and smiling as a bride adorned for her husband.

Ah! dear must be the daughter and sister for whose welcome even inanimate objects thus renew and beautify themselves!

Eulalia's expected return was indeed an era in the

quiet, monotonous life of our villagers. There was not a house whose inmates were not excited, in some degree, by the anticipation. Even strangers, and there were a few, who had sought the retirement of the valley, participated, through sympathy, with the all-pervading feeling. If such was the general interest, what must have been the emotions of the household where, as a young divinity, she was enshrined and worshipped? Yet, while every chord of their hearts was vibrating with hope and quivering with love, there were one or two little discordant notes mingling with this music of nature. Moreland, the planter, whose princely abode and broad possessions Eulalia had so often described, was more awe-inspiring than the stranger who had wooed her for his bride. Then, he merely visited them, now he must be domesticated; and the contrast between his own luxurious style of living, and their plain and necessarily economical habits, would be inevitably more conspicuous. Then his sister—they shrunk from the thought of her being admitted into their simple, unadorned circle, accustomed as she had been to all the appliances of wealth. The house was small, the rooms low and old-fashioned, the furniture, most of it, handed down from other generations. Mrs. Hastings, with all her genuine piety and sound good sense, could not help occasionally being troubled and careful about these things. It was one of the weaknesses to which poor human nature is liable, and, though one of the most excellent of her sex, she was still a woman, and had all a true woman's pride of appearance and self-respect.

Betsy was in a perfect fever of expectation and preparation. She scarcely slept at night, thinking of the morrow's work. The ghost that haunted her came in the shape of the negro nurse. Albert she knew, and did not care for him; but Netty must be proud and "sarcy," and would turn up her nose at everything she saw and heard. She would give all the world if Miss Eula had left her at home. She was willing to work her fingers to the bone herself—she did not mind that; but she could not bear to be interfered with, as she knew she should be. Yet such is the inconsistency of human nature, that while Betsy gave utterance to these misgivings, she liked to boast of the style in which Miss Eula was coming, and would have been quite ashamed to have had any one suppose that she had to attend to her baby herself. The way she scrubbed and cleaned and cooked was almost miraculous. The genius of Aladdin's lamp hardly wrought more wonders than Betsy out of her limited materials.

One day, after receiving a letter from the South, Mrs. Hastings entered the kitchen with a glowing countenance.

"Betsy!" she said, "I want you to look out for a young girl, who can help you while Eula is here—a nice, respectable young person, who can wait upon table and put the rooms in order."

Betsy opened her eyes wide, and dropped the shovel in her astonishment.

"That would be grand," she answered; "that's what I've been wanting all along, but I was afraid to say it, cause you allers said you couldn't afford any extras."

"We cannot do too much in honour of Mr. Moreland," said Mrs. Hastings. The letter of Eulalia was in her bosom, containing the munificent gift her husband had insisted upon her offering to her mother, and it was accompanied by words so sweet and affectionate, the most fastidious delicacy could not shrink from its reception. All that her warm and liberal heart had yearned to do, could now be done without impoverishing her husband, who was burdened with many cares.

"To-morrow they will be here," cried Reuben, now a graduate of ——— College, with the highest honours of the institution adorning his reputation, and who had been distinguished among his classmates as the eloquent champion of Southern rights.

"To-morrow and one day more, you mean," exclaimed Dora, in whose intelligent eyes and darkened hair the shade of three passing years softly rested. "How long the days are now! It seems as if they would never, *never* end!"

The morrow came and went; the one day more was nearly closed, and Dora, in her best white frock and curls smooth as satin, stood on the gate, and, shading her eyes with her hand, watched the road through the vista of lofty poplars, this side of the tavern. Reuben's glowing locks were seen leaning against the sycamore tree, which commanded the most distant view. Mrs. Hastings, too agitated to leave the house, gazed through the windows, which often grew dim as she gazed. Mr. Hastings's portly figure stalked up and down the yard, in its suit of Sunday broadcloth; and Betsy flourished about the kitchen in her finest calico frock, pinned up to be sure, and guarded by a blue-checked apron. Never were the setting-sun rays so anxiously watched. Every object seen through the poplar vista was a coming carriage. Sometimes it proved a black cow, sometimes a gentleman in black with a white vest, who was mistaken for a white-faced horse. The buzzing of a humble-bee was converted into the humming of distant wheels, and the haziness of twilight for the dust that heralded the approaching carriage. For hours, the supper stood untouched on the table, waiting for the expected guests, but they came not. Dora, who had soiled her white dress rubbing against the gate, and strained her eyes till they ached, and their clear white was streaked with little blood-shot veins, went supperless and weeping to bed. Betsy folded up her nice calico frock, grieved that she had tumbled it for nothing, and sighing over the flannel cakes so light and melting, and the muffins, white and porous as the froth of albumen.

"What was the reason folks never come when folks were ready and looking for them? 'Twas such a putty time to come about sundown, and have a whole night to rest in! One does hate to be cotched in their duds!"

Poor Betsy! people are so perverse they never will come at the exact moment,—they will take their own time, and it is generally the very worst in the world.

The morning was veiled in mist, so dense that not one solitary sunbeam could penetrate it. As Betsy said, "one could hardly see a hand before them." The disappointment of the preceding evening had cast a gloom over the family; and Dora wondered if it would be possible to live through another long day of expectation, —and foggy days were so dreary, they were longer than any other. But a short time before noon, the fog began slowly to lift up, like the curtain of a theatre, revealing the charming scenery concealed by its folds. It rose, becoming more and more thin, and brightening as it rose, till it assumed the appearance of transparent, silvery gauze, through which the green foliage was seen waving and sparkling, and the spring flowers softly glowing. It rested, a gossamer canopy, on the tops of the sycamores, then, melting into soft, bluish wreaths, floated up into the depths of ether. Just as the silver veil was slowly lifting, the sound of carriage-wheels was heard, right at the very gate, before any one was aware of their coming. Two carriages were there, and the steps of both let down before the door flew open, and the *welcome home* commenced. Oh! was not that glorious sunburst, penetrating the vaporous, gauze-like folds, an emblem of the joy of that meeting hour,—a joy shining through tears! That lovely youthful matron, with such a pale yet radiant face, who throws herself trembling in her mother's arms,—ah! that is sweet Eula Hastings, the flower of her native village! That beautiful boy, nestling, dove-like, in its father's bosom, and looking wonderingly at the strange faces that surround it,—that cherub boy is hers. For one moment, even Moreland was forgotten, who turned with glistening eyes to his sister, that seemed to say,

"You see, New England hearts are warm and tender as our own."

The Southern stranger was not chilled by her reception, though her own demonstrative nature exceeded its warmth. Her heart involuntarily sprang forward to meet Mrs. Hastings, whom she loved already, as the mother of Eulalia. When she came forward to greet her, with that air of subdued kindness which shows there is a well-spring flowing within, and extended her hand to the young creature clad in the sable weeds of widowhood, Ildegerte threw her arms round her neck, and exclaimed,

"Let me be your daughter, too!"

The warm embrace that followed this petition was a mute but expressive answer. Was this the lady whom her imagination had invested with such stately grace and aristocracy, whose coming she had secretly dreaded, this fair, pensive, loving being, who claimed so sweetly her maternal love?

The little black-eyed fairy, whose hand is already closely locked in Dora's, every one knows it is Effie, "the child of the sun," as Eula had often called her; Dora leads her into the house with such a protecting, motherly air, so confidential yet so patronizing, it is impossible to describe it. Dora has become such a precocious little woman, since Eula left her home, has so many responsibilities resting upon her, as the only *unmarried* daughter,—has so many of Eula's protegés to take care of, and her own reputation to sustain as the brightest scholar in school, that there is some danger of her losing some of the graces of childhood, without receiving a full equivalent. The wild and pranksome Effie will soon bring her back to the right level.

The "neat-handed Phillis," who had been engaged as Betsy's assistant, insisted upon relieving Netty of the carpet-bags and bundles which she was bearing, so that, fortunately, Netty's first impression of the village servants was, that they were very polite and well-bred; and Albert, who was never outdone in politeness, insisted upon taking them from the "neat-handed Phillis," who, on her part, thought the Southern slaves the best bred people in the world. But where was Betsy herself, that she had not appeared to welcome one whom she so dearly loved? She had been flying halfway up stairs, and halfway down stairs, in a state bordering on distraction,—resolving one moment she would change her domestic morning dress, the next, thinking it would take too long,—almost crying for joy at the thought of seeing Miss Eula's beautiful face once more, yet recoiling in imagination from the "sarcy" black negro, who accompanied her.

Eulalia's affectionate heart waited not for Betsy's vacillating and bewildered movements. Catching her baby in her arms, she sought the kitchen with eager steps, and found Betsy hovering, like Mahomet's coffin, between two counter influences.

"Why dear, good, faithful Betsy, how glad I am to see you!" cried she, her voice tremulous from excitement, and pressing Betsy's callous hand in her soft and rosy palm. "I have brought my boy to show you—my fair and beautiful Southern blossom."

Betsy gazed upon the mother and gazed upon the child with brimming eyes, that soon overflowed in a genuine heart-shower.

"Oh! you are puttier than ever, Miss Euly!" said she, laughing and crying in the same breath, "and just as good—better you couldn't be. And is this your own sweet precious baby—the beautifulest darling that ever my eyes sot upon!"

There was something in Betsy's homely, but honest, sterling features that attracted Master Russell's discriminating eyes, and, with a most engaging smile, he extended his snowy arms towards her.

"Bless his little heart and soul! I'm ashamed to touch him, that I am—all in my dirty morning working clothes. I dressed in my best last night and you didn't come, and now ain't I a sight to see?"

"You look very well indeed, Betsy, and your kitchen, as usual, as neat as wax. How is your poor lame brother, Betsy?"

"He is better off, a great deal, Miss Euly, for he's gone to Him that makes the lame to walk like the bounding roe. For a long time it seemed as if I'd nothing to live or work for; but them that has a plenty to do hasn't time to spend a grieving, and it's a mercy in the end."

It is not to be supposed that so important a personage as Eulalia would be suffered to remain alone in the kitchen, for the doorway was soon filled with those that followed her movements and hung upon her accents, as if her lips dropped manna. Moreland greeted Betsy with genuine cordiality, and Count D'Orsay himself could not have displayed more grace than Albert, in introducing his young and coquettish-looking bride to the sturdy, republican Yankee servant. Netty though herself vastly superior to Betsy, but she had been so well drilled by Albert in the *proprieties* of a Northern kitchen that she condescended to be very courteous and genteel. Indeed she stood too much in awe of her master to do anything which she knew would displease him

Betsy saw the vision of the insolent black woman fade away, and a trim, smiling, smooth-faced mulatto beaming in its place. From that moment she extended the hospitalities of the kitchen with excellent good-will. Betsy was an uncommon instance of unchanging devotion to one family, in the midst of general fluctuation. It is not often that you find, among Northern servants, one who remains, as she had done, a fixture in the household, identified with the best interests of the family, and participating heartily in all its joys and sorrows. But in a small inland town, where the tide of emigration does not come flowing in, there is less of the spirit of change than in the large cities. Those who prefer labouring in a family to toiling in the crowded factories, are generally of steady, domestic habits, and, having made up their minds to work as a necessity, see no advantage in rolling, like the stone that gathers no moss, from door to door.

Had Mr. Hastings become reconciled to his Southern son-in-law? One would suppose so, from the bright sparkling of his keen black eyes, the constant friction of his hands, and the "very happy to see you again," that repeatedly gladdened his lips. Not that he had voluntarily yielded one iota of his principles—he still persisted that they were as firm as Mount Atlas; but he was more guarded in the expression of his feelings, and the letters of his daughter had insensibly wrought a change in them greater than he himself was aware of.

He could not but respect and admire the character of Moreland, and rejoice in the happiness of Eulalia. He was proud, too, of the wealth of her husband, and the distinction his alliance had given the family.

The being, beloved as Eulalia was, returning after the absence, even of a few years, to the bosom of her family and friends, has an earnest of the bliss of reunion in the spirit-world. There was no mistaking the testimonies of joy and affection that greeted her wherever she moved. The venerable Dr. Ellery, her beloved pastor, shed tears of joy when he embraced her; and when, with all a mother's pride and tenderness, she placed her blooming boy in his arms, he raised it towards heaven, and blessed it with the inspiration of a prophet and the solemnity of a saint. Then gently drawing it to his bosom, he said,

"I remember you, my daughter, an innocent, smiling babe, thus nestling in my paternal arms. I love to look back to that period, seeing before me the fulfilment of my fondest prayers. I love to look forward to the future destiny of this child. The blood of the North and the South is blended in its veins, and may he be a representative of the reunion of these now too divided parties!"

"Amen!" exclaimed Mr. Hastings. The spirit certainly moved him to utter it, for he seemed as much electrified by its sound as any of his auditors. The truth was, that little child, with its soft, downy touch, had done more to make *Mount Atlas* shake, than the giant efforts of reason, or the strong though invisible pressure of conscience.

On the following Sunday, Eulalia, dressed as she was accustomed to do as a village maiden, in simple, unadorned white, took her place behind the green curtain with the choral throng. With but few exceptions the same choristers were there, composing the singing band, the same "Harmonicas Sacras" lay open, at the notes of the same old, majestic anthems, which were wont to usher in the morning worship of the temple. The temple itself was unchanged. Pure from the breath of sacrilege, its walls presented the same spotless surface, and the same spotless hands ministered at the altar. When the choir rose, and, with a simultaneous burst of melody, chanted the sublime hymn commencing thus—

> "Before Jehovah's awful throne,
> Ye nations bow with sacred joy;"

Eulalia met the uplifted eyes of her husband, and they both remembered the first time he had heard her voice sustaining the magnificent chorus. The memories of three years of wedded happiness, such as seldom is given to mortals to enjoy, were gathered in that single glance. Her heart swelled with adoring gratitude, and gave utterance to its emotions in strains of angelic sweetness and power. There were some, whose aged ears had never hoped to hear that voice again, save in the celestial orchestra, were moved to tears as they listened, and blessed the lips that still, pure from worldly guile, loved to sing the holy songs of Zion.

Nature itself harmonized with the spirit of the scene, and breathed forth its gentlest, balmiest influences. The air, soft and bland as the gales of the South, stole in through the half-opened blinds, reverently parting the white locks of age, and fluttering the ringlets of childhood. Effie's gipsy curls and Dora's light-brown tresses, as they sat side by side, unbonneted, as children usually are during the heat of summer, were twined together by the loving gale. Beautiful representatives of the North and the South, they sat, with hand linked with hand and heart meeting heart! Oh! that they might be typical of that harmony which ought to exist between two regions which God has so greatly glorified, so abundantly blessed!

Moreland was exceedingly gratified by the cordial manner in which the citizens expressed their congratulations for his return, greeting him at the door of the church, when the services of the morning were over Mr. Grimby's swarthy features wore quite a benignant glow.

"What a man soweth, that doth he also reap."

Moreland's charities, though unostentatiously bestowed by the gentle hands of his wife, had glided through the byways of the village, quietly as the stream that fertilized its soil, imparting, like its clear and shaded waters, greenness and bloom. The blessing of the poor rested upon him, neutralizing the curse of fanaticism,—the anathema of prejudice.

Where was the aged mother of Nancy? This was a question Moreland and Eulalia both asked. She dwelt in the almshouse, the abode she had so long dreaded to inhabit. After Nancy's death, it was impossible for her to remain alone, in her age and infirmity. Though all were kind to the lonely octogenarian, none could assume the heavy burden of her support. Few had a room to spare or time to devote to one requiring so much watchfulness in life's second childhood,—that sad, sad era, marked by the helplessness of infancy, without its innocence; the infirmity of age, without its majesty. So she was borne to the almshouse, where many of the poor, unhappy, scattered members of the great human family were doomed to meet. The building was ample and comfortable, their common wants were supplied; but the withered and rent associations of home were trailing after their weary steps, and hanging in mournful tangles round their broken hearts. Who, while they bless the benevolence that founded these institutions of mercy, does not pity the miserable beings who, deprived of all other shelter, are condemned to bear the cross of humiliation, and suffer the most melancholy of earthly privations? We would ask any unprejudiced person, if old Aunt Dicey, in her comfortable cabin, in the midst of home and its unbroken associations, was not happier than Dame Brown, the companion of the drivelling idiot, the imbecile, the crazed, the lame, the halt, and the blind?

The poor old creature wept like an infant, when Moreland and Eulalia sought her in her sad retreat. They tried to comfort her, but their own hearts were full. How strange it seemed, that she should be suffered to live, the survivor of all earthly ties and joys, with the clanking of life's broken chain ringing in her ears; and Nancy, the joy and comfort of her age, blighted and cut down in the flower of her youth!

Never had Eulalia felt such an oppression of the heart, as in quitting that melancholy abode. The inequality of happiness in this world struck her with a force that was appalling. Why was she so richly blessed, and others so barren of comfort? Were poverty and suffering the black clouds prepared as the background for the exhibition of Christian graces? Must the earth for ever be darkened by the smoke of human suffering, creation for ever groan beneath the burden of sorrow and of want? Eulalia gave utterance to these interrogations, on her homeward path, and Moreland answered thus,—

"I have pondered long and deeply over these things, and have come to the conclusion, that, if every individual would do all that he can to relieve the sorrows and trials of those *within his reach*, whom Heaven has placed under his immediate influence, the sum of human misery would gradually and surely diminish, and dwindle into nothing. But man places himself on the hill-top, and, overlooking the valley at his feet, stretches his hands afar, grasping at intangible objects, and wasting his energies in fruitless and impossible efforts. He is not obliged to lift up his voice, to appease the groaning poor at his side,—the world will not hear the soft hushings of his benevolence,—his name will not echo to the distant hills. Every once in a while, he mounts a hobby, whose thundering hoofs trample down all individual rights, and disturb the repose of nations. Anti-slavery is the monomania of the present day; and a black face, provided it belongs to a fugitive, irrespective of every moral claim, a passport to favour and distinction."

Moreland started, and a glow of pleasure illumined his serious and thoughtful countenance. Whom should he meet near the threshold of Mr. Hastings's door but his Western friend, Dr. Darley? The doctor was making a Northern tour, the present summer, and his route leading him through this beautiful village, he learnt, with joy, that he might have an opportunity of meeting his Southern friends. This unexpected addition to their happiness was duly appreciated by all, but most especially by the grateful Ildegerte, whose countenance became literally radiant with the joy of welcome. Mr. Hastings was "very, very happy to see Dr. Darley, and to entertain so distinguished a guest." He was proud of the honour—so proud and so happy that he almost rubbed the skin from his hands by incessant friction. The doctor, who was an enthusiastic and poetic lover of the beauties of nature, and who thought he had found the loveliest resting spot in creation, consented to remain few days, and, during that short time, he had an opportunity of exercising that commanding influence for the public good which he exerted wherever he went.

A placard had been put up at Mr. Grimby's tavern, and in the most conspicuous public places, announcing that Mr. Howard, a distinguished philanthropist, would lecture on such a night in the Lyceum hall. He was to be accompanied by a fugitive slave, who would relate some of the most startling and thrilling incidents of the horrible system from which he had recently escaped.

Mr. Hastings was placed in a very perplexing dilemma. His house had always been a kind of abolition-tavern, and all itinerant lecturers were received by him with all the honours of hospitality. They were sure to bring him letters of introduction, and he was sure to introduce them to the public with a glowing smile of patronage. Supposing this stranger came, with his sable satellite, expecting admission to his home, how could he receive him under the same roof with Moreland? Yet, if he refused, how recreant to the principles he had so often declared himself ready to die to defend! Dr. Darley, too, whose sentiments on the subject he had been careful to ascertain, and whose good opinion he was most anxious to secure, would consider himself insulted as well as Moreland, by his countenance of one, the avowed champion of a cause, against which he had thrown the weight of his talents and the influence of his reputation. Poor Mr. Hastings was sadly troubled and perplexed. The large, staring black letters on the placards seemed branded on his mind, and by a most painful introspection, he beheld them from "morn till noon, from noon till dewy eve."

"I want to hear this orator," said Moreland, "and his African colleague. If he has the eloquence of a Brainard, he may make every green leaf of the valley thrill. I want to hear Dr. Darley, too, on the other side of the question."

"Not when Mr. Moreland is present."

"Surely you, Dr. Darley, standing as you do on the borders of the West, with the North on one side and the South on the other, can speak with a far better grace than one whose personal interests are identified with either."

"It will be as the occasion prompts," replied the doctor. "I do not believe I ever stayed three days in a place without being called upon to make a public address, by the imperiousness of circumstances."

Moreland had related to him the history of Brainard, the insurrection he had plotted, the scene at the grave of Dilsy, and the after flight of Vulcan.

"Perhaps this is the self-same man, figuring under a new name," said Dr. Darley.

"I have been thinking so," replied Moreland.

"If so, we may anticipate some great scenes," said the doctor, the merry spark in his eye scintillating with unusual brilliancy.

This was not said in the presence of Mr. Hastings, who wandered like a restless ghost the whole afternoon of the appointed evening. Every knock made him start and change colour: but to his unspeakable relief his hospitality was unclaimed—the modern Howard had not yet made his appearance.

When they arrived at the Lyceum Hall, it was already crowded almost to suffocation, all the front seats being occupied by ladies, and the window sills by little boys, with long republican sticks in their hands, ready to applaud the coming orator. Neither Mrs. Hastings, Eulalia, or Ildegerte were present, and Moreland, for reasons well known to himself, took the most remote and obscure corner of the hall. Dr. Darley glided in very quietly and seated himself at his side, while Mr. Hastings, with a reddening brow, walked forward with slow and measured tread to his accustomed place of honour on the platform.

The appointed hour came and passed. Leads were constantly turning towards the door, shuffling feet betokened impatience, and there was an incessant coughing and hemming in the audience, as if they were endeavouring to fill up the awful pause of expectation. Some accident must have occurred to detain the orator: there was no use in remaining longer in that close, oppressive atmosphere. Just then, a commotion near the door caused a sudden revulsion of feeling, the crowd divided, and a tall and slender figure, of erect and dignified mien, passed on towards the platform, ushered by the obsequious Mr. Grimby, and followed by a stout, brawny framed negro, black as the shades of Erebus. Moreland gave a sudden start, and laid his hand on Dr. Darley. He understood the pressure, and smiled. Yes! that was the sinewy arm which had forged the weapons of rebellion in the midnight forge, which had been wrapped in straining coil round his master's form when paralyzed by Paul's avenging blow. Yes! there were the murky brow, the sullen, bloodshot eye, the fierce, vindictive mouth, and glittering teeth of the Herculean rebel. But the orator! Moreland gazed upon his face, doubting and bewildered. Was it, could it be the false, hypocritical Brainard, thus transformed? His hair was short, and pushed far back from his high, fair forehead; Brainard's long, sleek, and meekly parted on his brow. A thick, dark beard, clustered round his mouth and chin, giving it a massy and bold appearance; Brainard's was smooth and sharp, as little Effie's classic eye had at nce discovered;—yet there was the same half-sheathed, steel-like glance, and the voice, though more clear and ringing, had the same false, silver sound. The garb of the minister, the clothing of the sheep, were cast aside for the bolder lion's skin, but the wolf was apparent behind them all.

Moreland's blood began to seethe in his veins when he saw Vulcan, far more embruted and animal in appearance than when he defied him over the ashes of the dead, ascend the platform and sit down side by side with his own father-in-law; when he saw the vile impostor, whose path had been marked with the slime of the snake, the brand of the incendiary, and the steel of the assassin, standing in that elevated position, the centre of every gazing eye, assuming to be the champion of truth and humanity, while violating their most sacred rights. He announced himself as a traveller recently returned from the South, that beautiful, but accursed region, "where all save the spirit of man was divine." He had had the most abundant opportunities of studying and examining its social and domestic institutions, and he was prepared to lay the result before an intelligent and enlightened community. He began with the utmost calmness and deliberation, describing the delicious climate, the luxuriant vegetation, the gardens of roses, the bowers of jessamine, and groves of orange trees, which made an Eden of that smiling land. He dwelt with enthusiastic admiration on the grace and loveliness of its daughters, the brave and gallant bearing of its sons. One would have supposed that to praise was his only task; but he was making a flowering groundwork, to enhance by contrast, the effect of the hideous structure he was about to rear upon it. Anon the hand that had been gently scattering roses, began to hurl the hissing thunderbolt, and in the wild and thrilling eloquence which succeeded, Moreland found no difficulty in recognising the splendid orator of the African church. He heard himself (for in what other planter's home had he been so closely domesticated?) described as a demon of cruelty, his slaves the subjects of the most atrocious barbarity, his plantation the scene of horrors that baffled the power of imagination to conceive. The clanking chain, the excoriating manacle, the gashing scourge, the burning brand, were represented as tortures in daily, nay, even in hourly use; the shrieks of womanhood, the cries of infancy, and the lamentations of age, as no more regarded than the yelling of wild beasts or the whistling of the wind. The audience was becoming painfully excited. Ladies were passing little bottles containing the spirits of ammonia from one to the other, and covering their faces with their white handkerchiefs; men groaned audibly, and many a dark and sinister glance was turned to the dim corner, where the Southern planter sat, unseen as yet by the orator of the night.

"Hush, hush!" whispered Dr. Darley to the excited and indignant Moreland. "Not for worlds would I have you prematurely interrupt this scene. Wait, and you shall have a signal triumph."

It was a terrible struggle with Moreland, to keep

from rushing forward and hurling the wretch from the platform, exposing him at once to the crowd, whom he was deluding by his falsehoods and magnetising by his electrical eloquence.

"Behold," said Brainard, after having exhausted, for the time, the vocabulary of horrors, "behold one of the poor victims of Southern barbarity—behold his mutilated fingers, his branded and disfigured body. Hold out your hand, long-suffering son of Africa—and show the awful mark of your master's cruelty."

Vulcan stretched out his left hand, in which the two central fingers were wanting, making a sickening chasm. We have already related the accident which caused this loss, as well as the burn which had left such an enduring cicatrice.

"Look at this poor disfigured shoulder," continued Brainard, folding back the negro's shirt-collar and displaying a terrible-looking scar (probably embellished by a few touches of reddish paint). "This is but a small portion of the scars which seam and corrugate his whole body."

Groans and faint shrieks were now heard from every part of the house, and again Dr. Darley's restraining hand was laid on Moreland's quivering arm.

"Not yet, not yet! We must hear the negro's story. The climax is to come."

But, just as Vulcan opened his huge lips to speak, in obedience to a gesture of Brainard, and people were pressing forward, half standing in their eagerness to catch every word of the hideous speaker, a young man forced his way through the crowd in the doorway, and rushed to the centre of the hall. So sudden was his entrance, so rapid his movements, that no one recognised his colour till, slackening his pace and looking wildly round him, he disclosed the bright yellow hue and dark-beaming eyes of the mulatto.

"Master, master, Mars. Russell!" he exclaimed, breathlessly, pantingly; "where are you? Why don't you speak, and tell 'em they're all lies? Why don't you tell 'em it's Vulcan, that tried to kill you, and Master Brainard, that tried to make everybody kill you? You may kill me if you want to!" cried he, shaking his clenched fist at the astonished Brainard. "I don't care if you do! I'll call you a story-teller and a rogue. I'd a heap rather be killed, than stand still and hear the best master that ever lived made out a monster of a brute!"

It is impossible to give the faintest conception of the effect of this impassioned appeal. The young republicans in the windows brought down their sticks like rattling thunder, while, high above the din, several voices were heard exclaiming—

"Put him out, put him out!" and many leaped forward to execute the order.

"Stop!" exclaimed a voice of command, and Moreland, without waiting to make a passage through the people, sprang from bench to bench, till he reached the spot where Albert stood, directly opposite the platform, in the full glare of the lamplight. With glowing cheek and flashing eye, he faced the bold, but now pale impostor and cowering slave, then turning to the people—

"Let no one," he cried, "on their peril, touch this boy. He is under my protection, and I will defend him with my life. He has spoken the truth. This man is a vile impostor. Pretending to be a minister of God, he introduced himself into my household, and, under the cloak of religion, plotted the most damning designs. I received him as a friend, cherished him as a brother, and obtained for him the confidence of a generous and trusting community. I blush for my own weakness; I pity the delusion of others. As to the horrible charges he has brought against me and my Southern brethren, I scorn to deny them. If you could believe such atrocities of *any* man, your good opinion would be valueless to me. That you can believe them of *me*, knowing me, as most of you now do, I know it is impossible. Had he been less malignant, he had done me more evil."

"I have spoken the truth, and nothing but the truth," interrupted Brainard, grinding his teeth with suppressed rage; "our black brother can bear witness to all I have declared."

But "our black brother" did not seem disposed to back his falsehoods with the boldness he had anticipated. Though brute force, roused by long-continued excitement, had once triumphed over moral cowardice, it gave him no sustaining influence now, and he shrunk and quailed before the thrilling eye of his deserted and injured master. The influence of early habits and feelings resumed its sway, and gleamings of his better nature struggled through the darkness of falsehood and treachery. Notwithstanding the bluntness of his perceptions, he felt the power of Moreland's moral superiority over Brainard, and when he found himself called upon to confirm his unblushing lies in the pure light of his master's countenance, a sudden loathing for the white man who could stoop to such degradation, filled his mind; and a strong desire for the favour he had forfeited and the place he had lost, stirred his heart.

"Speak, Vulcan!" cried Moreland, who had marked the changes of his dark face with intense interest, "speak! and in the presence of an all-hearing God, say if this man utters the truth, or I."

"You, massa, you!" burst spontaneously from the lips of the negro, and it seemed as if a portion of blackness rolled away from his face, with the relieving consciousness of having borne testimony to the truth.

"Villain!" cried Brainard,—stamping his foot, and turning fiercely on the blacksmith,—"villain, you lie! you and your master—"

"Order, order!" exclaimed Mr. Hastings, who had been terribly agitated during this scene. Before he could add another syllable, Moreland, with one bound, stood upon the platform, and seizing Brainard by the arm, gave him a downward swing that sent him reeling against the living wall below. The act was instantaneous as lightning, and the mimic thunder of the pounding sticks followed the flash. Brainard could not, at any time, compete in strength with Moreland, and now, when indignation nerved the arm of the latter, it seemed to have a giant's sinews. Conscious of a great revulsion of feeling in the audience, since Vulcan's testimony against him, he began to feel the insecurity of his situation. Turning in desperation to the platform, like an animal at bay,

"Sir," said he, addressing Mr. Hastings, "I appeal to you for redress, and protection from insult and outrage. I appeal to this whole assembly, as a stranger foully wronged. I appeal to Northern justice, for defence against Southern insolence and aggression."

For one moment, there was a breathless stillness, awaiting the reply of Mr. Hastings. The face of Moreland crimsoned, and his heart throbbed audibly. Would Eulalia's father throw the shield of his protection round this man? If so, they must be for ever separated.

"Sir," cried Mr. Hastings,—coming forward and speaking with emphasis, though in an agitated voice,—"I have no protection to offer an impostor and a liar This people have no redress for one who insults them by asking it, in the face of such a shameful detection. He shall find to his cost, that Northern justice will protect the South from aggressions and slanders like his!"

A deafening shout went up as Mr. Hastings concluded, showing how warmly public sentiment was now enlisted in the cause of Moreland. Moreland, relieved from an intolerable dread, involuntarily grasped the hand of his father-in-law, and pressed it with more cordiality than he had ever felt before.

Where was Dr. Darley all this time? Was he a cool, indifferent spectator of this exciting scene? By no means. Look at his keen, scintillating eyes, sparkling right over Brainard's shoulder; see the ignited, glittering particles they emit, and say if he is cool,—think of coolness if you can, in the presence of that countenance of fire. He has been biding his time, and it has come.

"My friends," said he,—addressing Mr. Hastings and Moreland,—"may I stand by you a few moments? I have a few words which I would like to say to this good people, if they will permit me. I want this man to hear me, also,"—laying his hand on Brainard's shoulder,—"I pray you," turning courteously to the gentlemen in his rear, "not to suffer him to depart."

Mr. Hastings, who seemed quite inspired by the occasion, immediately descending the steps, led up Dr. Darley, and introduced him in the most flattering manner to the audience, as one of the most distinguished citizens of the American republic.

"You see before you a plain, blunt man," said the doctor,—bowing with great dignity to the audience,—"as deficient as the Roman Antony in the graces of oratory and the flowers of rhetoric. Yet, I am given to making long speeches, and if I chance to inflict one on you, you must impute it to the force of habit, rather than inclination. The man who has addressed you to-night, and who is a most wonderfully eloquent speaker, is not entirely unknown to me. No testimony of mine, however, is requisite, to add force to the words of Mr. Moreland, whom I am proud to call my friend, whose hospitality I have experienced, whose domestic virtues are fully known to me, and whose kindness to his black family I have myself witnessed and appreciated,—no testimony of mine is needed to give effect to the spontaneous tribute paid by this son of Africa to his master's truth and worth. Your own hearts have given the verdict, your own consciences bearing witness to the justice of the decree. But, I said before, I have some little knowledge of Mr. Howard,—alias, the Rev. Mr. Brainard,—alias, Mr. Hiram Coates."

"Alias Ichabod Jenkins," cried a voice from the back part of the house.

Brainard started as if he had been shot, but there was no egress through that mass of living beings.

"I doubt not that he has innumerable aliases," continued the doctor, "but my present business is with Mr

Hiram Coates, who figured rather extensively in the West several years since. His magnificent forgeries are even now the wonder of the Queen City, where I reside. Now, if a man is determined to be a villain, I like to see him go on a grand scale. If he sells his soul, he should set a lofty price. Gentlemen, I recognised this individual the moment I beheld him, as the accomplished criminal who broke the prison bars of the West, and eluded the punishment of his transgressions. His after course you have learned; and what his future will be, if his evil passions are allowed to have scope, it requires no prophetic inspiration to tell. He is a dangerous, unprincipled, and lawless man, who should no more be suffered to roam at large than the brindled tiger or the shaggy bear. If there is a sheriff present, I call upon him to arrest him, on my own responsibility. If not, I call upon every lover of the peace of society, every advocate for the rights of mankind, to assist in securing him, till proper legal measures can be taken."

The prompt response of the sheriff, who was present, proved the alacrity with which he obeyed the summons. There was no escape for Brainard. Wherever he turned, detection glared him in the face. The individual who had called out "Alias Ichabod Jenkins," now came forward, and begged permission to recall to the public mind an incident which occurred in the county many years since. He asked if there were not some present who remembered a boy of that name put in the penitentiary for theft, but whose sentence was mitigated in consequence of his extreme youth, and the influence of many benevolent individuals, who interested themselves largely in his behalf, and defrayed the expenses of his collegiate education. He reminded them of the notorious character the young man afterwards established, of his wonderful powers of dissimulation, and his successful villany. For years he had disappeared from public notice; but there he was, the self-same individual, and he would swear to his identity though hundred thousands were present endeavouring to prove the contrary.

It is singular, but there are oftentimes moments in the life of individuals, who have seemed to possess a supernatural power of elusion, when an accumulation of evidence suddenly falls upon them, and they are crushed as if with a thunderbolt from Heaven; when the keystone of the proud arch of their iniquity gives way, and they are buried beneath its ruins.

As they were bearing this man of many *aliases* out of the hall, he turned round, and bursting into a sardonic laugh, exclaimed—

"Fools! dupes that you are! who strain at a gnat and swallow a camel! if I had not known your credulity, and proneness to believe evil of your brethren, I never should have prepared the black and bitter pill ye have been rolling as a sweet morsel under your tongue. You had better profit by the lesson."

'Yes, my friends," said Dr. Darley, as soon as the

criminal had passed through the door, where the rabble received him with hootings and hissings of scorn, "it will be well to profit by a lesson which, though it comes from a polluted source, may be salutary to you. We are too prone to believe evil of others, to forget extenuating circumstances, to put our own consciences in other men's bosoms, to decide upon their motives of action, and shake them, at our own will and pleasure, over the borders of the flaming lake. I am a man of many faults, but there is one thing I claim as a virtue, and that is patriotism. I love my country—my whole country. I recognise no North or South, East or West in the affection I bear it. I find no cardinal points in my heart, though they are convenient to use for geographical purposes. Born in one of the Middle States, I emigrated, in my boyhood, to the West. Since I have been a man, I have devoted much of my time to travelling, and studying the great book of mankind. I have learned to respect the rights of my countrymen, wherever they reside; to appreciate their virtues, to judge kindly of their motives of action, and to mete them with the golden measure which I would have applied to myself. I have learned to consider the iron bed of Procrustes as an abomination of heathenism, and the shame of a Christian land. I do not believe that when you and I and the whole congregated universe shall be arraigned before the great God and Judge of all, that he will ask whether we came from the North or the South, the East or the

West (there will be no cardinal points in heaven either); that He will ask whether we were born in a free or a slave State: but whether we have been faithful to the responsibilities imposed upon us, faithful to our own peculiar duties; whether we have done all we could to advance the sum of human happiness, and to promote His sovereign glory."

It is not our intention to repeat all that Dr. Darley said, for he spoke at least two hours, yet they scarcely seemed more than two minutes, so intent was the interest that hung upon his words. Every one felt that it was a whole-souled, whole-hearted, high-minded man who addressed them, lifted above all party zeal or sectional feeling, acknowledging the great brotherhood of humanity, while respecting the distinctions the Almighty has made. The kindling eye, the earnest tone, the impressive rather than the graceful gesture, the whole countenance illuminated with intelligence and sensibility, riveted the attention and made it impossible for it to wander.

There was one present on whom the events of the evening and the eloquence they elicited had a most powerful and enduring influence—and that was Reuben Hastings. He had listened with unspeakable indignation to the false representations of Brainard, and with difficulty restrained himself from rushing forward as Albert had done, in defence of the slandered Moreland.

But the youth of New England are accustomed to

repress their emotions, and habits of self-control are woven in with the woof and warp of their existence. At his father's indignant denunciation of the impostor, he could not help waving his hat in the air, while he pressed the other hand on his lips to hold back the exulting hurrah. Nor was he the only one who responded in heart to Mr. Hastings's remarks.

"That was the best speech you ever made in your life, squire," said Mr. Grimby to him the next day. "You hit the nail right on the head. To tell the truth, squire, I begin to think we have been a *little* too hard on the Southern people. It won't do to believe everything we hear. I wouldn't feel as cheap another time as I did last night to be made President of the United States. Now, that doctor of the West is the right sort of man. He don't shut up one eye and squint with the other, but he looks wide awake all round him, and sees everything at once. There ain't many men could keep me standing two hours on my feet without knowing it, as he did. We needed just such a speech, and it will do us all good. I tell you what, squire, if all the Southern people were like your son-in-law, Mr. Moreland, I wouldn't say one word against them as long as I live."

"There are few such men anywhere as Mr. Moreland," replied Mr. Hastings, delighted to find that he had not injured his social position by the stand he had taken the previous night. "You know," he added, in a self-appreciating tone, while his palms gave each a friendly salute, "that I made a sacrifice, a great sacrifice, when I gave him my daughter; but, like every act of self-immolation, it has met its reward. If ever woman was happy in marriage, my Eulalia is."

"If ever woman deserved to be happy, she does," said Mr. Grimby. On this the two gentlemen shook hands very warmly, and Mr. Hastings seemed to be attacked with a sudden cold, for he blew his nose and cleared his throat several times before he continued the conversation.

Vulcan humbled himself in the dust before his master, begged to be reinstated in his favour and received again into his family, but this Moreland refused.

"I forgive you, Vulcan," said he, "but I cannot place that confidence in your fidelity necessary to the relation that has existed between us. I have always said that the moment one of my slaves became rebellious in feeling to me, they might go. I want no unwilling service. You have an excellent trade, and, if steady and industrious, can earn a comfortable living. If you want money, I will give it to you. Come to me if you are in trouble, and I will relieve you,—but the relation of master and servant must exist no longer."

Vulcan had one of those surly, animal natures, that grow affectionate and yielding under a stern, controlling will. He had not appreciated his master's favour while basking in its sunshine, but now it was withdrawn for ever, he crouched in abject submission at his feet.

"I forgive you," again repeated Moreland, "but the rebel arm which dared to lift itself against my life, must never more wield the hammer or strike the anvil for me. Nothing can change this resolution. Go—you are free."

Vulcan turned gloomily away, cursing the tempter who had lured him from the white-walled cabin, the "old plantation," and taught him to lift his hand against his once affectionate and indulgent master.

The stirring events and *denouement* of that memorable night furnished subjects of conversation that appeared inexhaustible. The result was the diffusion of a more liberal, charitable, and enlightened spirit in the whole community. But the change in Mr. Hastings was most remarkable. His very person seemed to alter. His eyes looked larger, and his hair had a more subdued colour. He was constantly quoting Dr. Darley's opinions, and inveighed with great bitterness against one-sided and prejudiced people. As Mr. Brooks said, when first describing him to Moreland, he always had a hobby, which he rode without mercy. As his last had given him such a terrible kick, he resolved to discard it, and mounting another, it was not long before he was in danger of being carried as fast and far in an opposite direction. He talked a great deal about "our visit to the South" next winter, or rather the winter after next, of the fine prospects of "my son Reuben," who was to be established there as a lawyer, under the patronage of "my son-in-law." He even spoke of the possibility of his remaining there himself, and opening a classical school.

Shall we describe the visit of the Northern family to Eulalia's Southern home? Not minutely, lest we weary the reader by recapitulation; but it was an event unparalleled in interest in the lives of our villagers. It was long before Mrs. Hastings yielded her consent to the journey, well knowing that they would be placed under new obligations to the generous and uncalculating Moreland. But he bore down at last all her scruples, and when he had obtained her promise to accede to their wishes, he insisted upon carrying with them the young Dora, as a hostage of its fulfilment.

When he told Betsy that she must accompany the family, as it would not be considered complete without her, she shook her head, and said,

"I thank you, from the bottom of my heart, for not being ashamed to ask me, but I ain't fit to travel about and wait on ladies. My place is in the kitchen, and I wouldn't feel at home anywhere else. I'd feel as strange as a fish out of water, anywhere, but where I had to knock about and scuffle with my work. People gets used to the way they live, and, though it mayn't be the best way, it's hard to turn 'em any other. Your fine niggers don't make fun of me here, 'cause they see me in the right place; but let me stick up as a lady's maid, and go among 'em, I'd be the biggest laughing-stock under the sun!"

Betsy was right, and Eula, feeling that she was, did not endeavour to shake her resolution. She had too much regard for her feelings to wish to see her in an uncongenial situation, where her visible awkwardness might expose her to ridicule, and her innate worth be undiscovered or unappreciated.

The family made their visit in the winter season; but they were not suffered to return till they had witnessed the beauty and magnificence of a Southern spring,—a spring which does not break forth at once, in the full glory of the Northern season; but comes stealing gently on the scarcely perceptible footsteps of departing winter, showering roses, and distilling the odours of Paradise. They were enchanted with the climate, the luxuriant vegetation, the wilderness of blossoms and profusion of sweets, and even *bondage*, which at a distance had seemed so dark and threatening, lightened up as they approached it, like the mist of their valley, and receded from their view.

They passed a week at the plantation, from which all traces of the arch-fiend Brainard were now removed, and their respect and admiration for Moreland were heightened, when they saw him in his true position of planter and master, and filling it with such dignity, firmness, and humanity. Mr. Hastings acknowledged, that, if all masters established as excellent regulations, and enforced them with the same kindness, wisdom, and decision, the spirit of Abolitionism would die away for want of fuel to feed its flames. He carried a memorandum-book in his pocket, which he filled with notes, as materials for a new course of lectures, with which he intended to illuminate the prejudices of the Northern people. He had relinquished the idea of the classical school, believing that he would not be considered as great a man at the South as in the little village of which he had long been the intellectual autocrat. His son Reuben was to remain as his representative, and among his parting injunctions, while rubbing his hands with serene self-complacency, he warned him from cultivating an illiberal, narrow spirit, and bade him sustain his father's reputation for candour and philanthropy.

Perhaps some young, romantic girl may ask, "Did Ildegerte never marry again?" Perhaps they may wish that Dr. Darley were a young man for her sake, or that he had not devoted himself with such matchless constancy to the memory of his buried wife. It is certain, that Ildegerte values his esteem and friendship now more than the admiration of more youthful men; but the time may come when her blighted affections will bloom afresh, and another fill the place of the departed Richard. She is still young and very beautiful, a charming representative of her native South, by the side of the Northern Eula.

We are loth to leave her, our sweet "Northern bride,"

now a wife and mother, far happier than the bride; but, committing her to the guardianship and kindness of a generous public, we bid her farewell.

We know there are some who will throw aside these pages, with the impression that they give false and exaggerated views of Southern life; but, with a conviction that a God of truth beholds the lines traced by the hand which He has formed, we give them to the world. We have not gone groping in dark by-lanes and foul dens for tales of horror, which might gratify a morbid and perverted taste; but we have described what we have seen and known, without the intention of enhancing what is fair or of softening what is repulsive. We believe the Southern character to be misunderstood, misrepresented, and wronged, and that it is the duty of those in whose minds this conviction is rooted, to vindicate it, as far as their influence extends, from calumny and animadversion.

Not merely in the expectation of honour or profit, have we entered the lists as a champion of the South, but from a motive which we glory in acknowledging. We love it as the home of noble, generous hearts, of ingenuous and lofty minds. We love the magnanimity and chivalry of its sons, the pure and high-toned spirit that animates its daughters. Shall we dwell in its beautiful bowers and see the canker-worm eating into the heart of its blossoms, without reaching out a hand to rescue their bloom from the destroyer? Shall we breathe its bland, delicious climate, and know that the noxious miasma is rising and spreading, without endeavouring to disperse its exhalations, or trying to counteract its deadly influence? We love the North—

> Land of the wild and wintry blast,
> Of spirits high and glowing,

of minds exalted and refined, of hearts steadfast and true; even its snows and icicles are dear to our bosom; but it needs no champion to assert its uninvaded rights. Enthroned on its granite hills, it reigns in unmolested grandeur and serene repose. No volcanic elements are heaving under its wintry shroud, or threatening to lay waste its summer bloom. But, should the burning lava of anarchy and servile war roll over the plains of the South, and bury, under its fiery waves, its social and domestic institutions, it will not suffer alone. The North and the South are branches of the same parent tree, and the lightning bolt that shivers the one, must scorch and wither the other.

THE END.